ALSO BY E.I

THE WORLD OF THE GATEWAY

The Gateway Trilogy (Series 1)

Spirit Legacy: Book 1 of The Gateway Trilogy
Spirit Prophecy: Book 2 of The Gateway Trilogy
Spirit Ascendancy: Book 3 of The Gateway Trilogy

The Gateway Trackers (Series 2)

Whispers of the Walker: The Gateway Trackers Book 1
Plague of the Shattered: The Gateway Trackers Book 2
Awakening of the Seer: The Gateway Trackers Book 3
Portraits of the Forsaken: The Gateway Trackers Book 4
Heart of the Rebellion: The Gateway Trackers Book 5
Soul of the Sentinel: The Gateway Trackers Book 6
Gift of the Darkness: The Gateway Trackers Book 7

AWAKENING OF THE SEER

AWAKENING OF THE SEER

The Gateway Trackers Book 3

E.E. HOLMES

Lily Faire Publishing

Lily Faire Publishing
Townsend, MA

www.lilyfairepublishing.com

ISBN 978-0-9984762-3-0 (Print edition)

ISBN 978-0-9984762-4-7 (Digital edition)

Cover design by James T. Egan of Bookfly Design LLC
Author photography by Cydney Scott Photography

For Mary Carey, who loved a good book more than anyone.

EPIGRAPH

The future: time's excuse
to frighten us; too vast
a project, too large a morsel
for the heart's mouth.

Future, who won't wait for you?
Everyone is going there.
It suffices you to deepen
the absence that we are.

-Rainer Maria Rilke

CONTENTS

I

STOLEN HOLIDAY

"STOP! STOP! I changed my mind! This is a terrible idea!" Hannah shouted.

"Don't be ridiculous. This idea is brilliant, just like all of my ideas," I shouted back.

"What if it falls? What if it gets stuck? We are going to get in so much trouble!" Hannah cried.

I leaned my whole torso out the window and glared down at her. "It's too late now! Just finish tying it already!"

Still muttering a stream of quiet objections, Hannah tied the rope to the base of the pine tree. I watched with a satisfied smile on my face as she gave me the thumbs up that she had finished.

"Okay, now back up in case we drop it!" I called, then turned to Savannah Todd, who stood beside me at the open window, sleeves pulled up and mischievous grin in place. "Ready, Sav?"

"Ain't I always?" she replied.

We both grabbed onto the rope and began to pull.

I wasn't generally the type of person who pulled Christmas trees in through castle windows in the dead of night, but desperate times called for desperate measures. There were three things in life I treated as matters of the utmost importance: snark, coffee, and Christmas trees. Usually, I could just go to a Christmas tree farm or a tree lot like a normal person and put a tree up in my living room. But this year, I would unexpectedly be spending my Christmas at Fairhaven Hall, and so adjustments had to be made.

Hannah and I had arrived at Fairhaven just shy of two weeks ago to represent our clan at the Airechtas, a very important meeting of the Durupinen that convened once every five years. Traditionally, the Northern Clans would gather for a week and vote on important issues and policies that affected our abilities to carry out our calling—to guard the Gateways that separate the worlds of the

I

living and the dead. If all had gone according to plan, Hannah and I would have been back home in the States, decorating a tree in our apartment. Instead, the proceedings had been upended by the arrival of a Shattered spirit, which spread through the castle possessing unwitting Durupinen and effectively halting the Airechtas until all the Shards of the spirit could be caught and joined to each other again.

So now, the meeting we'd come so reluctantly to attend hadn't even really started yet, and wouldn't reconvene until two days after Christmas. This was a big problem, because I had a long list of traditions that I indulged in every year without fail. During my whirlwind, nomadic childhood with my mother, Christmas was one of the only constants. No matter what crappy apartment we were living in, or how bad her drinking was, I could always count on the same familiar songs, the cookies baked from the same recipes, and, most memorably of all, falling asleep every night in the soft glow of the colored lights on our Christmas tree. There were many sacrifices I was willing to make for my role as a Durupinen, but celebrating Christmas wasn't one of them.

Hannah, whose own fractured childhood had been shored up with none of these traditions, was participating in this latest Christmas shenanigan only reluctantly. She'd have been much happier to leave the tree—and all chance of getting into trouble—back in the woods where we'd found it.

The tree seemed to want the same thing.

"It's snagging on something down there," said Savvy through gritted teeth. "Can you see what it's caught on?"

"I can't see anything, Sav, it's pitch black!" I panted.

At that moment, we both turned at the creaking sound of the bedroom door. I expected to see Hannah, and instead the friendly face of Mackenzie Miller peeked around my door.

"Knock, knock," she said. "Anyone home?"

"Hey, Mackie," I grunted, adjusting my grip on the rope and trying to tug at a different angle. "Come on in, but shut the door behind you."

Mackie eased the door closed, and then stepped around the bed so that she could see us properly. She narrowed her eyes at me. "What are you up to, then?"

I shrugged casually. "Who, me? I don't know. Definitely not hauling a nine-foot-tall Christmas tree through a third-story castle

2

window with a rope of dubious quality. That would be completely irresponsible."

"Oh blimey, Celeste will have your head!" Mackie said, rolling her eyes.

"Not if you get your arse over here and help us pull it in before we get caught," Savvy grunted. "Come on, then, be a chum."

Mackie sighed, but jogged over to give us a hand. Together, the three of us managed to squeeze the monstrous tree through the window and prop it up in the corner.

I ran back to the window and gave Hannah a thumbs-up. "Success! Come on back up so we can decorate it!"

I couldn't hear her reply, but there was definitely head-shaking and cursing involved. "Someone's going to end up on the naughty list!" I shouted down at her before pulling the window shut. A gusty swirl of snow floated in, making me shiver.

"It's... kind of monstrous, isn't it?" Mackie was asking as she looked the tree up and down. It could barely stand straight up in the makeshift stand we had jerry-rigged out of a giant old urn. "Where did you get it?"

"Didn't you hear us call timber over in the grove?" Savvy asked, looking disappointed.

"You chopped it down *on the grounds*?" Mackie asked incredulously, and then put up a hand. "You know what, no. Don't answer that. I'd rather not know."

"Ignorance is bliss, mate," Savvy agreed, slapping her jovially on the back. "You're not Head Girl anymore, so sod the rules and help us decorate this beauty!"

"Have you got decorations?" Mackie asked.

"Have we got decorations?" I snorted, and held up two enormous brown paper shopping bags, crammed with the gaudiest, most glittering Christmas décor we could find. "London has no Christmas left. We bought it all."

"What's in that bag, elf costumes? A Father Christmas suit?" Mackie asked, pointing to a third bag on my bed.

"Nah. That's some clothes from me mum," Savvy said. "She's a seamstress, so when I see something I like in a magazine, I send her the picture and she just knocks something up for me. She made this blouse." And she gave a twirl, showing it off.

"Nice," Mackie said, looking impressed. "Well, all right then. I helped you get it through the window, so I guess I'm an accomplice in this nonsense now. Hand me the tinsel."

We'd just managed to get the lights onto the tree when Hannah came through the door, panting. "Believe it or not I don't think anyone noticed that whole debacle."

"It's a Christmas miracle!" I cried, plugging in the final strand of lights. Savvy played along by making sound effects of angel voices.

Hannah rolled her eyes but laughed as well. She pulled off her hat and scarf, and started digging through the nearest bag for some ornaments.

"So, what's on the schedule for this Christmas party, then?" Mackie asked. "I'm almost afraid to ask, now that I've seen the tree. You haven't got an actual sleigh on the roof of the castle, have you?"

"No, no. Don't worry, it gets tamer from here," I said. "We persuaded one of the cooks to make a batch of all my favorite cookies." I pointed to the table by the fireplace, where a platter was heaped with gingerbread men and sugar cookies. "We are going to decorate them while watching bootlegged copies of *It's a Wonderful Life* and *Miracle on 34th Street* on my laptop. I also got us all stockings."

"To hang by the chimney with care?" Mackie laughed.

"Obviously," I said. "And now, mood music!" I cued up my playlist on my phone, and the sultry tones of Bing Crosby filled the room.

"Where've you been all afternoon, Mack?" Savvy asked. "We tried to find you to come shopping with us. Celeste got you working yourself to the bone again?"

Mackie sighed. "Yeah. It's been a real nightmare, keeping track of who's coming and who's going now that the Airechtas is happening after the holidays. We're trying to make sure we've got rooms for everyone, and that the kitchens are stocked for the right numbers of people. Seamus is having a devil of a time making sure that he's got enough Caomhnóir to handle security. And of course... well, everyone's worried about Finvarra."

We all looked at each other but didn't say anything. Finvarra, High Priestess of the Northern Clans, was very ill—so ill, in fact, that many worried she would not last through the entirety of the Airechtas. She had maintained her health for years through Leeching energy from spirits as they Crossed, but her health had

4

been steadily declining since the practice had been banned more than three years ago. No one had seen her out of her tower since the first day of the Airechtas, but the updates that trickled down through the ranks were troubling. As much as we didn't want to admit it, there was a very good chance that we would need to elect a new High Priestess before this Airechtas was over.

And I doubted anyone was as reluctant to admit this fact as Hannah and I were. The death of Finvarra meant the Crossing of her Spirit Guide and Caomhnóir Carrick, who just happened to be our estranged father. I knew I had to make some attempt at dealing with this fact, but my heart and brain had joined forces in refusing to let me. I made the next move in the epic chess game that was avoiding my own feelings by changing the subject before anyone could vocalize any of these things.

"Any idea if Lucida is still in the hospital wing?" I asked.

Check and mate. Take that, feelings.

Although I had directed the question at Mackie, it was Savvy who answered. "I had to go down there this morning for a follow-up with Mrs. Mistlemoore. Lucida is still there, and still unconscious from what I can tell."

"Celeste says the Shattering was a traumatic event, for the spirit and for Lucida. It's no wonder Lucida's still laid out," Mackie said.

"Eleanora," I blurted out.

"What's that?" Mackie asked.

"The spirit," I clarified. "Her name was Eleanora."

Mackie's cheeks colored, and she nodded solemnly. "That's right. Sorry, mate."

"No, don't apologize," I said quickly. "I... I guess I'm weirdly sensitive about it. Sorry, knee-jerk reaction."

"You don't need to explain weird sensitivities to me," Mackie said with a wink. "Empath, remember? I'm one big walking sensitivity."

I laughed. "Fair enough. So, no one's heard any word on when Lucida might be moved?"

"Nah. They can't move her until they can assess the damage, and they can't do that until she wakes up. If she wakes up," Savvy said and she shrugged, as though she could care less whether Lucida ever regained consciousness again—a sentiment I could heartily appreciate.

I heard a small, sniffling noise and looked over at Hannah. She was trying to open a package of ornaments but her hands were now shaking. Immediately I wanted to kick myself.

"Ah, shit, Hannah, I'm sorry," I said. I hopped down off the chair I was standing on and dropped to the floor beside her, throwing my arm around her shoulders. "That was a crappy topic to bring up. And here I am, talking about sensitivities like an idiot."

Hannah shook her head and rubbed ferociously at her eyes. "No, Jess, it's fine. I hate that she gets to me like this. I just need to get over it."

I opened my mouth to object, but Savvy beat me to it. "Oy!" she cried, making us all jump. "Not a single bloody word out of you about getting over things! That devious old blighter screwed up your life good and proper. You are allowed to feel however the hell you want for however the hell long you want, and don't you dare apologize for it, yeah?"

A smile crept over Hannah's initially shocked expression. "Yes, ma'am," she said, giving Savvy a military salute.

"That's right. But call me ma'am again and I will club you over the head with this angel," Savvy warned, swinging the angel around menacingly.

"In the true spirit of Christmas," Mackie said, and we all laughed.

I was very impressed with our collective holiday decorating skills. Within an hour, not only had we filled every inch of that enormous tree with glittering décor, but we had hung tinsel garlands all around the room, strung extra Christmas lights around the doors and window frames, and hung the stockings from the fireplace. We'd just put the finishing touches on a wreath on the inside of the door when Milo stuck his head through it. I yelped and dropped the ribbon I was holding.

"You will be visited by three ghosts, *clink-clink!*" he moaned in a spooky voice.

"*Clink-clink?*" I asked. "What the hell is '*clink-clink*' supposed to mean?"

"You know, chains? Jacob Marley? 'I forged these chains in life?' Read a book much?" Milo teased, sailing the rest of the way into the room and circling it once, taking in all our hard work. "Ugh, it looks like the dollar store threw up in here. Mine eyes cannot take all this glitter."

"Really? Isn't glitter the official currency of your people?" I teased.

Milo spun and narrowed his eyes at me. "Yes, and you are pending it *all wrong*. Now watch that sass or I will revoke your allowance."

I raised my hands in mock surrender. "Okay, okay!"

"So, are you done? Is it present time?" Milo asked, clapping his hands gleefully.

"No presents until tomorrow morning!" I said sharply.

Milo pouted. "Oh, come on! Aren't you at least going to give me a hint?"

"You were totally that kid who searched your house from attic to basement until you found all your Christmas gifts, weren't you?" I asked him.

"No need, my mother kept them all in the back of her closet every year," Milo said. "And besides, I never got what I asked for anyway, so what was the point?" He mimed ripping open a present and then gasping in surprise. "Oh, look! More sports ball accoutrements I don't know how to use for teams I don't want to join! Thanks, Mom and Dad!"

"Well, you are just going to have to wait until tomorrow. I am not spoiling this surprise, it's too good."

Milo gasped. "You can't just say stuff like that and then not tell me what the surprise is!"

I grinned an evil grin. "Of course, I can. Torturing you is part of my holiday fun."

Milo turned to Hannah, but she shook her head firmly before he could even open his mouth. "Don't even try it. I am not spoiling your Christmas present, either."

"Ugh, you are the meanest moms ever!" Milo grumbled, floating down to rest on Hannah's bed like a grumpy feather.

"Did you find Karen?" Hannah asked him.

"Yes," Milo said, still sounding sulky. "She just got back from what I can only assume was a guilt-induced shopping spree. I'm surprised she could carry all the bags." He looked over at me and pointed a judgmental finger at my all-black ensemble. "And Karen has flawless taste, so your wardrobe undoubtedly just got a major upgrade."

Our aunt had arrived a couple of days ago, after all the chaos of the Shattering had ended. Since she had stepped off the plane, she had subjected us to an almost uninterrupted stream of apologies for asking us to come to the Airechtas in her place. No matter how many times we told her that we didn't mind, and that we'd forgiven her, and that it wasn't her fault, she remained wracked with guilt. Unsurprisingly, she was now venting her guilt with her credit card. I used to give her a hard time about gifts, but now I knew it would be easiest to just accept whatever she bought me with a smile. She was never able to have any kids of her own, and she had missed out on eighteen years of spoiling us. Besides, she was still seething about how the Council had treated Hannah during the Shattering, so her ire was easily stoked right now. I was pretty sure I could still hear the distant echoes of the tempestuous tirade she had unleashed on the Council on her arrival—and barely a Council member had looked us in the eye since.

"Did you tell her about the movie night?" Hannah asked.

"She said she'll be up as soon as she finishes wrapping, but not to wait for her," Milo said. "And I warned her in advance of the foliage," he added, pointing to the tree.

"Good idea," Hannah said. "I still think we're going to get in trouble for having a tree in here. And I'm positive we're not supposed to be using that either." She pointed to the massive urn Savvy had found to stand the tree up in.

"Ah, no one's going to miss that old thing," Savvy said dismissively. "It was just gathering dust."

Mackie took a good look at the urn for the first time and her eyes widened. "Is... is that from the Grand Council Room?" she asked weakly.

"Yep," Savvy said. "Swiped it from beside the flag pole and told the Caomhnóir on duty I was taking it for Christmas polishing."

Mackie dropped her head into her hands. "Sav, that urn is from the 1500s. It's quite literally priceless."

"They've got another one just like it on the other side of the throne!" Savvy said, as though that solved the problem. "How priceless can it be if they've got a spare lying around? Besides, we haven't smashed it to bits, have we? We'll put it back on Boxing Day, good as new."

"Here Mack, have a cookie," I said quickly, shoving a fistful of sugar cookies into her hand before she had a chance to argue further. "It will all be fine. Holiday magic, okay?"

"Luckily for both of you, I'm more interested in eating this cookie than I am in that urn," Mackie said through an impressively large bite.

8

"Excellent," I said, and looked around me with a sigh of satisfaction. I had successfully conjured nearly all of my favorite traditions in one way or another. My room was a tacky glittering Christmas-fest. My favorite music was playing, and the scents of gingerbread and balsam sap were thick in the air. I'd gathered some of my favorite people around me, and it was going to be a lovely night. The Durupinen might have turned my world upside down, but I had managed, for this one night, to right it again. I crammed an entire sugar cookie into my mouth. It tasted like victory.

2

WOUNDS AND SCARS

T HE CASTLE WAS PITCH BLACK and eerily silent. The only light and movement came from the occasional drifting form of one of the resident spirits, who took as little notice of me as I did of them as I crept down the staircase and through the corridor toward the hospital ward.

I knew that Finn would be relieved of his shift guarding Lucida in the hospital ward right at midnight, and that he would head back to the barracks when he had finished to get some sleep before his shift in the morning. If I was going to see Finn on Christmas, and actually have a real conversation with him, this might be my only chance. I'd left everyone else sleeping in a Christmas cookie-induced torpor and snuck out without disturbing them.

I hovered in the stairwell at the end of the hallway, listening as the Caomhnóir conferred with each other in low voices. Then I waited with building anticipation as I heard Finn's footsteps come closer. I could tell they were his footsteps; he had a habit of landing a bit more heavily on his right foot, giving his strides a lopsided sound. Yes, I knew the sound of his walk. Pathetic, I know.

Finn rounded the corner and stopped short at the sight of me. I lifted a finger quickly to my lips, and he stifled whatever sound of surprise he was going to make. He followed me down a flight of stairs to a deserted landing two floors below where I finally felt it was safe to stop and talk.

"Hi," I said lamely.

"What are you doing here?" he asked by way of greeting.

"I... wanted to say merry Christmas to you, and I wasn't sure if I'd get the chance later," I said.

"Oh. I see. Yes, happy Christmas," Finn said stiffly.

What had I expected? We'd barely had two minutes to speak to each other since we'd gotten into a terrible disagreement. After a passionate tryst in a deserted hut in the woods, I had accidentally suggested that he quit being a Caomhnóir so that we could be together. I'd never seen him so angry, not at me, anyway. The distance between us had been palpable ever since.

I looked up into his gaze and felt like I could see it there—that distance—like a curtain shutting out the warmth in his eyes. Instantly, I felt embarrassed and angry with myself. "I'm sorry, I shouldn't have come. It was stupid. I just... have a good night. Merry Christmas."

"No, don't go," Finn said quickly. "I... I apologize. I'm tired. It has been a long shift."

"You're not just tired," I murmured. "You're still mad at me."

Finn's jaw tightened. "I'm not mad."

I laughed. "You're doing a really good impression of it."

His nostrils flared. "I am doing my best to keep up the façade that we both agreed was crucial to our cover while here."

"Finn, I'm not an idiot. There is no one else in this stairwell. We are totally alone. There's no reason for the façade right now. Just admit it. You're still angry with me."

He didn't reply.

"I'm really sorry about what I said, Finn. I don't think my role as a Durupinen is more important than yours as a Caomhnóir. Honestly, I don't. How could I? How many times have you saved my life now? No one appreciates how important Caomhnóir are more than I do. I was just upset and frustrated because our callings are standing in the way of... us."

Finn's expression softened just a bit. "Apology accepted. I share your frustration."

"Do you, though?" I asked quietly.

"I don't follow," Finn said.

"Well, it just feels like you're content to leave things the way they are."

"I still don't follow."

I sighed. "As it stands, this is the only way we can be together." I gestured around us. "Secretly. Stolen moments. Constantly pretending for the benefit of others that we can barely tolerate each other's company. It's exhausting and demoralizing, and yet you seem to feel no real motivation to change it."

"Jess, that's not fair. Of course, I wish that things were different. But there are certain realities of our relationship that must be

12

aced. We cannot wish them away, and dwelling on them will only
poil what time we do have together. We knew what we were getting
nto when we started this."

"I know. That doesn't make it any easier to deal with."

"So, would you rather we broke it off?" he asked bluntly.

"What? No! That's not what I'm saying! But nothing is going to
hange if we don't try to change it."

His expression morphed from truculent to wary. "Change it
now?"

"The Airechtas is almost over. If we're ever going to speak up—"

Finn put up a hand. "Stop. I know what you're going to say. We
an't, and you know it."

"But this might be the only chance we get to—"

"To what?" Finn hissed. "To ensure we are discovered? To watch
Seamus stand up before the Council and reveal what he knows? To
say goodbye before the Council reassigns me and we never see each
other again?"

"We don't know that will happen," I said in a tiny voice.

"You might not. I do," Finn said. "I want the freedom to be
together as badly as you do, Jess, but we're not going to get it like
this. It's too risky. I won't lose you in a foolish gamble against such
odds."

I looked at him, but couldn't finish the sentence. I didn't even
know what I wanted to say. I was too confused, too frustrated. This
wasn't how I wanted this conversation to go.

"It's Christmas. I don't want to do this right now," I finally said.

"No," Finn said. He dropped his arms and with them, his
combative tone. "Nor do I. Look, we're both under a lot of pressure
here. In just a week or so, the Airechtas will be over. It will be much
easier to be rational when we are finally well away from this bloody
castle. We will have more time and space to talk. We'll figure it out."

I almost told him about the Council seat. This was the moment
to do it. If I didn't do it now, it was tantamount to a lie. But the
words wouldn't come. I couldn't say them. I couldn't bear to further
damage this tiny, fragile snatch of time we had together. It was
foolish, but I couldn't do it.

"Yeah. We'll figure it out," I said instead. "You'd better get going.
They'll be wondering at the barracks what's keeping you."

I turned to go, but he stopped me. "What is that?"

13

I turned back to see him pointing at the parcel tucked under my arm.

"Nothing. It's just something I was going to give you."

"And now you're not going to give it to me?"

I shrugged. "I wasn't sure that you'd want it."

He extended a hand. "May I see it?"

Reluctantly, I pulled it out from under my arm and placed it on his outstretched palm. "It isn't anything big."

He didn't reply, but quietly undid the string and wrapping paper, revealing a small book.

"It's for your poetry," I muttered. "For you to write in."

"Oh, I see," Finn said, turning it over in his hand. "Well, thank you very much."

"You have to open it."

"Pardon?"

"You have to open it. It's not just a plain book. I... just open it," I said.

Looking puzzled, Finn began flipping through the book. His eyes grew wide. "Jess, this is... wonderful."

I had filled the pages of the book with hand-drawn borders and accent sketches, a sort of canvas of my art on which he could record his own.

"I know you love a good blank page. I mean, I do, too," I said. "But I thought this might... inspire you."

Even as he looked at the drawings, his face fell back into lines of misery. "I haven't anything to give you. I didn't think we would be here for Christmas, and I wasn't sure if we..."

"That's okay," I said quickly. "I don't need you to give me anything. I've just been working on this for a while, and so I thought Christmas was as good a time as any to give it to you."

"Well, thank you. I look very much forward to writing in it," he said.

"You're welcome," I said. We stood awkwardly, and every second that he didn't reach for me and kiss me expanded into an ocean between us.

"I should go," I said, and left without saying another word.

I made it to the bottom of the stairs before the tears started, and halfway down the next hallway before they really started blinding me. By the time I reached the entrance hall, I could barely stifle the

14

sobs. On the final landing of the grand staircase, I sank to the floor, dropped my face into my hands, and let the pain just wash over me.

"Jess? Are you okay? What are you doing?"

I looked up to see Milo hovering just a few feet from me at the base of the stairs. His face was twisted with sympathy.

"Sleepwalking," I replied, willing the tears out of my voice and keeping my face carefully hidden. "What are you doing down here?"

He shrugged. "It gets très dull while all you breathers are sleeping. I was just entertaining some floaters out on the grounds and killing time until I could wake you all up for gifts."

I nodded.

"So, you didn't answer my first question," Milo said, floating up the steps and coming to rest beside me on the rug.

"What question?"

"I asked if you were okay," Milo prompted quietly.

"I'm swell," I insisted.

"Would this 'swellness' have anything to do with why I just saw Finn storming out across the grounds?" Milo asked.

"He was storming?" I asked. Even to me, my voice sounded small.

"I think storming is an accurate description, yes," Milo said. "There was cursing, and kicking, and a pretty steady tirade of angry muttering under his breath. He didn't even acknowledge me when I said hello."

"Yeah. We're both swell," I said.

"Do you want to talk about it?" Milo asked quietly.

I kept my palms pressed to my closed eyes. The pressure seemed to relieve some of the aching. "There's nothing to talk about."

"Come on, Jess," Milo said, and for once there was no laugh in his voice, no sarcastic edge. "I'm not an idiot. I might be closer to your sister, but you and I— we're Bound, sweetness. We share an actual psychic connection. Sure, you've never told me outright that you two are together, but those feelings don't just shut off. They trickle through the connection. They color everything you say about him, every time he walks into the room."

Feeling colored me at that moment too, as I felt my cheeks burn with the shame of being so transparent. "Color? Really?"

"Oh, yeah," Milo said. "Your thoughts come through all rosy and gold as soon as Finn is involved. It's like that old French song. You talk about him, and suddenly it's 'La Vie en Rose' inside my brain.

But psychic connection aside, you are not nearly as good at hiding your emotions as you think you are."

"Is that so?" I said, keeping my now scarlet face safely behind my hands.

"Yes, that's so," Milo said. "You think I don't know what it looks like when someone has to hide their feelings for someone they love? Honey, that was the basis of my entire existence from the moment I hit puberty."

I didn't respond; I was trying too hard to push back the tears that were determinedly leaking from my eyes.

"You are tough as nails when you know you're being watched," Milo went on. "But it's those other moments—the ones when you think you're alone—that's when your shields come down, and at that point, sweetness, you might as well tattoo his name on your forehead."

"I didn't realize I was being so obvious," I said.

Milo chuckled, but the sound was hollow and sad. "Just be thankful that he loves you back. Okay, story time." I felt him move closer to me, felt his chill as the distance between us closed by a few more inches. "Back when I had a pulse, I was madly in love with a boy in my high school. He was your typical testosterone-fueled three-season jock, a vision of perfection in his musky game day jerseys. I was convinced I was flying completely under the radar. I had just transferred from another school, fresh out of one of my dad's 'scared straight' boot camps. After six weeks of learning how to be a man's man, I was sure no one would ever guess I was as gay as a Broadway kick line."

He laughed mirthlessly. "Oh, what a sweet, deluded little creature I was. He saw right through me, and for some reason, he loved what he saw. He absolutely loved that I was in love with him. No one is easier to fuck with than the queer boy who is not-so-secretly in love with you. I'm not really sure why he did it. Maybe he was secretly gay, full of self-loathing. Maybe he was just a narcissist with sociopathic tendencies. Maybe a little bit of both. Anyway, he made me think he was interested in me. He wasn't subtle about it either, let's just leave it at that. And I fell for it, hook, line, and sinker. I was supposed to meet him outside the door to the locker room late one night. I went, my heart pounding like a jack-hammer inside my chest. He was there; I couldn't believe it. He'd brought a six pack of beer—not that I drank that swill, but he'd already

16

opened one for me, so I took it. He told me he was going to run inside for a minute to see if the coast was clear. Then, he said, he had something really special he wanted to show me. Tingling with the anticipation of what that 'something' might be, I waited, and while I waited, because I had nothing better to do, I drank. I remember thinking, all of a sudden, that I felt really sleepy, and I sat down on the bench. That's the last thing I remember until I woke up, four hours later, practically hypothermic and with the word 'faggot' scrawled all over my face in permanent marker."

I kept my face hidden behind my hands, perhaps because I thought that if I looked at him in that moment, I would lose what little control I had left over the tears. "Jesus, Milo. I'm so sorry. That's horrible."

He sighed ruefully. "Whatever, I'm over it. That's one of the few perks to so much mandatory therapy; you get to work through shit like that. I'm not telling you because I need your sympathy, Jess. I'm telling you because I want you to know that I get it. I get how hard it is to fight against the feelings, and convince yourself you don't feel them. I know what it is to finally let someone in only to get annihilated. And I wouldn't wish that on anyone, really, but I especially wouldn't wish it on you."

"And why especially me?" I asked.

"Because I'm finally admitting to myself how alike we are, and that's probably why we create a lot of friction. We both have dealt with a lot of bullshit in our lives which has jaded us. We didn't have any real reason to trust anyone anymore, and so we built our walls of sarcasm and we piled on our armor of attitude and we hid behind them. And every once in a while, when someone would breach the defenses, they'd prove to us, all over again, that we were right to put up the walls in the first place. But those are the moments that betray us, you know. The cracks in the wall that let the love in are the same ones that let it shine through when we try to hide it."

"When did you get so sappy and poetic?" I asked him.

"I'm an undiscovered talent, what can I say?" Milo said. "Finn's emo love poems are nothing to my cheesy love advice. You're avoiding my question, though."

"I know. I'm trying to distract you so you won't notice. Is it working?"

"Nope."

I sighed. I took my hands away from my face, and there was

nothing to keep the tears from leaking out now. And so they did, dripping freely down my nose and dropping onto the knees of my pajamas.

"You're crying!" Milo said in surprise.

"Yup."

"I didn't realize... you don't do that very often."

"I know. It's one of the side effects of those walls you were talking about," I said. My voice broke as a sob bubbled to the surface.

"Oh, sweetness, I hear that," Milo said. "I was the queen of the clandestine ugly cry. You can go right ahead and let it out all over me, if you want. For once, I'm gonna pack the sass away. No judgment." He scooted over so that he closed the distance between us on the floor and rested the full spiritual weight of his form against me. The feeling was intensely cold and yet so comforting. I could feel our connection pulsing through him, much as I did when Hannah and I grasped hands.

And as much to my surprise as his, I did. I let it all out—every aching, wrenching frustrated tear until I was all cried out. And as I cried, I told him every single twist and turn in my relationship with Finn that had led us to this moment. It felt just terrible and wonderful at the same time to share it with someone, to lift the burden off myself and release it into the air. It was almost as if, by telling Milo, he was helping to carry the weight of it. At last, I sniffed into silence and looked up at Milo with swollen eyes.

"I never did understand how Hannah could stand a hug from a ghost, but I have to admit, it's helping."

"I'm glad, sweetness."

"I just... I don't know how I always manage to screw it up so badly. Is this genetic? Do I have some kind of self-destruct button on all of my relationships that I can't resist pushing?"

"It does sort of sound like you can't get out of your own way, sweetness," Milo said with a small, sad smile. "Is that why you're so upset? Because you have to keep things secret?"

"I feel like we have this one chance," I said, and despite thinking I had no tears left, I could feel them burning the corners of my eyes again. "This one chance with the Airechtas to change everything. This is our opportunity to make a proposal to overthrow the restrictions on Caomhnóir-Durupinen relationships. The Prophecy was the original reason for the restrictions in the first place, and

18

ow it's over. If we don't fight for us here, this week, I don't know if ve'll ever get another chance."

"And Finn doesn't want to?" Milo guessed.

I shook my head. "He thinks it will expose us. Why else would we sk to abolish the law, unless we were already breaking it?"

"Don't you think he has a point?" Milo asked. "No offense, but it vould be a pretty transparent request."

"I know. I know it would," I said. "But what's the alternative? ip-toe around for the rest of our lives? Constantly look over our houlders, convinced that the next kiss will be the one that finally petrays us? I can't live like that. It's only been two months and it's already driving me mad!"

Milo let out a low whistle. "That is some Capulet and Montague bullshit right there."

"No kidding. And we all know how that one ended."

Milo looked sternly at me. "I can't believe I'm saying this, but don't be dramatic, sweetness. No one is dying in this scenario."

"Maybe not," I said. "But it would still be a far cry from a happy ending."

"What would the Council do, theoretically, if they found out?" Milo asked.

"They'd send Finn away. They'd reassign him, as far from me as hey could place him. We would never see each other again," I said, and even the thought of it felt like a punch in the stomach.

Milo let out a low whistle. "Damn."

"I haven't even told you the worst part yet."

Milo's eyebrows disappeared into the artful sweep of his dark hair. "How can it get any worse?"

"Seamus knows," I said, and my voice sounded dead, defeated. "He caught on to what was happening three years ago, when we first got back from Fairhaven. He threatened Finn, and that was why we never... why nothing ever happened between us back then."

"Oh, shit."

"Yeah. Finn says he's sure the Caomhnóir don't have a clue about us now, but if we propose to the Council to lift the ban..."

"You're screwed."

"Bingo," I said. "And I get that. I get why he's scared. I'm scared, too. Terrified, actually. But the thing is, Finn is such a fighter. He's fought his whole life. It's how he's approached almost every situation he's ever faced. And I just wish… I just wish he would fight for us."

We sat together for a silent minute. Milo's chill continued to sap away the intensity of my sadness, dulling it, like ice on a wound.

"I haven't even told him about Hannah running for the Council seat," I confessed at last.

Milo's eyes widened. "He doesn't know?"

"No. He knows that Finvarra is going to nominate us, but he doesn't know that we're going to accept the nomination." I saw Milo staring at me, and added defensively, "There's been no time! We just decided the other day, and he's been constantly on duty!"

"But you were just talking to him alone. Why didn't you tell him then?" Milo asked.

"I couldn't do it," I said. The corners of my eyes burned, but I had no tears left to shed. "I know I should have, but I chickened out."

"So, he still thinks we're going home at the end of the week?" Milo asked.

"Yes," I said. "And let's be honest, we probably are. No one is actually going to vote for the Apocalypse twins for the Council."

"Yeah, but even so, you have to tell him, Jess," Milo said. "This is his life, too, and this is too big a decision to make without him, especially if you want to stand a chance of staying together."

"I know, I know!" I cried, dropping my face into my hands again. My head was beginning to pound with the monster of a headache that only a good cry could produce. "So, now you know everything. I've completely poured my heart out to you. You're my Spirit Guide—guide me! What should I do?"

"I don't think you should do anything," Milo said quietly.

"But—"

"Let me finish!" he said, putting up a hand. "I don't think you should do anything on your own. This isn't something you can do unilaterally, not when it affects you both so much. If the two of you want to wind up together, that's how you have to make the decision: together. You have to come clean about the nomination, and you have to promise him that you won't bring up a measure to abolish the relationship rule unless you both agree that it's the right thing to do."

I sniffed a few times, absorbing his words. "That is… really good advice," I said finally.

"Don't sound so surprised! My time as a Spirit Guide has made

20

me wise beyond my years," Milo said with a sigh. "It's exhausting, being so full of sage wisdom, and having to dole it out to all you foolish living people."

"Well, thank you. Thank you for exhausting yourself for my sake. I really do appreciate it," I told him.

"Anytime, sweetness," Milo said. "And I mean it. Talk to him. Talk to him again. Keep talking until the two of you talk yourself onto the same page. And another thing, too."

"What?"

"Just now you said that Finn has been a fighter his whole life, and that's how he approaches every situation, except this one. But really, that should show you how special you are to him. He knows that fights don't always go your way. Sometimes, you lose. And losing you? That must be unthinkable for him."

"Milo, don't tell anyone I said this, because I will deny it until my dying day, but you are the best. Seriously," I said.

"Don't worry, I won't rat you out," he said, with a trace of a laugh in his voice.

"And don't tell Hannah all this stuff about Finn. I want to tell her myself."

"Cross my heart and hope to... well, you know what I mean," Milo said with a smirk.

"Come on," I said, standing up.

Milo looked startled at my abrupt command. "Where are we going?"

"Upstairs to the room. It is," I checked my watch, "12:37, which makes it officially Christmas. I'm not going to make you wait a minute longer for your present."

"Wait, for real? I get it now?" Milo squealed, his face lighting up.

"Yes. Right now. Let's go."

3

MILO'S CLOSET

MILO BLINKED OUT to conserve energy, but I felt him with me all the way back up to our bedroom, hovering beside me like a candle I was using to light my way. Finally, I closed the door behind us and flicked on the lights.

"Jess? What's going on?" Hannah asked, rolling over and rubbing her eyes.

"Who's there? What the hell is happening?" Savvy cried, squinting in the brightness. Then she spotted me and seemed to remember where she was. "Mate, what time is it?"

"It's almost one o'clock, but Christmas is officially starting," I announced.

"Do I need to be conscious for it?" Savvy grumbled.

"You're going to want to be conscious for this. We're giving Milo his gift."

"Now?" Hannah mumbled.

"Right now! Cannot wait! Need to do it immediately!" I cried. I reached into the bag of Christmas trappings and tossed a Santa hat to each of them. Savvy pulled hers over her eyes and flopped back down on the couch. Hannah, however, sat up, rubbed her eyes, and put the hat on.

"Where's Mackie?" I asked, looking around for her, an extra Santa hat clutched in my hand.

"She went back to sleep in her own room," Hannah yawned. "She said if Savvy kicked her one more time, she'd have to kill her, and that wasn't in the spirit of Christmas."

"Oh," I said, thrusting the hat onto my own head instead. "Well, her loss. And I doubt Karen wants us to wake her up either, so let's just get started."

"But why are we doing this now? In the middle of the night?" Hannah asked again.

"Because Milo and I just had a moment and I can't wait anymore," I replied.

"Aw, you guys had a moment? Without me? But you know how much I love to see you getting along!" Hannah said, pouting.

"Yes. It was very touching. Don't get all excited, though. We aren't going to make a habit of it. It would mess with our love/hate dynamic," I assured her.

"Exactly. I don't think Jess and I could survive without a steady diet of witty banter," Milo added.

Hannah was still looking pouty. "It was a spontaneous moment, okay?" I said, waving my hand impatiently. "The point is that I needed to talk to someone and Milo was in the right place at the right time. And he was brilliant, so now we need to reinforce his good behavior with gifts." I plopped down on my bed, pulling my laptop from under it and flipping it open.

"What's going on?" Milo asked. "My present is on the computer?"

"Of course, it is! What did you think I was going to give you, a sweater? You don't have a corporeal form!" I pulled up what I was looking for on the screen, but I tilted it away from Milo so that he couldn't yet see it. "Okay, so do you remember last week when I dyed my hair and you flipped out on me?"

"Righteous indignation is hardly an overreaction when it comes to fashion, but, yes. Proceed," Milo said in a dignified voice.

"I was confused at the time. I couldn't understand why you were so mad at me. But then I figured it out," I said.

Milo's smile slipped. "Oh, really? And what exactly did you figure out, Sherlock?"

"Well, I already knew you had a real passion for the fashion world when you were alive," I said, trying to keep my voice light and even, refusing to give in to the sadness at the heart of what I was saying. "Hannah told me it was your dream to design your own couture line and have your own runway show at Fashion Week. Is that true?"

Milo shrugged, hoisting his armor on more securely against whatever emotions I was stirring up in him. "It was a pipe dream. Everyone's got one. You probably wanted to be Rembrandt. I didn't really think it was going to happen, or anything."

"I may never be Rembrandt, but it won't be because I didn't get the chance to try. That's not the case for you."

Hannah was looking wary. Even Savvy had sat up and pushed

he Santa hat up onto her forehead so she could see. Milo didn't espond. Maybe he couldn't. I went on, so that he didn't feel like he ad to.

"So, then I started thinking about all the times you've given me nsolicited fashion advice. All the times you've suggested what to lo with my hair, or my accessories. All the times you begged to upervise our make-up application. And I always give you such a ard time about it, because I always thought you were just nagging ne. But then I realized it was more than that."

"Not really," Milo said, with a too-careless wave of his hand. Someone had to take you in hand. Seriously, girl, you are tragic."

I smiled. "Nice try, but we're going to lay off the snark for a few ninutes because it's Christmas, and on Christmas, we get real," said. "I realized that helping Hannah and me is the only pportunity you get to do what you truly love. And it never occurred o me that I might actually be hurting you when I said no. I'm really orry, Milo."

Milo didn't speak; his face was twisted with long-repressed pain. or a moment, I wondered if I had gotten too real for him, and if he night just blink out to avoid the bluntness of what I had just said. 3ut then he nodded in acknowledgment of my apology.

"No one does more for us than you, Milo. And you do it all the ime, day and night, and you never complain, even though you lidn't know what you were getting yourself into when you Bound ourself to Hannah," I said.

"I don't regret that part," Milo blurted out. "I've got regrets, ut... not about being a Spirit Guide. Not many ghosts get that kind f chance—to do something really meaningful after they die. I do, .nd I'm grateful for it."

"I know. Hannah and I will never be able to thank you enough. 3ut we can do this one little thing to show you how much we .ppreciate you. So, merry Christmas."

I turned the computer around so that Milo could see the screen. Ie looked at it for a moment, then his eyes widened. He floated oward it, his mouth hanging open.

"What... is that?" he whispered. He pointed to the top corner, vhere the name of the blog curled across the screen in glittering uchsia script: *Milo's Closet.*

"It's a fashion design blog. Or at least, it will be, once it goes ive."

25

"I don't understand. No offense, but you don't know the first thing about fashion."

"True. But *you* do," I said.

Milo stared at the screen, then back at me. "I still don't get it," he said finally.

"It's a blog. For your designs. So that the world can see your ideas and know how stupidly talented you are," I said.

One corner of Milo's mouth twitched into a suggestion of a smile but he still looked utterly bewildered. "How is that supposed to work? I'm dead. I can't blog."

"Not by yourself, no. That's why we'll be here to help you. No seriously, listen, we've figured it all out!" I said, because he was still looking skeptical. "Here's how it will work. When you get a design idea, we Habitate. You can use me to sketch the design for you."

A slow smile began to spread over Milo's face. "So, we can post the sketches for people to see? That's pretty cool."

"No, no, it's more than that!" Hannah chimed in eagerly. "When the design is done, we use Savvy's mum to construct it for us."

"I've already asked her, and she's tickled to get started," Savvy said through a yawn. "She's dead clever with a sewing machine. She can make anything you like, quick as a wink."

"When the clothes are done, Savvy and Hannah and I can model and photograph the designs for you. Then you tell us what to write for the blog entry, and we post! You'll be famous in no time."

"You would do that... for me?" Milo whispered, his expression stunned.

"Of course," I said.

"But... you hate having your picture taken. Are you seriously going to let me dress you up in whatever I want and then spread the proof of it all over the internet?"

I shrugged. "You've lent us your soul for the next seventy-odd years, so we're lending you our bodies. I am your canvas." I quickly adopted a businesslike tone. "Of course, I absolutely refuse to be photographed wearing anything that isn't black. And you can only photograph me from my left side, with no up lighting. And under no circumstances can you force my giant feet into stilettos."

"And I won't wear nothing that don't show my girls off, so keep them dresses low-cut, yeah?' Sav added with a wink.

Milo threw his head back and laughed. "I can't believe this. This is just... incredible." His smile faded. "But what if people actually start reading it? Won't my cover be blown? Isn't this against the Durupinen code of secrecy? I don't want to wind up in front of the Council again."

I shrugged. "People pretend to be other people on the internet all the time. If anyone ever wants to interview the famous designer Milo Chang, they will have to do it over email or by phone. It will enhance your mystique."

Milo squealed. "This is... I can't even tell you how much this means to me!"

"But we haven't even told you the good part," I said.

Milo laughed. "The good part? What could possibly be better than this?"

I looked over at Hannah, who was so excited that she had pulled her pajama shirt up over her mouth to muffle the little squealing noises she was making.

"I put in a call to the one and only celebrity I know, who just happens to owe me a huge favor. Once we're up and running, and your first collection is done, she's going to wear one of your pieces out to one of her movie events."

Milo's form went pale. "I... you don't... you can't possibly mean..."

"Oh yes, I can, and I do. The one and only Talia Simms has agreed to be photographed, in public, in a Milo Chang original."

With a shiver and a pop, Milo vanished on the spot.

We all sat there for a moment, staring around for him.

"Milo? Are you okay?" Hannah called, a laugh in her voice.

"AM I OKAY? IF I HADN'T ALREADY DIED, I'D BE DEAD!" Milo shrieked through our connection, so that Hannah and I had to clamp our hands over our ears to stop them from ringing. "I don't... I can't even... I CAN'T REMEMBER HOW TO MANIFEST!"

I laughed aloud, despite the agonizing pain in my head. "Well, calm down and figure it out before you make my skull explode!"

"Sorry!" Milo sang. "This much fabulousness combined with this much excitement is just impossible to contain."

"So, you like it?" Hannah asked, rocking backward and forward on her knees. "I wasn't sure whether you would want to put your stuff out there. Aren't you worried it's going to be stressful, people critiquing your ideas?"

With what felt like a massive mental effort, Milo lifted himself out of the connection and wavered back into physical form. He was

27

grinning from ear to ear, and his eyes were shining. "Sweetness, if anyone understands the phrase 'life is too short,' it is yours truly. I never thought I'd get the *chance* for anyone to critique my ideas. People just don't get second chances like this. I'm not going to let a little fear stand in the way when I finally have the chance to get a taste of what I've always wanted."

He caught my eye and I winked at him. "Neither will I."

"Well, we're awake," Hannah said, shrugging. "Should we just exchange the rest of the presents?"

"Can my gift be more sleep?" Savvy moaned, flopping back over.

"Yeah, I'm too excited to go back to sleep now," I said. "Grab those stockings, and let's dig in."

§

All in all, it was a much better Christmas than I would have thought possible while being stuck at Fairhaven Hall. We tore through all the gifts under the tree in less than an hour, gorged ourselves on Christmas cookies, and slept the rest of the morning away. Mackie shuffled in with coffee around nine o'clock, and Karen turned up an hour later with an excessive number of gifts, which we dutifully opened and squealed over. The dining room was set up with a lavish breakfast buffet so delicious that we trekked down twice before we pronounced ourselves too stuffed to eat ever again. Around two o'clock, Tia interrupted our Christmas movie marathon with a Skype session, during which she lamented our absence, but gushed profusely over the British-themed box of gifts I'd mailed to her.

"When are you coming home?" she asked.

"I'll keep you posted," was all I could say. Of course, we had no idea what the answer to that question would be. If Hannah actually managed to win the Council seat—a long shot, it was true, but still—we wouldn't be coming home at all.

At four o'clock we somehow found ourselves hungry enough to stuff ourselves silly with a mouthwatering traditional English Christmas dinner. After several plates full of roast turkey and goose, goose-fat roasted potatoes, sage and onion stuffing, pigs-in-blankets, sprouts, Yorkshire pudding, mince pies, and Christmas pudding with brandy sauce, I thought Hannah was going to have to roll me up the stairs to our room.

"Wake me up for next year's Christmas dinner," I groaned, flopping onto my bed, which creaked more than usual.

"Same," Hannah sighed, collapsing into a chair by the fire. She was still wearing one of the tissue paper crowns that came inside the Christmas crackers Savvy gave us at the table. She had demanded that every single person wear their crown, and then forced us all to read the jokes aloud. She roared with laughter at every single one, whether it was funny or not.

"I must admit, I missed Christmas at Fairhaven," Karen said, stifling a yawn. "It was always such a wonderful celebration, and I see it hasn't changed." She sunk into a chair and sighed, kicking off her shoes and rubbing one of her feet. "Well, I'm glad you girls have decided to stay for the rest of the Airechtas. I think that you'll learn a lot, and I'm proud of you for sticking it out, in spite of how terribly it all went wrong in the beginning. But we'll be done soon, and then you won't have to be in that Council Room for another five years." She smiled.

I looked at Hannah. She shrugged her shoulders and nodded. I didn't need our connection to decode her answer to my unspoken question.

Yup. We have to tell her. It's now or never.

"Karen," I began, sliding off of my bed and coming to sit in the chair beside Hannah. "We need to talk to you."

Karen's expression was instantly wary. She dropped her aching foot and sat up straight. "I don't like the sound of that. What is it?" she asked.

"We have something we want to tell you, but it would be great if you would let us tell you the whole thing before you started... freaking out," I said.

"Jess, you can't begin a conversation with a statement like that and expect me *not* to start freaking out," Karen said exasperatedly.

"I'll get to the point then," I said. I looked at Hannah and she nodded encouragingly. "When we first got here for the Airechtas, Finvarra called us to her office. She said she had something important that she wanted to share with us."

"Okay," Karen said slowly. She was picking anxiously at a thread on the hem of her sweater. If she didn't calm down, she was going to unravel the whole damn thing into a pile of cashmere.

"She started by apologizing to us—well, to our whole clan, really. She said it was her fault that we lost our Council seat, and that she had lots of regrets about the way she treated our family in the wake of Mom's disappearance."

"As well she should," Karen said bitterly. "And she's not the only one, either."

"Finvarra told us that she wants to make it up to us by nominating our clan for the open Council seat," I said.

Karen just continued looking at me as though I had not spoken.

"Karen? Did you hear what I said?"

Karen gave her head a little shake. "She told you what, I'm sorry?"

"The open seat on the Council. The one that they stripped from Marion. She is going to nominate our clan for it," I repeated, a little more slowly.

Karen laughed incredulously. "And how exactly does that constitute an apology? It's an empty gesture. She already knows that I will have nothing to do with this Council. What does she hope to prove, by nominating me for a seat that she knows I will never run for?"

"Yeah, she knows you won't have anything to do with it. That's why she told us instead of you. She was hoping that Hannah or I would make a run for it."

Karen laughed again, louder this time. "Has she lost her mind?"

I looked at Hannah again. "Well, no, but Hannah and I might have."

Karen stopped laughing abruptly. "What do you mean?"

Hannah cleared her throat. "We... well, actually... we decided that I'm going to run for the seat."

Karen looked back and forth between the two of us with a strange half-smile on her face, looking to catch one of us in a lie. The smile slowly faded into a blank look of horror as she realized that there was no punchline.

"You cannot be serious!" she said weakly. "What in the world would possess you to do something like this?"

I jumped in because Hannah was already looking discouraged. "Well, before you jump to conclusions, you should know that no one else influenced this decision. We didn't tell anyone or ask for anyone's advice. We came to this decision totally on our own."

"We also didn't decide right away," Hannah added. "We've been thinking very carefully about it for days."

"Yes, but how you could be thinking carefully about it and yet

30

till come to this decision is what alarms me!" Karen cried, and then immediately closed her eyes and took a long, deep breath. No. No, I am not going to flip out on you." She looked up and caught my eye. "I can only assume that's why you didn't call me to tell me about it in the first place? You thought I'd go ballistic?"

"Something like that," I said. "And then the Shattering happened, and suddenly the Council seat was the last thing on anyone's mind."

"Right. Yes. Okay," Karen said, and she still gave the impression of someone fighting every natural impulse to lose her cool. "Why don't you start by telling me why you decided to do this. What was your logic? I want to understand."

"I was the first one to consider it," Hannah said, falling on her word as though she hoped to salvage my dignity. "I saw it as an opportunity to help shape Durupinen policies rather than being victimized by them all the time. Jess wanted nothing to do with it—wouldn't even entertain the idea, but then... she began to change her mind."

"I see," Karen said, her voice calm but her nostrils flaring. "And what was it that caused you to change your mind, Jess?"

"It was a lot of things, I think, but mostly it was the Shattered spirit, Eleanora. She was a Caller, and her Council destroyed her. No one was there to speak for her, or to protect her from the same fear-driven policies that followed us when we got here. She died because they thought she and her sister might be us. We can't change that, but we decided we couldn't ignore it, either."

Karen froze. Her eyes widened. All of the anger and exasperation drained from her face, and she suddenly looked less like a cutthroat lawyer and more like a lost little girl.

"From what you and Finvarra told us about our grandmother, it doesn't really sound like our family used our power or influence for good when we had it before," Hannah said.

Karen allowed herself a sardonic smile. "No. My mother saw power as little more than currency to barter for what she wanted. It would not have occurred to her to use it to help anyone but herself."

"A lot of the Council seems to feel that way," Hannah continued. "And most of those clans have been in power for a long time. In fact, most of those same clans held those seats when they sentenced Eleanora to imprisonment, including ours. We just thought...

maybe it's time for some fresh blood and a different perspective up there in the benches."

Karen's eyes were bright. Her defensive posture sagged. "You're right, of course," she said. "And I couldn't be prouder of you for wanting to make a difference, but—"

"You're worried that the rest of the clans are going to object?" I finished for her.

"That is an understatement. Objections we can weather. I feel like I'd be watching you throw yourselves to the wolves. I need hardly tell you what most of the Durupinen think of you and our clan. Just look at the way you've been treated in the past week."

"I know," Hannah said. "And I think that's why we have to do it."

"Look, it's a long shot," I said. "And we might really regret it. Marion has already promised to give us hell if we run—"

Karen gasped. "Marion knows about the seat? You didn't tell me she—ah," she sighed ruefully as the realization hit her. "Of course. That's why she's here, isn't it? She wants to stop you from taking the seat."

"Bingo," I said. "And, to be honest, it probably won't be hard to do. From the looks of it, the entirety of the Northern Clans will be lining up behind her for the chance to slam the door in our faces."

"But you want to do it anyway," Karen said.

"Yes," Hannah and I said together.

Karen took her glasses off, massaged the bridge of her nose, and replaced them. When she looked at us again, her expression was hard to read. "I'm not foolish enough to try to persuade you one way or the other. I know that you've both considered all of the factors at play here. You are clearly well aware of the animosity you will meet. You are also aware of the upheaval it will cause in your lives if you manage to secure the seat. I suppose all I can do is support you through this process."

"But what do you think, Karen?" Hannah asked. "We do value your opinion, even if we've made our own decision."

"I'm torn," Karen said with a helpless shrug. "I want to protect you. I want to shield you from an ugly and bitter struggle. I know you are adults, and I know it's not my job, but I just can't help it. Your mother and I grew up surrounded by Durupinen politics— we watched it spread its poison through our family. That's why I've refused to get involved with it again. At the same time, I want to support you, because I know that you are exactly what this broken, antiquated system needs. I know that you will do wonderful things, if someone will just give you the chance."

"Well, Finvarra's given us the chance, so we're going to take it," I said. "So, what do you say? Can you stand by us with this? We're going to need you, Karen. And after all, this is your clan, too, and it's going to affect you if we pull off the impossible and actually manage to win this seat."

Karen stood up, crossed to the sofa where Hannah and I sat, and squeezed herself in between us, throwing an arm around each of our shoulders. "Of course, I will stand by you. Try to stop me. I can't say I'm happy about it, but that's just my worry getting in the way of my courage. It's about time Clan Sassanaigh took charge of this place again, and I'm going to help you do it if I can. Just because I walked away from this part of our family legacy, doesn't mean that you can't take up the mantle."

"Thanks, Karen," Hannah said.

"No, thank you, girls. Here I am thinking I'm being the mature and level-headed one by staying away from the politics, but you've reminded me what real maturity looks like. Hiding our heads in the sand and cultivating our anger will not change the things that so desperately need to be changed. Only jumping back into the fray can do that. I've been too afraid of the fray."

"For good reason," I said darkly. "This may turn out to be a huge mistake. But it's a mistake we're going to make."

"Well, I'm not going to let you make it blindly," Karen said, and she jumped back up and started pacing with slow, thoughtful, deliberate steps. Hannah and I turned and grinned at each other—we both recognized Karen's lawyer prowl.

"The most important thing to do is to fend Marion off. She will do anything she can to prevent this seat being taken back by our clan," she said.

"Does it really matter who takes it? I mean, I know she hates us and all that, but any clan that takes the seat will essentially be stealing it from her. Won't she try to stop anyone who makes a bid for it?"

"Yes and no," Karen said. "The animosity between our clans goes back decades. Marion's family has been clawing their way up the ladder for several generations, and our family, in particular my mother, wanted nothing more than to kick them right back down to the bottom rung."

"Why?" I asked.

Karen grimaced. "My mother didn't need a reason. All upwardly mobile clans were a threat to be crushed, but Clan Gonachd was particularly manipulative. My mother didn't want to have to compete with anyone who played the game as well as they did—she preferred a stacked deck at all times."

"So, this isn't just about Mom," I said.

"Oh, no. It goes back much further than that," Karen said. "Marion would rather see that seat go to just about anyone, although she'll have her own handpicked candidate she'll be throwing her considerable weight behind. So, the first challenge will be to get you through the nomination process without her interference."

"What kind of interference?" I asked warily. "I assumed she would make trouble if we ran, but before?"

"Do not underestimate this woman," Karen said sharply. "She will not miss an opportunity to thwart you at any point in this process. Count on it."

"Okay," Hannah said. "How do we combat that?"

"Put her off her guard," Karen said, pressing the tips of her fingers to her chin and resuming her pacing. "Give her a false sense of security. We want her to think you aren't going to accept the nomination."

I threw my hands up in the air. "Well, I've already screwed up that angle. I told her we weren't sure what we were going to do. At the time I was just trying to piss her off, but I've probably set us up for something, haven't I?"

"It's probably not too late to convince her that the nomination won't move forward," Karen said. "There's a new factor in the equation now."

Hannah looked quizzically at me. "What factor is that?"

A slow smile bloomed over Karen's face. "Me," she said.

"You've got your evil plan face on," I said, pointing at her. "Explain."

"I can stage something—a loud argument, maybe—and make sure that news of it gets back to her. I'll make sure one of her Council friends is around to witness it."

"An argument about what? With who?" I prompted, still confused.

"Celeste, maybe? Or Siobhán? Someone close to Finvarra. I'll

34

corner someone publicly or near the Council room and let loose a tirade. Goodness knows I've got a reputation for them now," she said with a wry smirk.

"What will you shout about?" Hannah asked.

"Well, I'll start by proclaiming that I only just now found out about the intended nomination and demanding to know why I'd been left out of the loop on it. That part, at least, won't be an exaggeration. I'm still mad at the two of you, by the way, even if I've agreed to help you," she said severely, scowling at us.

"We know, we know, we're sorry, okay? You can yell at us later again, if it will make you feel better. Just tell us what you're going to say in your tirade!" I said impatiently.

"I'll tell them that they can just go straight to Finvarra and tell her to nominate someone else, because I've forbidden you to accept the nomination, and that you've agreed not to. Then I'll threaten that, if Finvarra does nominate our clan, all three of us will get on a plane home and refuse to stay for the rest of the Airechtas, rules be damned," Karen said. "That ought to raise enough eyebrows to send Marion's little spies running to spill what they've heard. That should at least keep her from causing too much trouble beforehand."

"And afterward?" Hannah asked.

Karen laughed. "There's nothing we can do about that. It will be a free-for-all once you accept. We'll just have to stay on our toes and fight back as best we can. She's lost a lot of credibility in recent years, and that will work in our favor, but she will surely still be a force to contend with."

"But that's in less than two days. Why bother? What damage can she do in two more days that she hasn't wrought already?" I asked, but then stopped short as I processed the incredulous looks on Karen and Hannah's faces. "Never mind," I said swiftly. "Monumentally stupid question."

4

GUIDANCE

A T TWO O'CLOCK in the morning, I awoke. It wasn't the kind of waking that happens gradually—the slow, sleepy rousing of early morning. Nor was it the sudden, heart-pounding waking that followed a nightmare. Instead, it was a strange, instantaneous waking, as though someone had flicked a switch. I was instantly, completely awake, all trace of sleepiness gone, my eyes wide and expectant. I was not surprised that I had woken. I knew exactly what time I would see on the clock when I turned my head, because I had wakened at this exact same time, in this exact same manner, every night since Eleanora had Crossed. And each time it happened, I had the distinct feeling that someone had just spoken my name. I never heard it, but it was as though I could still feel the echo of it in the air around me.

I looked around the room. Karen had sufficiently recovered from the revelation that Hannah was running for the Council seat, and after one last cup of hot cocoa, had headed off to her own room. Hannah was sound asleep, hands tucked under her cheek and a small smile on her lips, like the proverbial child with sugarplums dancing in her head. Milo was nowhere to be found, but that wasn't surprising—he typically spent his nights with other ghosts, rather than boring himself to death for hours on end watching the non-floaters snore and drool.

By the soft glow of the Christmas lights, I reached under my pillow and extracted a small, battered old diary from the pillowcase, where I had stashed it every night since the Shattering had ended. I flipped through the pages, picking random words out in Eleanora's elegant script. The depth of the connection I felt to her was something I couldn't even satisfactorily explain to myself. All I knew was that I could not shake the feeling that, though she had already slipped through the Aether to what lay beyond it, there

37

was a strand of substance—be it memory or empathy, or something less identifiable—that still stretched between us, and not even the closing of the Gateway could sever it. I was a girl who saw ghosts, but this was the first time that I felt truly, inexorably haunted.

I flipped to the back of the diary, where I had folded up the sketch I'd done of Eleanora. I pulled it out and unfolded it, so that I could examine, for what felt like the millionth time, that lovely, tortured face.

At the time I'd drawn it, I thought it was a typical, spirit-induced drawing. It was the most logical conclusion to come to; I was a Muse, and so spirits often reached out to me and used my artistic abilities to communicate. I had found and Crossed many spirits this way over the past few years, and it was a skill that I was constantly honing and mastering, with Fiona's expert—if reluctant—help. But in the last moments before Eleanora had Crossed, we'd had an exchange that I couldn't get out of my mind.

"It's much more my fault than yours," I'd told her. "You tried to reach out to me, but I didn't know what it meant. I only wish I could have discovered who you were before the Shattering happened. I could have prevented all of this."

"Reached out to you? What do you mean?" she had asked in confusion.

"The sketches. The psychic drawings I did of you—the ones that I showed you to help you remember who you were."

"What about the drawings? I didn't have anything to do with them."

"Of course, you did," I'd insisted. "You had to have reached out to me those nights while I was sleeping. How else could I have drawn them?"

"I haven't the faintest idea," Eleanora had replied. "I never saw the drawings, or you, until the moment you showed them to me. How could I have? I was still trapped in the *príosún*, unable to communicate."

Unable to communicate.

The more I ran over it in my head, the less sense it made. There could be no spirit drawing without spirit communication. There could be no Muse without a ghostly artist using her to create the art.

How, then, had these drawings come to be? Had I really produced them on my own, and if so, what did that mean? It was a question I could not fathom the answer to, not without help. And I knew who I had to ask for that help.

And she was just about the least helpful person I could think of.

"Jess? You okay?"

Startled, I looked up. Hannah's eyes were open, her head propped up on her hand.

"Hey. Yeah, I'm fine. Just can't sleep."

"I didn't know you still had that," Hannah said, pointing to the book.

"Yeah. No one really knew what to do with it when the Shattering was over, so I just sort of... kept it."

"Why?"

"I'm not sure."

Hannah furrowed her brow in an expression that I loved. It made her look like a small child faced with a reality of life she had never encountered before, but wouldn't accept—like an adult had just told her that she couldn't actually fly. "I think," she said slowly, considering each word as she let it fall, "that we did everything we could for her. We made sure that everyone knew her story. After all, that was why she left the diary in the first place. And we made sure that the entire Council read it. And then every Durupinen at the Airechtas was told about her, too. And of course, we Crossed her, which is what she wanted more than anything else. Do you think there was something else we could have done?"

"Short of inventing a time machine and going back in time to save her? No, there's nothing else," I said with a sigh, staring into those deep, dark eyes I now knew so well. "And logically, I know by now that's usually the case. We're sort of doomed to a life of helping people when it's too late to help them, you know?"

"Yeah," Hannah said sadly. "Yeah, I know."

"And the thing is, I've made my peace with that, mostly. I don't usually spend a lot of time dwelling over stuff we can't change. I can't let myself go there, or this whole Durupinen thing would just become too much to handle. But this," and I tapped the cover of the book, "this feels... different."

Hannah slipped off her bed, padded across the room, and curled up next to me. "Of course, it does," she said. "Eleanora's story could have been ours. It was like watching versions of us from another life, facing a fate that we barely escaped ourselves."

"Exactly," I said, swallowing back a lump in my throat. "And in a weird way, I feel responsible, because we're the ones her Council was afraid of. We are the ones they saw when they looked at Eleanora. I've only ever felt this guilty about a spirit once before, and that was Pierce."

"That was not your fault," Hannah said firmly.

"If he'd never met me, he would still be alive," I said.

"You don't know that. He could have walked off a sidewalk and been hit by a bus the next day. You can't torture yourself like that, Jess. There are too many intersecting paths and choices and coincidences in life to justify shouldering that kind of blame."

I didn't answer because I didn't want to argue. She understood my silence, though.

"I blame myself for Milo. Every single day," Hannah said.

I turned to look at her, horrified. "Hannah, come on! That was his choice to make. You did absolutely everything you could to prevent him from making it!"

Hannah shrugged. "It was because of me that he knew spirits exist. Maybe if he hadn't been sure of that fact, he might have been too scared to go through with it."

"Milo would be the first person to tell you it wasn't your fault," I said.

"And Pierce would be the first person to tell you the same thing, I expect," she replied. "So why don't we both agree to do our best to let it go?"

I narrowed my eyes at her. "You are too small to be this wise. Seriously, it's like being twins with a fortune cookie."

She allowed herself a tiny smile. "That's why people listen to me: the element of surprise."

I laughed, and felt a little of the suffocating weight lift from my chest. "Fine. I'll try."

"Me, too."

We lay in silence for a long time. A drowsiness began to steal over me, so that the Christmas lights about our heads began to wink in and out of focus.

"There is one more thing that we are doing for Eleanora," I said, stifling a yawn with the back of my hand.

"Mmmm?" Hannah asked, her voice muffled with sleepiness.

"The Airechtas. The open seat," I reminded her.

"Oh yes, that's right. Yes, I guess, in a way, it is for her," Hannah muttered.

Yes, I told Eleanora's image, before folding it up inside the book once more. *We are doing what we can to make it right.* And in the morning, I would go and see the one person who could help me understand why Eleanora and I connected in the first place.

§

"What fresh hell is this?"

"Hi, Fiona," I said, as cheerfully as I dared. "Have a good Christmas?"

An inch-wide strip of Fiona's face appeared through the crack in the door. "It was magical. Now, sod off." She tried to shut the door again, but I wedged my toe between the door and the jamb.

"Have you got a few minutes? I need your help with something," I said.

"No, I do not have a few minutes," she grumbled. The eye I could see squinting out at me was bloodshot and watery. "It's Boxing Day, and as is time-honored tradition, I intend to be hungover and snoring until well past noon. So, unless you've arrived to deliver two paracetamol and a greasy parcel of fish and chips, you can bugger off."

"Fiona, please. I wouldn't bother you if it wasn't really important," I said.

Fiona squinted at me still harder, and something in my expression gave her pause. "This is Muse-related, isn't it?"

"Yes."

She was silent for so long I thought maybe she'd fallen back to sleep standing up. Then she said, "I reserve the right, at any time, to boot you out in any manner I choose."

"So, the usual arrangement, then," I said dryly. "Look, I'll throw the chair at myself if this isn't worth your time, okay?"

Issuing a stream of unintelligible muttering, Fiona unfastened the deadbolt, flung the door wide, and shuffled back toward the chaise lounge in the corner of her studio. By the time I'd closed the door behind me, she had already flung herself facedown back onto it, so that her next words were muffled in pillows.

"Sit. Speak. Quietly."

I used a damp rag to wipe down the potter's bench that stood opposite the chaise, and then sat down on it. My heart was pounding unaccountably hard. I swallowed and began in a low voice. "Do you remember those two sketches of Eleanora Larkin that I brought to you a few days ago? The ones we used to identify her?"

"Jessica, I'm hungover, not brain dead. Of course, I remember them."

"Eleanora told me something about them right before she Crossed that I thought was kind of... weird."

"Weird in what way?" Fiona asked, face still buried in pillows.

"Well, I mentioned them to Eleanora because I wanted to apologize to her for not discovering her identity sooner. And she told me... well, she told me she never reached out to me to create those drawings."

Fiona was silent for a few seconds, then she lifted her face and turned to rest her cheek on the chaise so that she could look at me. "What are you on about?"

"Eleanora said she never communicated with me. She never made contact. The first time she even knew about the drawings was when I showed them to her when she was still Shattered into Shards."

Fiona shrugged. "That's not possible. She was still confused. Must have been the aftermath of the Shattering."

I shook my head. "No, I don't think so. She told me that she couldn't communicate with anyone outside of the *príosún*. She was under too many Castings as part of her imprisonment."

Fiona sat up, rubbed her eyes, and slapped her cheeks forcefully. Then she looked at me again, as though seeing me in her studio for the first time. "She claimed that your sketches were unsolicited spirit drawings?"

"Yes," I said, feeling relieved just to know that she was paying attention now. "We didn't have time to discuss it further, because Keira interrupted us a moment later to invite Eleanora to Cross. But she was adamant that she had nothing to do with the creation of those sketches."

Fiona took a last, longing look at her pillows. "Dogs!" she cursed under her breath, then sighed, holding out a hand. "You've got them with you, I suppose? Let's have them."

I handed them over at once. Fiona snatched them from me and brought them over to her desk, tripping over an errant broken bit of pottery as she went. She cleared the heap of clutter with a violent sweep of her arm, sending paint, paper, brushes, and jars of pencils kittering away across the floor. She reached up beyond her paint-pattered bandana into her tangled nest of hair and extracted a pair of bifocals, which she jammed onto her nose and then used to examine the sketches again. I watched the entire violent display with not a trace of surprise; Fiona generally displayed a complete disregard for all items—and people—that had the audacity to exist where she didn't want them to be.

"These are all of them, yeah? The only sketches you've done of her before or since?" Fiona shot at me after an intense minute of staring at the papers.

"Yes."

"And you completed both of them before the Shattering occurred?"

"Yes. One each night for the two nights before the Shattering happened."

"And you were asleep at the time, or in a psychic trance?"

"I told you all of this when I—"

"TELL ME AGAIN!" Fiona roared, slamming her hand on the desk and then wincing at the sound.

"Asleep both times," I said flatly.

"And did you wake up while you were still drawing? That is, did the completion of the drawing wake you?"

I had to think about this for a moment. "I still had the pencil in my hand each time. The first time I was definitely still sitting up. So yes, I think I woke up right away when I had finished."

"Do you ever remember having dreams that included Eleanora?" Fiona asked. "Either on the nights you completed these drawings or before?"

"Dreams? No," I said. "I just woke up from what felt like normal, dreamless sleep, and these drawings were there. I've had dreams about her since she Crossed, though."

"I'm not concerned about that," Fiona said dismissively, waving her hand. "I'd be surprised if half the castle wasn't dreaming about her after what she put us through."

"What *Lucida* put us through," I corrected her quietly, but Fiona wasn't listening to me. She had pulled her bandana down over her eyes and pressed her hands over it so she could think. She looked like she was about to play a game of blind man's bluff.

"It doesn't add up. Dogs! I cannot *think* under these conditions," she muttered to herself, then slapped her cheeks again and raised

43

her head, bandana still covering her eyes as she looked in my direction. "Right. I'm going to need you to find out some information for me," Fiona said. "I need to know what kinds of Castings were being used on Eleanora and for how long. I need to know the details of how she was contained at the *príosún*."

"Who can I talk to who would have access to that kind of information?" I asked.

"You're a Tracker now. Ask one of your Tracker mates," Fiona said.

"I don't have any Tracker mates," I said, rolling my eyes. "Catriona is the only other Tracker I know so far, and she's not up to researching anything. She's still recovering from being a Host."

"Hell's bells, Jessica, do you need me to hold your hand through this simple task or what? Just find another Tracker!" Fiona shouted.

"Okay, okay!" I cried. "I'll figure it out!"

"Too right you will, because I can't help you until you do. And there's one other thing."

"And what's that?" I asked, suppressing a childish urge to flip her off to her face while she couldn't see me.

"You need to talk to Lucida and find out about her interactions with Eleanora in the days leading up to the Shattering. There's a chance she could have lifted one or more of the Castings and enabled Eleanora to reach out to you, even if Eleanora was unaware that she was doing so."

My mouth had gone dry. My tongue felt like sandpaper in my mouth as I tried to swallow. "Talk to Lucida?" I repeated.

Fiona reached up and tugged the bandana back up into her hair so that she could survey me with her beady eyes. She squinted, looking shrewd. "You think you can handle that? I'm not saying you should be able to."

"I don't know," I said honestly. "I honestly don't know what I would do if I were sitting in front of her. I don't trust myself."

"You don't think you could talk to her?"

"Maybe not without assaulting her, no," I said truthfully. "Seriously, Fiona, I'm not trying to be funny here. I've done a damn good job of putting the Prophecy behind me. I've thought a lot about Lucida and what she did and why she did it. And the weird thing is, that I can forgive most of it—or at least understand it. But what she did to Hannah? How she manipulated her and used

44

her like that?" I shuddered with anger. "I'm not sure I trust myself, Fiona."

Fiona continued to glare at me, and for a moment, I thought she was going to pick something up and throw it at me, but instead she jerked her head once in a grudging nod and said, "Can't say that I blame you. Get another Tracker to do it. I dare say they will have questioned her anyway. You might be able to get the answer from whoever interrogated her."

I let out a sigh of relief I didn't realize I was holding. "Yeah. I'll try that first."

"Good. Good. Once we have as much information as we can gather about it, I might be able to tell you what happened here," Fiona said, tapping the sketches. "In the meantime, I'm going to hold on to them."

"Okay," I said, feeling the anxious knot in my gut loosening up. "Thank you, Fiona. I appreciate it, really. It's been weighing on me these past few days."

Fiona grunted in acknowledgement. Suddenly her curmudgeonly expression softened and she hesitated, mouth half-open, as though she were trying to decide whether to say something more. Then she snapped her jaw shut and pointed to the door.

I was dismissed. I had crossed the room and placed one hand on the doorknob when she called me back.

"Jess. Wait."

I watched her cross the room and wrench open one of the many drawers of an old, paint-splattered apothecary's chest. She pulled out a small velvet bag, its mouth puckered shut with a drawstring. Then she shuffled over to the door and thrust it at me.

"This is for you. Happy Christmas."

"Huh?" I said, sure I had heard her wrong.

"I realize I ought to have given it to you yesterday. But I'm shit with remembering things, so there you are," she said.

"Thank you," I said. "I'm sorry, I didn't think to—"

"Oh, bugger it with the formalities, will you?" Fiona snapped angrily. "What do I want with Christmas gifts? Anyway, it's not the fecking crown jewels for cripe's sake."

"Right," I said, and pulled open the bag before she yelled at me again. I turned it over and shook it, so that the object inside fell into my cupped hand. It was a silver, oval-shaped locket on a thick, heavy chain. There was a tiny shape etched into the face of it that looked like it might have been a map.

"It's your clan's ancestral territory," Fiona said, as she watched me stare at it, brow furrowed. "Back before we spread all over the globe, each clan used to lay claim to its own little piece of the world. Those were the lands under the spiritual control of Clan Sassanaigh over a thousand years ago."

"Wow," I whispered, running my fingers over the shape of it. "That's really cool, Fiona. Thanks a lot."

"Open it," she ordered.

I did, and gasped. Staring up out of the little frame inside was a tiny, exquisite portrait of my mother. She couldn't have been more than eighteen years old.

"Oh, Fiona," I breathed, feeling the tears rush to my eyes. I swiped them away, angry at them for obscuring my view of that face I so missed, even though I had never seen it so young and fresh and undamaged by the ravages of life. "Where did you get it?"

"I painted it," Fiona said, staring down at her own hands as though the sight of my emotion was unbearably indecent. "Do you remember last week, when we were trying to find out who Eleanora was, and Milo asked if official clan portraits were traditional? Well, they aren't, but it reminded me that I had this. Your grandmother commissioned it from me while I was still an apprentice here."

I tore my gaze from my mother's face to stare in surprise at Fiona. "You painted this yourself?"

"That's right. I wasn't always the curmudgeonly old artistic purist you see squinting before you. I was young and eager, not above trading on my gifts commercially," she admitted defensively. "You needn't look so bloody surprised. I was young once, too."

"It was the word 'eager' that threw me, actually," I said, smirking.

"Well, maybe eager isn't the right term," Fiona said, betraying a hint of a rare smile. "Let's call me 'grudgingly available' instead. I desperately needed to make some money, and that was one thing your grandmother had in abundance. She asked me to paint two portraits, one each of your mother and your aunt Karen, to be fitted into a brooch locket. But before I could finish them, your mother disappeared and your grandmother died. Wasn't sure what I should do with it. Thought about giving it to Karen, but..." Fiona shrugged, and I couldn't be sure, but I thought her cheeks reddened just a bit. "She was a good egg, your mum. Not a lot of the girls here bothered much with me, but she always had a kind word. She was the closest thing to a friend I had, apart from my sister, Nan. So, I suppose I wanted to keep it for myself, for a while. But now, I'd like you to have it. You lost a great deal more of her than I ever had to begin with."

I swallowed back my tears, mostly because I thought Fiona would find them absurd. "Thank you, Fiona. It really means a lot to me to have this."

"Right. Well, off you go then. And I don't want to see your face up here again until you've gotten that information from Lucida."

And she slammed the door in my face, though—I thought—with slightly less force than usual.

5

BOMBSHELL

"OH, GOD. Oh God, oh God, oh *God*."

"Hannah? Are you okay?"

I looked over at her as she stood in front of the mirror. She was gaping at her own reflection as though she had no idea who was staring back at her. Her complexion was ashen.

"Hannah?" I repeated.

"I can't do this. I *cannot* do this," she whispered.

"Are you panicking?" I asked her in a calm, gentle voice.

"Yes," she squeaked. "Yes, I am one hundred and fifty percent panicking."

"And what did you tell me to do if you started panicking?" I intoned.

"I... I don't remember," she gasped. "I can't remember things when I'm panicking."

"You told me to slap you across the face as hard as I could," I said.

She spun around, frowning at me. "No, I most certainly did not!"

I smiled at her. "You're right, you didn't. But I snapped you right out of that panic, didn't I?"

Hannah dropped her face into her hands and groaned. She sank down into the nearest chair. "I can't do this, Jess. I thought I could, but I can't."

I sat down beside her and rubbed her shoulders. The morning of the reopening of the Airechtas was upon us at last, and the delightful distractions of Christmas could no longer shield us from the grim reality of what was to come.

"You don't have to do this," I said.

Her head snapped up and she glared at me. "Yes, I do."

"Okay, fine. Yes, you do," I capitulated. "But you don't have to do it alone. I'll be right there with you, and so will Milo. Right, oh wise and magnanimous Spirit Guide?"

49

I sent this last question zinging through our connection where it met with a glowing warmth and then a laugh. "You know I've got your back, sweetness. Oh, and I'm now only answering to 'wise and magnanimous Spirit Guide,' so get used to it, girls." He popped into form at that very moment on the arm of the chair, just to punctuate the announcement.

There was a sharp knock on the door. Hannah jumped, but I squeezed her shoulder again. "It's just Finn, remember? He's escorting us down."

"Oh, right," Hannah said. Her body relaxed back into the chair, but her face was still tense with anxiety.

I stopped with my hand on the door. "I'm just going to... warn him," I said over my shoulder to Hannah. "If there is any chance of a negative reaction from the other Durupinen... well, you know Finn. He doesn't like to be taken by surprise."

Hannah didn't even look up. She just nodded her head, staring disconsolately down at her own hands. Milo turned to Hannah and said brightly, "Come on, sweetness, to the mirror. I'm not going to allow you to walk into that room with a blotchy face. One must always stare down the barrel of public ridicule with an even complexion. Jess, we'll meet you out there in a few minutes." He marched Hannah into the bathroom and, as he closed the door, he gave me a surreptitious little wink that seemed to say, "You've got this, girl."

I gave him a tiny smile in return and pulled open the door to see Finn looking down at me, his standard Caomhnóir scowl firmly in place upon his features.

"Hi," I said.

"Good morning," he replied inclining his head in a suggestion of a bow. "I've come to escort you all down to the Grand Council Room for this morning's session, if you are prepared to go."

"Thanks, but we're not quite ready to leave yet," I said. "I need to talk to you first."

Something woke up in Finn's eyes, and he was looking at me now with real concern. "What is it? Is everything all right?"

"Yes, although I'm sure you won't agree with me," I said. I looked up and down the corridor, which was deserted, and pulled Finn across the hallway where a large tapestry of a hunting scene concealed a windowed alcove. I shoved the tapestry aside and he followed me behind it, so that we were masked from anyone who might pass by.

"Jess, you're scaring me. What is it?" Finn whispered urgently.

I looked up into his face and suddenly couldn't find my nerve. I couldn't tell him. I just couldn't do it.

"Jess, answer me!"

"I'm trying!" I hissed back. "I just… I don't know how to tell you this, but I have to. We're about to head down into that meeting and you're going to find out anyway."

Then, to my utter surprise, Finn's expression cleared. He actually smiled in his relief. He reached out a hand and placed it gently on my cheek.

"It's okay, Jess. I already know what you're going to say."

"No, you really don't," I muttered.

"I promise you, I do." And then, stunning me still further, he stepped in to me and kissed me right on the lips.

Desire wiped what little of my thoughts hadn't already been erased by surprise. For a moment, all I could do was stand there, lost in the unexpected bliss of a kiss I wasn't sure I'd ever experience again. But then, slowly, reality seeped back in and I pulled away, breathless.

"I… you don't… I didn't deserve that," I said.

He smiled again. "Of course, you do."

I thrust a hand out between us, keeping him at arm's length. "Trust me, you are going to want to take that kiss back when you hear what I've got to tell you. And I won't be able to get the words out if you keep distracting me with… you."

Finn took hold of my hand now pressed against his chest and squeezed it. "If it's about the Council seat, Jess, I already know."

My mouth fell open. "I… you… what do you mean, you already know? What do you already know?"

"I know that Hannah is going to accept Finvarra's nomination on behalf of Clan Sassanaigh this morning," he said.

I pulled my hand back from him, waiting for the explosion, but his face was completely impassive. It was unnerving.

"You know," I repeated, more to let the information sink into my own brain than for him to confirm it.

"I know," he replied, still the picture of calm.

"How did you find out?" I asked.

"Bertie," Finn said, and the corner of his mouth turned up in a trace of a smile. "He stopped by your room on Christmas evening looking for Savannah and he heard Karen shouting about it. Naturally, he hastened right off to tell me. He seemed to think I should be prepared for a volley of attacks on your person from the other Durupinen and wanted to volunteer to be my second in case of violence."

"Your second?" I snorted. "As in, like, a duel?"

"That would be correct," Finn said. "Bertie's general perception of being a Caomhnóir is equal parts swashbuckling fantasy and fleeing in terror. I'm not quite sure how he's made it this far without Savannah simply knocking his block off."

"Neither am I, but I'm fairly confident that's how he'll meet his end," I said. "So, you've known for almost two days?"

"Yes," Finn replied.

"You don't seem... angry," I said tentatively.

"I'm not," he said, and there was no anger in his voice, repressed or otherwise. "I must admit, I am confused, though. I'm trying to understand why you didn't tell me yourself."

"I was trying to," I said. "And not just now. I tried to tell you on Christmas, too, when I brought you your gift. And at least half a dozen times before that. I just kept losing my nerve."

"Why? Were you just trying to avoid a row?" Finn asked.

I shook my head. "No, it wasn't that, exactly. The thing is that we never actually resolved the last row, and I was afraid that it would be that last straw, you know? Everything has been so strained, so stressful since we've been here. We're under so much more pressure to hide, and the fear that we'll be discovered is palpable all the time. And then we had that awful fight. I was just scared, Finn. I was terrified that this," and I gestured at the space between us as though it were a living, breathing thing, "wouldn't be able to survive it."

"Perhaps it wouldn't, if it were stretched so thin, so far as that," Finn said. Then he reached across that space and pulled me in against him. "But here. Together. Like this we are so much stronger," he said, his voice gruff with emotion. He gestured now at the inch of space between us. "Nothing you could tell me could break us when we're here, like this."

I leaned my head forward, pressing my forehead to his neck. I felt the warmth of his breath in my hair, and his kiss on the top of my head. "I'm sorry," I said. "I'm sorry you found out from someone other than me. It wasn't fair to you."

"I forgive you," Finn said. "And in turn, will you forgive me?"

I raised my head and looked up into his face, frowning. "For what? You didn't do anything wrong."

"That's not true. I let my own fears widen the space between us, too. I've pulled away from you while we've been here. I told myself it was to protect you, but it was selfish. I was protecting myself, putting my walls back up. I guess we're both good at that."

"Yeah, we are," I said. "My two attempts at relationships include a ghost and a guy I'm forbidden by ancient law to get involved with. It's almost as though I want to fail, isn't it?"

"Self-sabotage, definitely," Finn said with a smirk. "But at least you've moved from spirit to living person. That is definitely a step in the right direction."

"I'm still trying to understand why you aren't mad at me," I said. "I'm making things so much more complicated for us. The more time we're at Fairhaven, the more time we'll have to spend hiding, and the more chances someone will figure us out."

Finn shook his head. "Hannah winning the Council seat—if she can manage it—doesn't mean we have to be at Fairhaven all the time. We'll need to be nearby, certainly, but it's not as though we'll be moving back into the castle. Many of the Council members have lives and jobs outside of these walls. Catriona is only here between Tracker missions, for example." Finn paused, laughing at the stunned look on my face. "Didn't you realize you wouldn't have to live here in the castle?"

"I... should have. But I didn't," I said, a smile dawning on my face, but fading almost as quickly. "It will be nice to have a little bit of space, but it doesn't really solve our problem, does it?"

"That's true. But I've been thinking quite a lot about what you were saying before, about looking to have the law repealed," Finn said slowly.

I stared at him. "You completely shot down that idea when I brought it up. And you were right. It would be much too obvious if I stood up and pushed that agenda, especially given what Seamus already knows. What's changed?"

"I know I said it was too risky, but maybe, with Hannah on the Council, there might be a way to propose the change without giving ourselves away," Finn said.

53

I felt my heart lift. "Really? How?"

"Well it won't be you, for a start. And she would have leverage as a Council member. Their proposals are always considered thoroughly. She may even be able to find another member or two to co-sponsor the proposal. I think it's the best shot we have, if Hannah is willing to put herself out there on the issue."

"I'm sure she would, but we'll have to come clean with her first," I said.

"Yes, we certainly will," Finn said, and his brows contracted. "Do you think she'll be angry when she finds out?"

"I think she already knows."

Finn stepped back, looking shocked. "She does? But how—"

"Okay, well maybe she doesn't know, but I'm sure she must suspect it. Finn, I know all you Caomhnóir think you're James Bond, but we're not nearly as stealthy as we think we are," I said. "Milo figured it out ages ago. There's just no way we could all live in such close proximity to each other and keep this a secret."

Finn sighed. "Yes, I suppose that is true. But you will need to tell Hannah anyway, just to confirm it."

"Yes. Is that okay with you?"

"Yes, indeed. I daresay it will be a relief to have someone we don't have to hide from," Finn said.

Even as I thought about it, one of the tense knots in my stomach began to loosen. I looked up into Finn's face and felt, for the first time in days, that the invisible barrier there had been lifted. I could see straight through to the man I knew he was, rather than the façade of the man he pretended to be.

"There you are," I whispered. "God, I've missed you."

"And I you," he replied. "But we will need to miss each other a little longer, I fear. It is time to go. The Airechtas waits for no one."

§

Knowing the Durupinen love of pageantry, I was sure that we would be forced to participate all over again in the elaborate opening ceremony that we had marched in on the first day, but thankfully, the Council decided to plow forward with the meetings instead. This was a blessing, because I think if Hannah had to stand around biding her time amongst the other Durupinen in the entryway, she might have had enough time to talk herself out of

54

ntering the Grand Council room at all. She had no chance to bolt
or the doors, though, and before I knew it, she was sinking into her
eat beside me, her face pale, but set and determined.

Perhaps to spare her the indignity of another spectacle of an
ntrance, Finvarra's wheelchair was already stationed on the
latform near the podium. I wouldn't have thought it possible for
er to look frailer or more sickly than when last I'd seen her, but
was very wrong. She was skeletally thin now, and her skin had
aken on a waxy, yellowing quality, as though her body were already
reaking down even as her spirit fought to retain possession of it.
ler head lolled to one side as the seats filled before her, as though
he could barely keep herself awake. Carrick hovered beside her, his
ace set in a mask of repressed pain.

Hannah was staring at her, too, and the sight of Finvarra had a
trange effect on her. Her face suddenly flooded with color, and her
yes became bright, almost feverish.

I leaned over and whispered to her. "Are you okay?"

She kept her eyes on Finvarra. "Am I okay? Of course, I'm okay.
And no matter what happens today, no matter how terrible the
esponse, I will still be okay. Nothing we will face down today can
ver be as frightening as what she is facing down right now," she
aid, pointing up at Finvarra. "If she can battle her way down here
ust to nominate us for this seat, then I can certainly take a little
eat for accepting it."

"Hannah, someday maybe I'll remember that you are the
oughest cookie on the planet, but in the meantime, you continue
o impress me," I said. "I made something for today, but I hadn't
lecided if I was going to give it to you or not."

Hannah turned to me, her expression quizzical. "You made
omething?"

"Yeah."

"Well, what is it?"

I reached into my bag and pulled out a red and yellow striped
ag, which I thrust into her hands. The smell coming from it made
everal people around us turn in their seats to stare.

Hannah looked down, and then rolled her eyes. "Oh, my God,
less. You are so ridiculous."

"Every good spectacle needs popcorn, and I think it's safe to say
we're about to put on a real showstopper," I said, grinning. Hannah
tried to look stern, but her lips were trembling and twitching with

suppressed laughter. I grabbed a second bag and carried it across the aisle to Savannah.

"Here," I said, dropping it into her lap. You're going to need this."

"What's this, then?"

"Snacks."

She looked down, confused. "I'm not one to say no to nibbles, but are you taking the mickey?" she asked.

"A lot of the people in this room will probably think so, after this meeting," I said. "Enjoy the show, Sav." And without another word of explanation, I slipped back across the aisle just as the last of the Durupinen filed into their seats and the door closed with a resounding thud at the back of the room.

The Council members filed in from a side door in a long, orderly line, sliding into their benches and sitting in unison except for Celeste, who took her place at the podium and called the meeting to order.

"I welcome you all back to the 204th Airechtas of the Northern Clans. This has been an—ah—*eventful* gathering thus far, but I think it is safe for me to say that we can hope for a smooth and uneventful process from here on out."

"Famous last words," I muttered to Hannah, who smirked.

"If everyone can please open their itineraries to the first page, you will find our agenda for today. The first and most pressing matter is the filling of the vacant Council Seat. Siobhán will review the nomination process, and we will hear all nominations today."

Siobhán stood and took her place behind the podium, Celeste moving smartly aside to make room for her. I couldn't help but think, as I watched the two of them standing there, that only a few days ago, they were both possessed by Shards of a Shattered spirit in this very room. In fact, Siobhán had been standing in the precise spot she occupied now. Perhaps she was thinking the same thing, for she gave a wary look around her before she opened her massive tome of guidelines and the first few words of her speech were delivered with a tremor in her voice.

I supposed I ought to have been paying attention to the details of how we were about to handle the nomination, but it was difficult to concentrate on Siobhán's words when Marion was attempting to burn a hole through my head with her vicious stare. Not one to miss an opportunity to psych out a mortal enemy, I turned to her and winked, and then, for good measure, blew her a kiss. She betrayed no reaction but for a slight tightening at the corners of her mouth.

"That bitch just moved right to the top of my list," came Milo's hiss of a voice through the connection. I turned to see that he had manifested between Hannah and me, his arms crossed tightly over his chest and his lips puckered into a bitter little knot.

"You mean there were actually people above her?" I shot back, the thought zinging between us like a current.

"Not many," he admitted. "But they have officially been supplanted."

". . . at which point, every clan will be called upon to put forth their nomination, should they choose to make one. Please remember that you cannot nominate someone from your own clan, a clan that has been disqualified from running, or anyone who has already been put forward by another clan. Also, no single clan may occupy more than one seat on the Council. If your nomination meets with any of the aforementioned qualifications, it will be stricken from the record," Siobhán said, her voice cutting through our mental conversation. "Once all nominations have been put forward, the nominees will have the opportunity to accept or decline. Those who accept will be given formal paperwork to fill out and will attend a meeting this afternoon to further explain the election process. All nominees are permitted to drop out of the running at any time. Are there any questions?"

Heads turned and bodies shifted in their seats, but no one raised a hand or spoke. I could feel the tension mounting.

"Will there seriously be a nominee from every clan?" Milo asked through the connection. "That's ludicrous! How is anyone supposed to win a majority of votes that way?"

"Karen talked to us about it last night," I said, glancing over at Karen, who was sitting a few rows away, looking tense and combative. "She said that while the clans all have the chance to nominate, only the really powerful ones ever do."

"But why?" Milo asked. "How do they ever expect to get a voice if they don't nominate anyone?"

"Perceived power," Hannah's thoughts joined the conversation. "The more powerful clans form alliances for votes before the nomination process even begins by promising to address pet issues and concerns. They shut out the lesser clans from influence by stacking the deck ahead of time, or else secure their support by promising them something."

"So, in other words, Durupinen politics is just as dirty as every other kind of politics?" Milo asked.

"Yup," Hannah and I thought together, so that our voices rang inside our heads and we both winced.

"So, what's the point of even accepting the nomination, if the other clans have already rigged everything?" Milo asked.

"Well, there is the element of surprise," I pointed out. "As long as Marion has kept her mouth shut, the majority of clans probably don't know we're being nominated."

Milo snorted. "Marion keep her mouth shut? Fat chance."

"You never know. This might be the kind of information she doesn't want getting out, especially since she doesn't know if we'll accept or not," Hannah reminded him. "And besides, even if she told her little pack of minions, there's still the rest of the clans to consider. If they were looking for a way to take the power out of the hands of the current Council clans, we might be able to sway some of them to vote our way."

"Always assuming they don't run screaming the moment they see you approaching," Milo said.

"Assuming that, yes," Hannah said dryly.

"The point is that, by and large, we've got the element of surprise on our side," I said, "and that will probably help us as much as it hurts us. Marion might know the ins and outs of the political system, but she's at least as unpopular as we are these days, after the stunt she pulled three years ago."

"You mean she might have as much ugliness flying her way as we do?" Milo asked, his tone brightening.

"A girl can dream," I muttered, and then closed off the connection as Celeste raised her hands to signal our attention again. I couldn't be sure, but I thought her eyes flicked over to us just before she began speaking.

"If there are no questions as to the nomination process, we shall move forward. As is tradition, our High Priestess has the privilege of putting forth the first nomination," Celeste called.

Every eye in the room now fell upon Finvarra, who seemed to be in a light doze, but jerked to attention as Carrick bent his head and spoke to her. Her body managed to summon some blood from somewhere to faintly color her cheeks in embarrassment at being caught sleeping, but by the time she had cleared her throat, she was deathly pale once again. She did not have the chance to utter a single word, though.

"Deputy Priestess? Do forgive the interruption, but I am afraid I do indeed have a question," a familiar voice called over the loaded silence. I closed my eyes and took a deep, calming breath. Marion always did like the sound of her own voice within these walls.

Celeste, too, looked like she was praying for patience as she turned, slowly to acknowledge Marion. "Yes. The Council recognizes Marion Clark of Clan Gonachd with a question about the nomination process."

"Thank you," Marion said graciously, rising from her seat and smoothing a non-existent crease in her crisp skirt suit before continuing. "I should clarify that this is as much genuine concern as it is question."

"Bollocks," snorted Savvy from the back of the room. I turned, along with many others, to see her munching her popcorn while looking daggers at Marion.

Marion, however, ignored the comment, choosing instead to keep her back turned firmly on Savvy. Her voice, as she continued, was dripping with overplayed courteousness. "I am well aware that it is a long-standing tradition to give the High Priestess first nomination. I don't for a moment mean to disagree with the practice on principle—indeed, I think it only fitting that the leader of the Northern Clans be afforded such an honor. But I wonder—under this particular set of circumstances—if it is entirely... advisable?"

"Aaaaaaaand, here we go," Milo muttered. "Let the fireworks begin."

I threw a look over my shoulder at Karen, who raised an eyebrow at me as though to say, "Brace yourself. Here we go."

Finvarra shifted slightly in her wheelchair. Celeste might have been turned to stone, so still was she standing at the podium, her hands gripping either side of it with white-knuckled intensity. Her lips barely moved as she replied. "And what particular set of circumstances are those, just for clarification?"

Marion glanced around her and gave an incredulous little cough, as though she couldn't quite believe she was being made to clarify something so glaringly obvious. "I do not wish to be indelicate..."

"Like hell you don't," Savvy's mutter carried clearly.

". . . but I really think we must stop to consider the conditions under which our High Priestess is making this nomination."

Finvarra drew herself up to her full height in her chair, her face tense with anticipation of whatever callous machinations were about to fall from Marion's lips. Sure enough, Marion's next words set Finvarra's nostrils flaring. Beside her, Carrick was clenching and unclenching his fists in fury.

"Please do not make me ask for clarification again," Celeste said through gritted teeth. "Either make your intentions known regarding this interruption of the nomination process or risk your own nomination being stricken from consideration."

Marion put her hands up demurely on either side of her, as though she were surrendering. "Now, now, Deputy Priestess. Exercise a modicum of patience, if you please. You may not believe this, but I am endeavoring to be courteous, and in so doing, I am choosing my words carefully."

"Please. As if everything that's about to come out of her mouth hasn't been scripted and memorized since the day she found out about this nomination," Milo scoffed inside my head. "This woman has never improvised in her life."

"Calculating to the core," I agreed, but quickly tuned him out as Marion began to "choose her words carefully" once more.

"I do not mean to minimize the incredible hardships that the High Priestess has had to battle against as she has faced down this devastating illness." She placed a hand on her chest, as though scandalized by the very thought. "Indeed, quite the opposite. I think we should more strongly consider what the effects of those hardships have wrought upon her."

"Do you honestly mean to say," Finvarra said coldly, speaking for the first time in a hoarse whisper of a voice that nevertheless carried, "that there could possibly be one soul in this hall who cannot see the effects for themselves? I am quite literally on display before you."

Marion inclined her head toward Finvarra, a respectful gesture marred by the smile still playing about the corners of her mouth, giving her away. "We all applaud your bravery in making the effort to be here, High Priestess. Do we not, sisters?"

Marion gestured around, inviting the rest of the Durupinen to weigh in on this pronouncement. Most everyone looked far too vary to reply, though a few people murmured in agreement and others clapped awkwardly.

Fiona stood up, her face scarlet with anger. "The Council would like to move that Marion cease and desist with the theatrics and get to the fecking point."

Celeste banged the gavel, but Fiona was already waving her off and taking her seat again.

"Gladly, Fiona," Marion said, making the same phony little bow in Fiona's direction. "As I said, we commend you for your fortitude in attending the Airechtas at all, High Priestess. But I think it is also painfully obvious to all of us here, though it grieves me to say it, that you are in no fit state to be putting forth a nomination for consideration."

A wave of reaction swept through the crowd. A few, those surrounding Marion, mostly, were nodding sadly, as were a few Council members up in the benches. For the most part, however, the response was one of outrage. A few Durupinen in the front rows actually stood up and started shaking their fists at Marion.

"How dare you insinuate..."

"That is your High Priestess and you will show respect when..."

". . . unfair accusations..."

"Have you no decency..."

Under cover of the uproar, I leaned in to Hannah. "She's actually trying to argue diminished capacity, isn't she?"

Hannah nodded, laughing incredulously. "She's hoping she can get the nomination thrown out before it's even made by arguing that Finvarra's health is too compromised for her to participate at all."

"Can she do that?" Milo asked.

"She's doing it," I replied. "Bit of a hail Mary, don't you think?"

"Desperate times call for desperate measures," Hannah said grimly. "And she is definitely desperate."

"Mmm-hmm, and it is not a good look on her," Milo replied. "She must realize everyone knows exactly what she's doing."

"Of course, she does, but she doesn't care," I said. "As long as it gets her what she wants, she doesn't care how transparent it is."

Marion's voice rose up over the end of the tumult. "I understand how painful it must be for many of you to face this obvious truth, but I beg of you all, for the sake of our future, to consider it carefully. Our High Priestess is, forgive me, barely conscious. It's a miracle she's been able to make the journey from her bedchamber to this room! She has been on all manner of medications and drugs, and the toll it has taken on her body and her mind is no doubt severe. Perhaps you think me cruel for inviting you all to face reality in this manner. But our crucial election is not the moment for naïveté or wishful thinking. It is the moment to make the hard decisions that will place our sisterhood in the best possible position to retain its strength, resilience, and formidable leadership. I cannot believe, and nor do I think can many of you, that we can risk allowing Finvarra to put forth a candidate for nomination."

Celeste's gavel was pounding upon the podium, but it was another sound that brought the clamor in the hall to a ringing silence. From atop the platform, still somewhat slumped in her wheelchair, Finvarra was bringing her hands together in a slow, steady clapping motion.

"Brava. Brava, indeed," Finvarra said, raising her head to reveal, miraculously, an amused smile on her face. Everyone in the room dropped immediately into their seats with the exception of Marion, who remained on her feet, staring the High Priestess down defiantly.

"I rather thought, when I first heard you requested attendance at this meeting, that I should deny your request," Finvarra said. "But I knew, given who I was dealing with, that denying your physical presence was a waste of time. I knew it would not, for even a moment, obstruct your agenda."

Marion gave no outward sign of contempt save for a subtle tightening of her hands now clasped in front of her.

Finvarra went on, seeming to gain strength as she spoke, and each word twisted like a well-placed dagger. "You would no doubt have found a way, through a surrogate, to raise the same objections, and attempt to influence the same outcomes. Far better, I told myself, that you do so in the open, so that everyone could see exactly who was pulling the strings."

"Hear, hear!" shouted Savvy from the back. "Oh, sod off," she added as several people nearby tried to shush her.

"I told myself I wasn't going to do this, but facing my own mortality has burned away any desire I once had to maintain such fallacies as dignity," Finvarra said with a hoarse cackle, gesturing to the tragic theatre that was her wheelchair and IV. "And so, Marion, if you care not to maintain the façade of propriety, then neither do I. Consider your gauntlet thrown, and I have no intention of allowing you to pick it back up. It was just three years ago that you stood in this very room and presented a petition to have me removed from my office. Your stunt very nearly worked, but in the end, the leadership saw you for what you truly were; a power-hungry fearmonger."

"Oh, shit," Milo muttered, and I felt his mounting excitement through the connection. He lived for this kind of drama. Hannah, on the other hand, was flooding the connection with a steady gush of anxiety.

Finvarra looked almost fevered. Her eyes burned brightly, and I knew that she had little more than her own anger to keep her going through this impassioned speech. Carrick knew it, too. He kept throwing terrified glances over at Mrs. Mistlemoore, who sat perched on the very edge of her seat, as though she expected an imminent health crisis.

Finvarra went on, "Now, you attempt the very same stunt to strip me of what little authority is left me to shape the future of this Council. You wish to prove I am—what? Unhinged? Irrational? Senile? Devoid of my once impressive mental faculties? What proof do you have to support such accusations, or did you perhaps think that planting the seeds of doubt would be enough to leave me irrelevant in this, the last event of my priestesshood?"

Marion did not reply. She seemed too taken aback that Finvarra was responding in this manner. Finvarra made the same observation, for she let loose another laugh, stronger this time, and went on. "What's wrong, Marion? Cat got your tongue? Didn't think the old girl had this much fight left in her, did you?"

Several titters went up around the room. Even Hannah let out a squeak of laughter. Fiona was lounging back in her chair with an expression of unadulterated delight on her face, as though this were the first time in her life she'd ever enjoyed herself in this room. My own face had broken into a wide smile of its own. I had only ever seen Finvarra conduct herself with the utmost grace and decorum—there had always been a practically royal air to her, but now? Pretense was stripped away. Decorum be damned. She was staring down the barrel of her own mortality and had absolutely nothing left to lose.

And it was a *beautiful* thing to behold.

Finvarra drew another breath and plowed on. "I do not know how you found out about my intended nomination, and frankly, I don't care. I only care that you not be allowed to get away with your devious meddling. So again, I ask, what was your endgame? A vote, perhaps, on whether I was well enough to make this kind of pivotal decision? Allow me, then." She lifted her chin and addressed the entire assembly. "I move that a vote be taken now. If you believe that I, your ailing High Priestess, should be denied the opportunity, after years of service to this sisterhood, to put forth a single name into contention for the empty seat on this Council, please raise your hand and let your objection be known to the assembly."

Siobhán leapt to her feet, her mouth opening and closing like a fish's. Celeste too, looked thoroughly discombobulated, her gavel hovering in midair as she tried to decide if she needed to do something with it. Clearly, Finvarra had committed several breaches in meeting etiquette by rashly calling this vote, but it did not seem to matter. Not a single hand rose into the air. Not a single one, not even Marion's.

"Very well," Finvarra said. "Now, all those who agree that I should now be allowed to proceed with my nomination without further interruption?"

A massive shifting sound as every hand, save Marion's and a small knot of her clique, rose into the air in a sweeping show of solidarity.

Finvarra surveyed the room, satisfied, and turned back to Marion. "There we are. It seems the Durupinen here assembled are in agreement that I have earned the right to make this nomination. And so, with their mandate, I will proceed in doing so. But thank you for taking the time to express your feelings on the matter, Marion. It's one of the true benefits of this process, to allow members to show each other who we truly are."

Marion dropped her gaze to her feet for the first time since the confrontation had begun. Her face was twitching, as though she were swallowing something very bitter, and she lowered herself into her seat. Finvarra watched her for a long silent moment, relishing Marion's defeat before she spoke again.

"Thank you to our Deputy Priestess and our secretary for managing the many details of today's proceedings, and thank you to the entire assembly for your indulgence as I battle with my illness to fulfill my duties here," Finvarra said with an almost defiant return to her accustomed regality. "I have long considered this moment and the decision I would make, were I to live long enough to see it. I am grateful that I have, for I feel that I have the chance to right a great injustice today."

Mumbling broke out around the room, but no heads turned to look at us. It was clear that most of the Durupinen in the room had no clue what Finvarra was talking about. So we knew, at least, that Marion hadn't spread the word of Finvarra's choice indiscriminately. Keeping my eyes determinedly on Finvarra, I reached out to take Hannah's hand. She fumbled for my fingers and then squeezed them tightly.

Finvarra cleared her throat. Now that the adrenaline of confronting Marion was wearing off, her voice was fainter, and a bit quavery again. "Sometimes, in our efforts to preserve and protect our sisterhood, our individual clans are hurt. I have always excused such damage as collateral—unavoidable, and justified for the greater good. It was an unfortunate but necessary part of my job, and one that I undertook with little regret and, I am ashamed to say, little empathy. We have always kept our eyes on the spirit world, making our decisions with our calling in our hearts, but there ought to have been room there for the women that we walk with, and that we call sisters. Our calling is not all we share; we must share each other's pain and each other's burdens as well, especially when we have a hand in causing it."

No one moved. No one even whispered. The High Priestess had every soul in the room, living and dead, held in breathless anticipation. From somewhere deep inside her, Finvarra summoned the voice that put fear into the hearts of her adversaries and respect in the eyes of her supporters. She raised her chin and pointed with a firm, steady hand straight at Hannah and me.

"In light of their great history of service and contribution to the Northern Clans and, more importantly, in light of their recent bravery and commitment in the face of terrible prejudice and nearly insurmountable opposition, I choose to nominate Clan Sassanaigh for the open seat on the Council."

6

DESPERATE MEASURES

LOOKING BACK ON THE MOMENT after Finvarra uttered those words, I found that I was oddly peaceful. All around us, the room erupted in shouts and cries, objections and demands for explanations. I honestly couldn't tell you what exactly was said or who said it. It all sounded distant and unimportant. In fact, I found myself strangely insulated from the vitriol. My mind had created a little bubble for me, and I crawled into it.

Inside that bubble, though, everything was clear. The first thing I thought of was my mom. I thought about her not as I knew her—a troubled, self-medicated shell, but as I knew she had once been when she'd walked the halls of the castle. I saw the girl inside the tiny portrait Fiona had painted, the portrait I now held tucked inside a locket around my neck. Her eyes were bright and inquisitive, her tongue sharp and witty. She'd gazed around this very room, full of dreams of her future and plans to make her mark. She saw the injustices and absurdities of the system she was meant to accept without question, and she had the audacity to question them.

Something made me look up, and I found his eyes. Carrick was staring at me, and his expression was sagging with the same weight of memories. He pressed his lips together and nodded at me. I nodded back. He knew what I knew. She would have been proud. She would have taken that seat and moved mountains with it, carving her mark with the steady, crystal clear persistence of water through rock. My heart ached with the knowledge of what this moment could have meant if he and I had been more than strangers to each other.

It was strange and intimate, there in the eye of the storm, my father and I, sharing this unprecedented understanding. I tried to hold on to it, but the storm intruded at last, and violently.

Carrick's expression shifted. His eyes narrowed, and then widened trained on something just to the right of me. Then he flew forward just as a scream and a toppling of chairs startled me. I felt something hard and metal strike my shin and gasped.

A form was lunging toward me, limbs flailing, screeching words I couldn't comprehend. I wasn't even frightened; there was no time. My reflexes, so attuned to Visitations, simply kicked in without conscious thought. I pushed Hannah down across her seat, throwing my own body over her like a shield just as Carrick materialized in front of us, like a solid wall of ghostly energy. With a single thrust of his arms, he created an invisible barrier of spirit energy that sent our attacker reeling backward, arms flailing, through the air.

"Jess!"

I still hadn't even processed what was happening, and Finn was hoisting me out of my chair and dragging Hannah and me away from our row of seats as a pair of Caomhnóir wrestled with the struggling, writhing form of a woman I did not recognize. She had long silver hair braided back from her face, which was twisted into a leering snarl as she continued to lunge for us.

"Clan Sassanaigh will destroy us all! You are cursed! Cursed! Someone stop this! You cannot allow this curse to poison our sisterhood! It must be routed out! It must be destroyed!" she cried, tears streaming down her weathered face. I lost sight of her for a moment as Finn dragged us to a knot of Caomhnóir who had rushed forward to surround us, closing in like a slamming of human doors.

"They must be destroyed! We cannot allow this to happen! Someone, anyone stop them!" the woman squealed. Seamus yanked her arm sharply behind her back. She let out a cry and something clattered to the floor.

It was a knife.

Everything seemed to stop. I just stared at the thing blankly, as though I had never seen one before and couldn't comprehend what it was for. Finn stepped out from behind us and bent down to pick it up. It had a carved wooden handle and a curved, deadly looking blade.

"What the actual hell?" Milo cried as Finn held it up. A general outcry met the sight of it.

"A knife! She had a knife!" The voices rose up around us like instruments in an orchestra of fear. One voice in particular called

68

out over the others. It belonged to a woman with long, dark hair and a beautiful but stricken face.

"Please! Please don't hurt her!" the woman cried between terrified sobs. She pushed closer to where the Caomhnóir held our attacker, reaching for her, but Braxton stepped in and held her back. "She's not well! Please, don't hurt her!" she pleaded with him.

"Order! I will have order immediately! Caomhnóir remove her from the hall at once," Celeste was shouting over the chaos.

The attacker, whoever she was, was still shrieking about curses and something about "dooming us all" as Seamus and a second Caomhnóir dragged her up the aisle and out the back door. All around the hall, Caomhnóir were ordering people back into their seats. In the back corner, Savvy was standing on her chair, mouth hanging open and her popcorn spilled all over the floor. I nodded at her, as though to say, "I'm all right," but she just continued to stare in shock. Then another figure drew my gaze, not because of its frantic motion, but instead for its utter stillness. Marion sat in her chair, looking almost bored. She saw me looking at her and lifted the corner of her mouth in a satisfied smirk before turning away to converse with the woman sitting beside her.

Hannah shook my arm. "Jess? Jess, are you okay? Did she hurt you?"

"What?" I asked, tearing my eyes from Marion and dazedly looking around. Hannah was pointing down at my leg, which was bleeding through my pant leg.

"I... no, I don't think so," I said, trying to think through the adrenaline. I reached down and pulled up the pant leg. I didn't even realize that I was injured until I saw the blood, and suddenly aches rushed through my shin, like I had flicked some switch. "Oh, I guess I am hurt."

"You mean... she actually..." Hannah couldn't even finish the sentence, but she didn't need to. I was already shaking my head.

"No, it was that chair in front of us. It got knocked over and caught me in the leg. It's just a scrape, seriously," I said, reconfirming the truth of this even as I said it, trying to replay the moment in my head to see if I even remembered it clearly. I thought I did.

Finn jogged back to where we were standing behind our wall of Caomhnóir, having handed the knife over to a younger guardian I didn't recognize. This younger Caomhnóir produced a plastic bag from nowhere, suggesting he regularly carried evidence collection equipment around with him as a hobby. I opened my mouth to ask Finn if he carried such items on his person as well, but he cut me off in a panicked staccato, words firing off like a machine gun.

"Are you two all right? Jess, why are you bleeding?" Finn asked, zoning in on the wound like a shark scenting blood in the water.

"Calm down, Finn. It was just a chair, not the knife," I said, as calmly as I could, though the shock was starting to wear off and my voice now had an audible tremor in it.

"JESSICA! HANNAH!" Karen cried hysterically, stumbling over chairs and shoving Durupinen aside right and left to reach us. "Out of my way! Let me through! Those are my sister's girls!"

At a nod from Finn, two of the Caomhnóir parted, letting her through. She grabbed us to her in a smothering hug, her body shaking with fear and barely contained sobs.

"It's okay, Karen, everything's okay," I said, my face muffled against her shoulder. "We're fine. Just try to get a grip, all right?"

Carrick materialized beside Finn, though his form was flickering feebly after the massive drain on his energy he had made by throwing the woman back.

"We're fine, we're fine," I said to him before he could properly open his mouth.

"Carrick, thank God you saw her coming," Karen gasped, releasing her grip on us and looking anxiously into our faces as though expecting to see someone irreparably damaged staring back at her.

"Thank you so much, Carrick," Hannah said breathlessly, pulling her face out of Karen's grip and turning to Carrick. "I... I don't even want to think of what might have happened if you hadn't..."

"Let's not consider it," Carrick said gravely. "And there is no need to thank me. I'm your... I would do anything in my power to protect you, always, and without hesitation."

Hannah nodded at him, and I did as well, all of us choosing to skate over the awkward omission of the word, "father." There was no time to dwell on it, anyhow. Celeste was desperately attempting to restore order and call our attention to her.

"Please! Please, everyone take your seats and calm down," Celeste was shouting. Her Caomhnóir broke away from the knot surrounding us and ascended the podium to whisper in her ear. She listened intently for a moment, nodded her head curtly, and turned back to the room at large, which was slowly starting to settle again, due in large part to the Caomhnóir circulating amongst them, silencing their anxious questions and guiding them back into chairs.

"Come on, let's go sit," I said to Hannah, who nodded and made to follow me. We were met with a solid wall of scowling testosterone.

"Excuse us," I said, with as much authority as I could muster. "We would like to rejoin the group."

"We have not been authorized to break ranks," the nearest Caomhnóir growled at me.

"I just authorized you," I replied through gritted teeth. "You may not have noticed, but both the weapon and the woman holding it have been removed from the room."

I looked at Karen for support, but she was still a mess, wiping at her streaming eyes and stroking Hannah's hair like a missing child she'd just been reunited with.

The Caomhnóir opened his mouth, presumably to argue with me some more, but Finn stepped in. "The threat has been contained. As Caomhnóir for this clan, I am authorizing you to break ranks and allow these ladies to return to their seats."

They didn't look happy about it—hell, when did they ever look happy about anything?—but they parted, and Hannah, Karen, Milo, and I made our way back to our seats. Carrick, after satisfying himself that there would be no further need for him, vanished and rematerialized almost immediately beside Finvarra, who was being assessed by Mrs. Mistlemoore in the wake of the excitement. Karen did not return to the place she'd been sitting before, but followed us up to our row, where the neighboring Durupinen hastened to make room for her and offer her a chair.

Our reemergence from our security detail was evidently exciting enough that everyone finally stopped talking and chose instead to watch us take our seats. I tried to ignore all the pairs of eyes on us, and instead looked expectantly up at Celeste, waiting for her to say something—anything—that would turn the general attention her way again.

Celeste spoke, but we were not out of the spotlight yet. "Jessica. Hannah. My Caomhnóir tells me that you are both uninjured?"

"Yes," I replied, and felt relieved to hear that my voice had stopped shaking.

Celeste turned to Finvarra, presumably to give her the opportunity to speak, but Mrs. Mistlemoore was now providing her with oxygen, and she seemed unable to address the assembly, so Celeste went on. "I cannot begin to express my horror at what has just occurred. We will be taking a recess for the remainder of the afternoon so that we may investigate further. Let me just say this: never in the history of our sisterhood have we allowed fear and division to halt our democratic process, and today shall be no different. When we reconvene tomorrow morning, our nomination process shall continue unabated. Clan Sassanaigh, I will ask that all members of your clan here present please proceed to my office forthwith."

We all nodded. I had expected that. Surely someone was going to tell us more about what the hell had just happened to us and why.

"Very well, then," Celeste said, "In that case, I would like to adjourn the—"

But Hannah had stood up, her hand raised high in the air. I looked curiously at her, but she did not acknowledge me.

Celeste lowered her gavel and pointed to Hannah. "Yes, the Council acknowledges Hannah Ballard of Clan Sassanaigh."

"Thank you," Hannah said. "I just wanted to know if we would be given the opportunity to respond to our nomination?"

Celeste looked taken aback. "Well, yes, of course. Every clan will have the chance to do so. But you've just been through quite an ordeal. We hardly expect you to make any sort of decision under the—"

"We accept," Hannah said firmly. "And I will personally be running for the seat."

7

BAGGAGE

"**U**NBELIEVABLE. Truly unbelievable," Milo said, shaking his head and laughing.

"Which part?" Hannah asked dryly.

Milo, Hannah, Karen, Finn, and I were sitting in the Council office, waiting to meet with Celeste. Several other Durupinen were loitering around outside; I could see the shadows of their pacing feet stretching underneath the doorway.

"The part where you upstaged an attempted coup and a failed assassination," Milo said.

Hannah rolled her eyes. "If by 'upstaged' you mean that I still somehow managed to be the most horrifying thing to happen in that meeting, then yes, I guess you're right."

"It was pretty epic, though, Hannah, you've got to admit it," I said. "I mean, just accepting right there on the spot, minutes after that woman attacked us? Awesome."

"I wasn't trying to be awesome," Hannah said, still not cracking a smile. "I was trying to get the acceptance over with so that I wouldn't have time to talk myself out of it before tomorrow's meeting."

"Yeah, well, no one in that room knew that," Milo said. "I've never heard a silence that loud in my life. It was sheer awe."

Hannah snorted. "Sheer horror, more like. I'm surprised no more knife-wielding Durupinen leapt from the crowd to finish us off."

"That's not funny," Karen said quietly. She had barely spoken a word since we'd left the Grand Council Room. She sat between us, arms folded tightly across her chest as though to keep all the emotions from spilling out.

"Sorry," Hannah murmured. "I know it's not. Do you know who that woman was?"

Karen nodded stiffly but did not elaborate, and we had no chance

73

to ask her to do so. At that moment, the door to the hallway opened and Celeste swept into the room. As she had so often recently, she looked harassed and rather tired. I wasn't convinced that she'd given herself enough time to recover from the harrowing experience of being a Host during the Shattering.

"Thank you for your patience," Celeste said to us, dropping into the chair behind the desk with a wan smile. "I wanted to be sure I had as much information as I could gather before I met with you."

"Of course," I said. "I think we'd all like to know whatever you can tell us about the random lunatic who tried to kill us, if possible."

Celeste tried to smile at my joke, but couldn't quite pull it off.

"Clan Sgàil is one of our oldest documented clans in the north, and one of the proudest. They have a long history of staying well clear of Durupinen politics and often had to be dragged to the Airechtas under threat of repercussions. They were also one of the largest clans, maintaining a Geatgrima on their native land, and seeking very little protection or power from the hierarchy. But that all changed about twenty-five years ago," Celeste began.

Beside me, Karen sat rigidly in her chair. She seemed barely to be breathing.

"The woman who attacked you today is Bernadette Ainsley. She had a... falling out with your grandmother," Celeste said, clearly choosing her words very carefully. "She has never fully recovered from what she considers to be the injustice of it and, from what I understand from what her daughters just told me, has become increasingly unstable over the years because of it."

"What kind of falling out?" I asked. "I mean, I know our grandmother made a lot of enemies over the years, but I didn't think any of them would actually want to kill us."

Celeste glanced at Karen again, who was looking determinedly at the wall over Celeste's shoulder. "Karen, do you..."

"No, I do not," Karen said stiffly. "You can tell them."

"Bernadette is a Muse, just like you, Jessica. When your mother and your aunt were just starting at Fairhaven, she made a spirit-induced sculpture that she did not fully understand. She interpreted it as a warning about the Prophecy and brought it from her clan seat to Fairhaven to inform the Council. When she arrived, she passed your mother in the entrance hall and realized that it was her face in the sculpture."

"Our mother?" Hannah and I both gasped at the same time.

74

"Yes," Celeste said. "The Council studied the sculpture at length and came to the conclusion that the face could not be positively identified. The work was incomplete, and the carving was rather crude. Of course, knowing what we know now..." Celeste shook her head regretfully. "However, at the time, the Council decided to dismiss the claim as unsubstantiated."

"That's it?" I asked incredulously. "That's why she tried to kill us?"

Karen let out a sharp bark of bitter laughter. "Of course, that wasn't it. Haven't I taught you anything about your grandmother?"

Hannah threw her a wary look. "What do you mean?"

Karen dropped her hands into her lap. "Mother was livid. I don't know if I'd ever seen her so angry, until Lizzie vanished, of course."

"But why?" I asked. "The sculpture was rejected. The Council dismissed it. What did it matter?"

"Any stain on our family reputation, no matter how small, was an utterly unforgivable offence. Your grandmother would not rest until Bernadette was so thoroughly discredited that no one would believe a word she uttered again in her life," Karen said.

"So, what did she do?" I asked tentatively.

"She waged an all-out war on Clan Sgàil," Karen said bluntly. "She dragged Bernadette before committee after committee, demanding that her abilities as a Muse be tested over and over and over again. She used Council legislation to strip Clan Sgàil of their honors one at a time, first finding a pretext to shrink their territory, then placing their stewardship of the Sgàil Geatgrima under advisement, then slapping them with sanctions for infractions they probably weren't even committing. And all the while, Bernadette Ainsley was desperately trying to prove that her sculpture was a legitimate piece of spirit-induced art. She soon found herself banned from seeking audiences because of her constant harassment of Council members, and, from what I understand, she spent years searching fruitlessly for the inspiration that led her to create the piece in the first place. Over time, it's become rather an obsession for her, and her mental and physical health have suffered for it."

"Yes, I have heard that as well. I haven't seen her here in years," Celeste said. "Her elder daughter has been looking after her."

"Why didn't we ever hear about her?" I asked. "When people

were telling us about the Prophecy and explaining the history of it, why didn't she ever come up?"

"We agreed that knowing about her might negatively impact one of your relationships here," Celeste said.

"What do you mean?" I pressed. "Which relationship?"

"Ours," said a voice from the doorway.

I spun in my seat to see Fiona standing there, framed in the doorway, her face looking so long and tired that her paint-spattered bandana might have been holding it on. She smiled sadly. "Bernadette is my mother."

I gaped. "Your... your mother just tried to kill us?"

"My dear old mum, that's right," Fiona said.

"I... can't believe... wow," was all I could muster in response. I had no idea what to say. I half-wanted to apologize, although something about the absurdity of the situation—that somehow I owed someone an apology when I was the one who'd just had a knife swung at her—gave me pause.

"Yeah, well, sometimes I can't believe it myself," Fiona said tartly before turning to Celeste with a grim expression. "Nan's here and she'd like to tell you something."

Celeste sat up a little straighter in her chair. "Very well, she may enter."

Fiona looked over her shoulder and jerked her head sharply. The woman called Nan shuffled out from behind her, her long dark hair half-concealing a freckled, tear-stained face. She did not look up or speak but continued to sniffle piteously. I recognized her as the woman who had been pleading with the Caomhnóir not to hurt Bernadette.

"Out with it then, you bloody fool," Fiona spat at her. "Tell them what you've done."

Nan jumped and began to speak quickly, so that she tripped over her words in her effort to get them out. "I brought my mother here today even though I knew she was unstable."

"And why did you do that?" Celeste demanded. "You knew that Fiona would vote on behalf of your clan. Neither of your presences was required."

"I know that," Nan said, nodding. "But then Marion came to see us."

Karen, who until now had seemed reluctant to even turn to look at Nan, whipped her head around. "Marion? When? For what purpose?"

"On Christmas Day," Nan said. "We were not expecting her. I don't think I've spoken to her since our school days at Fairhaven."

"Lucky you," muttered Fiona.

"She asked to come in, and we saw no reason to refuse her," Nan said, as Fiona snorted derisively. "She explained to us that she had long felt our family had been ill-used by the Council, and that she wanted to right some of the wrongs that had been committed against us. I was skeptical at first. I could not understand why she would care one way or the other about our clan. She'd given us nary a thought before, as far as I could see."

"Your instinct was correct, and you ought to have followed it, you useless twit," Fiona snapped.

Nan sniffed louder and when she continued, there was a pleading note in her voice. "I told her that I couldn't see what she could do to help us. We had heard all about her fall from power after the Prophecy came to pass. What could she do, when my own sister, who was sitting on the Council, couldn't even repair the damage that had been done?"

Fiona and Nan glared at each other. It was impossible to tell which face held more contempt.

"How did Marion respond to that?" Celeste prompted quickly, in an obvious attempt to defuse the situation.

"She explained that, while she wasn't technically on the Council anymore, her influence within the Council, and within the other powerful clans, was still strong. She could pull the right strings, if we would help her."

"Are you saying," Karen said in a deadly quiet voice, "that she orchestrated the attack on these girls?"

"No!" Nan cried, looking horrified. "No, of course not! She wasn't asking us to hurt anyone and I had no idea that... that my mother would ever..." she burst into hysterical sobs.

"All right, Nan. All right. Get ahold of yourself, now. There are still many questions to be answered here, and no one's got time for your useless tears," Fiona said impatiently.

"What did Marion want you to do, and what, specifically, did she offer you in return?" Celeste asked.

It took Nan several more false starts and deep shuddering breaths before she could continue with her story. "She wanted us to come to

77

the rest of the Airechtas. She said there was a chance that someone was going to nominate Clan Sassanaigh back onto the Council. She would not let that happen, she said, and she needed our help to ensure that they did not win back the seat." Here, Nan threw a half-ashamed, half-defiant look at Karen. "Karen, you know I hold no ill-feelings toward you personally, but your mother has ground our clan into the very dust. We cannot forgive such crimes against us."

"I do not deny it, and I deeply regret that our clan has caused yours so much grief," Karen said stiffly. "My mother was not a compassionate person and her legacy as a Council member is not one I wear with pride."

Nan blinked once, and then nodded stiffly in acknowledgment of Karen's words before continuing. "Marion asked for us to attend the Airechtas and, if needed, to testify against the nomination of Clan Sassanaigh. She also asked us to persuade as many of our ally clans as possible to vote against them. She thought just the sight of my mother there would be a stark reminder to many at the Airechtas of the damage Clan Sassanaigh has wrought within the Council. If possible, we were also supposed to convince Fiona to vote against them."

Hannah was watching Nan with a horrified expression, pulling obsessively on the sleeves of her shirt. Beneath her trembling fingers, one of them had begun to fray.

"And in return?" Celeste prompted again.

Nan swallowed. "In return, Marion would ensure a request for full restoration of our ancestral lands would be brought before the Council for a vote, and that she had the support to pass it."

Fiona scoffed. "I've tried it twice already, so I can't see why you'd fall for that load of tosh."

"Marion said she has far more influence amongst the sitting clans than you'll ever have," Nan shot back. "And I daresay it's true."

Fiona scowled, but did not answer. From all I'd ever seen, she was certainly the black sheep of the Council. I silently wondered how she'd ever been elected in the first place, and made a mental note to ask Karen about it later.

"And your mother? How did she feel about coming?" Celeste asked.

"She wouldn't let it go, once we'd heard Marion's offer," Nan said. "It wasn't the return of our lands that tempted her, though he was pleased to hear that Marion intended to make it happen. she was terrified that Clan Sassanaigh would get the Council seat back."

"Of course she bloody was, which was why you should have kept her far away from this place!" Fiona said. "Nan, she hasn't been stable for years and you know it! What were you thinking, bringing her here?"

"She wouldn't let it go, Fiona!" Nan cried.

"And so, you just let her have her way, like some spoiled child?" Fiona shouted.

"You don't understand what it's like, caring for her day in and day out!" Nan spat, and her eyes began to fill with tears again. "You've no idea the hardships I put up with while you sit up in your little tower playing with your paints and your clay!"

Fiona reached right out and slapped her sister, as hard as she could, across the face. Nan stumbled back, clutching her cheek and staring at her sister in horror. Celeste stood as though readying herself to step in, but Nan did not move to retaliate.

"Never," said Fiona in a deadly quiet voice, "degrade my work like that again. You chose to care for Mother. You wanted the job. You said you could do it. This," she held up her paint- and plaster-spattered hands. "I never asked for this. Some days I'd like to cut these hands open and let the Muse drain out of me. Then I might get some peace. I expect Mother has felt the same way."

No one spoke, because no one knew what to say. I had never heard Fiona speak of her gift as a Muse as anything other than just that: a gift. I'd always accepted her artistic temperament—her mood swings, her quirks, her obsessions—as a sign of her devotion to her work, rather than a sign that she was struggling with it. I felt as though I was seeing her clearly for the first time.

So, perhaps, was Celeste, for when she spoke again, it was in a gentler tone than she had yet used. "You have both done much in service of your clan; that is not in question here. Nan, at any time did Marion suggest that your mother take matters into her own hands?"

"No!" Nan said, sounding horrified. "No, of course not! I would never have come if such a thing had been suggested!"

"And your mother never gave any indication that she wanted to hurt or harm anyone?" Celeste asked.

"No!" Nan said, and then she bit her lip. "She... she was really anxious about what would happen if Clan Sassanaigh retook the seat. You know what she went through, and then the Prophecy came to pass... she... I think she was very scared it might happen."

"And the knife? Did the Caomhnóir show it to you?" Celeste asked.

"Yes."

"It was extremely distinctive. Have you ever seen it before?"

Nan shot a nervous glance at Fiona. "Yes. It's a clan heirloom. It usually resides in a case over our fireplace with other clan relics. She must have taken it out and concealed it before we left. I didn't notice it was missing."

Fiona literally stuck her fist in her mouth and bit down on it to stop herself from shouting at her sister again.

"Very well," Celeste said, perhaps sensing the same mounting tension. "Finn, please escort Nan to the hospital wing. Nan, you may await news of your mother there, but I must insist that you remain until I have spoken to you again. I am sure that there will be further questions for you."

"No, wait!" Nan said. "I need to know... what is going to happen to my mother? Her mind isn't... she isn't responsible for... please, don't lock her away. She's not well."

"I can make no promises about your mother, Nan," Celeste said, and though her voice was firm, it was not without empathy. "The crime she attempted to commit is very serious. Were it not for the expeditious responses of Mr. Carey and the other Caomhnóir, both Hannah and Jess could have been killed. There is much to consider, but I do give you my word that we will take your mother's mental state under advisement. Many here are already well-acquainted with her history."

Nan sniffed, nodded miserably, and turned to go, still rubbing at her scarlet cheek.

Finn stepped forward, clicking his heels together and bowing at the waist. "Deputy Priestess, I would be more comfortable leaving my clan if I knew all elements of the situation are under control."

Celeste frowned slightly. "What elements are those, Mr. Carey?"

"He means Marion," Milo said, his tone and expression fierce. He and Finn locked eyes, an unspoken agreement flowing between them like a current. "He wants to know what you've done with her. Personally, I'd be most comfortable if you told me she's chained up somewhere."

80

"So would I," Karen muttered.

It was Fiona, not Celeste, who answered. "After Seamus questioned Nan, he sent Braxton to fetch Marion and escort her to the Caomhnóir office for interrogation. I expect she's there, or at least on her way."

"Very well," Celeste said, nodding. "Mr. Carey? Spirit Guide Chang? Does that control the elements of this situation to your satisfaction?"

"Does the Caomhnóir office have handcuffs and leg irons?" Milo grumbled.

Finn gave me a swift look that seemed to ask, "Are you okay if I go?" I gave him the tiniest nod I could manage. "I will be on guard outside your quarters as soon as I am finished. I will gather as much information about Marion's interrogation as I can," he told us, and marched out, Nan scurrying ahead of him.

"Thank you, Finn," Karen said.

We watched in silence as Finn closed the door behind him.

"With your permission, I'd like to take the girls back to their room. They've had a trying morning," Karen said to Celeste, and though she was asking permission, she was already standing expectantly.

"Very well," Celeste agreed. "I'll send Seamus along, if there is anything else to tell you."

Fiona stepped quickly forward. "Could Jess and I have a moment?" she asked, addressing Karen, but looking at me.

"Yeah, okay," I said.

Karen looked as though she wanted to refuse, but she just sighed instead. "We'll be waiting for you out in the hallway, Jess," she said, and headed for the door. Hannah and Milo stood to follow her. Hannah squeezed my shoulder as she passed, and Milo sent his silent support zinging through the connection. After a few very long, very loaded moments, Fiona finally spoke, though she had to clear her throat a couple of times to coax the words into an audible volume.

"What a fecking mess this is, eh?"

"That's an accurate summary of the morning, yeah."

"Look, I'm sorry I never told you, Jess. I didn't want you to think I... that I couldn't mentor you fairly, just because of the history between our clans. I'm not my mother, and you're not your

81

grandmother. I've always known that, and I can promise I've never let their troubles affect how I've treated you."

"So, you're saying you throw that many chairs at everyone?" I asked, with a spark of a smile.

Fiona's tense face relaxed, and she actually grinned. "Exactly that many chairs. Sometimes more, if I'm honest."

"We're good, then," I said.

Fiona's grinned faded. "Are you sure that you—"

"We're good," I said firmly. "And... I'm really sorry about your mother. I understand what it's like, having a mom who's been swallowed whole by all of this."

"I know you do. We'll get her sorted. I just hope the Council sees clear to send her home instead of locking her up," Fiona said.

"Karen will talk to them, and so will we, if we need to. I know the last thing Hannah would want is for anyone to be locked up when what they really need is help."

Fiona nearly managed a smile, but then frowned once again. "Look, have you spoken to Lucida yet?"

My stomach lurched. "No. With all we've had to do to prepare for today, I haven't had a chance." *I'm also purposely avoiding it*, I added silently to myself.

Fiona bit her lip. "Right, yeah. Well, just make sure you do, and soon. I'm working on those sketches for you, but there are some questions I need answered if we're going to get to the bottom of them. It's strange territory—jumping to conclusions isn't an option. It's probably the last thing you want to do, but..." she didn't finish the sentence, but I understood her anyway. What I wanted wasn't really a factor.

"I'll speak to Finn and Mrs. Mistlemoore," I told her. "And I'll come to see you when it's done."

"Good. And... don't let her mess with you."

"What do you mean, 'mess with me?'"

Fiona rolled her eyes. "It's Lucida. Use your imagination."

8

PLEDGES

KAREN, MILO, HANNAH, and I walked back to our room in silence. Perhaps we were all still reeling from what had happened. I, for one, still hadn't actually allowed myself to absorb the reality of it all. It felt like my brain was trying to protect itself by keeping the memory at a safe distance. Even as I tried to recall it, many of the details fell into a blurry state, like I was trying to remember something while half-asleep. I was sure that the trauma of it would hit me, and soon, but for the moment, I was grateful for my well-developed defense mechanisms.

The entrance hall was nearly deserted as we passed by it on our way to our room. Nearly.

"Oi! Jess! Hannah!"

Savvy was jogging up the staircase toward us, looking uncharacteristically serious. "Bloody hell! Are you all right? I've been looking for you two everywhere!"

"Yeah, we're fine," I told her. "As predicted, we are super popular."

Savvy made a sound that was half-laugh, half-sigh of relief. "I don't know whether to hug you or slap you, mate!"

"Why would you slap me? Did the attempted stabbing not add enough shock value for you?"

"No, I mean, the nomination itself! I can't believe you knew it was coming and you didn't tell me!"

"Sorry, Savvy," Hannah said. "I didn't want anyone to know, just in case I changed my mind. Unfortunately, the wrong people still found out."

"Yeah, but you showed 'em all, didn't you? When you accepted like that..." she let out a long whistle. "That was brilliant! I actually saw steam come out of Marion's ears."

"Yeah, I think we're lucky she didn't drop a cartoon anvil on our heads," I said, smiling back in spite of myself. "Although, she may have done worse."

"How do you mean?"

"Walk with us upstairs. I'll explain everything."

I used the walk back to our room to fill Savvy in on all of the details of our meeting in Celeste's office. Her mouth hung further and further open with each new revelation.

"Fiona's *mum*?!"

"Yeah."

"And you think there's a chance that Marion actually told her to attack you?"

"It's Marion," I scoffed. "She probably sharpened the knife for her."

"No," Karen said, chiming in for the first time as we closed the door to our room. "Marion is much too smart to make an error like that. She would never leave any sort of trail, verbal or otherwise, that could directly connect her to that attack. Of course, that doesn't mean that she still didn't orchestrate it all the same."

"Orchestrate it how?" I asked.

"She created the perfect set of circumstances," Karen said, her tone curt and clipped in her anger. "She knew Bernadette was unwell. She knew her animosity for our clan was fierce. Marion brought Bernadette here knowing that Bernadette would have to sit there and watch her greatest fear come to pass: Clan Sassanaigh gaining power once again. She must have known that Bernadette would react strongly, and there was plenty she could have said to Bernadette to ensure her panic was heightened. I do not doubt for a second that Marion hoped something like this would happen."

Hannah and I looked at each other solemnly, and I saw the same resignation in her face. This was going to be over before it had even begun.

"We're in over our heads, aren't we?" Hannah asked quietly. "You're going to ask us to pull out of the race."

Karen gave her a long, hard look and then said, "No."

Hannah looked shocked. "No?"

"No," Karen repeated. "I want to. I want to put you on a plane home tonight, Airechtas be damned, and lock you in your room like a pair of unruly teenagers. But I can't."

"Why not?" Hannah asked.

84

Karen hesitated. "I'll tell you, Hannah, but I'm not sure how you're going to feel about it."

"Tell me anyway," Hannah urged her.

Karen sighed. "Because the way you stood up in there, just moments after that woman attacked you, and coolly, confidently, and without a hint of fear, told Celeste that you accepted the nomination—all I could see in that moment was your mother."

Hannah's face went blank. "My mother?"

"Yes. Your mother, whatever you may think about her, was an incredibly brave person. I never once saw her hesitate to stand up against something she believed was wrong. In fact, she was the reason I decided to become a lawyer. She inspired me to confront injustice wherever I saw it. Whatever else she may have battled against, whatever demons got the better of her, whatever mistakes she may have made, she was one of the bravest women I ever knew. And watching you in there today—I would never have been foolish enough to stand in your mother's way, and I won't be foolish enough to stand in yours."

Hannah's face was flushed and her eyes were bright. She didn't say anything, but dropped her gaze to her own hands, now clasped in her lap.

Karen seemed to realize that she'd touched a nerve and quickly changed the subject. "Will the two of you be okay here without me? I have a few people I need to speak to, and I'd like to do it now, while Marion is still being questioned," she said.

"We'll be fine," I said quickly. "Finn should be back here soon, anyway."

"And I'm a right old brawler when I need to be," Savvy said, clapping Karen on the back. "Don't you worry 'bout a thing."

Karen looked for a moment as though Savvy's words had given her a whole new reason to worry, but she took a deep breath and swallowed her misgivings for the time being. "I'll be back soon. I'd rather you didn't venture down to the dining room quite yet. It's bound to be crowded and I don't want you to have to navigate the rough waters without me, all right? Humor me."

We knew better than to argue. Instead we assured her and reassured her all the way across the room and out the door.

"I'll wait to go down to lunch, too, then," Savvy said, flopping down on my bed. "Hope she's back soon, though. I'm bloody starving. I spilled half my popcorn."

"Here, take mine," I said, reaching into my messenger bag and thrusting the crumpled popcorn bag into her hands. "I was too busy hyperventilating and dodging knives to eat any of it."

"Cheers," Savvy said, snatching it from me and plunging her hand inside.

"Here, take mine, too," Hannah said, handing her bag over.

"What have you got against popcorn, then?" Savvy asked, starting to look suspicious.

"Nothing," Hannah replied. "I just didn't appreciate the joke."

"Oh, please, I'm hilarious and you know it," I said. "I was just trying to get you to smile a bit. How was I supposed to know what was going to happen?"

Hannah didn't respond. Instead, she lay on her bed and looked intently up into her canopy, as though she might find a solution to this mess tucked up in the folds of fabric.

"Well, anyway, I didn't just come here to swipe all your nibbles," Savvy said, standing up and looking, for a moment, slightly embarrassed. "I actually came to give you this."

She reached into the back pocket of her jeans and drew out a slightly crumpled envelope. She held it out to me, and I took it, turning it over to examine it curiously. It was made of thick, fibrous parchment and had a purple wax seal on the front. The design stamped into the circle of wax was that of a triskele.

"What is this, Sav?" I asked.

"Just open it, mate," Savvy said. "Both of you."

Mystified, I carried the envelope over to Hannah's bed and slid up onto the mattress beside her, Milo floating along behind me. Hannah sat up, her own face mirroring my confusion. As the three of us bent over it, I broke the seal, unfolded the heavy vellum paper within, and read the words aloud.

"Clan Lunnainn does hereby pledge its faith, its support, and its sworn vote to the Clan Sassanaigh for the post of Council Member for the Northern Clans on this, the third day of the 204th Airechtas of the Northern Clans. Bound in word, bound in sisterhood, and sealed in blood."

"Damn," Milo whispered. "Blood? Seriously?"

"It's a metaphor," Savvy said. "I didn't actually... y'know... bleed on it, or anything."

I looked up, stunned. "What is this?" I repeated.

Savvy frowned. "Didn't you read it? That's my vote. Well, my clan's vote. For you. For the Council."

I looked at Hannah, who gaped. "What do you mean?"

"You've voted already?" Milo asked. "But they haven't even finished the nominations yet."

"That's what's called a pledge," Savvy explained. "Every clan has the choice to put one in writing and deliver it to the candidate clan before the final vote."

"A pledge?" Hannah repeated, still looking dumbfounded.

"I hope I've done it all right," Savvy said, looking a little sheepish. "I followed what the book told me to do, copied the exact words and all. Nearly burned my bloody finger off trying to seal it. But it's binding."

"Sav, how did you even know to do this?" I asked, dumbfounded.

Savvy shrugged sheepishly. "I read about it."

"You read about it? In... in a book?" Hannah asked.

"Yes, in a bloody book!" Savvy replied defensively. "Frankie was asking me questions about the Airechtas and I didn't know the answers. I thought that was bad form for a mentor, so I went to the library and got a book about the Airechtas from one of the Scribes. I've been reading it so Frankie don't think I'm a tosser for not knowing what's going on."

A slow grin spread over my face. "You found the library?"

Savvy rolled her eyes and held her hand out, snapping her fingers. "I'll have it back if you're going to be a—"

"No, no!" Hannah cried, taking the pledge and holding it to her chest. "It's... this is..." But instead of completing the thought, Hannah slid off the bed, bounded across the room, and threw herself at Savvy in a fierce hug.

"Whoa, there, wee one!" Savvy laughed, stumbling backward with the force of the embrace, but flinging her arms around Hannah and hugging her back. "You pack quite the punch, don't you?"

"In hugs as in life, don't let appearances fool you," I said, smiling. "Tiny but tough."

Hannah broke away from Savvy, still grinning, but with suspiciously bright eyes. "Thank you, Sav. This means so much to us—to me."

Savvy's cheeks went pink. "It's nothing. Surely you knew I'd be voting for you."

"I'm still confused, though," Milo said. "If everyone is just going to make pledges ahead of time, what's the point of having a vote? If everyone's already pledged, we'll know who won before we even reach the voting, won't we?"

"Not quite," Savvy said. "Well, I guess you might, if it was a landslide. But for one thing, a lot of clans won't make pledges. They don't like the idea of showing their hand or taking the chance that their vote might go to someone else, because pledges are transferable, mate. You can do what you want with it."

Hannah frowned. "What would I do with it, besides keep it?"

"Oh, I read all about it," Savvy said, throwing her chest out importantly. "You can use pledges like currency. They give you leverage, see?"

"No, I don't see. A vote is a vote, right?" Hannah said.

"Nah, pledges are even better," Savvy said. "You can use them to bargain. So, if other clans can see that you're racking them up, right, they may start trying to negotiate with you. Trade pledges for campaign promises, or support on future legislation, rubbish like that."

"Oh, I see," Hannah said. "This process is more complicated than I realized. I hope Celeste is planning to explain all this to us in the nominee meeting tomorrow."

"I'm sure she will. You'll need to be prepared. You know people like Marion will be gaming this part of the system for all it's worth," Milo said.

Hannah looked at me, and I could tell she was worried. This was an element of the election we had not been prepared for. If everything Savvy said about pledges was true, there was going to be a lot more to this process than we'd thought.

"Who else do you reckon is going to be nominated? Besides me, obviously. We all know I'm a shoo-in," Savvy said, flipping her hair.

"No idea," I said. "But you know Marion will have her handpicked candidate in the mix. If you ask me, that will be the person to beat."

"And whoever she is can probably already count on a stack of these," Milo said, gesturing to Savvy's pledge.

"I wonder how many she'll be able to count on when word gets out that Marion set Fiona's mum on you like a rabid dog," Savvy said grimly. "That's not bound to sit well with a lot of folks."

A timorous knock interrupted our conversation. We all froze, looking around at each other cautiously.

"Who is it?" I called.

"It's Bertie," came a tremulous voice from the other side of the door. Is Savannah there? Could I trouble her for a word? I must discuss the afternoon's security plans with her."

"Christ on a bike," Savvy groaned. "He is unbelievable. What other Caomhnóir needs to review their schedule of activities five bloody times a day? Does Finn put you through this kind of nonsense?"

"Not anymore," I said. "He's mellowing out in his old age."

"A mellow Caomhnóir? That's an oxymoron, if ever I've heard one," Milo snorted.

"I'll see you all later, then," Savvy said, and wrenched open the door. We caught a brief glimpse of Bertie's pale, terrified face and a few seconds of glorious Cockney-accented tirade before the door slammed shut behind her.

§

For all my talk about Finn mellowing out, he was insistent that we attend the next day's Airechtas session with a full complement of additional security. Before I could open my mouth to complain, Karen added that he had arranged it on her orders and it was a condition of continuing to attend the meetings.

"I stand by everything I said yesterday. I trust you both completely to handle yourselves in there. I just don't trust anyone else," she said, arms folded truculently across her chest.

Security inside the Grand Council Room had obviously been increased as well. There were almost twice as many Caomhnóir as the previous day, and we could hardly miss the fact that several of them were stationed in the area immediately surrounding our seats. I fully intended to complain about it when the meeting was called to order, but Hannah gave me a long warning look to keep my mouth shut. She had no interest in drawing any unnecessary attention to us today.

And for once, the Airechtas was exactly as boring as it was always meant to be. Celeste made a few remarks at the opening of the meeting, explaining that the matter of our attack was being handled by a committee of Trackers, and that no further outbursts would be tolerated. Marion was unusually quiet. In fact, the only really interesting moment of the meeting occurred when her clan was called to put forth a nominee.

"Clan Gonachd has chosen to abstain from putting forth a nominee for this seat," she said smoothly before taking her seat and continuing to stare directly ahead of her, ignoring all of the muttering that had broken out around her.

Hannah gaped. "You've got to be kidding me! She concocts this elaborate plan to interfere with our nomination, and then she doesn't even put forth someone else to run against us? This makes no sense!"

"It makes perfect sense," Karen said, glaring at Marion through narrowed eyes. "She knows she's being watched closely now that her role in your attack has been uncovered. Our clan isn't the only one outraged by what happened to you, and she knows she's lost a lot of credibility now."

"Now?" Milo laughed incredulously. "You mean to imply she actually had any credibility left when she dragged her sorry, treasonous ass back in here?"

"With some people, sadly, yes," Karen said. "But even those who remain loyal to her may want to distance themselves now. Remaining allies with Marion only makes sense if her power plays are successful."

"So, you think she's going to stay out of things now?" I asked, dubious.

"Not a chance," Karen replied. "But I do think she'll work behind the scenes. She'll have asked another clan to put forth her choice, and she will be putting her considerable efforts behind that candidate to get her elected, whoever she may be, but she'll do it quietly. At this point, Marion is as much of a liability as she is a powerful ally, and her little tribe is starting to realize it."

In the end, though over a hundred clans were present, only five other candidates were put forth for the Council seat. The clans currently represented on the Council were not eligible to nominate anyone, though they could vote in the election. As Karen had predicted, none of the nominations came from the newer, unfamiliar clans, all seated toward the back of the Council Room. All five nominations came from the first few rows, where the oldest, most powerful clans held court. It seemed no one wanted to challenge their authority by creating more competition. The last of the five nominations was a woman named Diana McLennon. As she rose gracefully from her seat to accept the nomination on behalf of her clan, I recognized her as one of the women always drifting ıaughtily along in Marion's wake, casting resentful looks at anyone ᴠho dared exist without her express permission.

"That's her," Karen said, cocking her head at Diana. "She'll be the ⵐne to beat."

Milo nudged Hannah in the ribs and winked at her. "Favorites are ⵐo predictable. Give me a dark horse any day."

9

FACING DOWN DEMONS

"**W**HAT ARE YOU STARING AT?" Hannah asked, looking up for the tenth time to see me checking the clock over her head on the mantle.

"Nothing," I said. "Just keeping an eye on the time."

My would-be casual tone did not fool her in the least. The meeting with Lucida was in fifteen minutes, and I felt like I'd swallowed a basket of angry snakes.

Hannah bent her head back over her notebook and began scribbling again.

"How is the speech going?" I asked, eager to talk about anything other than Lucida.

Hannah sighed, setting the pen down and looking pensive. Among the many things she'd learned at the meeting of nominees the previous afternoon was that each of them would be required to stand up in front of the entire assembly of the Airechtas and give a sort of campaign speech. It seemed like she'd spent every hour since either bent over a notebook or lost in deep contemplation. I'd done my best not to interrupt her, but I was too nervous in this moment to be left to my own devices.

"I'm not really sure. I feel like I'm rambling," Hannah said, biting her lower lip. "But I just have so much I want to say. I think I'll have to reorganize it all eventually, but for now, I'm just trying to get all the thoughts down onto the paper."

"That seems like a good place to start," I said. "I'm sure it will be great."

"When it's done, could I use you as a test audience?" she asked hesitantly.

"Of course!" I said, attempting a smile. "I'd love to hear it, when it's ready."

"I wish I had more time to work on it," Hannah said, looking back down at the notebook and shaking her head. "Two days is not a lot of time to come up with a whole platform. I bet some of the other nominees have been working on theirs for months, if not years."

"I've got faith in you," I said. "You know what you want to change, and I think you're the right person to do it. And I think the others will, too, once they're given the chance to hear you speak."

"Always assuming I don't pass out when I get up there and see all those people staring at me," Hannah said with a shiver.

"Well, yeah, I mean, trying to stay conscious is one of the basic tenets of public speaking," I replied, winking at her. "But you've gotten up in front of your grad class for a presentation. This should be a piece of cake."

Hannah threw her pen at me.

When I sat back up after ducking out of the way of the projectile, the last of the Lucida-free minutes had ticked by. I stood up.

"I'm going to head down now. I'll see you when I'm done."

In answer, Hannah closed her notebook and stood up.

"What are you doing?" I asked.

"I'm coming with you."

"You bloody well are not!"

Hannah's face split into a grin. "Bloody well? What, are you British now?"

"I've been spending too much time with Savvy. It was bound to rub off on me eventually," I snapped. "But in all seriousness, you are not coming with me."

Hannah scowled fiercely at me. She looked so much like our mother in that moment that I took an involuntary step back from her.

"That is my decision, not yours," Hannah said.

"Yes, I'm aware of that. I'm also aware that, just a few days ago, the very thought of Lucida reposing at the other end of the same room left you close to nervous collapse. What in the world would possess you to think you'd like to go have a cozy little chat with her?"

Hannah folded her arms across her chest, looking defiant. "I don't want to have a cozy little chat with her. I want to be there to support you when you face her."

"That's very touching, Hannah, but I won't have much chance to demand answers from Lucida if I'm too busy holding you together at the seams," I said.

94

Even as I'd sat there the night before, telling her about the meeting with Lucida, I knew that I was probably going to regret it. Either she'd be so fearful of my going that she'd harass me endlessly to cancel it, or else, she'd pull something like this. But I could hardly make a decision like this and not tell Hannah. It was impossible— almost as impossible as not telling Finn.

"I'm going to support you, not the other way around!" Hannah said hotly.

"Okay, okay, I'm sorry. That wasn't fair," I said. "But seriously, Hannah, I'll just be in mama bear mode the entire time if you're there. It's going to be hard enough to focus on what I need to do if I'm squandering all my energy on trying not to rip her hair out."

Hannah's face twitched as she suppressed a smile, then her shoulders sagged. "Okay, fine. I'll stay here. But I need you to give her this for me."

She held out a sealed envelope with Lucida's name written on the front.

"What is this?" I asked warily.

"It's everything I want to say to Lucida but I've been too nervous to say to her face," Hannah said with a deep breath. "I've argued with myself since they brought her here about whether to go see her or not. This way, I don't have to."

"I'll give it to her. I promise," I said.

"Make sure she actually reads it!" Hannah called after me.

I looked back over my shoulder. "If I have to read it to her myself, I'll make sure she knows what's in here."

As I reached toward the door handle, a crinkling sound near my feet made me look down. I had just trodden upon a small pile of envelopes that someone had shoved under the door.

"What are these?" I asked.

"What are what?" Hannah asked without looking up at me. She had picked up her notebook and returned to her speech.

"All these envelopes on the—" I stopped short as I spotted it: a wax seal, imprinted with a triskele, peeking out from under the top envelope. "Oh my God."

Hannah looked up now, alarmed at the tone of my voice. "Jess? What is it? What's wrong?"

"Nothing's wrong. It's... I think we got more pledges."

Hannah's mouth fell open. "What?"

I reached down and scooped the envelopes up off the floor. There were four of them, each bearing a wax seal with the same triskele design pressed into it.

"See for yourself, but they look just like the one Savvy gave us," I said, handing them to her.

Hannah opened each one in turn, her expression becoming more and more bewildered. "I can't believe this. I don't know any of these clans personally, do you?"

I read the names of them over her shoulder. "No, I don't think so," I said after a moment of racking my brain. "I think I remember hearing their names in the roll call, but it's hard to keep track."

"Look at this one," she said, and read a note scrawled at the bottom of the formal letter. "'Your family has endured enough tragedy and deserves a voice again.' And this one, 'We don't believe the Council has led us wisely during this tumultuous time and are eager to see what your voice can do to temper them.'"

I read a third aloud as she unfolded it, "'We have been impressed with your actions throughout the Airechtas, choosing to help us even as certain Durupinen continued to vilify you. You have our wholehearted support.' Hannah, this is... amazing! You haven't even given your speech yet, and people are already supporting you!"

"I... I don't think I ever expected anyone to actually vote for me," Hannah said, almost in a whisper. She was staring down at the pledges as though they were precious jewels cradled in her hands.

"I don't think I did either," I said frankly, turning back toward the door. "That's only five votes, though. We've got a long way to go, but it's a start. Sorry, Hannah. I've got to go or I'll be late. Don't worry about me. Finn will be with me, so everything will be fine."

Hannah barely nodded her head. She seemed not to really hear me. At least she was no longer insisting on coming with me. Deciding it was better to slip out while she was distracted, instead of taking the chance that she might change her mind again, I pulled open the door. Finn was already standing on the other side of it, waiting for me.

"There you are," he said as I pulled the door shut behind me. "I was starting to think you might be getting cold feet."

"My feet are roasty-toasty, thank you," I said, sounding surlier than I intended in my anxiety. "Let's get this over with."

We strode along in silence. It wasn't in Finn's nature to appear relaxed almost ever, but he looked much calmer than I'd

nticipated, given who we were going to see. When I'd told him
vhat I meant to do, I couldn't believe how calmly he'd taken it.

"Very well. I'll arrange it with the Caomhnóir on duty," he had
.aid.

I'd blinked. "That's... that's it?"

"What's it?"

"You aren't going to freak out? Demand I cancel? Suggest that
.omeone else could meet with her to answer my questions?" I
.uggested.

Finn had shrugged. "What would be the point? You'd just meet
vith her anyway. This way, I've got some modicum of control over
he circumstances. It's a far sight better than finding out about it
ifter you've already done it without consulting me."

And I had to admit that it was. I felt better, knowing that Finn
1ad arranged all of the details of the meeting. I felt more secure,
:nowing he was fully briefed on the security measures that kept
.ucida safely in her bed and incapable of wreaking her own
)ersonal brand of havoc on Fairhaven. He would be there with me,
)repared for anything, and it was only that knowledge that made it
)ossible for me to walk into that hospital wing and sit calmly down
)eside her bed.

Lucida was still in a light doze, and she did not rouse right
iway. Her eyes were sunken in her gaunt face and ringed with
leep purple circles. Her collarbone stuck out unnaturally, and her
fingers, resting on her stomach, were bulging at the knuckles. She
looked so frail, so harmless, that I felt my fear of her melt away.
Stung by her own treachery at last, Lucida was little more than a
shell of our former nemesis. Just as this thought crossed my mind,
1er eyelids fluttered and opened.

"Well, well, well," Lucida said, a suggestion of a smile flitting
across her features. "I was right."

I didn't ask what she was right about. Doing so would feel like
handing over the keys before we'd even gotten in the car, and I
had no intention of letting Lucida drive this conversation off the
nearest cliff.

Lucida seemed to decide that my silence was a request for
clarification because she went on. "Cat told me that you'd never be
down to see me while I was here. She said you'd want nothing to do
with me. But I knew different."

"Really? You knew? How omnipotent of you," I said dryly.

"Oh, yeah," Lucida said, with a spark of her old confidence, even as her voice cracked and broke. "How could you resist? The traitor is on display in the hospital wing. It was only a matter of time."

"Is that so?" I asked, taking a deep breath as I said it. There was no point in losing my temper, not yet. I needed information, and she had it. I needed to play nice, at least for the moment.

"That's right," Lucida said. "Cat thinks you've moved on from the events of the Prophecy, but I know different. I wasn't sure of much when I woke up here, but I was sure that I'd see you before I left."

"And why is that?" I asked blandly, knowing that she was going to tell me whether I asked her to or not.

"Because I'm sure that, until I showed up here, you thought you'd never see me again," Lucida said. "You probably thought you'd missed your chance to say whatever it was you wanted to say to me. Surely, you've got a speech prepared, love."

"No, I don't," I said, drawing deeply from a well of calm I didn't know I had. "I'm not here to monologue by your bedside, however much I may want to give you a piece of my mind. And I'm not here to be a victim, yet again, of your mind games. I've wasted enough of my energy and feelings and thoughts on you. I'm here because I have questions about the Shattering, and once you've answered them, I fully intend to dedicate myself entirely to forgetting you've ever existed."

Lucida raised an eyebrow. "And why should I answer any questions for you?"

I tilted my head to the side. "Oh, you mean other than the fact that you nearly destroyed the entire Durupinen sisterhood and would cheerfully have seen Hannah and me killed in the process? You'd like a reason besides that one? Because, I have to be honest, that one feels pretty legit to me."

"The sisterhood has had it coming for centuries. I was just the last in a long line of Callers who was raked over the coals, poked and prodded and mistrusted because of how I was born. They got what they deserved, and nothing less," Lucida said dismissively.

"And what about Hannah? What about me? What about all the spirits you destroyed in the process? Did we all have it coming to us, too?" I demanded.

Lucida shrugged. "Can't make an omelet without breaking a few eggs. There was no other way."

"There were lots of other ways."

"Don't be naïve, love. The Prophecy was the only way. It was coming. It was bigger than you, and it was bigger than me, and all we could do was choose a side, fight like hell, and hope we chose right. You chose right. I chose wrong. But if I had it to do over again, I wouldn't change my mind. It was worth it, taking my chance at burying this place. I regret only that it's still standing."

"And what about Cat? What about what you did to her with the Shattering? What about everything you put her through for your long shot at revenge? Not even a tiny bit of regret there?"

Lucida's face tightened for a moment. "Cat understands," she said shortly. Her defiance was almost pitiable as she lay there, too weakened even to sit up.

I shook my head in disgust and moved on. I needed to stay focused on why I was here. I was letting her get to me the way only Lucida could, and if I carried on like this, she would derail me completely. *Get in, get the answers you need, and get out, Jess.* I took a slow, steady breath.

"Look, I didn't come here to rehash your considerable resume of screwing over people who have trusted you. You can do that on your own time. I'm here because I need some details about how you communicated with Eleanora Larkin in the *príosún.*"

"What does that matter to you?" Lucida asked, betraying her first hint of genuine interest in what I had to say.

"Since when do you care what matters to anyone? Just answer the question."

She probably would have stayed silent out of pure spite, but I had piqued her curiosity with the unexpectedness of my question. "Callers can connect in ways that the Durupinen don't understand. We sensed each other inside the *príosún* and, over time, we connected by Cross-Calling."

"Cross-Calling?"

"Called each other, like. One soul to another. She reached out, and I reached out, and we connected. It took time and practice, but we learned to communicate."

"But there are wards all over that prison to stop you from being able to communicate with spirits, aren't there?"

"Oh sure, but Eleanora was forgotten, wasn't she? Buried in the rubble years ago. No one was checking up on her, making sure she was contained or restricted. Mind you, there were still dozens of Castings around the ruins of her cell, so she couldn't break free. But not one of those Castings can stop two Callers from connecting if they work at it long enough. At first, we could only communicate for brief moments. Then over time, the connection itself grew clearer and stronger."

"How?"

"Think of it with a prison break metaphor, if you will," Lucida said with a hint of a wry smile. "We were digging a tunnel with bloody psychic spoons, yeah? And we just kept digging and digging, clawing and poking, until we broke through. And once our connection was strong enough, I was able to Call her right out of her cell and straight to me."

"And she was free to move around and communicate once you had Called her out?"

"That's right."

"So, at that point, could she have communicated with someone outside of the *príosún*?"

"Unlikely," Lucida said, shaking her head.

"Why is it unlikely?" I asked.

"Because within moments of her breaking free, she had Shattered. She didn't have the time or the desire to communicate with anyone else. Her singular focus was to Cross."

"And your singular focus was to destroy her," I said, clenching my teeth to stop myself from shouting at her. "How in the world did you convince her she'd be able to Cross without the other half of your Gateway there? She was a Durupinen, too. She knew how Crossings work."

"She was desperate, vulnerable," Lucida said, her voice dispassionate. "I told her a few lies about the nature of our Cross-Calling connection, told her it would open the Gateway right up for her. She didn't understand very much about her own gift, so she believed me."

I bit back a livid diatribe about Lucida's victimization of Eleanora. What was the point? The woman in front of me was utterly incapable of remorse, and there were still several important points I needed to clarify.

"So, in the days leading up to the Shattering, the only person that Eleanora could possibly have communicated with was you?"

"That's right," Lucida said.

A strange thought occurred to me. Eleanora had traversed Lucida and Catriona's connection when she Shattered. She had possessed

Catriona, even though she hadn't ever communicated with her directly. What if she had done something similar with me?

"What about another Caller?" I asked.

Lucida frowned. "What are you on about, then? Another Caller, what?"

"I mean, could Eleanora have reached out and communicated with another Caller? One that was outside the walls of the *príosún*?"

"Like who?" Lucida asked.

"Like Hannah," I answered.

Lucida narrowed her eyes at me. "Why do you think that—"

"Just answer the goddamn question, would you please?" I snapped.

"In a word, no. Cross-Calling only works if both Callers are actively attempting to communicate at the same time. Hannah—and the rest of the castle, for that matter—didn't even know Eleanora existed before the Shattering, did they? So, there's no way that Eleanora and Hannah could have established any kind of communication, accidental or otherwise."

I remained silent as her words settled onto me, weighing me down, like stones in my pockets. It really didn't seem that Eleanora could possibly have reached out to me in any way. So, where in the world had the sketches come from?

"Is that it, then? Is that all you wanted to know?" Lucida asked, breaking into my tangle of thoughts.

"Yes," I said, standing. I couldn't bring myself to thank her, so I just sort of nodded at her. I had already turned to leave when I remembered. "Wait. No, actually, that's not it," I said, and I reached into my pocket for Hannah's letter. "Hannah wrote this and asked me to give it to you. I told her I would wait while you read it."

Lucida cast a wary look at the letter, as though expecting it to explode. "Have you read it?"

"No. I have no idea what it says. That's between you and Hannah," I said.

Lucida hesitated, then reached out for the letter, but a sudden loud banging noise made her jerk her hand back. I turned to see Hannah striding purposefully up the ward. I leapt to my feet, instinctively placing my body right in front of Lucida, as though I could prevent Hannah from having to look directly at her.

"Hannah, what are you—"

"Don't, Jess. Don't give her the letter. I want to say it for myself."

"Hannah, you don't need to do that. You've got everything you want to say right here." I held the letter up and shook it at her. "Why put yourself through a—"

"I know you want to protect me, but I don't need you to," Hannah said. "I have something I need to say to her and I'm going to say it."

"But, Hannah, she's—"

But Hannah had already pushed her way past me. I stumbled backward with the force of it. I watched helplessly as Hannah marched right up to the edge of Lucida's bed, squared her shoulders and said, "I came to apologize to you, Lucida."

If I looked surprised to hear these words come out of Hannah's mouth, it was nothing to the expression on Lucida's face. Whatever snide remark she may have been concocting died on her lips, and her trademark smirk slipped right off her features to be replaced with a wide-eyed look of shock. She looked, for a moment, like a child in the throes of a nightmare.

"I'm sorry," Hannah went on, and her voice shuddered with emotion. "I'm sorry that you grew up under terrible scrutiny and suspicion. I'm sorry that your own sisterhood made you feel like a dangerous outsider. I'm sorry that their cold detachment caused you to seek acceptance elsewhere, and I'm sorry that the Necromancers were there to provide it. I'm sorry that I was the cause of it. I was the one the Durupinen rightfully feared, and many, many lives were destroyed in anticipation of my arrival, including yours."

I finally found my voice. "Hannah, stop. You don't owe her any—"

Hannah spun and glared at me, her expression so fierce that I sat right back down on my chair again. "Maybe not. But the people who do owe it to her will never admit it, so someone has to acknowledge it. Someone has to stand up and say that this wasn't right."

Her face was so fierce that I leaned away from her. She turned back to Lucida. "You deserve to hear these things, even if I'm not the one that owes them to you. But that's okay. It costs me nothing to say them."

Lucida's face spasmed with emotions I couldn't identify, and then settled into an unsettlingly blank expression. "I suppose this is when you expect me to apologize to you in turn. Is that why you're doing this? Some naïve, misguided attempt at the myth of closure?"

Hannah shook her head. "No. I don't want your apology. I don't need it. I don't for a second believe that you've got the capacity to say the words and mean them, and I've watched you lie to me too many times already to subject myself to it again."

Lucida attempted a smirk and failed. Her mouth just sagged crookedly. She blinked convulsively, like she was fending off tears. "Come off it, pet. I know you've been dreaming of the day I beg your forgiveness for my wicked ways."

Hannah laughed—actually laughed. "I used to. As recently as an hour ago, the thought of facing you absolutely terrified me. But something happened to me this past week. I took charge of myself. I finally admitted that my role in the Prophecy wasn't something to forget. I stopped trying to move on from it. I stopped trying to bury it. I took it out and I dusted it off, and I put it on. People didn't like it, at first. They were clinging onto their fears and their prejudices, and I expected that. One of them even decided to take a swing at us with a knife the other day. But we persisted, and we spoke our truth, and now we've got these." And she held up a stack of papers I recognized at once as the pledges we'd found stuffed under our door, except there were seven of them now. Perhaps Lucida realized what they were, too, for her eyes widened at the sight of the rainbow of broken seals. "They just keep showing up—two more of them, just since Jess left to come down here. And whether I win or not, it doesn't matter. People understand the enormity of their mistake and they are trying to atone for it. And so, I'll be wearing that Prophecy like a badge of honor from now on. It's a new kind of battle scar and I'm done covering it up."

Lucida laughed, too—a single, humorless bark of a laugh. "Badge of honor, eh? Don't fool yourself. They'll keep tearing at you, love, just like they did me. They'll keep tearing and pulling and ripping that scar wide open just to watch you bleed."

But miraculously, Hannah was smiling. "If I believed that, I would have reversed the Gateway for good. But I don't. And I never will." She held up the pledges again. "I have a chance to change things, and I'm going to change them. I'm sorry that it was too late to help you, and Eleanora, and all of the Callers who came before you, but it won't be too late for the next Caller who comes through these doors, that I can promise you." She sighed deeply. "So, I guess that's it. That's all I wanted to say to you. I suppose Jess could have given you the letter, but I needed you to see for yourself that I'm not broken, as hard as you tried to break me."

She turned and walked away. Lucida stared blankly after her for a moment, then, her eyes filling with the tears she'd been trying to hold back, she struggled up onto one elbow and called after her, "I don't regret it. Any of it. And I don't need you swooping in here and bestowing your pardon on me like the bloody Queen of England. I don't need your forgiveness!"

Hannah stopped, one hand on the door handle. "Well, that's good, Lucida. Because if you think back over our conversation, you'll find that I never gave you my forgiveness. And I never will."

And without so much as a backward glance, my sister closed the door on Lucida in every possible sense of the word.

IO

SCOUTING

I T SEEMED THAT Hannah Ballard could not and would not be
stopped.

There was a new confidence in her step, a new gleam in her
eye. Her strength had always been there, a molten core beneath her
seemingly delicate surface, but now it was on display for everyone
to see. Free of her fear of Lucida, and armed with the pledges, she
walked through Fairhaven with a sense of belonging there.

Milo had nearly died all over again when he found out she went
to see Lucida without him.

"I mean, I'm your best friend and your Spirit Guide! How do you
just leave me out of something like that?" he'd shouted.

"Because as my best friend and my Spirit Guide, you would have
done everything in your power to talk me out of it," Hannah had
calmly replied. "And I would have listened to you, and then I
wouldn't have been able to close that door. I'm sorry, Milo, but I
had to do that on my own."

"But I missed it! I need transcripts! I need a dramatic
reenactment! Can you just do the whole thing again?" Milo cried.

"Sorry, sweetness," she said, sympathetically. "That was a one-
night-only performance."

I was happy that Hannah had found so much closure, but I was
still left with more questions than answers. I managed to catch
Fiona at the end of the next day's Airechtas session to tell her
everything I'd learned from Lucida about Cross-Calling. I couldn't
be sure, because she was so difficult to read, but I thought I saw
something like fear flash in her eyes.

"Right," she said finally, avoiding my questioning gaze. "Right.
Well, then. Cheers." And she turned abruptly away from me and
stalked toward the staircase.

"Fiona!" I called after her, more than a little annoyed that she hadn't at least acknowledged how difficult it must have been to face Lucida. "Wait! Does that... what does that mean, for the sketches?"

Fiona stopped, but did not turn to look at me. "It means Eleanora was telling the truth. And I have some more work to do." And she walked away without saying another word.

I muttered to myself all the way back to my room. My brain felt fried. The morning's session of voting on obscure and seemingly meaningless measures had sapped me of the will to live. To get a little of it back, I planned to dig out my sketchbook and bring it with me, along with some lunch, down to the conservatory. It was a beautiful little spot I'd discovered during this stay, where several of the Durupinen were in charge of growing a variety of plants and herbs commonly used in Castings. It was warm and full of dappled green light, and it smelled like sage and lavender and springtime. It was like an oasis in the icy white desert of the English winter, and the perfect place to forget where I was and why I was there. It would also get me out of Hannah's hair for a while. She planned to spend the afternoon putting the finishing touches on her speech, and for some reason, me sitting there staring at her wasn't helping her concentrate.

As I turned the final corner, I saw someone standing outside our bedroom door, bent down as though examining something on the floor. As she tucked her curtain of dark hair behind her ear, I recognized her.

"Róisín?"

Róisín straightened hastily and spun on the spot, looking startled. I could see her sister Riley standing waiting for her on the other side of the doorframe, arms folded sulkily across her chest. It occurred to me that I had never actually seen her smile.

Róisín, however, flashed a brilliant one at me as she walked over to meet me.

"Hi," she said, through those glittering teeth.

"Hi," I replied warily. "Uh, what's going on? What are you doing here?" I was having unpleasantly vivid flashbacks of arriving back at our room on our very first day at Fairhaven and finding "Go home, traitors!" splashed across it in red paint. Ugh, this castle was just teeming with fond memories.

"I'm just... running an errand. For our clan," Róisín said, her smile tipping into a sheepish expression.

"What errand?" I asked.

"Well—"

"Róisín, we're just supposed to deliver it and go!" Riley said in a clipped voice. She was determinedly not looking at me and tapping her foot against the floor, where it made a disproportionately loud noise against the ancient stones.

"Well then, you go," Róisín snapped back. "I want to talk to Jess for a minute."

Riley looked like she was chewing on something nasty she wanted to say, but swallowed it back. With a huffy sigh, she turned and stalked up the corridor and out of sight.

"Sorry about her," Róisín said, cocking her head back over her shoulder where her sister had vanished. "She's not very good at shaking off old prejudices."

"I get that sense, actually," I said. "Don't worry about it. We aren't here for the adulation, although, as you can see, it is pouring in from all sides."

Róisín allowed herself a laugh, but then her face quickly sagged into a frown. "I still can't believe what happened to you the other day. I was just shocked. We all were."

"Don't worry about us. Actually, that's one of the better receptions we've gotten in that room."

Róisín smiled. "I daresay that's true. Still, I'm sure you and Hannah are both a bit shaken."

"I'm not a good enough actress to convince you that's not true," I conceded.

"Nor do I expect you to," Róisín said. "It was terrifying merely to watch it happen, let alone experience it. But I'm so pleased that you haven't allowed the attack to derail your clan's candidacy. That would have given your opponents exactly what they wanted."

I opened my mouth to say something, but couldn't figure out how to say what I was thinking without sounding like a huge bitch, so I closed it again. Róisín was too observant to miss it, though.

"What? What were you going to say?"

I hesitated again. "It's... it's going to sound rude."

Róisín rolled her eyes. "Jessica, I once helped kidnap you in the dead of night in a hazing ritual that could have killed you. Whatever you have to say, I think you're owed the right to say it without worrying that I may be offended."

I smirked. "Good point. Well, it's just that you're talking about our opponents like they are these separate, foreign entities, but...

well, your mother is right in Marion's inner circle, isn't she? Don't you think she and—by extension, you—should be counted amongst those opponents?"

Róisín didn't look offended at all. "A year ago, I would have agreed with you. But friendships like my mother's and Marion's are based on alliances and advantages, not affection. Marion's influence is fading, struggle as she may to wield it as she once did. I think her involvement in your attack, however indirect, was a turning point for my mother."

I raised my eyebrows. "Seriously?"

"Oh, yes. In fact, that's why I'm here," Róisín said and, with a deep breath, held out a wax-sealed envelope I recognized at once.

"Holy shit," I gasped, reaching my hand out for it.

"I gather from your colorful reaction that you know what this is," Róisín said, grinning rather broadly now.

"Yeah, I... we've seen a few of these already," I said vaguely. I wasn't sure what the rules were regarding telling people about pledges from other clans. If Hannah were indeed building some kind of momentum, I didn't want to be the one to screw it up.

"I don't know what you intend to do with the other pledges you get, but this one is rather valuable. I'd hang on to it, if I were you," Róisín said, and there was an edge of clan pride in her voice that she couldn't quite suppress.

I just nodded, reluctant to let her see just how ignorant of this upcoming election I really was.

"I feel obligated to warn you that this is a purely political maneuver on my mother's part," Róisín said, looking down at the pledge and frowning. "You shouldn't expect a sudden surge of acceptance or friendliness from the senior clans. They aren't looking to be chums, and both you and Hannah would have a long road of proving yourselves should you manage to pull off a victory. But you do have real supporters as well, and I count myself among them. My mother and I are not the same person. I love and respect her, but she holds prejudices and grudges that prevent her from seeing clearly, sometimes. She looks so diligently for the value in political connections that I think she sometimes fails to see the far deeper value in personal ones."

She was looking at me expectantly, so I replied, "I agree with you. I just didn't expect any members of current Council families to feel that way."

108

Róisín waved a hand airily. "You mustn't lump all of us together, ess. I personally feel there is quite a disconnect between our mothers' generation and our own. We don't cling to politics and history the way they do."

I arched a single, sardonic eyebrow, and Róisín blushed a little.

"You probably think I have quite a bit of nerve, making a statement like that. We were all terrible to you when you arrived here for Apprentice training. But a lot has changed since then. Even Peyton has come a long way in seeing the damage her mother's blind ambition caused. I mean, my goodness, just look at their entire clan. They're in utter disgrace. And the rest of us were lucky to escape with our lives when the Necromancers came. Some Durupinen will always focus on what could have happened, but many of us choose to focus on what did happen: you and your sister saved us that day. You saved the entire Gateway system. And then with the Shattering—my mother might still be a Host if it weren't for you and your sister discovering the identity of the Shattered Spirit. We ought to be thanking you, not punishing you."

I finally shook off enough of my shock to smile at her. "Thank you, Róisín. Seriously, it means a lot to hear you say that. To hear anyone say that, really."

"You're welcome. And please do share my words with your sister. I was hoping to catch her, but she must be out. No one answered the door," Róisín said.

"She's in Karen's rooms, I think, preparing for the speech," I said.

"Oh, of course. She must be quite nervous. Well, please tell her that I, for one, look very much forward to hearing what she has to say."

"I'll tell her. I know she'll be grateful to hear it," I said.

At that moment, a cloud outside shifted and a ray of sunlight shot through the nearby window, casting rainbow sparkles onto the walls around us. I looked down and saw that the light had fallen directly on Róisín's left hand, where an enormous diamond glittered on a delicate gold band.

"Oh, my God!" I exclaimed.

"What?" Róisín asked, looking alarmed.

"I... sorry, I just noticed your ring," I said, pointing unnecessarily as the offending jewelry sent another glimmer of multicolored lights shooting off across the wall.

Róisín looked down in surprise and then back up at me, a relieved half-smile on her face. "Is that all? I thought you'd spotted something terrifying!"

"I did," I said without thinking.

"What?" Róisín asked frowning in confusion.

"Nothing, nothing," I said. "It just surprised me, that's all. It's beautiful. Is it... are you engaged?"

"Oh, yes," Róisín said with a smile as dazzling as her ring. "Last summer. The wedding is this June."

"Wow," I said, trying to look delighted instead of horrified. "Congratulations."

"Thank you," Róisín gushed. "I'll be very glad to have the wedding over and done with. It's been a good deal of work and planning, and my mother has been insufferable. You've seen how she can be in Council meetings. Just imagine trying to have a say when she's in charge of planning an event."

I just nodded, attempting to look politely interested, but Róisín smirked at me.

"You look like you're going to be ill," she said with a little laugh.

I smiled sheepishly. "Sorry. I'm... I guess I'm not in the marriage frame of mind yet. I'm still usually living on ramen and pretending to be an adult."

"Oh, I see," Róisín said. "Of course, you haven't grown up in a traditional Durupinen atmosphere. I expect this seems rather young to be married to you, doesn't it?"

"Isn't it?" I asked hesitantly.

"Not for a Durupinen, no," Róisín said, looking surprised. "I'm one of the last of my circle to be married. Peyton married two summers ago, and Olivia was married last winter."

I gaped at her. "But... you're all the same age as me, aren't you?" I asked blankly.

"Yes," Róisín sighed. "Twenty-two. Practically an old maid in Durupinen terms."

For some reason, I was starting to feel a bit claustrophobic. "Is this one of those ancient traditions you all cling to?" I asked.

Róisín looked puzzled again, but then laughed, shaking her head. "Oh, of course. You weren't here for the whole second year of training, were you? And I expect Karen didn't subject you to the social grooming aspect of Durupinen life under her instruction."

"Social grooming?" I repeated blankly. The walls were closing in on me.

"Oh, yes," Róisín said, and she suddenly took on a very businesslike tone, like she was pitching a presentation to a board room. "Obviously, it was a priority from the earliest days to make sure that the Gateways were passed down from mother to daughter through the clans. It was a mark of distinction to produce your clan's next Gateway, and a particular accomplishment to produce both Passage and Key."

"Produce?" I said, and my voice sounded like it was coming from the end of a long tunnel. "You're talking about... pregnancy?"

"Of course," Róisín said. "Every clan wanted to ensure the continuation of their calling, and so producing the next Gateway was approached with the same fervor as monarchs felt to produce the next heir to the throne. Although, Durupinen value female offspring rather than male offspring. Of course, the optimum window for having healthy children really is so small that it makes perfect sense to start early. And when there are lots of girls in your family, a little healthy competition helps to move things along as well. I don't want Riley getting all the glory." She winked. "Mother's been insufferable about it. I expect she'll be throwing baby clothes at me instead of rice as I walk up the aisle."

I think I laughed at the joke, but I couldn't be sure. I was too busy fighting against a sensation that I was falling down a deep, dark hole.

"It was more difficult to find a suitable partner in previous centuries because of all of the rules about total secrecy and whatnot. Now, at least there are accommodations that can be made if your spouse finds out about your calling. And of course, the Council offers excellent scouting services, so that makes finding a suitable partner that much easier."

"What are scouting services?" I asked, my mouth very dry.

Róisín snorted. "It's a ridiculous title, isn't it? Really, it's just a glorified matchmaking operation. But the older clans often avail themselves of the scouting services just for the sake of convenience. And honestly, who wouldn't want to have the option of having their future prospects pre-screened for suitability? I, for one, found it to be very handy. Goodness knows that dating is difficult enough without wondering what kind of riff-raff you might be getting involved with. I knew Jeremy had all the qualities I was looking for—gorgeous, wealthy family, athletic, excellent job—before I ever even had to meet him."

"Wow, that's... great for you," I said with barely concealed distaste.

"Of course, scouting goes far beyond that. With the benefit of the Trackers, any match made through scouting has been background checked, health-screened, and even been put through full behavioral and psychological analysis," Róisín said. It sounded as though she wanted to impress me, but my face obviously suggested that her efforts were fruitless. "You needn't look so horrified, Jess. Why let any of those factors be nasty surprises later in life if you can avoid them? I mean, honestly, wouldn't you rather know?"

"Yeah, maybe," I said, not even really paying attention to what I was agreeing to. My brain was too busy trying to process what I was hearing.

"I'm surprised you haven't heard of scouting before, what with your role in the Trackers," Róisín said, looking genuinely surprised. "I believe collecting information for scouting is a fairly sizeable portion of the workload for them."

"No one ever mentioned it," I said, starting to feel a dull anger spreading through my body, waking up my shocked sensibilities. "I assure you, it wasn't in my job description or I wouldn't have taken the job."

Róisín threw her head back and laughed. "Oh honestly, Jessica, you needn't look so shocked. Surely, you've been around the Durupinen long enough to realize how we cling to tradition, and to our power. Scouting is just another tool that helps us to do that. Disastrous marriages and tainted gene pools were very real threats in centuries past. Now we have a better chance than anyone of finding lasting success in our marriages."

"I'm not even sure I want to get married," I said.

Róisín raised her eyebrows. "Why ever not?"

"I don't know," I said. "It seems very... restrictive. And permanent."

Róisín laughed. "Good heavens, you make it sound like a prison sentence."

"If the metaphor fits..." I muttered under my breath as she continued to giggle at me. I had never been witness to a proper marriage growing up with just my mom, and I'd never lived in one place long enough to watch anyone else's marriage function for any meaningful amount of time. I'd grown used to the idea of people as independent beings, fending for themselves, looking out for their autonomy in a world determined to snatch it from them, either by dire happenstance or insidious social construct.

Okay, there was definitely a good chance that I was the one screwed up here, not Róisín.

Róisín patted me on the arm, pulling me out of my internal self-analysis. "Well, do try to rein in your horror. No one is going to force you into matrimony. But for those of us who choose it," she smiled and flashed her ring at me again, "the assistance of scouting is much appreciated. It's like having a personal shopper for dating."

"Yeah. I'll keep that in mind. Thanks for the tip," I muttered darkly. "I, uh... I'm going to see how Hannah's doing with that speech. I'll see you later. Congratulations again."

§

I flung the door to Karen's room open so hard that Karen leapt up from her seat and Milo vanished on the spot. Hannah yelped and the speech she was rehearsing fluttered to the floor at her feet.

"Jess? What is it? What's wrong?" Hannah asked breathlessly.

"Scouting," I said, without further illumination. Hannah just stared at me blankly, having clearly never heard of it before. Milo popped back into form, cursing under his breath. Karen, however, looked up at the ceiling as though praying for patience.

"What about it?" Karen asked calmly.

"What about it? What about it?" I cried. "Uh, well, it exists, how about that for a start?"

"What is scouting?" Milo asked tentatively, as though not really sure he wanted to risk the explosion that might come with further explanation.

"It is a Durupinen tradition of matchmaking. It was customary many years ago to match young Durupinen with suitable men that gave us the best chance of maintaining our secrecy and carrying on the Gateways within the established clans. Some of the older clans still participate in it," Karen explained.

Hannah looked from Karen to me as though she had missed something. "Okay. And... that's bad?"

"Well, not when you say it like that!" I said, throwing my hands up in the air. Where the hell was everyone else's righteous feminist anger, for heaven's sake? "It's basically arranged marriages! You expect that kind of thing hundreds of years ago, I guess, but not in the twenty-first century. Not with people we know! Did you know that Róisín is engaged?"

Hannah looked mildly interested. "Oh, no, I didn't. That's nice."

"Nice? Are you... what are you even... she's barely twenty-two!"

Hannah shrugged. "I guess that's kind of younger than average. But she's an adult, Jess. It's not like anyone's forcing her, is it?"

"Well, no, but... it's cultural, Hannah! It's encouraged! Just like the Caomhnóir are running around as kids learning that Durupinen are evil temptresses, Durupinen girls are being told on their mother's knee that their biggest goal in life should be to marry and mate for the good of the clan! Apparently, Peyton and Olivia are both already married. Róisín actually called herself an 'old maid!' At twenty-two!"

Hannah's face fell. "Okay, that's a little weird."

"Damn right, it is! And it gets worse! She was going on and on about how the point was to produce the next Gateway!"

Hannah's eyes grew wide. "Produce... ?"

"Yes!" I said, happy to see a little of my own horror finally reflected on another face. "I mean, what kind of dystopian, anti-feminist fuckery have we landed ourselves in? Here I am, soothing myself with all of this bullshit about how this is a matriarchal society, and women are in charge, and wow, isn't that refreshing. Aren't I lucky to be born into a sisterhood that, if nothing else, acknowledges the power of women? And doesn't that sort of make up for the constant hauntings and the overbearing male protectors? And all the while, there's this cultural practice of marrying us off and knocking us up as soon as we can breed just to ensure the continuation of the Gateways?"

Karen put her hands up. "Jess, you're getting a little over-dramatic here."

"I've never been over-dramatic in my life!" I shrieked.

"Oh, honey," Milo cooed, patting my shoulder so that it tingled with cold. "If you'd only been alive for the last five minutes, that still wouldn't be a true statement."

"I understand what you're so upset about," Karen jumped in before I could turn my anger on Milo. "Scouting is a ridiculous practice. In fact, that's the reason I never mentioned it to you. I knew you would find it as ridiculous and antiquated as I did. I refused flat out to participate when I was in training here, as did your mother. And believe me, in our family, that was tantamount ɔ mutiny. After all, your grandmother met and married your randfather as a result of a scouting match. If it weren't for couting, none of us would even be here."

"Oh, God, I think I'm going to throw up," I said.

"Please don't," Milo suggested, floating several feet further away rom me.

Karen smirked at me. "Your mom and I felt the same way. Your randmother was beside herself with anger when we both refused he scouting services."

I gaped at Karen. "They actually tried to rope you and Mom into his insanity?"

"Oh yes," Karen said with a wry smile. "But Mother nderestimated our father's influence over his girls."

"What do you mean?" Hannah asked.

"Your grandfather was a lot of things. He was quiet and tubbornly set in his ways. He was devoutly religious, and that ften made him intractable on issues of morality. But he was also great lover of books and learning, and unlike many men of his eneration, he did not believe that education was a privilege eserved for boys. He instilled a fierce work ethic and drive in both our mother and me. Your grandmother didn't mind at first, as ve could apply that work ethic anywhere in life, including to our)urupinen calling. But she didn't count on how it would stoke our rofessional ambitions. At eighteen, she found her two daughters unning for ivy league schools, not diamond rings. I need hardly ay she was less than pleased."

"What did she do?" I asked, momentarily forgetting to yell.

"She spent the better part of our training shoving files on eligible achelors under our noses," Karen said, rolling her eyes. "We topped going to restaurants with her, because we would always rrive to find two young men waiting for us. It didn't get any better vhen we arrived at Harvard. Upstanding young man after ipstanding young man was paraded past us—thrown across our)ath masquerading as chance encounters or else introduced as a riend of a friend. Each one was rebuffed on principle, I promise ou, even the good-looking ones."

"Well, that sounds hasty," Milo said, with every appearance of rying to sound reasonable.

Karen smiled. "Perhaps so, but we couldn't in good conscience bandon our teenage rebellion. Anyway, circumstances beyond our control soon put a stop to it." No one replied. Karen was referring to the permanent incapacitation of our grandfather, the death of our grandmother, and the disappearance of our mother, none of which qualified as topics we wanted to revisit, and so didn't require her to elaborate on them. "Anyway, with our Gateway Bound and our family in disgrace, no one cared very much who I dated after that. I met Noah my first year of law school and I didn't bother to consult anyone regarding his suitability. And as for producing another Gateway..." Karen shrugged in a gesture that tried to play casual but instead made her look, for a moment, incredibly vulnerable, as though the subtle rise of her shoulders had shifted things and revealed a glimpse of aching heart between her ribs. "Well, little did I know that your mother had already taken care of that. And my body never would rise to that particular challenge, so... c'est la vie."

I shuffled my feet around beneath me, my insides writhing with guilt. Here I was, ranting about Durupinen being bred like cattle, and I'd completely forgotten about Karen's struggle with infertility. Seriously, was there a point in life when I would stop walking around with my foot perpetually in my mouth, or was this a lifelong affliction?

"Anyway," Karen went on, "like most matters, it basically comes down to money, power, and politics. The ruling clans want to remain ruling clans. They don't want to risk losing their position, power, or influence because they failed to carry on the line, just like the stories you've heard about kings and queens obsessing over producing heirs to their thrones."

"All that Henry VIII craziness, right?" Milo said with a shudder. "Bear me a son or off with your head?"

Karen smiled. "That is one of the more famous examples, yes. The Durupinen are no different. That's why it will be so wonderful to have a voice on the Council who doesn't think the same way." She nudged Hannah gently with her elbow. "Let's add it to your official platform: no more outdated, sexist dating and marriage practices."

Hannah grinned. "That's catchy. I'll put it on some campaign posters."

"I'll design some t-shirts," Milo added. "Only you'll have to belt them and wear them as off-the-shoulder mini dresses because t-shirts are so over."

"Okay, well, I'm glad you all think this is funny," I grumbled. "But Róisín told me the Trackers are the ones who research the eligible bachelors. Did you know that? Did you know we are nothing more than anti-feminist foot soldiers? That's not what I signed up for!"

"Nor is it what you will be doing," Karen said patiently. "The Trackers who handle the scouting are not field agents, like you and Hannah. They are trained in computer research and document analysis. But if you're really so worried that you might unwittingly assist in marrying one of your classmates off to a millionaire, just talk to Catriona and make it clear that you want no part of it."

"Fine, I will," I said, feeling more foolish by the second as Karen's cool-headed logic began to prevail. "And I want to take an ax to that policy as soon as Hannah's on the Council."

"Duly noted," Hannah said, giving me a little salute.

"Okay, then. Sorry if I overreacted, but..." and I brushed my finger on the outside of my bag, where Eleanora's diary sat nestled amongst my art supplies, "you do realize that all this scouting nonsense is the reason Eleanora is dead? If the Council hadn't scouted out that bastard Harry and if he hadn't attacked her—"

"Then her Calling abilities would have revealed themselves anyway, at another juncture, and poor Eleanora would have met the very same fate," Karen said calmly. "Besides, Eleanora's experience with scouting was very different than what it is today. The Council is not forcing arranged marriages on anyone, and clans are completely free to participate in the scouting or not, although," and here Karen pursed her lips, "I have no doubt that some clans consider the practice just shy of compulsory, for social reasons. Still, your friend Róisín is not being dragged, kicking and screaming, to the altar, as Eleanora would have been. Scouting is antiquated and absurd, Jess, but it is not the root of all evil here. If we are really going to use this Council seat to make a difference, let's try to keep focused on the real problems. Scouting is a symptom of the larger issues. If we resolve them, things like scouting will crumble by association."

I took a deep breath. "Fine. But if I get a whiff of a scouting assignment in the Tracker Office, I'm burning this shit to the ground."

"I can help with that, as I recall," Hannah said with a mischievous little grin.

Milo threw back his head and cackled loudly. My mouth dropped open.

"Yes, Hannah! *Yes!* Have we finally arrived at a place where we can joke about this?"

"We've thrown ourselves into the lion's den for this election," Hannah said, her grin fading just a little as she picked her speech back up off the floor. "I'm pretty sure we're going to need all the laughs we can get."

II

THE CALLER SPEAKS

T HE GRAND COUNCIL ROOM was silent, and yet it was buzzing with anticipation. No one moved. No one spoke. Every eye was trained on the diminutive figure standing at the podium in front of us.

My heart was hammering against my ribcage. I was wrestling with a mad desire to pounce on everybody in the room and tear their eyes out for the way they were staring at her. I wanted to shield her with my body, to offer some kind of tangible, physical protection for her. But there was nothing I could do. She had to do this, and she had to do it alone.

I wasn't the only one on edge. Milo's energy was so intense that the inside of my head sounded like a swarm of angry bees. Beside me, his figure was blurred at the edges, vibrating with the intensity of his nerves.

"I know," I said through the connection, replying to his unspoken and yet deafening exclamation. "I know."

"If you two do not calm down, I'm going to have to close the connection," Hannah's angry energy came thrumming through to us. "I'm nervous enough without piling yours on top! Seriously, pull yourselves together!"

"Sorry," Milo and I said through the connection, and together we made a concerted effort to calm ourselves down.

We'd sat through four speeches already, because obviously Hannah was slated for last, purely to ratchet up our own unbearable tension. I told Hannah in a whisper that her first order of business if she won should be to find the person who set the speaking order and slap her.

"I'll get right on that, Jess," she had replied through gritted teeth.

Finvarra was noticeably absent from the proceedings, as was Carrick. This unnerved me more than I would have thought. Of course, we understood Celeste's explanation that Finvarra was too ill to attend, that her condition continued to decline, and that we would all be kept informed if there were any changes, but I still felt unsettled. I'd been subconsciously counting on both Finvarra and Carrick to be there, silent but steady in their support for us. To see the empty space where they ought to have sat left me feeling almost panicked, knowing it surely would not be long before their places would be vacant forever. This realization was shouting to be dealt with, but I couldn't do it—not then, not with Hannah's speech about to happen. I turned my attention to the other speakers instead, desperate for the distraction.

The first speech had been given by an old Scottish woman we could barely understand through her thick brogue. Karen leaned in and told us that she was part of Moira's clan—Moira was the eccentric old keeper of the Léarscáil—and that someone from her clan was nominated every time a seat came up, but had never been elected. She spoke for a rambling ten minutes about honor, duty, and the particular strength and resilience of her clan, which hailed from deep in the Highlands. She didn't offer a single policy idea or make a single campaign promise. She capped it all by singing a strange little Highland song and toddled to her seat amidst scattered, befuddled applause.

"One down," Milo had muttered.

The next speech was a barely concealed diatribe against the establishment. The woman, who was in her mid-40s, had violently purple hair (which, let's face it, I could appreciate) paired with a degree of angst that had even me rolling my eyes. She railed at the Council and shook her fist quite a bit, and then tried to get us all to join in a chant of "New times, new laws!" which only a handful of people half-heartedly joined. Every single Council member looked as though she had been forced to eat something disgusting, and Celeste looked nothing short of relieved when the woman finally sat down. Milo followed her speech with sound effects of falling and exploding.

"Is it me, or is the competition... not much of a competition so far?" I asked in a whisper to Karen. "Am I missing something here?"

"You're right," Karen hissed back, with a hint of a chuckle. "It's by design, though. The older, more influential clans buy up the loyalty of anyone who might put forth a real contender, or else ominate a candidate that will draw away a few votes from other, ess-desirable candidates, but will ultimately lose."

The third speech was monotonal and uninspired, read by a middle-aged woman with her face a half-inch from the paper. It sounded, from what little I managed to pay attention to, like a steady stream of old-clan propaganda, promoting the purity of the old bloodlines and the importance of clinging ferociously to old traditions. I could appreciate that the speech was well-written, and that, in the hands of a fiery orator, it could have been rousing, and even inspiring, but for all the wrong reasons. It sounded vaguely authoritarian, but the woman delivering it was so devoid of authority, that the words just bounced off her audience and rolled away across the floor. The newer, less powerful clans responded to her speech with a stony silence. She did get some enthusiastic applause from the first few rows, though, as well as from the Council benches.

"Some good old-fashioned authoritarian dogma, just for kicks," Karen whispered, responding as though my thoughts had floated into her head. "This is what the party line sounds like. This is the kind of speech my mother used to give back in the day, although she delivered it much better."

"It's kind of..." I hesitated, searching for the right word.

"Disturbing? Elitist? Smacking of fascism?" Karen suggested.

"Uh... yeah. All of those," I said.

"Too few, with too much power, for too long," she muttered, her nose wrinkled as though a noxious smell was wafting under it. "The thought of inclusion or change both terrifies and unites them. It's why it's so hard for new clans to break into the ranks."

Diana McLennon was by far the most accomplished speaker of the group. Tall and stately, with a noble bearing and a powerful authority in her voice, she would have been the most impressive candidate regardless of the content of her speech. She commanded the attention of the room almost instantly, and many Council members and Durupinen in the rows around us watched her with satisfied smiles on their faces. She spent the first few minutes of her speech stroking our collective ego; she went on and on about the importance of our role in the living and spirit worlds, praising our commitment and our bravery and our selflessness.

"If I hadn't already decided to hate her, I'd like her," I whispered to Hannah, in an attempt to wipe the tense look off her face. She forced a little smile but didn't respond.

Having thoroughly charmed her audience, Diana shifted gear to attack her competition, and it seemed that only one other candidate was worth her time.

"We are well acquainted with the dangers outside of our sisterhood, and we have met them head on. But we must be vigilant—very vigilant—of the dangers that nest deep within the fold," she said smoothly. Her eyes rested briefly on Hannah before she went on. "There is much we still do not understand about the fulfillment of the Prophecy. Have the repercussions of it truly passed? Have those involved truly left the past behind? We cannot be sure. Our failure to act when the Prophecy loomed before us is perhaps our greatest mistake. We were not decisive and we did not properly heed warnings that might have protected all that we hold dear. We cannot make these mistakes again. We cannot hope for positive outcomes; we must fight for them. We cannot consider opportunities; we must seize them. And we cannot allow guilt to guide us in a dangerous direction."

She glided to her seat, carried aloft by a tumult of clapping and adulation for the utterly predictable arguments she'd made. Not everyone was impressed, though. Many of the newer clans toward the back of the room sat with their hands folded in their laps, not even bothering to acknowledge Diana's speech with a polite round of applause.

And now, finally, here we were, watching Hannah take her place at the podium, watching her square her narrow shoulders and clear her throat. My God, she looked almost like a child up there. There was nothing childlike about her voice when she spoke, though.

"I first want to thank Finvarra for the honor of being nominated for this prestigious position. I am sorry that she was not well enough to hear this speech today, but I hope that it would have met with her approval," Hannah began, nodding her head toward the empty throne to the right of the podium.

"I want to talk to you all today about identity. Most of you, from a very early age, knew exactly who you were, and what your destiny would be. I didn't have that luxury. Growing up as a kid in the foster care system, my identity was always a mystery. Who was I? Where had I come from? Why could I see and talk to people that no one else could see? Would knowing more about where I came from help me to understand my gift—which I always thought was a curse—or would it always be an enigma? With no explanations to guide me, and no people around who would believe me, I invented wild theories about why I was haunted. I was being punished for something terrible I'd done in a past life. Or else that I hailed from a family of witches, and had been left here among normal people like a changeling in a fairytale. As I grew older, and my mind clung less and less to fantasy, I accepted what the doctors and foster families and therapists insisted was the truth: I was just crazy.

"They didn't use the word crazy, of course. There was a long string of medical terms and an even longer list of medications that I won't bore you with. But once I had accepted it, it became part of my identity: I was sick. I was broken."

Hannah paused to take a deep breath, and when she did, I breathed with her, only realizing in that moment that I had been holding it. Milo was as still as a carved image, his tension so palpable that he actually seemed corporeal in the space beside me. On my other side, Karen was shaking with suppressed sobs.

Hannah went on, her voice gaining in power and surety. "Then everything changed. My sister found me. Our aunt finally explained who we were, and why spirits sought us out. For the first time in my life, I knew, at least in part, who I was, but I was overwhelmed by that knowledge, because, as you all know, a great deal of responsibility comes along with it. Still, I was eager to learn how to help the spirits who had been plaguing me for so many years. At last, their pleas would not have to go unanswered. My sister and I embraced our heritage, but it did not embrace us back.

"It was a struggle from the moment we arrived here. I was told by the very people who should have been my sisters, that I was a threat, someone to be feared, someone who should be locked up. I don't blame you for believing it. I believed it myself. And in my confusion, I was taken advantage of. I was manipulated into fulfilling the Prophecy. Luckily, I had a wonderful sister by my side. She knew exactly who I was, and she helped me to see it, too. And that is how the Prophecy came to be thwarted. Because at the moment it mattered most, I could finally see the truth of who I was meant to be."

Hannah smiled at me. Every fiber of my being wanted to stand and whoop and cheer right there, but I knew the speech wasn't over, so I contented myself with a silent fist pump.

"Identity is a struggle because parts of it are always changing. There are so many factors to identity, and owning each one is important. I am a sister. I am a friend. I am a woman. I am a Durupinen. I am a Caller. But knowing when to cast them aside is also vital. There is a difference between who you were, and who you are, and there are many things that used to be a part of my identity that are no longer part of who I am. I am no longer a victim. I am no longer a threat. I am no longer a dangerous answer to a riddle you've all been trying to solve. The days of the Prophecy have passed, and I will no longer define myself by them." Hannah turned her head and looked right at Marion. "And I will not allow others to define me by them either.

"If you still see me in this way, you are stuck in the past, and the Northern Clans cannot afford to be stuck in the past. We must look forward in order to continue serving the spirit world to the very best of our abilities. I believe that the capacity in which I can best serve the spirit world, and the rest of you, my sisterhood, is as a member of the Council.

"And so, I am inviting you all to look to the future with me, and see all the potential in it. We can take what we've learned and grow together, strengthening our bonds both to each other and to the spirits we serve. We can embrace new clans and new Durupinen and realize that the newness of their gifts is not a liability, but an asset. We can work through the old rules and policies that divide us, and find a renewed strength in our unity. We can provide better support for those who are struggling to come to terms with who they are, and help them on the days when their gift feels far more like a burden. We can unshackle ourselves from old rules that do not serve us in our modern-day mission, and realize that, just because our gifts are thousands of years old, our policies don't need to be. Tradition is beautiful when it serves the present. History is crucial to understanding how we arrived at who we are today. But adaptation is the key to survival, and if we are to find our identity and our place in the world together, we must adapt. We must learn, and grow together so that in this new day, in this new time, our collective identity as the Keepers of the Gateways is strong, protected, and celebrated. I humbly ask for your vote, so that I may be a catalyst in building the future of the Northern Clans. I promise to work tirelessly for our sisterhood. Thank you for allowing me to speak today."

The silence hung for an instant, like that moment when you know the very first raindrop of a storm is about to hit the ground, and the world seems to slow to a standstill waiting for the tumult to break.

And then the tumult did indeed break.

Maybe the lesser clans had never heard words spoken in this room that so definitively included them, but the effect was instantaneous. The back two-thirds of the room rose to their feet, as did a scattered number of the front benches and even a few members of the Council, including Fiona, Celeste, and Siobhán. Beside me, Karen was barely remembering to clap as she stared around, open-mouthed, at the response. Any pretense of decorum forgotten, Savvy leapt up onto her chair, whooping loudly and whistling shrilly with two fingers shoved into her mouth. Behind her, Frankie, who had come along to witness the proceedings for the first time, was waving her hands wildly over her head, eyes sparkling with tears. Even Catriona's permanently bored expression had slipped from her features, leaving her wide-eyed and clapping along with everyone else. Even those who were not clapping showed no hostility on their faces; their masks of shock left no room for animosity.

No one, however, looked nearly as shocked as Hannah, whose chalky white face was now bright crimson as she shrunk away from the initial burst of applause, as though the sounds were being hurled at her like projectiles. Then, as she realized that she was being applauded, she gathered up her pages, twitched her hand in an awkward little wave of acknowledgment, and scurried back to the bench behind her, face still glowing like an ember. All of the other nominees were applauding politely except for Diana, who shifted slightly away from Hannah as she sat, nostrils flared as though she had suddenly scented something unpleasant.

"Thank you to all of our nominees for your words today. You have given the electorate much to think about," Celeste said, her voice quelling the end of the applause. "I encourage all of the clans to discuss with their fellow members the speeches you have heard here today. If there are any more pledges to be made, the deadline to do so is midnight tonight. Pledges may be delivered to the nominees directly, or to me. Nominees, I salute you all for the interest and commitment you have shown in your sisterhood by choosing to run for the Council. I wish you all much success in the vote ahead. A reminder to everyone to look over the formal platforms that have been submitted by each nominee. They have been posted outside of my office door, as well as in the case right outside the entrance to the dining room. Please review them to inform your votes. The Airechtas will reconvene tomorrow morning at 9AM with the hearing of requests for clan redistricting. I hereby dismiss the assembly. Go in peace to serve the spirit world."

Hannah scuttled down off the platform and over to where we stood. I wrapped my arms around her and kissed the top of her head about a dozen times, stuttering out words of congratulations between sobs and incredulous peals of laughter.

"Someone just hand this girl a tiara and a fancy robe or whatever, and be done with it!" Milo crowed over the scraping of chair legs against the stone floors. The elder clans around us were pulling themselves together and composing themselves into haughty, dignified silences as they rose to leave. Those nearest gave us a wide berth, looking anywhere except in our direction. Róisín reached over the back of my chair to squeeze Hannah's shoulder and say, "Well done! Very inspiring speech!" before following Riley up the aisle with the crowd.

"Thank you, Róisín!" Hannah's muffled voice sounded from somewhere near my armpit. "Milo, I don't think tiaras are part of the job description. Jess, could you, uh, let me out of the headlock? It's hard to breathe."

I released her, and turned, still laughing and crying simultaneously, to look at Marion. She was sitting so still, so determinedly without expression, that she might have been carved from an exceptionally bitchy block of marble. The sight of her only made me laugh harder.

Hannah's escape, meanwhile, had been brief. When I turned back to her, she was being strangled by Karen, whose praise for the speech was nearly unintelligible amidst her blubbering. Hannah got the gist of it, however.

"You were right, Karen," she said, smiling a little more now that she wasn't in the glare of the spotlight. "There really are a lot of Durupinen who feel they aren't represented up there on those benches."

"There always have been," Karen said, nodding and wiping her eyes. "I'm very proud of you, Hannah. And if there's one thing they've never seen up there before, it's a clan who had it all, lost it

ll, and now wants to fight for them instead of for itself. It's still a
ong shot, but you might just have a chance to mend our Council
egacy yet."

"Long shot? Seriously? Did you hear that applause? Can't they
ist call it now, like on game shows?" Milo asked. "Is that a thing, a
Durupinen applause-o-meter?"

Hannah rolled her eyes. "I gave one decent speech, Milo. Don't
et ahead of yourself."

"Oh, yes," said a voice from behind me. Marion had finally
acated her seat and was sweeping up the aisle, Diana beside her.
There are still three days to go. An awful lot can happen in three
ays."

"It certainly can," Karen shot back, before Hannah, Milo, or I
ould open our mouths. "Just think, three days ago there were
eople in this assembly who still thought you had credibility."

It seemed Marion had no retort for this. She continued up the
isle, ear inclined toward Diana as she murmured something to her.

§

Anywhere we went through the castle for the rest of the
fternoon, people stopped to wring Hannah's hand and
ongratulate her on her speech. Others stopped her to plead with
er about a particular grievance they had, or to ask her if she would
neet with them to discuss an issue that concerned them.

"It's like they think she's already on the Council," Milo whispered
o me, after the fifth time it happened.

"They must think she has a real chance or they wouldn't bother,"
said, watching Hannah as an elderly Durupinen spoke earnestly
vith her. The woman had reached out with her gnarled old hand,
nd Hannah had taken it and was patting it empathetically as she
istened intently to the woman's words.

"I bet no current Council member has ever given that poor lady
he time of day," I whispered back. "And just look at Hannah. She's
o approachable and gentle with everyone. And people can finally
ee that, now that the pall of the Prophecy isn't overshadowing her
nymore."

When we returned to our room that night, there was another
tack of pledges shoved under the door—at least twenty of them.
Iannah went through them one by one, reading the notes and

writing down the clan names on a list that Karen had insisted she keep. She held two of them up for me to see.

"Fiona," she said, smiling. "And Celeste, too."

We had just decided to settle down to bed when there was a knock on the door. I looked at the clock. It was five minutes before midnight.

Hannah slid off the bed and paused by the door, her hand resting on the handle. "Who is it?" she asked.

"It's Marion."

12

WORTH A THOUSAND WORDS

H ANNAH WHIPPED HER HEAD around to stare at me, her eyes full of animal terror. "What should I do?" she mouthed.

I jumped down off of my own bed and joined her, my heart pounding.

"What do you want?" I asked.

"I simply wish to speak with Hannah," came Marion's bored reply.

"Let me go out there and tell her what she can do with her wishes," Milo hissed through clenched teeth as he floated over to join us.

"I've got a better idea," I told him through the connection, so that Marion could not possibly hear. "Go find Finn and bring him here."

Milo scowled. "I don't want to leave you two here with—"

"Please, Milo," I urged. "Please. I don't think she's stupid enough to make any more obvious attacks on us, but I'd feel a lot better if she had to conduct whatever business she has here with Finn standing over her shoulder."

Milo made another impatient grimace, but then vanished on the spot.

I nodded to Hannah and then opened the door just a crack. I did not pull the chain.

"What do you want?" I repeated.

"Are we really going to converse on either side of a locked door?" Marion asked, pointing to the chain and raising an amused eyebrow.

"Yes," I said. "And you don't even deserve that. So get on with it, before we slam it in your face again."

"First of all, I wish to apologize for my role in bringing Bernadette Ainsley to the Airechtas. While I did hope that her presence would encourage others to vote against you, I did not believe that she was a physical threat."

I blinked. I'd never expected Marion to admit to her involvement with Bernadette, let alone apologize for it. I cleared my throat.

"Is that all?" I asked.

"No," Marion said. "I wished to discuss the possibility of a pledge bargain."

Again, Hannah and I stared at each other. Karen had told us a bit about pledge bargains. Clans could trade pledges for campaign promises. "Should we go get Karen?" Hannah mouthed.

I shook my head. "Let's hear what she has to say first. If Karen shows up she might kill her."

Hannah nodded, and then turned back to the door. "Fine, then. Let's hear it," Hannah said. Her hands were trembling, but her voice was steady.

"As I'm sure you've gathered, I am campaigning for Diana McLennon. She has years of committee experience and comes from one of our oldest, most respected clans. She will be able to do far more, with her connections and expertise, than you could ever hope to accomplish as someone barely acquainted with our ways."

"You really suck at flattering people," I interrupted. "Did you miss that day in charm school? If you want people to cooperate with you, telling them how inadequate they are isn't really the best way to start out."

Marion pursed her lips. Up close, the fine lines and wrinkles were visible beneath her expensive make-up, and her heavily applied foundation could not quite conceal the shadows under her eyes. The perfect façade was finally starting to crack under the stress and strain of watching her power slip away.

"Have you received pledges?" she asked bluntly.

"Yes," Hannah said.

"How many?" Marion asked.

Hannah glanced at me, then said, "That's not a piece of information I want you to have."

Marion clicked her tongue. "I thought you might say that. I have come on behalf of Diana to make an offer to you, in exchange for your pledges."

"Without even knowing how many I have?" Hannah asked.

"But she knows how many Diana *doesn't* have," I said, a satisfied smile spreading across my face. "They're desperate, or she wouldn't be here."

"The vote is nearly upon us. Time is running out. Do you wish to hear my proposal or not?" Marion snapped.

"Fine," Hannah said, crossing her arms. "Let's hear it."

"We wish to offer Clan Sassanaigh a full pardon, by official decree, for all events as they related to the Isherwood Prophecy," Marion said.

Hannah's eyes widened. "What... what do you mean?"

"I mean," Marion said, and she smiled now, knowing she had gotten our attention, "that your entire family—your grandmother, your aunt, your mother, and even the two of you—would be officially absolved of any responsibility. It would be put in writing, signed by the entire Council, and proclaimed to the entirety of the Northern Clans. It would be filed with the International Council as well. No more tarnish upon the memories of your mother and grandmother. All responsibility, all blame, all culpability would be lifted permanently from your shoulders."

Hannah and I looked at each other, speechless. I don't know what I had been expecting Marion to say, but it certainly hadn't been that. The idea that she would permanently relinquish the only weapon she held over our heads was absurd, and yet here she was, relinquishing it.

Playing for time, I asked, "If we did decide to entertain your offer, how do we know that you would keep your word?"

"All pledge bargains are made in writing and signed by the participating clans," Marion said quickly. She could not hide her eagerness, now that we had not slammed the door in her face. She pulled a thick parchment envelope out of her handbag. "We have already drafted a copy. Then the signed bargain would be made public record with the Council. I could not break the promise even if I wanted to."

Hannah bit her lip. I could tell that she was tempted. She'd spent years trying to crawl out from under the crushing burden of her guilt, and here was Marion, offering to cast it away for good.

"Give us a moment, please," Hannah muttered, and shut the door. She turned to me, and her eyes were glistening with tears. "What do you think?"

"I don't think a piece of paper is going to change anything in there," I said, tapping a finger gently on Hannah's chest.

"Do you think it would matter to the rest of the clans? Do you think it would really change the way they see us?" Hannah asked.

I shrugged. "Maybe. They do love their traditions. I bet a lot of them would accept our innocence, if the Council proclaimed it officially, but..." I hesitated.

"But what?" Hannah urged me.

"Look at that stack of pledges," I said. "Look at the response to your speech. The other clans are already starting to see that we aren't the enemy. And, more importantly, look at the way you've been walking around this castle since you spoke to Lucida. Do you really need Marion or the Council to tell you that the time for blaming yourself is passed?"

"The pledges might not be enough. What if I lose? What if I can't repair our clan's legacy by getting back on the Council?"

"What if you can?"

Hannah stalled, biting at her thumbnail. Then she lifted her face and asked a question I never thought I'd hear her ask ever in our lives.

"What would Mom do?"

It was difficult to speak, not because I didn't know the answer, but because I couldn't get the words past the spasm of emotion in my throat. Finally, I choked out, "Honestly? She'd tell Marion to fuck off."

The corner of Hannah's mouth trembled with the suggestion of a smile. She reached out and gave me a fierce hug and planted a kiss on my cheek. Then she walked back to the door, pulled the chain, and opened it wide just in time to see Finn striding down the hallway, looking tense, and Milo floating in his wake.

"Is everything all right here?" Finn asked.

"Everything is great," Hannah told him, and then turned to Marion.

"Fuck off," she announced, and promptly slammed the door in Marion's face.

§

The pain in my hand woke me from my sleep. It was radiating up my arm in dull, aching waves. I opened and closed my hand to dispel the sensation, and realized that I was holding the stump of a charcoal pencil.

"Oh, great," I moaned. "Just what I need. Who is it this time?"

I fumbled around in the dark until I found the switch that turned on my reading light, and then squinted like a nocturnal creature in the brightness for a few moments until my eyes adjusted. I glanced at the clock. It was just after 4AM. I'd been so hyped up by our encounter with Marion that it had taken me until nearly 2AM to fall asleep. I dropped the charcoal pencil into the jar I kept on the bedside table—the jar from which I had plucked it in my sleep to produce whatever sketch was now waiting for me on the wall.

I rubbed at my eyes, still blurry with sleep, and focused my exhausted gaze. What was I looking at?

Two figures. Women. One standing, looking down over the other.

No, one figure. Because the woman standing and the woman lying on the ground were the same woman. She was looking down upon herself.

Wait, was that right? I examined them more closely. Yes, the same hawkish profile. The same wild, tousled hair.

Oh, my God.

"Oh, my God!" I whispered. I knew her. I knew that face, and that hair, and that defiant, singularly stubborn expression.

"Annabelle."

My brain was trying desperately to catch up to my eyes, but then, as it did, a numb horror started to set in, and suddenly I wanted to unsee it, to unknow it, to tear it from the wall and deny its very existence.

In the sketch, Annabelle lay on the ground, her body sprawled in grass, her mouth slightly open and her wild hair fanned out around her like the rays of a sun. But Annabelle also stood above herself, staring down into her own face with a shocked and disbelieving expression.

"No," I murmured, my voice rising to a frantic pitch. "No, no, no, no, no!"

I stumbled out of my bed and across the room to the desk, where I knew my phone lay plugged into its charger. The bangs and scrapings of my frantic movements woke Hannah from her sleep. She sat bolt upright, staring wildly around for the source of the sudden commotion until she spotted me fumbling to disconnect the phone from its charger.

"Jess? What's going on? Are you okay?" she murmured, her words still slurred and muddied with sleep.

133

"No, nothing is okay," I cried, and I cursed loudly as my fingers clumsily refused to press the right numbers to unlock the screen. "Come ON!"

"Jess, you're scaring me!" Hannah said, reaching over to turn on her own light. "Tell me what's happening!"

"It's Annabelle!" I said, my voice rising hysterically. "I don't... can't remember her number."

"It's in your contacts, just type in her name," Hannah said in a slow, calm voice, almost a monotone—her attempt to relax some sense into me. "What is it, Jess? What about Annabelle?"

"The picture! Just look at the picture," I cried, gesticulating wildly at the image now hovering like a specter next to my bed. It took three times to type Annabelle's name correctly with my shaking fingers, and when I stared down at it—completed, meaningful—I wanted to fling the phone away from me. If I called her... if she didn't answer . . .

I heard Hannah's quiet gasp over my shoulder as she examined the sketch, but I didn't acknowledge her. I hit send and waited for the call to connect, my teeth chattering so that I could barely hear the crackling ringing sound.

Please, please, please let her answer. Please. The thought felt less a prayer and more a wild, aimless thing flapping off into the empty air. A prayer had a destination, but these words felt desperately untethered from any comfort that might anchor them—or me—against my fear.

"Hello?"

Had I ever heard anything so wonderful as that voice, shot through with a thread of annoyance?

"Annabelle?" I breathed a sigh that was half a sob. "Is that you? Are you okay?"

"Jessica? Yes, of course it's me. It's my phone, isn't it? Who else would be answering?"

"Where are you?"

"I'm in bed, like most normal people at eleven o'clock on a Tuesday night," she sighed.

"And you weren't trying to... get in touch with me, at all?" I asked, looking back over at the drawing.

"Get in touch with you? No, of course not! I was reading a book and starting to nod off to sleep. You are the one who called me, remember?"

"Right, yeah," I replied, trying to rein in my breathing.

"I know there's a big time difference, but it's late for a phone call, don't you think?" she snapped.

"It's... yeah, sorry about that," I said.

"Hang on. That means it must be..." I could almost hear her calculating the time difference, hear as her annoyance morphed into concern, ". . . four in the morning over there! What's wrong? Why are you calling me in the middle of the night to ask if I'm okay?"

I cast wildly around for an excuse, realizing that I hadn't for a moment considered what I would say to Annabelle if she answered the phone, because I was so convinced that she wouldn't. "I... I'm so sorry. I had this awful dream," I stammered.

"A dream? About what?" Annabelle asked urgently, all trace of annoyance gone. As a sensitive and a psychic medium, Annabelle didn't underestimate the potential significance of dreams.

I hesitated, then blurted out. "Pierce. It was a nightmare about Pierce. And I woke up so upset. Sorry, I was still half asleep when I dialed the phone."

"Oh, Jess." Annabelle sighed, and I was relieved to hear that the fear had gone from her tone. "I understand. I still dream about David, too, every now and then. Do you need to talk?"

"I... no, it's okay. I'll be fine. Sorry I bothered you," I muttered. "I... how are you? Is everything okay with you?"

"Same old, same old," Annabelle said. "Shop is doing well. It's not such a madhouse anymore, but holiday sales are good. The boys miss you," she added, and I knew she was talking about Pierce's old ghost-hunting team; Iggy, Oscar, and Dan. "They keep asking when we'll be off on our next adventure."

I tried to smile, hoping she might hear it in my voice. "Tell them I miss them, too, and that I'm working on our next gig. I'll send information along when I've got something."

"I'll let them know," Annabelle said. "And you're sure you're all right?"

"Yes. Honestly, it's nothing. I was disoriented from the dream. Sorry I bothered you."

"Not a bother. Glad to hear from you. Be sure to stop in and let me know when you're home from Fairhaven."

"I will," I agreed. "I... take care of yourself, Annabelle."

"I always do," she said, and she hung up.

I sat staring at the phone, where Annabelle's name still glowed up at me from the screen, the length of the call flashing beneath it. I stared and stared at it until the screen went black.

"Jess?"

I jumped, having all but forgotten that Hannah was even in the room with me. Milo was sitting cross-legged beside her; apparently, she had summoned him during my phone call.

"It's okay. She's okay," I said, dropping the phone back onto the desk and my head into my hands. I could feel a bad headache coming.

"Well, if she's all right, then what's happening?" Milo asked.

I shook my head, eyes shut tight, warding off the moment when I would have to look at the sketch again. "I don't know. I woke up from a psychic drawing episode to find that hanging next to me. I panicked. I thought..."

I lifted my head to look at them. Both Hannah and Milo were staring at the sketch in fascinated horror.

"You thought Annabelle was dead," Milo said, his voice barely more than a whisper.

"Yeah."

Hannah was so close to the image now that her nose was barely an inch from the paper. "It's definitely her. There's no mistaking it, Jess, your likenesses are too good."

"I know."

"So then, why..."

"I don't know!" I shouted, and instantly regretted it. The pounding in my head increased tenfold at the sound of my own frightened voice. "This isn't how the psychic drawings are supposed to work! A spirit wants to communicate, it reaches out, and I produce an image. Usually it helps me identify who the spirit is, or gives me an idea of what's kept him from Crossing. But this..." I gestured helplessly at the picture again.

"That's not what this is," Milo said quietly. "This is... different."

"Yeah. And it scares the shit out of me," I said. I stood up and paced around the room, my mind racing, my heart refusing to slow its pounding. "Something is happening with my gift. It's changing. This isn't a spirit drawing. This is something else. I mean, just look at it. Look at that drawing and tell me what your first thought is when you look at it."

Milo floated so close to the sketch that his nose nearly brushed

136

against it. "I would think that Annabelle was dead," he blurted out, as though saying the words quickly would make them less awful to think about. "And I would assume that her spirit was reaching out to me for help."

I nodded frantically. "Exactly. There's no other way to interpret that sketch, is there? That is a body and a spirit, separated from each other."

"And... did you notice... here, by her hand," Milo whispered.

Hannah and I both joined him on the bed and examined the spot where he was pointing.

"Is that... a knife?" Hannah murmured.

I hadn't noticed it before, but it was unmistakably a knife lying on the ground next to Annabelle's limp hand.

We all sat for a few loaded silent moments, letting the horror of it seep into us, just as the life seemed to have seeped out of the Annabelle on the ground.

"So," I said, looking away from the image and finding my voice again, "I call Annabelle in a panic, and she's fine. She's not dead. She's not hurt. She sounds as though absolutely nothing out of the ordinary has happened to her. 'Same old, same old' she tells me. What am I supposed to think?"

"Could she be lying to you? Do you think something has happened, and she doesn't want to tell you about it?" Milo suggested, though without much conviction.

"No, I really don't think so. Annabelle puts a lot of stock in dreams and visions and the importance of symbols and signs. Everything has meaning to her, everything is worthy of interpretation. If I called her out of the blue, asking if something was wrong with her, and something terrible really had just happened, I don't think she would ignore that coincidence."

"Could another spirit be contacting you about Annabelle? Could another spirit be trying to warn you about something?" Hannah asked.

"About something that hasn't happened yet?" I shook my head. "That's never happened to me before. I've never had a visit from a spirit without getting a sense of who the spirit was. If this was someone other than Annabelle, he swooped in, planted this image, and swooped out again without leaving a single trace of his presence. That just seems so unlikely."

"You need to bring this to Fiona, too. She needs to see this," Hannah said finally.

"Yeah, I'll bring it to her first thing tomorrow, but... why is this happening? I mean, I've been a Muse for years, and it's always worked the same way. Why is it changing now?"

Hannah and Milo stared back at me, their faces empty of answers, only reflecting my own questions back to me.

§

I sprinted up to Fiona's tower first thing in the morning, trying to catch her before the Airechtas session that day, but she did not answer the door. *Maybe it's for the best*, I told myself. No need for both of us to be impossibly distracted when we were supposed to be paying attention and voting on critical policy matters. Between my preoccupation with Annabelle and my lack of sleep, I knew I'd be lucky to absorb a single word that was uttered all day.

I did manage to catch Finn before breakfast and tell him, briefly, about the drawing. He agreed that it was best to show it to Fiona, but did not share my sense of panic.

"Spirit drawings are cryptic, Jess," he said to me in his frustratingly logical tone. "You can't jump to conclusions about what they mean or how they might be interpreted. Like you said, Annabelle is fine. I'm sure there is a perfectly reasonable explanation for it."

I had neither the time, nor the inclination to argue with him, but my gut was telling me that reasonable explanations were quickly turning into a thing of the past.

Finally, after two three-hour sessions and a lunch break, during which I couldn't even look at food, Celeste's gavel hit the podium, jolting me out of my stupor and marking the end of the day's meetings. I jumped to my feet and fought against the tide of Durupinen heading for the back doors.

"Fiona!" I called. "Fiona, wait up!"

Fiona, who had been gathering up her things and preparing to leave the Council benches, paused and watched me elbow my way toward her. Before I could put a foot onto the platform, though, I was intercepted.

"Jess, I'm glad I caught you," Celeste said, placing a hand on my shoulder. "I've been asked to give you a message."

"Message?" I said blankly. I waved to Fiona to wait for me. "What ind of message?"

"A message from your... from Carrick," Celeste said awkwardly.

I looked at her properly, focused for the first time since I'd ntered the room. "Oh. I... what is it?"

"He says that he would like to speak with you, but that he cannot ave Finvarra anymore. She is... she doesn't have a lot of time left."

I blinked. "I... when you say, 'not a lot of time'..."

Celeste swallowed hard. "Mrs. Mistlemoore is not sure. A few ays. Perhaps less. It all depends on whether Finvarra decides to eep fighting or chooses to let go."

"Oh," I said again. I tried to collect my thoughts, to sift through hem to find something to say. "Is... is he up in her tower?"

Celeste nodded. "He says he understands if you do not want to ome, but... but that he would like you to."

My mouth was dry. I had no idea how to respond to the request, o I cast around for something else to say. "How... how would we all now if she... will there be a meeting? Or an announcement?"

"The castle bells will toll thirteen," Celeste said. "And black anners of mourning will be hung from her tower windows."

"I, uh... okay. Thank you, Celeste. I'll... I'll let Hannah know bout what Carrick requested," I said, my voice barely more than a vhisper.

Celeste squeezed my shoulder. Her face was full of a pity I ouldn't stand to see there. Luckily, she didn't force me to give ny further answer, but turned and headed back to the podium to ollect her things.

"Oy! Jess!"

I looked up. Fiona was glaring expectantly at me, and I shook off he numbness of dread as I climbed the steps to reach her.

"Well?" she said curtly. "What is it?"

Without preamble, I thrust the sketch of Annabelle into her ands and told her everything about the previous night's events. iona stared down at the sketch, frozen. She didn't move or speak or so long that I started to panic. Finally, the anticipation verwhelmed me.

"Fiona, will you please say something before I lose my mind over ere?"

Her lips barely moved. "Have you shown this to anyone else?"

"No. Well, just Hannah and Milo, but they don't really c—"

Her hand shot out and grasped onto my forearm. She pulled me in close to her, so that her lips were brushing against my ear as she whispered, "Meet me up on the fourth floor landing near the East Tower tonight at midnight. Tell no one you are coming."

"What? Why?" I murmured back, but she was already pulling away, thrusting me from her with a rough gesture.

"Don't ask me anything else right now. Don't speak a word about this drawing to anyone else. If you meet anyone else on your way to meet me, lie and say you are going somewhere else. No one can know. Do you understand?"

"Yes," I said, although I didn't understand at all. Her look was so fierce, though, that I didn't dare return any other answer.

"Midnight," Fiona repeated, and hurried away, folding up my drawing and tucking it into the pocket of her overalls as she went.

13

THE SEER

MY TREK TO THE FOURTH FLOOR landing of the North corridor was uneventful, but for the increasingly wild speculation multiplying inside my own head as to why Fiona wanted me to meet her there. I'd told Hannah that I was meeting Fiona, just so she wouldn't panic if she woke up and found me missing, though I hadn't mentioned the cryptic manner in which Fiona had demanded the meeting. No need to spread my own near-crippling panic to anyone else, at least until I knew there was definitely something to panic about.

The moon was nearly full—it would be time for another lunar Crossing tomorrow night—and the light of it slanted in through the windows, casting elongated shadows upon the stones and leaching the color and warmth from every surface it touched. My breath preceded me in tiny damp puffs, like I was a jittery steam locomotive mounting the castle stairs.

I think I can't, I think I can't.

I turned the final corner to the landing and barely managed to muffle a shriek. Fiona stood so close to the top step that I slammed right into her, nearly knocking the oil lamp from her hand and setting us both on fire.

"Damn it, Fiona!" I hissed at her. "You scared the shit out of me."

"I've not even begun to scare the shit out of you," Fiona said wryly.

"The details blatantly ripped off from Victorian Gothic novels are helping," I shot back. "A darkened castle stairway? An oil lamp? For Christ's sake, haven't you ever heard of a flashlight?"

"Batteries were dead," she said dismissively. "Follow me and stop stamping your feet like that. I heard you coming a mile away and so will anyone else if you don't keep it down."

"Where are we—" I began, but Fiona was halfway up the next set of stairs, moving with surprising speed for someone who usually stumped around in leather slippers two sizes too large. I hastened to keep up with her, and though I repeated my question twice more, she had no intention of answering it. I gave up, and used my breath for climbing instead.

Soon, we were hurrying down a corridor I recognized. It was the same hallway that Mackie had lead me down the first time she showed me to Fiona's studio. It was called the Gallery of High Priestesses, and it was lined with tapestries depicting the High Priestesses through the ages. I had seen the tapestries recently; they had been moved down to the Grand Council Room for the opening ceremonies of the Airechtas. Apparently, someone had decided it was time to relegate them back to their gloomy home in this forgotten corridor. I searched out the face I knew, the face that linked my family, and this place, and the terrible Prophecy that nearly destroyed us all. Agnes Isherwood gazed down upon me from the shadowy folds of her tapestry. The wavering light from Fiona's oil lamp gave an eerie life to her features, as though the very fibers from which she was woven were now imbued with both sentience and magic.

"In here!"

I tore my eyes from the tapestry to find Fiona beckoning angrily from the end of the hall. I jogged to catch up with her. She was standing directly in front of another tapestry, one I had never seen before, that depicted Fairhaven itself at the center of an idyllic-looking landscape.

"What are we—" I began, but stopped as Fiona located a cord tucked behind the tapestry and gave it a sharp yank. The tapestry slid aside like a curtain to reveal a door hidden behind it. Fiona slipped a massive iron skeleton key into the lock and twisted it with both hands until we both heard the mechanism clunk into position. Then she pushed it open with one hand and gestured me into the darkened room with the other.

The space was long, narrow, and very cold, as though the heat from the rest of the castle could not penetrate the walls—which were not really walls at all, but row upon row of shelves. Fiona walked the length of it, turning on lights as she went, illuminating the room bit by bit. Long wooden tables with benches were placed end to end along the middle of the room, dotted with magnifying glasses, pencils, stacks of paper, paint brushes, and bottles of cleaning solution.

"Where are we?" I asked, momentarily forgetting my fear and staring around in wonder.

"This is the Archive," Fiona said with a last flick of a switch that bathed the far end of the room in soft, golden light. "I am the only person in the castle who is allowed in here, with the exception of the head Scribe. If you ever tell anyone I let you enter it, I will deny it, you understand me?"

"Yes," I said. "But... what is it? It looks like a library research room."

"It is where we store all records—written, verbal, and artistic—of all Durupinen prophecies."

My heart leapt into my throat, constricting my voice and my ability to respond.

"I've something I want to show you," Fiona said, pulling out the nearest bench with her foot and pointing to it. "Sit."

I promptly sat. My legs were feeling shaky anyway.

Fiona walked along to a display rather like stores use to display posters for sale, except that each panel contained a piece of artwork carefully preserved between two pieces of Plexiglas. Carefully, she began to flip through the panels until she reached the one she was looking for. Unhooking the entire panel from its wooden arm, she carried it over to the table and laid it down in front of me.

I gasped and pushed the bench back from the table.

"Sorry to spring this on you, but you've got to see it. Scoot back over here, now," Fiona said firmly, but not unkindly.

I tried to swallow, but my mouth and throat had gone instantly, horribly dry. I pulled the bench back under the table and leaned cautiously over the panel again, unable to quell the feeling that the image there would reach out and attack me.

Because, in a way, it already had.

Within the panel was a painting that had been done on an ancient and frayed canvas. Time had faded and worn the artwork, but it was undeniably the very same image I had once, in a spirit-induced fervor, scrawled all over the walls and ceiling of the entrance hall in the rather unique medium of ashes mixed with my own blood.

"This is the Prophecy," I whispered.

"Yes."

"It's the same image I drew. Exactly the same image."

"Nearly."

I tore my eyes from it to frown up at Fiona. "Nearly?"

"Here," she said, and she tapped the finger against the center of the painting. The Geatgrima stood open, light and power and spirit hordes flooding out of it, but . . .

"No Hannah," I said softly.

"No Hannah," Fiona agreed.

"I don't understand," I said. "I thought the Prophecy was made in words, not images."

"The Prophecy was made in many forms over time," Fiona said. She swung her leg over the bench and straddled it as she sat down to face me. "The words you heard were the most complete record of it. But this image—and several other incomplete images like it—came first. They were collected, interpreted, rejected, re-interpreted, and eventually, confirmed in the form of the written prophecy, which was made, as you know, by your ancestor, Agnes Isherwood."

I scrambled to compose myself so that this new information wouldn't just bounce off me. "Why are you showing me this?"

"Not all drawings produced by Muses are spirit-induced drawings. Some are of a different nature entirely," Fiona said.

"What does that mean? What different nature?"

Fiona rubbed her fists into her eyes like a sleepy child. When she looked at me again, her eyes looked bloodshot and her expression weary. "Many Durupinen have extra gifts. Muses, Empaths, Callers, and so forth. There is another gift—a very rare one—that can appear in Durupinen. It is the gift that created this painting, as well as every recorded mention of the Prophecy up to and including when it was made in full by Agnes Isherwood. Every one was created by a Seer."

"A Seer?" I asked breathlessly.

"Yes. A Durupinen who can make predictions in some form. We have not had a Seer at Fairhaven since my grandmother."

"Your grandmother was a Seer?" I gasped. "Did she..." I gestured rather helplessly to the images scattered before me.

"No, no. She never foresaw anything to do with this Prophecy. But that didn't stop the other Durupinen from fearing her."

"Why?" I asked.

"You know that rather clichéd phrase about shooting the

144

messenger? They didn't actually shoot her, mind!" Fiona added hastily, for something in my face must have betrayed my alarm. But when you dislike the message, it is easy to project that dislike into the bringer of that message. My grandmother was brilliant and troubled, not unlike myself," Fiona said, glancing sideways to see if I would take the bait and laugh at the joke. I didn't. "Her marriage to my grandfather fell apart under the combined strain of the Visitations and the barrage of Seer episodes." And she pointed to a large, half-formed bust of a woman whose mouth was open in a fearful scream.

"Your grandmother made that?" I gasped.

"Indeed. Carving was her Seer medium, which is one of the reasons I work in sculpture so often. Seer sculpture is powerful, but incredibly draining and often difficult to interpret. It was nearly impossible for my grandmother to create a complete image before the vision dissipated. The Council demanded answers that she didn't have. They were paranoid that every single carving was a dire warning in need of faultless understanding. My grandmother, she began to crack under the pressure. She became obsessed with interpreting her creations, but most of them were barely half-finished. She began trying to induce Seer episodes, but mostly she was left frustrated and confused. It drove her mad in the end. We had her committed, but she kept trying to carve any surface she could get her hands on—walls, tables, floors. It was like the second coming of the Marquis de Sade."

"That's terrible," I whispered.

"Yeah, it bloody well was," Fiona said grimly. "Luckily she'd already passed her Gateway on to my mother and aunt. We had to find her for her own safety, just to stop the Visitations. And then, of course, you met my mother. Apple and the tree, and all that. My mother was never a great Seer in the sense that my grandmother was. She was a Muse, though, and it seemed she had a touch of the Seer gift, because she made that sculpture of your mother. And well... you know how that turned out for her."

"Why are you telling me all of this?"

"The night you turned the entrance hall into a life-size portrait of the apocalypse, I knew something was off. The Silent Child showed you the Prophecy as it had been portrayed before, in this image, but you added to it. Never until that night was the image of your sister a part of this record, or the Council would have recognized her right away as the Caller from the Prophecy. Of course, this was just an insignificant detail amid the chaos, and no one—including myself—stopped to wonder why you had added your sister to the image. But the truth is that the Prophecy was speaking through you. You were supplying the final piece of the puzzle. You were Seeing."

The room spun. I shook my head to clear the dizziness, but it gripped me like an attacker, shaking me to my core.

"I ought to have realized it then," Fiona murmured, knocking her fists against her temples as though she could knock this piece of knowledge into her past self. "I ought to have noticed that you had produced something new, a detail no Seer had yet provided. And then of course, when it was all over, no one wanted to dwell on the Prophecy anymore, not in the way we once obsessed about it. We wanted to lock all evidence of it away—to finally be free of its clutches."

My brain whirred into a defensive mode. "No, it can't have been Seeing," I reasoned, and in my own ears my voice sounded so calm and rational, even as my fear whimpered and moaned inside me. "It was spirit-induced. The Silent Child was using me like a vessel. If anyone was Seeing, it had to be her."

"I might have said the same thing until three days ago, when you brought me these," Fiona said, and she spread my own drawings of Eleanora out before me. "You heard what Lucida said. There was no way that Eleanora could communicate outside of those *priosún* walls. It was impossible. And even if she had, how would she have found you? How could she have known that you, of all people, would need to know her identity? She had not yet Shattered. What reason was there to warn you?"

A shudder ran from the top of my head down through my body and out through my toes, leaving me clammy and cold, doused in my own fear.

"These images were prophetic. You produced them as foreknowledge of the Shattering. There is no other logical—or even illogical—explanation for it," Fiona went on mercilessly. "And now we have this." She unfolded my sketch of the two Annabelles—body and spirit—in the forest clearing. "Your friend is very much alive right now, and so you must ask yourself: what does this image show and why?"

I could barely bring myself to look at it again—the way her eyes

146

stared out blankly from her prone body, cold and unseeing as marbles. The Annabelle that stood above was so pale, her edges so blurred. If I stared hard enough, I could make out the shape of the trees behind her, like she was a foggy window masking the woods beyond.

"It… it looks like she might be… she's dead," I whispered.

"And as you spoke to her just last night, you know that's not happened yet," Fiona said. "Which can only mean this drawing is a premonition of sorts, a warning of what is to come."

I opened and closed my mouth like a fish, feeling as though I could not breathe the air around me.

"One time is a fluke. Two times is cause for interest. Three times is a bloody charm," Fiona said. She clapped a hand on my back.

"The Durupinen have found another Seer at last, and it's you, Jess."

§

"No."

"I'm sorry?"

"No."

Fiona frowned. "What are you on about? What do you mean, no?"

"I mean, no," I said blankly. "No, I'm not a Seer."

"You're a Seer if I say you're a Seer," Fiona said, scowling confrontationally. "It's not up for debate. The evidence all points that way."

"No. I can't. It's too much."

"What are you—"

"There is such a thing as too much!" I cried, and it was all I could do not to sweep my arm across the table top and send all the artwork cascading to the floor. "No one in this castle seems familiar with the concept, but normal people—people who grew up outside of this insanity—reach limits of what they can handle. There needs to be a point where the weird stuff stops rolling in or they can't function. This is mine. I've hit it. No more."

"Jess, you haven't a choice whether—"

"Yes, I have! I have a choice! And I'm making it! I'm already a Durupinen—as if that weren't enough to drive the average person right off the deep end. Then I'm also a Muse, with spirits using my body while I sleep, invading my space like I'm just a new pair of jeans they just want to try on for a bit to see how I feel. And I've absorbed it. I've found a way to make myself okay with it. But, oh wait, Jess, that wasn't quite enough? We haven't broken you yet? Fine, you're a Walker, too. You can slip out of your body like that same pair of jeans and just leave it on the floor of your room, but be careful, or you could cause yourself to go insane. Like it would matter. Like insanity could actually be worse than my own personal version of reality. At this point, insanity would probably be a relief!"

Fiona sat patiently, watching me lose my shit with the calm demeanor of a yogi in meditation, which only made my anger peak. I wanted to slap that calm look right off her face, so that she would feel some of the pain and anger and confusion that was rising in me like a tide I couldn't stop because I half-wanted to drown in it.

"And then, of course, I was also the subject of that Prophecy. So, just as a recap, Jess, not only are you a ghost-magnet, a ghost-artist, and a corporeal vanishing act, but you also have to dive headlong into a portal to the afterlife in order to save the spirit world from total annihilation.

"And I did it! I fucking did it! So, you would think, after all of that, that the universe would say, 'Okay, Jess, I'm done with you. I'm not going to pile anything else on top of the teetering balancing act that is your life, because I can see that you are precariously close to toppling over and letting it all come crashing down on top of you.' But no. NO. Now I have to be a Seer, too? Well, I refuse. Take it back. Give it to someone else. I reject it. I refuse it. I am done."

All through this freak-out, Fiona waited patiently for me to rant and rave myself into silence. Finally, as I sat heaving with a combination of sobs and panicked gasps, she squinted at me, scratching her cheek.

"You about finished, then?"

"Yes, on multiple levels you could say that I am finished," I spat back.

"Right, then. Well, I hope that little tantrum helped you feel better, because it sure as shit did nothing to change the reality of your situation."

"Of course, it did. Didn't you hear what I said? I'm rejecting this particular aspect of reality. I'm finished with it. I won't have anything to do with it."

"You sound like a bloody child," Fiona spat, her usual fire breaking through the Zen exterior.

"Good. I want to sound like a child. I never really got to be one, so I'm starting now." I stood up abruptly. "If you need me I'll be in my room, picking the marshmallows out of breakfast cereal and coloring with some crayons in a blanket fort."

"Jessica, you can't run from this," Fiona called after me.

"Watch me," I replied, halfway to the door already.

"And what about your mate Annabelle, then? Not bothered to find out what this means? No interest in why you've gone and predicted her death?" Fiona shouted.

I stopped, my hand gripping the door handle, feeling as though a giant fist was squeezing my insides.

"Ah, that's got your attention, has it? Enough of this foolishness, now. Sit your arse back down here."

I turned and slouched back to the table, feeling my anger give way to tears of terror and helplessness. I sank onto the bench, but I kept my eyes averted from the image Fiona was now shoving under my nose.

"It is a hard, cold fact that Seers are rare and that their predictions are highly valued. It is also a fact that most of their predictions come to absolutely nothing."

I looked up, frowning. "What do you mean? They predict things that don't come true?"

"That's right."

"I don't get it. Isn't the whole point of a prediction that it does come true?"

"Prophecies are tricky things. They are only true in the moment they are made. A hundred factors could change in the interim, and then the outcome will change with them. The real test is how this prediction changes over time, if at all."

A hint of curiosity sparked in my overwrought brain. "Changes how?"

"I haven't the foggiest. The idea that the universe has a master plan is a load of bollocks. My experience with the world has taught me that it is a random chaos of intersecting paths over which we have no control. Today's prophecy might just be tomorrow's scrap paper. It all depends how all of those paths cross with each other. You follow?"

I shook my head. "But the Isherwood Prophecy. That remained unchanged for hundreds of years."

"But it didn't! That's what I'm telling you! Yes, it foretold your coming, but look at these images!" Fiona mashed a finger against the glass of the painting. "Look at this chaos! Look at that destruction! None of this actually came to pass!"

"Of course, it did! Hannah reversed the Gateway! The spirits came out!"

"And yet here we all sit, with the Gateways back intact and order restored to our sisterhood! This image, and the image you created, showed the worst-case scenario, don't you see? They showed us what could happen if you failed. It was only one possibility, not a foregone conclusion!"

I blinked. Never, in all my time of dwelling on the Prophecy, had this thought occurred to me.

"All this time you've been thinking that you were the subject of a Prophecy that came true, but rather, you were the subject of a Prophecy that was foiled. The Seers could account for many things, but in the end, they couldn't account for *you*."

"Me?"

"You! You were the variable! Even the written version of the Prophecy left us with a huge gaping question mark because it could not predict the choices that you would make. The same is true of every prophecy ever made! In the end, they are only glimpses of the ends of the paths we are currently on. It cannot account for the detours, the delays, or the possibility that we might just say 'sod it!' sprout wings, and soar off the fecking path and into the sky!" Fiona cried.

"Fiona, I enjoy a good extended metaphor as much as the next girl, but can you please just get to the point?" I sighed. "You just finished telling me that your mother and grandmother were driven mad by this so-called 'gift,' so you'll pardon me if I'm not up for reading between the lines."

"What I'm getting at is, you should treat this as you would treat any other spirit drawing. So, answer me this, eh? How often does the spirit who sends you an image actually establish meaningful contact?"

I shrugged. "As often as not," I said. "Lots of times, the spirits just leave a passing image and I never hear from them again."

"Exactly! The same will be true for what you See. As often as ot, the images will come to nothing, rubbed out of existence by he many variables still in play, irrelevant before you even finish rawing them. To dwell on them too much will be unhealthy and a vaste of your energy."

I sputtered incoherently for a moment as I groped, incredulous, or my reply. "How could I not dwell on this?" I cried finally, pointing a shaking finger at the image of Annabelle's body. "My ift—or the universe, or whatever is responsible for this—obviously hought this was something that I would want to know about, ight?"

"You need to take your cues from your gift. If you have a single passing vision of an event, chances are your gift isn't really forming true prophecy. It's just... plucking possibilities from the air, if ou will," Fiona explained. "But if a vision comes to you over and ver again, even if the details change with each new drawing, that s your clue that you are experiencing something significant in ature, something that will come to pass in some form."

"And what do I do if that happens?" I asked, a note of desperation n my voice.

"You come straight to me. We will take it from there," Fiona said.

"But the Council—"

"The Council shouldn't know anything about this. Not yet, nyway," Fiona said sharply.

I swallowed hard. "Why?"

"Because the Council is full of superstitious, biased fools," Fiona pat. "Women who already harbor ill will toward your family. I annot say for sure what they would make of the information that ou are a Seer, and so for the time being, I'd rather not give them he chance to make anything of it at all."

"Okay, but ... worst-case scenario. Why could it be bad for them o know?" I tried to sound merely curious, in an academic sense, ather than terrified to the point of tears.

Fiona laughed, but it was a humorless and bitter sound. "The Council has always looked at every gift as a tool to be used for heir own benefit. The more gifts the Northern Clans have, the nore powerful we are, and the more influence we can yield among he other Councils around the world. Some tools are more useful nd powerful than others, but a Seer?" She laughed again. "You vould be the crown jewel in their collection. They would flaunt you nd parade you about like a trophy. They would also pump you for information at every given opportunity, demanding answers you don't have and details your gift has not yet provided you. I'm your mentor and I am telling you right here and now that I will not allow it." She looked me right in the eye, and for maybe the first time ever I saw a flash of real affection there. "Is that absolutely clear? I will not allow it."

"Okay," I said, taking heart from her fierce determination. "So what do I do now, if I'm not going to tell the Council? What is this going to look like as a part of my life now?"

Fiona blew out a breath, and for first time I realized that she hadn't been nearly as calm about the situation as she'd appeared on the surface. She looked frankly relieved that I was listening to reason. "You're going to have to be very cognizant of your drawings. We will work together to catalogue them separately as spirit drawings and Seer drawings. Soon you will be able to tell the difference just by looking at them—but that will come with time. Then we will track patterns in any Seer drawings that seem related. If they come together in any meaningful way, and it seems like a prophecy that will have far-reaching consequences, then we'll bring it to the Council, but only if we must, and only as a last resort."

I took several slow, deep breaths. "Okay. And Annabelle?"

"Have you done any drawings of her since?" Fiona asked.

"No, but this was just last night," I answered.

"So, we wait. I know how that sounds," Fiona said, cutting me off with a raised hand. "It sounds as though we are allowing this image to come to pass. But the truth is that you've determined that your friend is fine, and you can continue to stay in contact with her. Find an excuse to stay in touch with her more closely. Hound her, if it makes you feel better. However, unless you produce further images related to this first one, I think your friend is safe. A prediction this serious—if it is still a possibility—will not leave you alone, I can promise you that."

I tried to process this information in a way that made me feel even a tiny bit better, but I couldn't really manage it. "I'll figure something out so that I can keep tabs on Annabelle."

"Good. Now, keep this between us, all right?" Fiona asked.

"Hannah and Milo already know," I said. "And I wouldn't keep it from them even if I could."

Fiona nodded. "Fair enough. You're too closely connected, and we know you can trust them. Most likely pointless to keep things from them anyway. And you ought to tell your Caomhnóir, too."

"What about Karen?" I asked.

Fiona frowned, considering. Honestly, I was conflicted about it, too. On the one hand, Karen was a wonderful champion to have in our corner, and she'd never let us down, at least since she had been forced into telling us about our Durupinen heritage, and I'd long since forgiven her for the breaches of trust that came before that.

"She can fret quite a bit, your aunt," Fiona said at last. "Best not give her anything to worry about until there's some worrying that needs to be done."

"Okay. What about the Council seat?" I asked. "If Hannah wins that seat, she'll be obligated to inform the Council, won't she?"

Fiona arched an eyebrow at me. "Are you daft, girl? I'm on the Council, and you don't see me running to inform them, do you?"

I grinned sheepishly, relieved to find that I had it in me to smile. "Sorry, Fiona. You're such a loose cannon that I forget sometimes that you're part of the establishment."

"Yeah, well, I spend most of my time trying to forget it as well. Sometimes, I'd just say to hell with it and give up the seat. It was a pity appointment anyway. They only voted me in as a way to make amends for the way my family was treated, and I only accepted it to appease my clan. But I cringe to think how much more damage that Council would wreak if all the sensible ones started jumping ship."

I stifled a laugh at the idea that Fiona might be deemed the sensible one in any scenario, but in a backward sort of way, she had a point.

Fiona sighed. "But as far as your sister and the Council, let's cross that bridge if we get to it. We've got enough to worry about as it is, and the odds of her landing that seat are not ones that I would fancy a flutter on."

"Fair enough. One catastrophe at a time, right?"

Fiona almost smiled. "Consider that our new philosophy."

14

DUTY CALLS

WHEN I WOKE THE MORNING after the revelations in the Archive, I lay with my eyes on the ceiling for a full five minutes, frozen with fear and unwilling even to twitch my gaze in the direction of the wall. I was terrified of what I might see there—convinced that another image of Annabelle's demise would be leaping in graphic detail from the paper hung there. I frantically assessed my right hand, testing for any tiny hint of the stiffness or muscle fatigue that typically accompanied a spirit-induced drawing. I felt nothing. I turned my head away from the wall and let my eyes fall upon the bedside table. The charcoal pencil I had placed there was still upright in its mason jar, still sharpened to a perfect point. I took in a long, deep breath, held it, and turned to face the wall.

No Annabelle. No drawing at all. Just blessedly blank, white paper.

I laughed giddily with relief and sat up to find Hannah staring at me with wary eyes.

"How are you this morning, Jess? Are you okay?"

Unable to sleep because of all the excitement of the nominations, Hannah had been sitting up waiting for me when I'd arrived back to our room from my meeting with Fiona. The entire walk back, I told myself that I would not burden her with the news that I was a Seer—not yet, not until this election was over and that terrible pressure was lifted from her shoulders. She didn't deserve more worry piled on top of the worry she already carried, I lectured myself firmly, stiffening my resolve with every corridor, every staircase. Then I'd opened the door, taken one look at her stricken face, and dropped it all on her like a bombshell.

Luckily, my sister was basically indestructible. I really should have remembered that—I rarely gave her credit for what a powerhouse she was because she appeared so tiny and fragile. She held me curled in her lap for an hour, stroking my hair and taming every fear I had like a snake charmer. And by the end of our conversation—though I was by no means happy about the prospect of being a Seer—I was at least ready to face it rather than run screaming from it.

"After all," she'd said, and there was steel behind the gentle timbre of her voice, "if I could face being the Caller destined to bring about the apocalypse, you can handle drawing a few sketches of predictions that may or may not come true."

I'd gasped and tried to sound offended, but ruined the affect by laughing. "May or may not come true? How do you know? How do you know I'm not the Seer that brings about the next apocalyptic prophecy?"

Hannah had snorted. "No way. You're not that cool."

Now, in the light of morning, she examined my face anxiously, trying to assess if the talk from the night before had really helped me, or if I was back in panic mode. I tried to smile and found, to my relief, that the muscles in my face were willing to cooperate.

I tried to look confident and unconcerned, though fully aware she'd just watched my bizarre new morning ritual. "Yeah. I'm okay. No drawings last night. That's a good sign. How about you?"

Hannah shrugged. "No pitchforks or torches outside our window last night. That's a good sign, too, I guess."

"I'm sorry. I was so distracted by the Seer news that I let you take care of me last night when we should have been taking care of each other," I said. "I feel really guilty about it."

"Don't you worry, sweetness," Milo said, sailing gracefully through the wall behind me and coming to rest on the chair between our beds, fluttering down as though he were a feather composed entirely of sass. "I was here with her all night, too. We had a good long talk while we were waiting for you to get back, and our girl is more than up to whatever desperate ploys Marion may have left up her devious sleeves. I gave you two your space last night so that you could talk, but now the Spirit Guide needs the dish. Let's have it. Spill."

Milo took the news that I was a Seer better than I thought he would, quickly tempering his initial shock with a nonchalant air. "Well, you know, I don't play Spirit Guide to just any old Durupinen. It is widely known among the floaters that I only ssociate myself with the very best—exceptional guidance needs xceptional guide-ees, after all. We already knew Hannah was xceptional. You were just a late bloomer, that's all."

"Excuse me? I'm a Muse and a Walker! I foiled the Prophecy! Vhat more do you want from me?" I asked.

Milo shrugged and winked at me. "Drawing and floating are retty tame, Jess, let's be honest. But predicting the future? Your tock just went way up, sweetness."

I rolled my eyes. "Ugh, you are *such* a stage parent."

"Well, in that case, we just went from community theatre to Iroadway, baby!" Milo sang. "Stop moping around and show a little ride! We are putting the 'sass' back in Clan Sassanaigh, and the est of the clans best be ready for it!"

"It's amazing how often I want to slap you and hug you almost imultaneously," I told him.

"You are not the first person to tell me that, sweetness, and you von't be the last," Milo said. He took his finger and drew a little 1alo around his head and immediately followed it up with a pair of levil horns.

"Well, since there are no new prophecies to deal with this norning, I'm going to deliver these down to the Council office o Celeste can record them along with the others," Hannah said, icking up the stack of pledges off her bedside table and waving hem at me. "And then I have to sign my final platform changes efore the session starts today, so that Siobhán can read it along vith the others before the vote tonight. Do you want to come with ne, or should I meet you down at breakfast?"

"Platform changes?" I dropped my face into my hands and ;roaned. "Oh, no. I forgot."

"Forgot what?" Hannah asked, frowning.

I sighed. "With everything going on, I forgot to talk to you. I vas supposed to do it before you finished your platform. I promised 'inn that I would."

I saw Milo stiffen as he realized what I must be talking about. But Iannah continued to frown. "What is it, Jess?"

I felt the color rush to my face. I dropped my eyes to my hands 1ow twisting uncomfortably in my lap. "I... I have something I have o tell you. Something kind of big."

"Something else? You can't be serious!" Hannah said with an

incredulous note of laughter. "What else can you possibly have to tell me that will top the news that you can see the future?"

I dropped my face into my hands, speaking into the darkness inside them. "It's about me and Finn."

Silence.

I let it build unbearably for several seconds before I could find the nerve to steal a glance at Hannah and Milo. When I finally did it was to see them desperately trying to control their features as repressed laughter twisted and contorted them.

"What are you laughing for?" I asked indignantly, dropping my hands.

A giggle slipped from between Hannah's tightly pressed lips. She quickly arranged her face into a serious, thoughtful look. "What about you and Finn?"

I pointed an accusatory finger at Milo. "You told her, didn't you? You told me you weren't going to."

"Oh, honey," Milo sighed. "I didn't need to. She already knew. We both already knew. Bless your heart, but the two of you aren't exactly the masters of mystery you fancy yourselves to be."

I looked back at Hannah, who shrugged apologetically. "Sorry, but it's true. You two basically get those cartoon eyes that turn into hearts when you see each other."

"You could have said something!" I cried, throwing my hands up in exasperation.

"So could you," Hannah pointed out. "But you didn't, and I took my cues from you. I wasn't going to out you if you weren't ready to talk about it."

"I thought you were catching on to something, but I guess I thought we were more careful than cartoon heart eyes," I said, sighing. "You're not mad that I didn't tell you, are you?"

Hannah smiled. "Of course not. It's your business. I knew you would tell me when you were ready."

"I'm mad at you," Milo said. "But mostly for being predictable. I mean, really, Jess? Your bodyguard? Ugh. How chick flick of you."

I rolled my eyes. "Sorry, Milo. Next time I'll consider your need for plot twists before falling for someone in my actual life."

"I appreciate that, thank you," Milo said in a lofty, dignified voice.

"There is one part of all this that makes a Milo-worthy plot twist, though," Hannah said, her smile slipping. "The relationship ban. What are you going to do?"

I felt my smile vanish, too. "There isn't really anything that we can do. At least, not without giving ourselves away. Seamus would expose us instantly, and Finn would be on the next plane to the middle of nowhere, reassigned to some outpost where I'd be guaranteed never to see him again. So that's why I wanted to talk to you about the platform."

Hannah smiled gently at me. "You don't need to talk to me about it."

"I don't?"

Still smiling, she came to sit down beside me, pointing down at the bottom of the page. "Here. The last item on my campaign platform. Read it."

I looked where she was pointing and read aloud. "I promise to revisit laws governing the interactions between Durupinen and Caomhnóir, in the interest of improving relationships between the groups and creating guidelines that reflect our modern-day circumstances." I looked up at her. "Does this mean what I think it means?"

"Of course," she said. "I couldn't come right out and say it, for obvious reasons, but if I get elected, this will be the first thing I tackle."

"Hannah, this is amazing!" I said, pulling her into a hug. "You know this won't be popular. A lot of people won't like this kind of a shake-up."

"Gee, being unpopular in the Council Room," Hannah said gazing up dreamily. "I wonder what that feels like." She looked back at me and winked. "It will be worth it. No one can deny the whole system needs improving. It's outdated and absurdly polarizing. Everyone admits it, even if they don't want to change it. It will benefit everyone, not just you, even if you are the reason I want to tackle it."

"Thank you," I said. "Honestly, Hannah. You're going to take a lot of shit for this, so I'm sorry in advance but... just... thank you."

Hannah smiled. "You're welcome. And about the cartoon heart eyes: don't panic. You are doing a really good job of hiding it in public. I just... know you better."

§

The dining room was a sea of staring eyes. I panicked for a full ten seconds—convinced that somehow everyone had found out I was a Seer—before I remembered that Hannah had just emerged as the unexpected favorite in the race for the Council seat. These were just the usual stares. These I could handle.

"Oi!" Savvy cried, flagging us down from across the room. She was sitting with Frankie over in our traditional corner of misfits. We filled our plates and rushed to join her.

"You cheeky little bugger!" she roared, slapping Hannah on the back. "You make like you're all quiet and shy, and then you get up there and you turn into Winston bloody Churchill! Why didn't you give me a sneak peek, eh?"

"We... uh... wanted to keep the speech under wraps," Hannah said hesitantly.

When Savvy looked puzzled, I added, "Sav, we love you, but you've got a big mouth."

Savvy looked almost offended. "I have not!" Then looked sheepishly around as she realized she was shouting. "I can keep a secret when I need to."

"We know that, Savvy. We trust you, I promise. I was just really nervous about giving the speech. Karen was the only one who heard the whole thing before the meeting, and that's because she helped me write it," Hannah explained.

"Ah, never mind, then," Savvy said, her annoyance melting with the warmth of her own grin. "It was worth it for the shock value alone! I've never seen so many sticks go so far up so many arses all at once." She chuckled reminiscently. "That was brilliant, that was. Even if you never get near that Council seat, it was worth running just for the looks on all of their faces when the cheap seats exploded in applause."

"It was a wonderful speech, Hannah," Frankie chimed in. "Definitely a great thing to hear my first time in the Grand Council Room."

"Thanks, Frankie," Hannah said, smiling at her. "How is your training going?"

"It's... an adjustment," Frankie said carefully. "But it's been better since I started accepting reality."

"Have you been able to sort things out with your school?" Hannah asked.

"Yes," Frankie said. "Siobhán assigned some of the Trackers to handle all of the details, to make sure I'm getting the tutoring I need to stay at the top of my class and graduate on time. With any luck, I'll be applying to a university medical program as planned."

"That's wonderful," Hannah said, but her smile was fading. "I suppose I may have some decisions to make about school myself if..."

"If you get onto the Council? Don't get too far ahead of yourself," said a purr of a voice from behind us.

I spun to see Catriona standing just behind us, her arms crossed over her chest and her signature bored smirk back on her face. "It's still a long shot. But I must admit, you have made for a very entertaining first week back to the Council," she added.

"Hi, Catriona," Hannah said stiffly, her cheeks blushing pink. "How are you feeling?"

"Oh, I'm in tip-top shape again, thank you," Catriona said, brushing a stray hair from her face. "A bit fatigued perhaps, but that's to be expected when your body is used like a vacant motel suite."

"I'm glad to hear it. We were all worried about you," I said.

Catriona snorted. "Yes, I'm sure you were just devastated. I daresay you wouldn't have minded another week or two without me, but you mustn't be too disappointed. Say what you will about me, but I'm resilient, if nothing else."

"Fair enough," I said. "So, to what do we owe the pleasure?"

"Well, I'm now about several weeks behind on my paperwork for the Trackers," Catriona sighed. She raised a hand to silence us as we all opened our mouths to protest. "I know, I know, but the spirit world slows down for no one, not even the Host of a Shattering. Some cases were put on hold, of course, but others plowed right along without me."

My heart began to race. Only one case could bring her here, to talk to us. I silently begged that she wouldn't continue, but my pleas went unanswered.

"I came down to ask if I might have a word with you, Jess," Catriona went on, "about that Traveler Walker you caught on the Campbell case. Won't take long."

"Uh, sure, that's fine," I said. "I just need to be back in time for the Airechtas session."

Catriona rolled her eyes. "Jessica, we both have to be back in time for the Airechtas session." She pointed at herself. "Council member, remember?"

"Yeah, right," I mumbled, standing up and cramming the rest of my muffin into my mouth. "See you guys later," I said, waving at Savvy and giving Hannah a reassuring nod.

We walked along in silence for several minutes, Catriona several long strides ahead of me, before she spoke again.

"Quite the power play, going for the Council seat."

I scowled at the back of her golden head. "Power play?"

"I'm not trying to insult you. In fact, I'm impressed," Catriona said, though there was something playful in her tone. "I didn't realize you two were so cunning to recognize this kind of opportunity, much less bold enough to seize on it."

"Catriona, I don't know what you're talking about, so either explain yourself, or leave me alone," I said through clenched teeth. It was remarkable how quickly she managed to bring all of my contempt rushing to the surface. Perhaps it was the fact that her droll manner so recalled her cousin Lucida, but I could already feel my blood starting to bubble under the surface. I took a deep breath, reminding myself that, however much I might dislike her, Catriona was essentially my boss now.

"Oh, come now. The leadership is in shambles at the moment, you must realize that," Catriona said languidly. "We don't know whether we're coming or going, and it's really down to you and your sister."

"How refreshing. We're getting blamed for something else," I grumbled.

Catriona tossed her cascade of curls aside so that she could throw a contemptuous look over her shoulder at me. "It's not personal. It's simply fact. Between Finvarra's illness, scrambling to install a new High Priestess, and the Airechtas, we're all flailing around like chickens with our heads cut off. The clans are divided on who ought to lead, and there is considerable dissention in the ranks about where the Northern Clans should go from here. Some long for a return to the familiar, but many others would be just delighted to shake things up and watch the ruling clans topple."

I didn't reply. This was the first I'd heard of any of this.

"Many of them aren't very vocal, because they aren't the ones holding the cards, but they will make themselves heard with their votes, and no mistake. I understand your sister has already found an eager little fan club amongst those who are in favor of a change of the guard." She smirked at me. "Surely this was part of your scheme."

"No," I said shortly.

"Well, Finvarra surely knows it. I can't imagine how you persuaded her to nominate your clan. But I suppose the family connection must help."

"What family connection?"

Catriona laughed. "Oh Jessica, you are such a terrible fake at innocence. Your father, pet. Your dear father who spends his afterlife dangling on Finvarra's arm. We all know she values his opinion very highly, perhaps more than anyone else's, even in spite of the obvious betrayal of trust. Do you honestly mean to tell me that he hasn't been lobbying on your behalf?"

I could feel my nostrils flaring like an angry bull. "My father is a virtual stranger to me. Our relationship, or lack thereof, is absolutely none of your business. But because I don't want your Council friends walking around with a false perception, you should know that Carrick had nothing to do with Finvarra's decision to nominate us. I think he'd be happier if we put as much space between ourselves and the Council as possible."

Catriona pursed her lips at me and inclined her head. "Whatever you say." It couldn't have been clearer that she didn't believe a word I'd said. But her words jolted me. In all of the insanity of discovering I was a Seer, I'd completely forgotten Celeste's message from the day before.

"Do you know... how is Finvarra doing?"

Even Catriona couldn't remain smug as she replied, "Poorly. Very poorly."

"But she's still—"

"Yes, she's still alive. I don't know what she's hanging on for, but she's not done fighting yet, for whatever reason."

I let out a breath I had realized I'd been holding, and resolved to tell Hannah, as soon as I saw her, about Carrick's request. We would have to decide together whether we would go, and what the hell we would say when we got there.

I followed Catriona into the Tracker office, trying my best not to relive the last time we'd been here, when Catriona had become the first victim of the Shattering. The windows had since been repaired, and the tapestry that Catriona had used to try to smother the fire had been whisked away to Fiona's studio to be repaired another tapestry had unceremoniously taken its place, completing the illusion that nothing amiss had ever happened here.

"So, I looked through the transcripts you and your sister signed My thanks to both of you for finishing that while I was... indisposed," Catriona said.

"No problem," I said.

"I sent them off to the Traveler Council several days ago, and they've reviewed them, along with the entire file for the Walker's case."

"You mean Irina," I said defensively.

"Does it really matter what I call her?" Catriona asked, with a bored roll of her eyes.

"Does it matter what I call you?" I countered.

She ignored the question. "The Travelers have set a trial date for Irina next week. They have requested that either you or your sister attend to testify."

I clasped my hands together in my lap to keep them from shaking. "Why? They have our full statements. What else do they need?"

"That's not my concern," Catriona said. "I'm simply informing you that as your Tracker mentor, I've assigned the task to you."

"Why me?" I asked.

"Are you going to question everything I tell you while you're here? If you are, please do let me know now, so that I can adjust my schedule for the rest of the day," Catriona drawled, lounging back in her chair and putting both of her feet up on the desk.

"I didn't realize I wasn't allowed to ask questions," I said shortly.

"I'm choosing you because you have a longer history with the Walker. You have more experience interacting with her, and your insights on her behavior are therefore more relevant than your sister's. Secondly, I am choosing you because you are available," Catriona said dryly. "Your sister may or may not be otherwise engaged next week, trying to learn the ropes of the Council. Even though it's doubtful that she will win, I think it better to send the twin with the empty dance card."

I bit my lip, refusing to rise to Catriona's bait. I had too many important questions.

"Am I allowed to ask another question?"

"If you must."

"What will this trial be like? I mean, what will I have to... do?" My only experience with courts or trials was what I had seen on television, and somehow, I didn't think a Durupinen Traveler tribunal was likely to bear much resemblance to an episode of *Law and Order*.

"Every enclave has its own policies and procedures, but generally, you will have to sit in front of some sort of jury and answer questions about what happened at Whispering Seraph. It should be very straightforward. Just tell them what happened so that they have an accurate account of Irina's crimes."

"I... I'm not in any sort of trouble with the Travelers, am I?" I ventured.

Catriona frowned. "Why would you be in any trouble?"

I shrugged. "I didn't know if maybe... the fact that we tried to Cross Irina instead of turning her in..."

"Oh, that," Catriona said, rolling her eyes yet again. "The only people you might have gotten in trouble with for that foolishness were the Trackers, and luckily for you, they reviewed my notes and decided to chalk it up to your inexperience and a callow tendency toward empathy that the rest of us have all but forgotten we once possessed. No, the Travelers only care that Irina was returned to them. But if you are looking to avoid their ill-will, just be sure to emphasize the time-sensitive nature of the situation. You had to make a decision on the spot. You did not know when we would arrive. You felt the best way to minimize the threat was to Cross her. Leave it at that."

Only then, as I felt my body relax, did I realize how much tension I'd been holding inside. I took a long, slow breath and attempted a smile. "That's good to know. Thanks."

Catriona ignored my thanks, reaching instead into her desk and pulling out a folder, which she slid across the desktop to me. "Details of your travel plans are all in here. Your Caomhnóir will accompany you to the Traveler camp. Hannah can find adequate protection here among the castle Caomhnóir until your return."

I picked up the folder without opening it. My mind was racing. "Great. Is there anything else?"

"Not from me, no. Shall I brace myself for a barrage of questions, or can you spare me the agony?" Catriona asked, her expression innocent, but her voice dripping with sarcasm.

"I'll spare you," I said, shortly, and walked out of the room.

There was no room left in my frazzled consciousness to deal with Catriona and her predictably sardonic attitude. All I wanted to do was to get away from her as quickly as possible so that I could think. I started off down her corridor and just kept walking.

Irina's life had been hell on earth from the moment she began to Walk—a practice she took on purely at the command of the Durupinen. They wanted to explore her abilities and mine her for a myriad of possible uses. They knew the practice was dangerous, but the Durupinen pushed Irina further and further to explore Walking, until her love of existence in the spirit form trumped her loyalty to them. When they realized they had lost control over her, the Durupinen trapped her back in her own body and concocted a crude prison for her, using chains to restrain her body and Castings to restrain her spirit. That was how I had first encountered her; imprisoned in a broken-down wagon like an abused circus animal, driven insane with the intensity of her longing to be free of her body.

I knew I would never forget the pitiful sight of her, and the agony of her cries. Even as she taught me to Walk, at the behest of the Durupinen, Irina thought of nothing but her own freedom. Something in me gave me the ability to Walk without experiencing the same intense pain and longing, but it did not prevent me from pitying Irina. And so, when an Unmasking revealed her to be the culprit at Whispering Seraph, and I was presented with the opportunity to free her forever—to allow her to Cross—I leapt at it. I could never right the many wrongs she had been subjected to, but I could, at the very least, prevent further travesties from being inflicted upon her.

It was Catriona who had prevented that Crossing, forcing us instead to Cage Irina and turn her over to the Traveler Durupinen to face "justice" for her crimes. I would not deny that Irina's actions at Whispering Seraph hurt a lot of people, but the thought of punishing her was unforgivable. It was because of the severity of her mistreatment that she committed her crimes in the first place. I suppose I didn't expect Catriona to have pity for Irina; Catriona didn't seem to have pity for anyone. I had hoped the Traveler

Durupinen might find it in their hearts to just let Irina go, knowing the awful torture they themselves had put her through, but I could not be sure that they would make the right decision.

And so, I had made Irina a promise. I swore that I would find a way to free her. It was an irrational, reckless promise, born of pity and fear and anger. It was a promise I didn't have the power or authority to make, and I had no real plan how I would be able to keep it. But now, it seemed, the moment to figure it out was upon me. I was out of time. Irina's fate would be decided at this trial, and I would have to be prepared to free her if the Travelers would not.

And I had absolutely no idea how the hell I was going to do it.

15

THE RISE AND THE FALL

I ONLY MADE IT BACK to the Grand Council Room just in time for the start of the morning's session, which had already begun as I slid into my seat.

"What did I miss?" I whispered.

"Celeste lit a candle for Finvarra and asked us all to keep her in our thoughts. She's really not doing well," Hannah answered. She pointed to the empty throne, on which now burned a tall white taper in a golden candleholder.

I bit my lip. The trauma of discovering I was a Seer had driven Carrick's request right out of my mind. My God, would the barrage of unfaceable realities never let up?

"I have to tell you something," I whispered, and leaned in, imparting the entirety of my conversation with Celeste into Hannah's ear.

Her expression was heavy with a mixture of conflicting emotions that I recognized all too well.

"I mean... we'll have to go, won't we?" she asked.

"I'm not sure," I replied.

"It just seems like... I know Finvarra is the one dying, but..."

"I know, I know," I said, and I dropped my head against the table. "If we don't go, it's like we're denying a deathbed wish or something."

"Well... yeah," Hannah said quietly.

I lifted my head to look at her. "I don't know what to say to him."

"Neither do I," she admitted. "But maybe that's not what it's about. Maybe he has things to say to us. Don't we owe him the chance to say them?"

I didn't answer, but I bristled at the thought of owing him anything. Finally, I sighed. "I don't know. But I'll go if you want to."

"I'm not sure that I *want* to," Hannah said. "But I think we should. Let's get through the vote this evening, and maybe we can go in the morning?"

"Okay."

We both turned our attention to Celeste, who was walking us all through the voting process.

"This evening at six o'clock, the doors to the Grand Council Room will open, and each clan will be called forth to place their vote here." She gestured to a large, carved wooden box, rather like a small steamer trunk, that had appeared on a pedestal during the lunch break. "When all of the votes have been cast, the clans will convene in the central courtyard around the Geatgrima while the votes are counted. When the winner of the election has been determined, that clan's banner will be hung from the highest window of the South Tower."

I looked over at Hannah. Her eyes were glazed over, and I wondered if she was imagining the same sight as I was: the deep purple banner of Clan Sassanaigh unfurling across the gray stonework high above our heads. It was the first time that the faint possibility of winning the election filled me with a sense of pride and excitement, rather than fear and trepidation. But then, the dread seeped back in as I glanced across the breadth of the hall to where Finn stood, the picture of duty and sacrifice. I could see his pride and his surety in the thrust of his jaw, the squaring of his shoulders.

Suddenly, I wanted nothing more than to shake him, to take his hand and pull him into a run. I wanted to run and run and run as far as we could go, until things like duty and clan and calling could no longer ensnare us with their grasping, greedy, entitled fingers. It was so difficult for the two of us to speak freely here, that I hadn't even had a chance to tell him about my meeting with Fiona the previous night. My entire world had changed, and I couldn't even clue him in. How could we ever sustain a bond together when this place—and everyone in it—continually drove wedges between us?

Ugh. The more I thought about it, the more I sounded like a whiny romance heroine, and I wanted to slap myself soundly right across the stupid face.

The last few hours of the Airechtas dragged more slowly than I would have thought possible. Surely some sadist with a love of bureaucracy had put a Casting on the clocks to prevent the hands from budging. I knew I wasn't the only one impatient for the meetings to end; all around us, fingers and pencils were tapping nervously, and eyes darted around from the clock, to the windows, and back down to the interminable agendas. At long, long, last, a bell tolled, and the Airechtas officially came to an end.

As a small crowd of Durupinen descended on Hannah, offering good luck and extending last minute offers of support, I slipped away and caught Finn's attention. As the rest of the Caomhnóir filed out of the hall, he broke ranks and met me in the back corner of the hall.

"Jess, what..."

"I have to tell you something."

He frowned at me, then turned and pushed open a side door. I followed him into a deserted corridor, down a flight of stairs, and into an empty classroom. He pulled the door shut behind us.

"What is it?" he asked, after ensuring the door was secure and the hallway beyond it still vacant.

Without preamble, because I didn't know how much time we had, I launched into the story of my meeting with Fiona. Perhaps it was because I had already had time to process it all, but I felt calmer explaining it to him than I had when I'd unloaded on Hannah. He did not interrupt with terse questions, as I had expected, but let me talk myself into silence, his expression attentive.

"So... that's it," I finished lamely.

He continued to stare. I could actually see the gears turning, his brain trying to take it all in. Finally, he lifted his hands to either side of my face and pressed his lips gently to my forehead.

"How are you?" he asked earnestly.

"Honestly? Completely freaked out," I admitted. I leaned into him, so that he kissed my forehead again. "This is helping."

He chuckled softly. "Well, I must admit, I've been expecting something like this to happen."

I pulled back and looked up into his face. "What are you talking about? You don't expect me to believe that you already guessed I was a Seer?"

"No, of course not," he said. "But, it's you, isn't it? Never a dull moment. You like to keep me on my toes."

"Do you have any real thoughts about this?" I asked him, frowning. "Not that I don't appreciate your newfound ability to tell a joke."

"Apologies, love," Finn said. "I'm just trying to diffuse the tension. I don't mean to diminish how serious this is." He reached down for my hands, and held them tightly in his. "But the truth is that your Muse gift has always been something rather extraordinary. I have often wondered if there might be more to it than we realized. And I agree with Fiona. This is information we should keep to ourselves until we have no choice."

"And what about Annabelle?" I asked. "Aren't you worried?"

"Of course," Finn said. "But you mustn't forget what Fiona told you. Prophecies are fleeting, and you are doing everything in your power to keep Annabelle safe and accounted for. I'm sure it's a frustrating prospect to face, but let's wait and see. If Annabelle is truly in danger, I have no doubt that your gift will illuminate things further."

"When did Mr. Overprotective become so calm and reasonable?" I asked, laughing in spite of myself.

Finn shrugged. "If my time as your guardian has taught me anything, it is this: whatever the spirit world throws at us, it is likely that we have already faced—and overcome—far worse."

"That's true," I said.

"Put this out of your mind for the moment," Finn said. "At least until the election is over. Your sister is going to need you, regardless of the outcome."

§

The waiting was almost unbearable.

In the center of the courtyard, the Geatgrima rose like a monument to the most terrifying and defining moment of my life. All around it, the clans stood assembled, clutching their candles and whispering excitedly to each other. On one side of me, Hannah was shivering with cold and anticipation. Milo was so tense that he had blinked out just to save his energy, but I could feel him buzzing like an oversized insect trapped in our connection. On my other side, Karen was gripping my arm so tightly that my fingers were starting to go numb.

"Karen. Lighten up," I whispered, shaking her off.

"Sorry," she murmured. "I'm just..."

"I know. Me, too."

A chill wind swept the grounds, causing us all to shudder.

"Hannah, whatever happens, I am so proud of you," I breathed in her ear.

Hannah squeezed my hand, but did not take her eyes from the South Tower, where the winning clan's banner would appear.

"Come *on*," I heard Savvy groan from somewhere nearby. "How bloody long does it take to count a few votes?"

I closed my eyes to center myself, just as a collective gasp rose from the Durupinen.

"Oh, my God," Hannah whispered.

When I opened my eyes, the first thing I saw was Marion's face. She was staring across at us, and the bitter defeat in her expression told me what I would see when I cast my gaze up to the tower.

I smiled at her.

And the courtyard erupted in cheers beneath the crest of the Clan Sassanaigh. A crowd descended upon us, hands reaching out to shake Hannah's hand, to pat her shoulders. Mackie had thrust two fingers into her mouth and let lose a piercing whistle. Savvy was shouting hoarsely, hoisting us both into a violent hug.

"You did it! You bloody well did it!" she shrieked.

Karen was sobbing uncontrollably, and her words to Hannah were entirely unintelligible as she wrenched us away from Savvy and into her own embrace. All around us, the Caomhnóir were closing in, attempting to break up the crowd, to ensure that we were safe. Milo kept popping in and out of form, blinking and wavering with unrestrainable emotion.

"I knew it! I knew it, I knew it, I knew it!" he crowed whenever he reappeared.

I freed myself from Karen to wrap my arms around Hannah, whose face was still blank with disbelief.

"Is this real?" she asked me. "Tell me it's real."

"It's real," I told her. "You did it, Hannah. You won."

Her face split into a grin that quickly crumpled into tears, and we hugged and sobbed together as the celebration continued to explode all around us.

Siobhán appeared beside us, smiling and beckoning Hannah to follow her through the crowd. Hannah took her hand and they shoved their way through, hands still reaching out to her as she went. Karen, Milo, and I followed, congratulations raining down on us from all sides. Siobhán led Hannah up onto the central dais to stand beside Celeste, who was beaming from ear to ear.

And there, on the very spot where the Prophecy had almost destroyed everything, Hannah reclaimed our family's honor as the Council robes were draped upon her shoulders.

Of course, there were those who did not smile. There were plenty who stood like statues of disapproval, watching Hannah's triumph with disdain and even fury. They did not matter. Not now.

I shouted myself hoarse as Celeste placed the Council circlet on Hannah's dark curls. As I waved my arms over my head at her, Finn's voice was suddenly in my ear. "And here I thought you didn't buy into any of this Durupinen political drama."

"I don't," I insisted through my tears and laughter. "It's a boring and meaningless bunch of nonsense."

As the crowd began to disperse, walking back toward the castle in twos and threes, Hannah stumbled down the stone steps, catching the overly long robe up into her hands to prevent herself from falling. Her face was as bright as a star as she beamed at me.

"I still can't believe it!" she cried.

"Nor can I," Karen said. "I think it will take quite a while to sink in, and not just for us." She jerked her head over her shoulder. Marion was striding toward us.

I stiffened, ready to fend off whatever bitter, nasty words she was preparing to fling at us, but she never had the chance. As she opened her mouth, the bell in the North Tower began to toll. Cries and gasps rose to meet the echoes that reverberated across the grounds.

Hannah looked at her watch, then up at me in alarm. "It's not seven o'clock yet," she whispered.

Staring into each other's eyes, we began to count, hearts hammering.

Seven. Eight. Nine . . .

"Please, no," Hannah whispered.

Eleven. Twelve. Thirteen.

I couldn't breathe. The last clang of the bell was echoing endlessly in my head.

All around us, cries and screams rose like a flock of birds into the darkening sky. I whipped around and stared up at Finvarra's tower just in time to see a long black banner unfurl into the twilight, flapping gently in the breeze.

"Oh, my God," Karen murmured.

"She's gone," I said.

174

"*He's* gone," Hannah whispered.

The courtyard shrank down around me, smothering me in our collective shock and grief. I didn't know what to do. I didn't know what to feel. I wanted to scream and break things while also crawling into a hole and pulling the dirt down on top of me. I wanted to curse something, and I also wanted to breathe a sigh of relief. What was this? How did I deal with it? Did I even want to deal with it? Maybe I could just stuff it away into the dark corners of myself, where the rest of the painful things nested. My armor would not keep the pain out, but I could choose to let it keep the pain in. I could do that.

"She must have been hanging on to see what would happen with the election," Karen said, choking back tears. "She must have been waiting for our banner to fly."

The Durupinen all around us were bowing their heads in silent prayer, or else consoling each other. The Caomhnóir all fell, as one, to their knees, their right fists pressed over their hearts. And with a gust of spirit energy that seemed to steal all the air from the grounds, every spirit that haunted the halls of Fairhaven rose into the sky and gathered in a ring around the tower. They hung there in silent, respectful tribute, a grief-stricken cloud of souls.

I felt a hand on my shoulder and whirled around. It was Celeste.

"I need you and Hannah to come up to the High Priestess's chambers. Quickly," she said. Her face was streaked with tears, but her voice was urgent.

"Us? Why?" I asked, alarmed.

"Just follow me. Now, please," she said, and started walking back toward the castle.

I stared at Hannah, who shrugged in a bewildered way and then started following in Celeste's wake. I forced my feet to follow.

It wasn't like Celeste to be so brusque or so cryptic. She was one of the few Durupinen that could be counted on to show a little more sensitivity in situations like this. Still, she spoke not another word as we followed her into the castle and all the way up to the top of the North Tower.

"In there," she said. She could barely meet our eyes.

"What's going on, Celeste?" I asked, my voice cracking with anxiety and, for some reason, fear.

"You're wasting time. Just go in. I'm not allowed to accompany you," she said. There was a tear trembling on the end of her nose.

Hannah pulled in a shuddering breath and pushed the door open. We both walked through it, and I closed it tightly behind me.

The room was in semi-darkness. There were candles burning low in brackets all around. Chairs had been grouped in a circle around a bed in the corner. The floor around them was scattered with tissues, blankets, and mugs: the remnants of a bedside vigil. Whoever had been sitting in those chairs were gone now.

As was the woman whose body was lying in the bed.

It staggered me how a body, having been alive just minutes before, could be so utterly, visibly changed by the exit of the soul. It was instantaneously recognizable that this was no longer a person that I knew. This was merely a shell now, an empty shell. It didn't even look as though the breadth of Finvarra's soul had ever expanded and animated this shrunken, feeble body that lay before us. And it could not have looked more desolate or abandoned now that the chairs around it sat empty, the machines silenced, the light outside fading from the room.

"Jess, what are you doing?" Hannah hissed urgently.

Without realizing it, I had drifted across the room, closing the distance between myself and the bed. I had no idea why I had done it. I didn't want to see this. I didn't want to see Finvarra this way, nor did I think she would have wanted anyone to see her this way. It felt indecent, like spying. And yet, I kept walking until I stood right over her, looking down into her sunken face. Her eyes were closed, and yet I kept imagining them open, the fierce light inside them extinguished at last.

I felt Hannah fill the empty space beside me. She slipped her small, cold hand into mine and squeezed.

"What are we doing here?" she whispered.

"I don't know," I whispered back. Why either of us was whispering, I had no idea. It wasn't as though there was anyone left in the room who could hear us. It was just what you did, wasn't it, in the presence of death?

"Jessica. Hannah."

I screamed and leapt back, knocking one of the chairs over and stumbling into the end table, scattering its litter of pill bottles and medical supplies all over the floor. Hannah had frozen where she stood in her shock. It was not the sound of an unexpected voice that startled us; God knows we'd grown accustomed to unexpected voices. It was the fact that the sound of that voice—*that voice*—should have been impossible, gone from the world forever.

I turned. Carrick was standing there, barely distinguishable from the shadows.

"What... how... you're supposed to be gone," I whispered.

"Yes, by all rights I should be gone. And I will be, very very soon," Carrick said. His voice had an echo to it, as though he were already halfway down the long path he was about to travel.

"But, how are you still here?" Hannah's voice broke through, strangled with emotion. "I thought you had to Cross when Finvarra did." She whipped her head around and stared at Finvarra's body again, scanning it for signs of life she already knew to be gone.

"I do. But our High Priestess, in a display of loyalty I neither expected, nor deserved, has given this small space of time to me."

"What do you mean?" I breathed.

"Over our many years Bound to each other, Finvarra has grown to know me very well; at times she has more insight into me than I have into myself. She knew, for instance, that in spite of all of my training and my posturing and my shows of strength, I am a coward at heart."

Hannah shook her head. "You're not a coward."

But it was me, in my silence, that Carrick looked at now. "Your sister does not dispute this assessment," he said, and though I blushed a little, I did not speak.

Carrick went on, "She is right. I am a coward, and I always have been, in matters of the heart. I used to blame it on years of military training, where I was taught to suppress all emotion as weakness, but I shall not lean on such excuses in these final moments. Deep down, I have always been so. I own it now."

Still I did not speak. And yet, inside my armor, I squirmed a little at how familiar his words felt, as though they could have been coming from my own mouth, if I had been brave enough to speak them. Which, of course, I wasn't.

"It was my cowardice that kept me from your mother all those years until my death. It was my cowardice that kept me from getting to know the two of you once you came here. And it was my cowardice that kept me from saying a proper goodbye to you. Finvarra, as I have said, knew this about me. She knew I was avoiding this last moment. She also knew I would regret having avoided it. And so, she arranged this."

"But what is this? What's happening? How are you still here if she is gone?" Hannah asked.

"She is gone, isn't she?" I added. "It would be really difficult for her to stay. Durupinen don't often become ghosts, do they?" I had wondered for a long time after my mother died if I would turn one day to see her spirit walking alongside me. Karen had explained to me that Durupinen had a special protection that ran in their blood, a sort of immunity to the pull of the Gateway; otherwise their souls would have been torn from their bodies every time they performed a Crossing. But once a Durupinen had passed away, and her soul left her body, the need to Cross would be almost insurmountable. Only spirits like the Silent Child, who was so wildly desperate to remain behind so that her truth could be told, would be able to resist the pull of it.

"Finvarra encouraged me to say my goodbyes to you before it was too late. I assured her that I would, and yet even as I watched her fail, I delayed. I was in denial, I think, that her time was so short, but I also did not know what to say, or how to even begin. As the end grew near, I panicked, and sent a message to you, asking you to come. But this was perhaps the most cowardly act of all, for I thrust all responsibility, all onus onto the two of you, where it did not belong. I lied to myself, insisting that I was respecting you by giving you a choice, but really, I was avoiding having to make the choice myself. But I delayed too long. Finvarra passed and I had to pass with her."

"But you're here," Hannah said slowly.

"In her final days, Finvarra instructed that a Casting be placed upon her. I was not aware that she had done so until she died, and I was not immediately pulled with her."

"What was the Casting?" I asked in a hushed voice.

"It is called a Tether. Finvarra and I are still connected, but the Tether allows me to stay behind as long as she remains in the Aether. Even now she delays her own Crossing so that I can rectify this mistake. As always, she is more generous to me than I deserve," Carrick said. He could not tear his eyes from the specter of his boots.

Hannah and I looked at each other, and I saw the same blind panic I was feeling misting over her eyes, giving her a glazed and wild look.

"I... this is... how long do we have?" she managed to choke out.

"I do not know. Not long. A few minutes, maybe less. She cannot remain in the Aether indefinitely. No Casting we have is any match for the Gateway itself."

I stood there, frozen. My brain refused to function, except to scream, "How dare you!" over and over and over again against the insides of my skull. It was all I could do to stop those words from bursting involuntarily from my lips.

"So, I suppose, I should say—" Carrick began, but I could no longer contain the explosion.

"You suppose you should say? No. I don't want to hear it. I don't want to hear anything that you didn't have the guts to say in the time we had left!" I cried.

Hannah turned to stone beside me. I, meanwhile, could not stem the uncensored thoughts tumbling over each other to get out. "This time should be for us! For me, and for Hannah, to say all the things we want to say to you!"

Carrick seemed totally unfazed by my outburst. In fact, he seemed almost to be expecting it. This only made me angrier. "Then take it," he said quietly. "Take it. It's yours."

"I DON'T WANT IT!" I shouted, and tears joined the mass exodus from my body. "I don't want to be responsible for fucking this up, when I didn't even ask for it! How dare she, how dare she force us into this!"

"You don't have to say anything. No one is forcing you to—"

"But how do we live with ourselves if we say nothing? We have to say the right things! We have to express them just the right way! But how can we, when we don't even know what that is? We can't let the moment go by, but we can't make it count the way it needs to! No matter what, we will walk away from this feeling miserable and full of regret, because we didn't say something, or we said it the wrong way. You can't just spring this kind of goodbye on someone! You can't just say, 'Okay, real quick, just perfectly express the most complicated emotional fucking mess you've ever had to deal with, and please hurry, the door is closing.'"

"Jess..." Hannah murmured, but I ignored her.

"I hate you!" I cried. "I hate what you did to our mother! I hate you for never speaking up! I hate you for leaving us to drown in that mess! And I hate myself for hating you, because who hates their own father? And then I hate you again for making me feel that way!

179

There are so many levels of awful here that I can't get out from under them!"

"That's okay," Carrick said, and his voice shook. And in that little tremor, another crushing blow of guilt.

"I don't need you to tell me it's okay!" I yelled, and the yell crumbled into a sob. "I need to feel it for myself, and I can't! There's not enough time! I haven't had enough time to forgive you!"

I sank to the floor and let the tears overtake me. Hannah knelt beside me, laying her head on mine and stroking my back in a gentle, steady motion, her own silent tears trickling down into my hair. At last, the sobs slowed, and softened, and finally subsided. Carrick said nothing. He did not approach any closer. He just stood there, letting me cry myself out.

"Do you want me to go?" he asked, when I had quieted.

"No," I said. "Wait, don't… it's not all anger. You saved our lives from the Elemental. You watched over us from afar for a long time, and you protected us in what ways you could. I'm grateful for all of that. I need you to know that I… I will forgive you. I'm not there yet, and I don't know how long it will be, but I won't carry these feelings forever. That's the best I can do, and I'm sorry."

I looked up at Carrick, and there was actually the smallest of smiles on his face. "That," he murmured, "is far more than I ever had the hope to expect."

Hannah cleared her throat. We both looked at her.

"You loved her. I think, if you'd have the chance, you would have loved us. That's enough for me," she said in barely more than a whisper.

Carrick nodded his gratitude to her. "I have nothing but pride in my heart when I look at the two of you. At the women you are. There is so much of her in you, and so little of me. I thank God for that. You are better for it, and the world will be, as well."

Carrick's voice faded out for a moment, and his eyes widened. "I'm going. I can feel it."

"Tell her we're okay," I said suddenly, wildly. "Tell her I love her, and we have each other, and we're going to be fine."

Carrick's face spasmed with emotion. "I will do that. I promise you, if it is within my power, I will do that for you."

Hannah's hands had tightened on my shoulders. I could feel the pressure of her fingernails in my flesh. I looked up at her and saw er face was contorted. I watched as she struggled for a moment hen blurted out, "I forgive her. Tell her I forgive her. Please."

Carrick nodded. "Of course. As soon as I—"

His voice faded out, and his form dimmed into the shadows. For a moment, I could still see the shape of him, one hand raised in farewell, as though imprinted on the air.

But then I blinked, and the image faded. Our father was gone.

16

INTO THE WOODS

"**I** CAN'T BELIEVE I have to go do this."

I stood by the open door of one of the Caomhnóir's fleet of sleek, black SUVs, my backpack by my feet.

"I know. But the quicker you get it over with, the sooner you'll be back," Hannah said, giving my shoulder a squeeze.

It had been less than forty-eight hours since the black banners had flown from the towers of Fairhaven, and we had to face saying goodbye to our father. It had been less than twenty-four hours since we all stood in the central courtyard, candles aloft, and watched Finvarra's silk-draped body laid to rest in the Tomb of Priestesses that lay concealed beneath the Geatgrima's ancient stone dais. The awful truth of it all still hung like a fog over the castle, and yet life was grinding back into motion. Hannah had to attend her very first meeting of the Council, at which they would discuss the election of the new High Priestess, and I had to reluctantly slip back into my role as a Tracker, and attend Irina's trial at the Traveler camp.

"Are you sure you're going to be all right? Maybe I can talk to Catriona and see if we can delay—"

Hannah was already shaking her head. "I will be fine."

"You would say that even if you were the furthest you've ever been from fine," I pointed out.

"She would, but I wouldn't," Milo said, floating around the front of the car and coming to rest at Hannah's side. "I'll be right here with her, raining Milo-style destruction down on anyone who dares give her a moment's disquiet while you're gone."

"Promise?" I muttered.

"Spirit Guide's honor," he said, crossing his heart with a swoop of his finger.

"Jess, we've got to get a move on, or we'll be late for our escort," Finn said stiffly, putting on a show of indifference for the Caomhnóir by the gates.

"Okay, okay," I said grouchily. I pulled Hannah into a one-armed hug. "Good luck."

"You, too," she said.

"I'm going to need more than luck," I said under my breath as I slid into the car, slamming the door shut behind me.

Several hours later, Finn and I stood together in the bitter cold on the outskirts of a deep patch of woods. A hundred yards behind us, our SUV was pulled off the road and out of sight into a clump of bushes.

"We've already been to the camp. Is this really necessary?" I complained.

"This is where they told us to wait," Finn replied. Though his voice was soft, it sounded like a trumpet in the utter stillness of the snow-blanketed countryside. We were both bouncing up and down on the balls of our feet, though he was doing it to cope with the tension, whereas I was doing it to keep my blood flowing so I didn't freeze to death.

"I know. It's just, why the secrecy? They know they can trust us already," I said through slightly chattering teeth.

Finn chuckled. "The Travelers trust no one outside their clans. It doesn't matter who you are or what you've done for them in the past; unless you have Traveler blood, you are assumed the enemy."

"The enemy? That's a bit over-the-top, don't you think?" I asked.

Finn shrugged. "Think what you like. But as Caomhnóir we were taught to be cautious in our dealings with the Traveler Clans. They will choose blood over all else, no matter what, and betrayal of blood is unforgivable."

I mulled his words over as we stared into the dark, silent edge of the woods. Finn could definitely err on the side of cynicism, but he knew much more about Durupinen culture than I did, having been raised in the heart of it. If what he said of Traveler culture was true, that did not bode well for Irina. Her betrayal would surely be considered one of blood, both of family and of calling. If she were found guilty... a shiver ran through me that had nothing to do with the cold.

"Here they come at last," Finn said, pointing into the trees.

Several orange lights were bouncing toward us, looking at first like the flitting lights of fireflies. As they got closer, they grew and resolved into the dancing flames of three torches, held aloft by three hulking young Caomhnóir with olive complexions and dark hair. Their voices drifted out to us, raucous and, unless I was mistaken, a bit intoxicated.

By the time they reached us, Finn's expression had hardened from wary to stony.

"You're late," he said, the moment the three Caomhnóir came to a stop in front of us.

"Did you have somewhere else you needed to be, Northerner?" the Caomhnóir in the middle asked, almost jeeringly. He was by far the biggest of the three, barrel-chested and thick-necked.

"Other than freezing on the edge of the woods, you mean? Yes, we were meant to have been greeted by the High Priestess at her tent ten minutes ago," Finn said dryly.

Another of the Caomhnóir, taller and ganglier than the first, laughed. My nose, well-acquainted with the scent of booze on breath, wrinkled in distaste at the sharp smell that his laughter expelled at me. "You're lucky anyone bothered to come for you at all," he sneered. "More trouble than you're worth, you Settlers."

"Charming," Finn said dryly. "What a delightful welcoming committee."

"You know full bloody well we don't welcome anyone here," the third Caomhnóir spat. His expression was more hostile than the other two, totally devoid of humor. His hair was closely cropped to his head, unusual for a Traveler male. "Every outsider here is an unnecessary threat to our safety and security."

"Right, then. Cheers," Finn said blandly. "Lead on."

At first, it looked as though the Traveler Caomhnóir were disappointed for some reason. One of them even opened his mouth again, looking combative, but the short-haired one jabbed him in the ribs with his elbow and jerked his head back toward the forest.

We followed them at a distance, having no desire to interact with such hostile hosts. Soon they were several yards ahead of us, and I felt safe talking to Finn without being overheard.

"What the hell is their problem?" I muttered, the crunching sound of the frozen leaves and twigs masking our conversation from the Caomhnóir, who in any case now seemed to be ignoring us, teasing and shoving each other around as they walked. "They weren't like this the last time we were here."

Finn smirked at me and raised his eyebrows as if to say, "I told you so," but instead said, "We were with Annabelle the last time we were here. And even then, they were extremely wary about letting us enter the camp. You could hardly have called them welcoming."

"I know, but they weren't so..." I gestured ahead at the Caomhnóir, searching for the right word.

"Rude? Combative?"

"I was going to say drunken frat boy, but yeah, that works," I murmured.

"They were also scared of you the last time we were here," Finn pointed out. "Last time, you were at the center of the Prophecy. Their prejudice was somewhat tempered by their fear. Now that they know you're just an average Durupinen again, well," he shrugged dismissively.

"Oh, thanks very much," I said coolly.

Finn grinned. "You know what I mean. Anyway, I intend to have a word about them with Dragos. This is entirely unprofessional. We are here on official clan business, at the request of the Traveler Council, no less. They ought to know and respect the difference."

We fell into silence as we walked, and my mind, ill-at-ease from the less-than-warm welcome, thought back to our first arrival here, and then, onto Annabelle. Hearing Finn speak her name had caused a cold, clammy feeling in my stomach, like I had swallowed a block of ice that was just sitting in there now, chilling me from the inside. I hadn't heard Annabelle's voice since my frantic late-night phone call, though I had found excuses to text or email her almost every day since. I'd also been checking her social media accounts multiple times a day like a creepy stalker. She posted her daily horoscopes on her shop's page every morning without fail, and updated her customers with inventory news regularly. She even posted a selfie with some friends who were watching a band play at a local bar the previous night. Everything seemed... completely normal. So normal, in fact, that I had started to doubt everything that Fiona had told me about being a Seer. And yet, I couldn't shake the feeling—stronger, now that I was walking into the heart of her heritage—that my sketch was still on a winding, dimly lit path to fruition, unless I could figure out its meaning.

The trees began to thin, and the sultry scent of campfire smoke wafted out to meet us like beckoning fingers. Another sensation greeted us, too: the unmistakable tingle of spirit energy, thick in the air like swarming bees. Just like at Fairhaven, the concentrated presence of multiple Gateways caused spirits in the area to congregate like moths to a flame.

A single battered tent stood on the outskirts of the clearing. Beyond it, I could see the collections of other dwellings, each able, at short notice, to be picked up and relocated should the Travelers so choose. It was hard to tell—because it was dim and the grove looked very different in the winter time—but I thought we might have been in a different part of the forest than we had been three years previously.

"Oy! Andrei!" the tall gangly Caomhnóir called sharply.

A bleary-eyed and unshaven old Caomhnóir poked his head out of the tent, his expression cantankerous.

"What are you on about?" he growled, squinting as though even the half-light hurt his eyes, one of which was hidden under a heavy bandage. I noticed bandages around his left arm and peeking out from under the left side of his misbuttoned flannel shirt.

"You're supposed to be guarding the northern crossing point, you useless parasite," the Caomhnóir spat in disgust. "What good are you if you can't even stay sober for a four-hour shift?"

Andrei muttered something that contained the words "spoiled children," but did not address the Caomhnóir directly. He pulled a battered book out of the depths of the tent with his good hand and scribbled something into it with the stump of a pencil.

"This the Northern Walker and her guardian?" he grumbled, slurring the last word ever so slightly as he jabbed the pencil stub in my direction.

"That's right. Now splash some water on that mug and pull yourself together before I report you to Dragos," the short-haired Caomhnóir growled.

Andrei pulled into the tent like a curmudgeonly turtle back into his shell and our escorts stalked past. I could still see the old man's eyes shining in the dark interior of the tent, following us as we passed.

"Why was Andrei all bandaged like that?" I asked their indifferent backs. "What happened to him?"

"His own incompetence happened to him, nothing more," the burly Caomhnóir replied without even glancing over his shoulder. "Good for nothing but mopping up spilled liquor, that one."

"Oh what, because you're so sober?" I shot back, firing up. "I've been to frat houses that smell less like beer than the three of you."

The gangly one turned, frowning perplexedly. "Frat houses?"

I rolled my eyes. "It's a Northerner thing," I said.

"The difference is that we can hold our liquor," the short-haired Caomhnóir said. "Andrei is little better than a sponge, and half as useful."

Finn gave me a warning look, so I bit back my retort. Perhaps I was more defensive than most when I heard people dragging someone with a drinking problem, having spent the better part of my childhood cleaning up after my mother, whose self-medication of choice dwelled at the bottom of a cheap bottle of chardonnay, but that wasn't the only reason I was angry. I knew Andrei—not well, it was true—but I'd met him three years ago, dozing outside of Irina's wagon. He'd not only been charged with guarding her; he was also her nephew. If I'd had to watch one of my own family members endure what Irina had suffered, and then been required to help enforce it, I would probably have drunk myself into a stupor, too.

We followed them to the left, down a path that seemed to lead away from the rest of the encampment. This path led to the lavish tent where Ileana, the High Priestess of the Traveler Clans, resided. I could feel my heart starting to race as the tent loomed out of the darkness, tendrils of smoke unfurling from its roof like kite tails.

Dragos met us at the entrance of the tent, arms folded across his chest like bolts barring a door.

"You're late," Dragos barked. I opened my mouth to argue that we had arrived on time, but closed it again when I saw he was looking not at us, but at the three young men who had escorted us.

"These Northerners are slow walkers," the tall one replied, barely able to keep his face straight, particularly when the burly one beside him snorted with laughter.

"Do not blame the visitors for your shortcomings, Ruslo," Dragos snapped at him. "Now all of you, make yourselves useful at the bonfire." All three of the Caomhnóir jogged off back down the path, roaring with laughter and trying to shove each other into snowbanks.

"Ileana would like to welcome you to the camp," Dragos said stiffly to me, as the laughter died away. "You may go inside. I will find someone to bring you to your accommodations when the High Priestess dismisses you." He turned to Finn. "I would like to fill you in on security procedures while you are here. If you would follow me, please."

Finn hesitated. He turned to me, but I answered the question before he could form it. "I will be perfectly fine here. Do what you need to do."

Finn nodded curtly, partly in show of the cold distant relationship we were supposed to be maintaining, and partly because I knew he wasn't happy about leaving me there on my own. He glanced back at me once before turning and following Dragos down the path the other Caomhnóir had followed.

My heart suddenly began to drum inside my chest as I stepped through the tent flaps. The interior of the tent was exactly how I remembered it, full of Durupinen relics and old, antique furniture jumbled together to give the appearance of having walked into a smuggler's den of treasures. And there, lounging casually on her great carved throne . . .

"High Priestess," I said, bowing my head in deference.

"And here she is at last," Ileana replied. Her wild hair was knotted back from her weathered old face in a scarf that rattled with a fringe of gold coins. "I thought, when you left this place a smoking ruin, that we would never see you again, at least not alive. But here you are."

"Here I am," I said stiffly, unsure how to respond to her words, which seemed to contain some sort of accusation.

"Couldn't believe my ears when I heard you'd actually done it," Ileana went on. She clucked her tongue and held out her arm. With a startling flutter of shining black wings, a one-eyed raven swooped down from the shadowy eaves of the tent and came to rest on her forearm. I'd released the very same raven from its cage when the Necromancers attacked. Evidently it saw fit to return to its mistress rather than make a permanent bid for freedom. Ileana cracked a peanut open with her teeth, spat the shell out on the floor, and held the nut out for the bird, who snapped it up greedily. "Thought you'd Walk yourself right into oblivion and leave us all to the mercy of the Wraiths," she chuckled. "But you surprised us all, including yourself, I daresay."

I just nodded, since I was pretty sure I was being insulted.

"There are many," she went on, nudging the bird with her finger so that he hopped up onto her shoulder instead, "that consider you a bit of a bad omen, Jessica."

"Yeah, I get a bit of that back at Fairhaven, too," I said, attempting a smile. "Must be this raincloud that keeps following me around."

Ileana did not acknowledge the joke. "We appreciate what you did for the Durupinen, make no mistake. But the pall of the Prophecy doesn't wash off so easy."

"Is this how you welcome all your guests?" I asked dryly. "Seriously, the hospitality is overwhelming."

"I'm trying to warn you to keep your head down while you're here," Ileana said, cracking another nut and tossing it into her own mouth.

"I'm here at your request," I said. "Believe me, I wasn't fishing for an invitation. You ordered me here, and that's the only reason I've come."

"And there are many who have criticized my decision to summon you," Ileana snapped. "But it seems that the stories of the two Walkers are too closely intertwined to examine one without including the other."

I swallowed back a spasm of fear. It was almost as if she knew.

"Would you like me to leave then?"

"I would like you to be on your guard."

"I am happy to provide my testimony and get out of here as quickly as I can," I said after a moment's awkward silence.

"And we thank you for your cooperation in this process," Ileana said with a sardonic grin. "Welcome back."

I laughed. "Am I dismissed?"

"You are, indeed," Ileana said, stroking the raven's feathers with the tip of one arthritic finger. "Dragos will inform you when we are ready for your testimony before the Traveler Council."

"Thank you," I said curtly, and turned to exit the tent.

I'd barely had a moment to take a deep breath of cold air when a soft, familiar voice called out, "Well, well, well, if it isn't the Northern Girl."

I smiled before I had even turned. "Well, well, well," I replied. "If it isn't the keeper of the world's weirdest mobile library."

Flavia walked toward me, a slow grin blooming across her face. Her hair was shaved on one side, and tousled over one eye in shades of turquoise and green. A tiny silver nose ring glittered in the side of her nose like a dewdrop on grass, and her wide brown eyes were framed by dark, rectangular glasses. A new tattoo peaked up from the neckline of her tattered red sweater; I could just make out the curve of several black feathers inked over her collarbone. I hadn't seen her in over three years, since the night the Necromancers attacked the Traveler camp. It had been one of the most terrifying nights of my life—and of hers too, I imagine. In a tearful, panicked burst of genius, she had smeared me in a dead Traveler's blood and begged me to Walk to save my own life. If I hadn't done as she'd urged... well, I tried not to think about it too much. I already spent way more time dwelling on the finer points of mortality than any relatively young and healthy person should.

Flavia closed the last few steps between us and enclosed me in a warm hug. "Welcome back. How have you been?" she asked me.

"I'm fine," I said, knowing full well it was a bullshit answer. No reason to unload on the poor girl the moment I saw her. "How is Scribe life?"

Flavia rolled her eyes. "A thrill a minute, just how I like it," she said. "Has anyone showed you to your wagon yet?"

"Oh, uh," I looked back over my shoulder. "Finn went to check in with Dragos. They were supposed to send someone to—"

Flavia was already shaking her head. "Don't hold your breath. Traveler Caomhnóir aren't exactly renowned for their reliability. They'll start sparring and drinking and forget all about you."

"Wow, really?" I asked, eyebrows raised. "We can hardly get rid of ours at Fairhaven."

Flavia grinned again and stooped over to scoop my backpack off the grass where I'd dropped it when I'd entered the tent. "Come on. I'll show you where you're staying."

We wandered through the encampment, a semi-permanent little settlement of colorful tents and old wooden wagons, as though a traveling sideshow circus had dropped anchor or else sprung up from the ground like mushrooms amongst the copses of ancient trees. Each cluster of dwellings was connected to those around it by well-worn footpaths, the grass and moss trodden away by scurrying feet. On all sides, smoke blossomed out of tin chimney stacks and swirled up from cooking fires crackling away in stone-circled firepits and old, cracked chimeneas. Here and there, a bedraggled horse nibbled at the patches of grass around its feet and barefoot children darted in and out of the shadows, their laughter as sudden and bright as the patches of sunlight that filtered down through the trees. Though I'd been unbearably cold while waiting on the outskirts of the forest, here amidst the campfires it felt unseasonably warm, and I found myself wishing I'd dispensed with the parka.

"I wasn't sure if you'd still be here," I said to Flavia as we walked.

"I wouldn't be, if I had the choice," Flavia said over her shoulder. "I finished my PhD in linguistics last year, but times are hard for an academic without university connections. I'm hoping some college takes pity on me soon so that I can finally get out on my own. Oh, don't tell anyone I said that," she added, stopping short and turning to look at me, looking slightly alarmed. "Our Council doesn't take kindly to deserters."

"Deserters?" I asked incredulously. "Isn't that a little harsh? You'll still be a Durupinen after all, won't you?"

"Not by Traveler standards," Flavia said. "I'd be an outcast."

"But," I said, sputtering. "Do they really expect you to just... stay in the woods your entire life? I mean," I grimaced. "Sorry, that sounded really rude."

"It's fine. I'm not offended," Flavia said gently. "Not many outsiders can wrap their heads around how we live. Most of the other clans have integrated into modern society, but the Traveler Clans remain an utter anachronism. We're a much smaller band of clans. As nomads, we've always had to band together for protection, and over the years it has built a rather xenophobic culture. Breaking away from the encampment for more than a short time is considered a great betrayal of our way of life. We stick together like a pack, normally."

"So, how did you go to school, then?"

"It wasn't easy," Flavia admitted. "I had to present my case before the Council, proving how the degree would help my work as a Scribe. And it will!" she said defensively. "I still want to do Scribe work. I still remain committed to our clans, but there is so much more out there to study, and learn, and I just..." she gestured helplessly around the clearing.

"You don't have to convince me," I said. "I would have tied one of those horses to a wagon and ridden out of here a long time ago if it were me."

Flavia laughed into the back of her hand. "Those horses wouldn't get you far. They're old, spoiled, and fat. God forbid we ever have to move this encampment more than a mile or two. We'll be carrying those horses on our backs rather than the other way around."

We followed the footpath around the back of a silver Airstream trailer that looked like a rusty zeppelin on wheels and Flavia stopped, pointing ahead of us. "Just over here," she said. It was a wooden wagon just like the one I'd stayed in the last time I'd been here, except this one had been painted bright blue with gold trim and was outfitted with just one set of bunks instead of two. Two green glass lanterns, shaped like stars, swung gently on gold chains on either side of the Dutch doors.

"It's been all set up for you," Flavia said. "I saw Andrei loading up the wood stove earlier today. You should be nice and warm in here."

With the unmistakable feeling that I was stepping over some invisible threshold into one of the Grimm Brothers' imaginations, I followed Flavia inside.

Flavia was right; the little wagon was downright toasty. She sat on a little wooden bench with her arms around her knees, watching me as I disgorged the contents of my bag into the built-in wooden drawers beneath the sleeping loft at the far end. I tried to smooth them out, but as I had shoved them so unceremoniously into the bag to begin with, I closed the drawer on a hopelessly wrinkled jumble. Oh, well. Who was I afraid was going to judge my wardrobe in the middle of the woods? I opened a few of the cabinets and found chipped porcelain plates and bowls, a few Mason jars, some tarnished silverware, a wrought iron kettle, and some ancient tins of oatmeal, sugar, and tea.

"You don't need to worry about cooking," Flavia said. "Everyone just meets at the bonfire at the center of the encampment to eat. It's like a potluck three times a day."

I nodded. "As long as there's coffee, I'll be fine."

"A cauldron full of it. Very black and very strong," Flavia promised.

"Music to my ears," I replied. I climbed up onto the bed and sighed. "So."

"So?"

"Irina."

Flavia's smile faded. A furrow appeared between her eyebrows. "Yes."

"What can you tell me? How is she?"

Flavia shook her head. "It's been terrible. They shut her back up in her wagon when the Trackers brought her home. But she's... not taking it well."

193

"I could have figured that much out for myself. Can you be a little more specific?" I asked.

Flavia leaned forward and spoke just above a whisper, as though saying the words more quietly would protect us from their horror. "The first night she was back she set the wagon on fire."

I gasped. "What? How? I thought they kept her chained up so she couldn't hurt herself?"

Flavia grimaced. "It was Andrei. He fell asleep with that blasted pipe hanging out of his mouth, and somehow she managed to get ahold of it and drop it in the hay."

"We saw Andrei on the way in. Is that why he's all bandaged up?" It wasn't hard to imagine him landing himself in a compromising position like falling asleep with a lit pipe in his mouth.

"Yes," Flavia said. "His injuries were fairly superficial, but Irina was burned very badly. They barely managed to pull her from the flames, and as soon as they did, she attempted to Walk. They had to perform an emergency Caging and then got permission to heal her body with Leeching."

"Jesus," I muttered, horrified. "Was she trying to kill herself, or just get out of the boundaries of the Castings so she could Walk?"

Flavia shook her head sadly. "She wouldn't say, but does it matter? Either way she would have had a chance of escape."

A white-hot anger flashed through me so intensely that, for a moment, my vision actually went dark. "What the hell is wrong with them? Don't they realize that the only humane thing to do is to release her? Whether they want to admit it or not, every minute she spends in that body is cruel and unusual punishment. If she's willing to burn herself alive rather than stay inside that body, why don't they just let her go?"

Flavia's hands jerked upward in a helpless gesture. "Somewhere in this mess she stopped being a person to them and started being something that needed to be tamed into submission. They fear she will wreak havoc upon them when she's free."

"Is she well enough to stand trial?" I asked through gritted teeth.

Flavia nodded. "They healed her body, if that's what you mean. But she remains as volatile and desperate as ever in her mind."

"What do you think they'll do to her?" I asked quietly. "Do you think she stands a chance of being freed?"

Flavia bit her lip. "I won't venture to say. But they've gone to great pains to recapture and contain her. I find it hard to believe they will simply let her go. When she escaped, she confirmed all their worst fears. Is it really true? Did she attempt to take control of a Geatgrima in America? That's the rumor around the camp."

"Yeah, it's true," I said.

"Then I fear her fate will be one of confinement," Flavia said. "It is not in the culture of the Traveler Clans to forgive such base betrayal."

"But," I sputtered incredulously, "surely they can understand why she did it!"

"Logically, I'm sure they can. But logic matters little in matters of clan loyalty. I assure you, the stereotype of gypsy passion is far from exaggerated," Flavia said.

A sharp rap sounded on the bottom half of the Dutch door. Finn stood framed in the opening, his jaw set and tense. "Apologies for the interruption."

"Not at all," Flavia said, standing up at once. "I was just helping to get Jessica settled. I'll leave you both to it. Dinner around the bonfire in about two hours, if you're hungry."

"We'll see you there," I assured her. "And Flavia?"

"Yes?"

"Ileana told me that many of the Travelers wouldn't want me here, because they would see my presence as a bad omen. So, I guess, thanks for not running screaming when you saw me."

"I'm not the running and screaming type, usually," she said with a laugh. Then she pushed her glasses back up the bridge of her nose, and left.

"What are you looking so delighted about?" I inquired of Finn's stony expression.

"The Caomhnóir operation here is... less than ideal," he said, with an air of great restraint.

"Would you care to elaborate?" I asked.

"No," he said shortly. "Suffice it to say that I'm not in the least surprised that the Necromancers were able to stage their attack so successfully three years ago. Utter incompetence in the ranks, and they just shrug it off."

I tried not to smile. "I suppose you'll just have to protect everyone, then," I said.

Finn glared at me. "I bloody well may have to. No shift changes, no reports system to speak of, no accountability. What a farce."

"They seemed on top of their game the last time we were here," I said. "Well, that Andrei was clearly a weak link, but otherwise they seemed competent." And I told him what Flavia had divulged about Andrei and the pipe.

"That is precisely what I'm talking about!" Finn cried. "That man should never have been allowed to guard anything, let alone a dangerous prisoner with a penchant for violent escapes! He ought to have been relieved of duty long ago, when his commitment to remaining perpetually pissed outstripped his commitment to protecting his clan." He was so worked up that specks of spit were flying from his mouth like a Shakespearean actor in the throes of a soliloquy. He took a deep breath to calm himself. "I don't mean to paint every one of them with the same brush, mind you. There are a few who take their duty seriously. Dragos, for one, is clearly more than competent, but I would expect little else from the Caomhnóir assigned to the High Priestess. But the younger crop are a rebellious lot. All bluster and no discipline, which is a dangerous combination. They need a semester at Fairhaven to whip them into shape."

"Little whippersnappers," I said, then laughed as he scowled at me. "Come on, Finn, lighten up. Who cares if the Traveler Caomhnóir are a mess? It's not your problem! We'll be out of here in a few days."

"I don't like the idea of any Durupinen saddled with unreliable protection, whether they're my problem or not," Finn said, his scowl deepening at the sound of my laughter. "I have half a mind to report them to the International Grand Council, though, of course, they're notorious for their inaction in regional matters. There's a reason the Caomhnóir exist, you know, and it's not simply to cramp your style."

My smile faded. "I know that. I'm sorry, Finn. I was just trying to lighten the mood."

Finn sighed, and sagged a bit. "I'm sorry, too. I hate being back here. It's forcing me to relive memories I would much rather forget."

"I don't like it very much myself," I admitted. I reached out and took his hand.

"You do realize that just a few yards from here is the spot I found you and thought you were..." he couldn't even finish the sentence, choking on the last word and swallowing it back.

"I know," I said. "But I wasn't. Try not to think about it."

He nodded, but still looked troubled.

I stepped in close to him and caressed his cheek with my hand. "It was also the first place we ever did this." And I kissed him gently.

I felt his body relax, felt him lean into the kiss, felt his lips tremble before pulling away to lean his forehead against mine. "There is that," he said with a soft chuckle.

The smell of him, the taste of his lips, left me dizzy. Although we were alone in the wagon, with the shades drawn, I knew it wasn't safe to get carried away here, surrounded by Durupinen we could not trust. Reluctantly, I stepped away from him and sat down on the bench Flavia had just vacated.

"Were you able to find out any more about the trial?" I asked, in an effort to change the subject.

Finn shook his head as though to clear it, and when he spoke again, he sounded like his usual brisk self. "The Traveler Council has been hearing witnesses and evidence during the last week. So far, there have been three days of testimony pertaining to Irina's alleged crimes leading up to the events at Whispering Seraph. Your testimony will conclude the evidentiary portion of the trial. Then the Court can choose to hear character witnesses."

"What are character witnesses?" I asked.

"They give their opinion about the defendant. So, for example, if they know from experience that the accused is violent, or kind, or what have you. They provide their observations so that the Council has a clearer picture as to what kind of person the accused really is. It is meant to sway them, one way or the other, in the sentencing process. The Council will decide on innocence or guilt by simple majority, and will recommend a sentence to the High Priestess, but it will ultimately be up to Ileana how and if Irina is punished."

I bit my lip. "So, it comes down to Ileana's mercy?"

"Or lack thereof, yes," Finn said grimly.

We lapsed into silence, each consumed by our own thoughts about what was to come. I had no idea if Ileana would be disposed to forgive Irina. She was certainly possessed of the unpredictable, mercurial nature that seemed a hallmark of the Traveler Clans, and I did not think she would take Irina's betrayal lightly.

One of the first things I needed to do, before the trial began, was to talk to Irina. I had no idea how I would pull it off; it didn't seem likely that she'd be allowed to have visitors, not when she was treating bystanders like kindling, but there had to be a way to let her know I was here. I didn't want the first time she saw me to be sitting on a witness stand, perhaps unintentionally sealing her fate with my account of her actions at Whispering Seraph. I needed her to know that I hadn't forgotten my promise, that I was here to help her... even if I still had no clue how I was going to do it.

I also needed to decide if I was going to tell Finn. Keeping my promise to Irina would be difficult enough without Finn hovering over me, weighing the dangers of every decision, but then his help, if he were actually on board, could be invaluable. Only Milo knew about my promise to free Irina. I hadn't even told Hannah, which I knew was shitty of me, because she deserved to know, but I couldn't bear the idea of adding any more stress to her life than she already had to deal with as the newest, most controversial member of the Council. She had her whole life to sort out: school, work, moving to a new country, not to mention the onerous responsibilities of her new position. She didn't need to know that I was entering into pacts with an unpredictable, half-mad woman who would betray me in a moment if it meant her own freedom.

Nor did I need to deliver on this pact, I told myself repeatedly, in my most reasonable, grown-up, logical voice. I could walk away from this. I could do my utmost to free Irina with my testimony. I could beg on bended knee before the Traveler Council to let her go, to show her mercy. But if that didn't work, I was under no further obligation to her.

I flopped down onto the bunk and sighed to myself. *Silly, Jess. You know you never listen to that voice.*

Ever.

17

SIREN SONG

A T FIRST, THE SINGING did not wake me.

It wound itself into the tendrils of a dark and terrifying dream, issuing first from the mouth of my own sister, then from the mouth of the Silent Child—silent no more—then from the gaping twin mouths of the Elemental, when it had taken the form of two girls on the night of the fulfillment of the Prophecy.

When I did finally wake from the dream, drenched in an icy sweat and gasping for air, the singing continued. At first, as I attempted to slow my galloping heart rate and calm my heaving breaths, I thought the singing was simply reverberating in my head, the echoing aftermath of a nightmare. Surely it would fade in a few moments, leaving me in the silent embrace of the winter woods, and I would drift back off into a deep and—please God—dreamless sleep.

But it did not fade. The haunting voice continued to drift into my wagon on the current of the frigid night air, sending shivers down my spine and a cold shaft of fear through my heart. An instinctive warning was nudging its icy little fingers into my ribs.

This song was dangerous.

"Finn? Do you hear that?" I whispered in a voice still cracked with sleep.

No answer. I squinted across into Finn's bunk, but he was not in it. The covers had been thrown back. I knew he wasn't in the wagon; it was much too small to hide anyone, and much too cramped for him not to have heard my call, even if he'd been just outside. I glanced over at the wood stove, the only source of heat and light in the room, and saw that the little curved door had been left open. There was nothing but embers, pulsing with a red glow, inside the belly of the stove, and no logs left in the basket beside it. Before I had time to panic about where he might have gone, I knew.

Finn had gone to get us more firewood so that we wouldn't freeze to death in the night.

Even as I breathed a sigh of relief at this realization, my ear was drawn, again, to the song. I slid out of my bed, dragging my thick blanket with me as I shuffled across the floorboards to the door. I unlatched the two halves and swung open the top one. The camp was entirely still, almost perfectly silent, except for that voice.

I couldn't understand the words; it was in a language I did not recognize, though I hazarded a guess that it was an Eastern European dialect. This particular band of Travelers were at least partly Romanian—this much I knew from Annabelle. The song itself was haunting, a sort of lullaby that lured the listener on the lilts of a melancholy, minor key that intrigued the heart as much as it shattered it. I couldn't have stopped listening to it if I'd wanted to, so alluring was the sound.

Had I been thinking logically, I never would have done what I did next, but the song eviscerated logic. I pulled the blanket more tightly around me, slid my feet into my slippers, and pushed open the bottom half of the door. I stumbled trying to descend the wooden steps, but caught myself before I fell flat into the frosty grass. Regaining my balance, I shuffled off down the path, snatching a lantern from a post beside our wagon to light my way.

On all sides, wagons and tents loomed up out of the darkness. Their stillness disturbed me. Why was no one else awake? Why was no one else following the call of this song, seductive as the call of land for a sea-weary sailor? Surely other people could hear it?

Disturbed, I considered two possible explanations. The first was that I was dreaming, though the bone-deep chill of the night air made this one seem unlikely. The second was that I—and only I—could hear the song. Was it possible the song was just for me?

This thought, rather than pulling me up short, acted as a bizarre sort of stimulant, propelling me up the pathway even more eagerly. Was there something I needed to know? Was some spirit trying to send me a message? My fear and doubt about my role here was so all-consuming that even a creepy, middle-of-the-night ballad was welcome if it could help me figure out what the hell I was supposed to do.

I was so eager to arrive at the source of the song that I didn't take stock of my surroundings, didn't stop to wonder if I was headed in a direction I had traversed before. If I had, I might have realized sooner where I was headed. Instead, I tripped out into the tiny clearing and felt my heart judder to a stop at the sight of the wagon before me.

Old and decrepit. Covered in runes. A wagon turned prison for the dangerous woman inside.

Irina.

The song was issuing from the wagon, though I could not see the singer. She was hidden somewhere in the shadowy recesses of the wagon's rounded wooden belly, but her voice was free, drifting through the clearing like a bird coasting on a breeze. Now that I knew who was singing, I wondered how I didn't know it from the very first note. Who else could weave a musical web of such profound sadness, for who in this wide world had suffered as she did now?

I had just decided to take a few steps closer when a muffled crashing sound sent me stumbling back into the cover of shrubs. A second figure had barreled into the clearing even less gracefully than I had done and landed sprawled in the powdery snow so that it rose up around him like a cloud of sparkling dust. It took a few moments of watching him curse as he untangled his gangling arms and legs before I recognized him: it was the tall lanky Caomhnóir who had led us to the camp, the one Dragos had called Ruslo.

Ruslo brushed the snow from his pant legs and then straightened up, staring in a mix of fear and wonder at the wagon before him. I opened my mouth to call to him, but then a movement in the darkened mouth of the wagon caught my eye, and I turned to see what he was gaping at.

Irina stood framed like a goddess immortalized on canvas by a Renaissance master. Her hair, a tousled, feral halo of curls, seemed to float around her face. She was stark naked save for the shackles around her ankles. The pale, moonlit curves of her body were made all the more mysterious by the many runes that had been inked onto them. She moved with a sinuous fluidity, a seductive primality more alluring than anything I had ever seen. Her lips caressed each word of the song that was issuing from her mouth, and her hips swayed to the sultry rhythm of it.

The vision of her was nearly enough to draw me from my hiding place, but it was Ruslo who shuffled forward, mouth agape, toward the wagon. The sound of his clumsy footsteps snapped me back to reality, and to the danger of what we had both stumbled upon.

"Ruslo!" I called, but almost no sound came out. I cleared my throat and tried again. "Ruslo! Don't!"

Something was wrong with the air. The sound of my voice was muffled, as though I had shouted the words into a pillow rather than into the open space of the clearing. Ruslo did not seem to have even heard me. I took a deep breath and tried again. "Ruslo! Don't go near her! She's dangerous!"

He did not even turn. My words fell uselessly at my own feet. My heart sped up. The idiot was drifting right to her, a storm-tossed ship guided by Irina's siren call, and he did not even see that he was about to be dashed to pieces on the rocks.

"Ruslo! RUSLO! Come back here!" I flung the blanket off my shoulders and scrambled to my feet, determined to catch him and drag him back. But I'd only taken a few steps when I ran smack into something solid and was knocked to the ground again. Dazedly, I shook my head and stared around. I couldn't understand what I'd hit. Only an open stretch of clearing lay before me. I stood up, wincing at the pain in my hip; I'd landed hard on a tree root sticking out of the ground. Moving cautiously this time, I put my hands out in front of me and walked slowly forward. Within seconds, my hands met with an invisible barrier, as though Irina's clearing existed on the other side of a glass wall. I pressed. I prodded. I reached out a fist and pounded as hard as I could. It made no sound. It felt like air that had been turned solid. I jogged first to the left, and then to the right, hands extended, probing for a weak spot, an end to the obstruction, but I could not find one. I could not move beyond it, but what *was* it? And why was Ruslo able to get through it, while I was stranded like a helpless spectator on the other side?

Ruslo.

I looked up and saw to my horror that he was now only a few yards from Irina's wagon. In desperation, though I knew it was useless, I flung my shoulder against the barrier over and over again, shouting so loudly that my voice cracked with the effort.

"Ruslo, no! Don't listen to her! Get out of there! You're not safe!" I shrieked.

An eerie silence met my words. Irina had stopped singing, though she made no sign that she had heard me. She draped herself in the doorway of the wagon, and she was cocking her finger invitingly at Ruslo, who stood in the grass before her.

"You've followed my song. Now taste of the pleasure it promised," she cooed.

Ruslo shook his head slightly, as though the end of the song had brought him, at least partially, to his senses. "What pleasure can a man have from you, you crazy old witch?" he said, though his voice shook with barely suppressed desire.

Irina laughed, and even the laugh sounded like a seduction. "Old, am I? My soul may be old, Guardian, but this body is young and supple. See for yourself." She turned slowly on the spot, and Ruslo seemed to shiver.

"So, I come in there with you and you light me on fire? I saw what you did to Andrei," he said, crossing his arms defiantly.

Irina threw back her head and laughed. The sound crackled with raw desire. "That decrepit old man? You truly believe that I could overpower a strong young man like you? Do you truly believe you could not have your way with this body, to bend it to your will?"

Ruslo shifted nervously. He licked his lips. "Of course, I could, but that's not the point. You want to attack me. You want to attack everyone. That's why they put you out here." His voice was slurred slightly; he had obviously been drinking again. Irina heard it too and smiled; it was almost as though she knew her prey was that much weaker, that much more vulnerable to attack.

Irina slunk another step closer to the edge of the wagon, and Ruslo took another involuntary step toward her. "They put me here because they fear me. They are weak. Cowards. But not you. You follow a song filled with danger. You face down the monster in her lair, don't you, Guardian? You take what you want. And you want this body. I can see it in your eyes."

I watched, paralyzed with panic. Ruslo's feeble resistance was cracking. I mean, hell, *I* half-wanted to throw myself into the wagon. There was something beyond natural allure at work here, of that I was damn certain. Was there a Casting that could make a Durupinen irresistible?

I didn't know what to do. Should I run back to the camp for help? It would take me several minutes just to reach the nearest tent, and by then, Ruslo would surely have fallen victim to the latest of Irina's increasingly frenzied bids for freedom. Desperately, I called back over my shoulder toward the camp.

"Help! Help us, please! It's Irina, she's attacking, help!"

Neither Irina nor Ruslo acknowledged the sound of my voice;

the barrier must have been designed to keep both my voice and my body from crossing through into the clearing, or else they were both too wrapped up in the power of their attraction to spare me a thought.

"What is a body for, if not to feel pleasure?" Irina whispered, her voice little more than a caress. She began to take deep, shuddering breaths, undulating each through her body in a hypnotic sort of dance. "What are desires for but to be fulfilled? I can see it in your eyes, guardian. Are you a fool who denies yourself what you so desperately desire? Or are you a man who takes it for his own?"

Ruslo licked his lips again. Even from several yards away, I could see his hands trembling.

"Take me," Irina breathed.

And Ruslo broke. With an animal moan of longing he charged forward, and leapt into the mouth of the wagon. He grabbed Irina by the arm and pulled her roughly in against his body. He grabbed a fistful of her hair and kissed her violently on the mouth. Irina's arms reached up around Ruslo's neck. Her own hands wound through his hair. And then, I saw Irina's eyes open, saw her lips curl into a half-smile around the kiss.

And for one last, passionate moment Ruslo truly believed that he was the mighty conqueror.

Fucking fool.

It happened faster than I could process it. One moment Ruslo was kissing her, and the next, he was sprawled on the ground, Irina's legs locked around his torso and the chains of her shackles wrapped tightly around his neck. Irina twisted the chain up into her hand. Ruslo jerked and twitched, but seemed unable to free himself. His feet dangled, twisting madly over the edge of the wagon.

"Help!" I shrieked. "Help! Someone, anyone, please!"

I pounded uselessly against the barrier, my cries turning to sobs, convinced I was about to watch a man be murdered right in front of me, and then I froze in horror. Irina was struggling to hold Ruslo still while she stretched across his body to reach something on his belt. A glint of silver at the end of a leather-bound handle. A knife. She was staring at that knife as though it were the singular most beautiful thing she had ever seen.

And I realized. She wasn't trying to kill him. She was trying to kill herself.

I stopped screaming. I stopped pacing. I stopped breathing. All I could do was stare in horror at Irina's struggle for the knife, wishing I could stop her from reaching it and yet also wishing I could simply hand it to her.

Ruslo continued to flail, reaching an arm up behind him in an attempt to grab at her face, but Irina, pulling from a freakishly deep well of strength, wound the chain once again around her leg and pulled it tight, so that it cut still deeper into Ruslo's neck. As he gasped and choked, she pulled him closer in a twisted mockery of an embrace as her fingers scrabbled for the tip of the knife handle.

A flash of movement from beneath the wagon caught my eye. A shape was crawling beneath it, slithering along on its belly like a predator stalking prey. For one wild moment, I thought a jungle cat had found its way into the British countryside, but before the idea could take hold, the lantern dangling from the far end of the wagon dropped to the ground and illuminated the figure.

It was Finn.

With a single swift movement, he swung his arm up, grabbed hold of the knife, pulled it out of its sheath, and flung it away across the grass. Irina, realizing what was happening, let out a savage scream of outrage and tried to haul Ruslo's twitching body up into the wagon, but too late. Finn leapt deftly up into the wagon and descended upon her. In a few sharp movements he had forced Irina facedown onto the floor of the wagon, and had pinned both of her arms behind her back. Holding her in this position with only his knee, he used both hands to unwind the chain from Ruslo's neck and shove him out of the wagon and down onto the ground where he lay sprawled in a heap, retching and spluttering.

"Get up, you useless sack of excrement, and go for Dragos!" Finn spat at him. Ruslo did not respond, but instead rolled onto his side and vomited violently into the grass, still gasping and choking for breath.

Swearing loudly, Finn released his hold on Irina and jumped from the wagon. He bent over Ruslo and, a moment later, had swept him up across his shoulders in a fireman's carry and started running with him back toward the camp.

Realizing he was barreling right toward me, I leapt back out of the way. Finn crossed the barrier as though it weren't even there and started at the sight of me, nearly dropping the now unconscious Ruslo.

"Jess, there you are!" he panted. "I... I heard you calling for help, but I came out over there and couldn't see you, and then I saw what Irina was doing... are you all right?"

"Don't worry about me, I'm fine. It's him we have to worry about," I said, pointing to Ruslo, whose breathing sounded ragged and strained. "Is he going to be okay?"

"Can't say for sure," Finn said. "She could have crushed his windpipe. We have to get him back to the camp. He may be an utterly useless prat, but we can't just let him die."

I had a million other questions, but they could all wait until we got Ruslo the help he clearly needed. "I... can I help you?" I asked, though I couldn't see how I could do anything but get in the way.

"Yes, you can," Finn said, nodding toward the lantern I had dropped to the ground. The flame was still alive inside it. "Pick that up and light the way for me, so I don't drop him."

"Yeah, sure. Of course," I said breathlessly, snatching up the lantern. "This is the path here."

I had time to steal only one glance back over my shoulder at Irina. She lay curled in a ball just inside the wagon, her shoulders heaving with sobs. She was mourning, yet again, the nearness of her escape from the body she now knew only as her prison.

18

WHAT'S IN A NAME

"WEAPONIZED SEX," I said, shaking my head. "Well, you can't say it wasn't an effective plan."

Finn and I sat outside the Herbalist's tent, waiting for news about Ruslo's condition. We'd only made it a few yards into the woods when a group of Traveler Caomhnóir met us, having heard my cries for help. After a hurried explanation from Finn about what had happened, the group had split in half, three of them running off toward Irina's wagon to secure her perimeter and check in on her, while the other three took Ruslo and jogged him off for medical attention. We had followed, unsure of what else to do. There was no chance of sleep, not now, and there was a blazing fire outside of the tent, so it was as comfortable a place as any to wait for news.

"Effective indeed," Finn said through gritted teeth. "Was he supposed to be the Caomhnóir on guard duty?"

"I can't say for sure, but I don't think so," I said. "The music seems to have drawn him to the clearing just as it did me."

"What music?" Finn asked. "You didn't mention music before."

"Oh, right. Sorry, the nude seduction and attempted murder must have put that right out of my head," I said, rolling my eyes. "That's how I wound up at Irina's clearing. I wasn't just out for a nighttime stroll. I heard her singing and followed it there."

Finn raised his eyebrows incredulously. "Four years in the spirit world, and you haven't learned that following mysterious music off into the woods in the dead of night is a bad idea?"

"It's not like I got into that wagon with her," I said defensively. "Save your lectures for Ruslo, he's the idiot who got within arm's reach of her." Now that he said it, though, even I had to admit it was one of the dumbest things I'd ever done. I mean, my God, how many horror films had I seen, and I had just turned into the girl who gets murdered in the first five minutes of the movie.

To distract from the looming truth of my own stupidity, I changed the subject. "How the hell did you get into the clearing? There was some kind of invisible barrier there. I couldn't get any further than the edge of the tree line."

Finn pushed up his sleeve and showed me a rune inked onto his forearm, just above his wrist. "There's a protective circle around that clearing. The Caomhnóir cast it to protect the rest of the camp from Irina's continued attempts to escape. The only people who can cross its border are the ones who have been marked with this rune. Dragos put it on me when I first checked in with him, just as a precautionary measure. He thought, given why we were here, I may have to interact with Irina during our stay."

"Oh. That makes sense, then," I said. "I just can't believe that Ruslo would cave like that. I mean, besides the fact Irina is incredibly dangerous, what about the ban on Durupinen-Caomhnóir relationships? Why would he risk losing his post?"

"I'm risking losing mine," Finn said.

"I know, but... for a one-off fling? And with a woman who will likely try to kill you? That doesn't make sense," I said.

"You're right, it wouldn't, if the Travelers had the same rules that we have," Finn said.

"What do you mean? Don't all Durupinen everywhere have the same rules?" I asked.

"Of course not," Finn said. "Don't you remember the Travelers' response when they heard about the Leeching that was running rampant in the Northern Clans? A single instance of Leeching could strip you of your Gateway for life under their Council's rules."

"Oh, that's right. I'd forgotten about that," I muttered. If only the Northern Clan's rules had been as strong—or at least as strongly enforced—there wouldn't have been a horde of spirits trapped in the Aether awaiting their destiny of being turned into a Wraith Army for the Necromancers. I took a deep breath and then expelled the negative thought with the air. I had no time or energy to waste on dwelling in a past I couldn't change.

Well, look at me, being all Zen and shit.

"So, what are the rules for relationships between Caomhnóir and Durupinen?" I asked in a much calmer tone.

"They aren't forbidden," Finn replied. "Of course, they aren't encouraged either, but when clans live cut off from the rest of society like this, social protocols are very different."

My mouth fell open. "So, you're saying that Durupinen and Caomhnóir can date?"

"Date, marry, what have you," Finn said, nodding his head. "But this is the trade-off for lax relationships between Caomhnóir and Durupinen; they aren't taught to resist temptation the way we are, and so they are subject to just this kind of weakness. Couple that with a lack of discipline in general, and suddenly it's the protectors who need protecting from themselves."

I scooted my foot over and nudged Finn's boot with my toe. "Oh, yes. You, for one, are excellent at avoiding the temptation of those Durupinen vixens."

He smirked down at his boots and then looked up at me. I waggled my eyebrows at him and his smirk split into a sheepish grin. "All right, all right. Well played, that." The smile vanished as quickly as it had come. "But this is just the kind of objections that will be raised when Hannah proposes the change to the relationship laws. And I must say, I can see the logic."

I frowned at him. "The logic? What logic? You can't justify upholding a law just because of one person's bad decision."

"They created the law in the first place over just one Prophecy," Finn pointed out. "Hundreds and hundreds of years' worth of Caomhnóir-Durupinen relationships, restricted and policed over what would eventually come down to just one person's decision. Well, two people, really, but you understand my meaning."

I tried to find a retort for this, but whether I was too exhausted or his reasoning was too sound, racking my brain yielded nothing of consequence.

"I'm starting to wonder whose side you're on," I murmured. "You do want the law to be overturned, don't you?"

"Jess, that's not fair. Of course, I do," Finn said, and though I half expected him to bristle at my words, his voice was gentle. "But it won't do us any good to pretend it won't be a struggle."

"Actually, I think it might," I said, looking up to find his eyes watching me intently. "Hope isn't a crime, Finn. It might not be practical or logical, but it isn't a crime. And sometimes people need it to keep moving forward."

"All right, love," Finn whispered. "Hope, then. For both of us."

The flap of the tent behind us swung open. Startled, Finn and I both leapt to our feet like two teenagers caught in a parked car.

"How is he?" we both blurted out at the same time.

Dragos nodded grimly. "He'll be fine," he said. "He's quite lucky she didn't strangle him to death."

"I was thinking the same thing," I said.

"Was he supposed to be on duty?" Finn asked. "Is that why he was in the clearing?"

Dragos nodded again. "He admitted to me that he left his post to relieve himself and get something to eat. He was on his way back when he heard the singing. He has offered no excuse for allowing the Walker to seduce him."

"That's because there is no excuse," Finn said curtly.

"Quite," Dragos agreed.

"What will happen to Irina?" I asked.

Dragos turned a sharp expression on me, as though I were an impertinent child rather than an equal participant in a conversation between adults. "What do you mean?"

"I mean, will she be punished for what she did tonight?" I asked trying to sound curious, rather than concerned.

"The Walker will likely find another charge added to her extensive list of crimes," Dragos said.

I bit back the urge to tell him to call her by her name. It wouldn't do Irina any favors to lose my temper with someone like Dragos. The last thing I needed was for any of the Travelers to think I was biased in Irina's favor, or they may not take my testimony seriously when it came time to speak before them at the trial.

"We are grateful to you for your intervention, but encourage you to give the Walker's clearing a wide berth. We cannot guarantee your safety if you venture into it again," Dragos said to Finn.

Finn nodded, but did not speak. I could tell from the set line of his jaw that he, too, was withholding some harsh words for Dragos.

"If there is nothing else, we will return to the wagon," Finn said. Dragos waved a hand in dismissal and disappeared back into the tent.

"Come on, then," Finn said to me. "May as well try to get some sleep before the sun comes up."

I didn't reply, sure that sleep would elude me for the rest of the night as surely as Irina's freedom had slipped through her fingers.

Surprisingly, I did manage to nod off for an hour or two, but what found waiting for me when I woke up made me wish desperately that I'd stayed awake.

"Jess? What's wrong?" Finn asked, startling me. I hadn't realized he was awake. I tore my eyes from the sketchpad in my lap and found him staring at me with concern.

"I... it's another spirit drawing. I did it just now while I was sleeping," I said quietly.

"What did you draw?" he prompted, though the hesitation in his voice made it obvious that he already knew what I would say.

Rather than answer him, I turned the sketchpad around and held it up so that he could see it. There again, the image of Annabelle, slightly transparent, staring down in horror at her own body lying on the ground.

Finn pressed his lips into a thin line. "Is this the same as the last one?" he asked after a few moments of grim silence.

I nodded. "As far as I can tell, it's identical."

"What are you going to do?" Finn asked.

"I don't know. I want to tell her, but what do I say? I don't know what this means. I don't know why I keep seeing it. I don't know where or when it will happen, so all I'll be doing is frightening her for no good reason."

"What's the alternative?" Finn asked.

I threw the sketchbook down onto the bed. "I don't know. Keep finding excuses to call and make sure she's okay? She's going to start thinking I'm stalking her."

"Better than the alternative," Finn said. "Still, there must be something you can do to help interpret this? What did Fiona suggest?"

"Nothing particularly helpful. She just told me that I need to try to be 'open' to the visions, but how am I supposed to do that while I'm sleeping?"

"Perhaps she just means that you need to accept the idea that you are a Seer. Not just accept it, but embrace it," Finn said.

I didn't reply right away. If I was honest with myself, I knew he was right. I would never understand these Seer visions if I didn't explore this new gift. The problem was that the idea of being a Seer, of having these visions of death and destruction for the rest of my life, was just about the most unwelcome "gift" I could possibly imagine. I didn't want to embrace it. I wanted to set it on fire and run screaming from it as far as my legs and my fear would take me.

"I don't think I can do that," I said finally.

"I don't blame you, love," Finn said. He leaned across the narrow aisle between the bunks and kissed me softly on each eyelid. "These eyes have had enough of prophecies to last an eternity, haven't they?"

His tender expression became a blur as my eyes filled with tears. "Yeah. Yeah, they have."

§

I tried repeatedly to find a cell phone signal as we walked to the central fire for breakfast, but it was no use. Instead, I reached out into my connection with Milo, and asked him to relay the message to Hannah.

"No worries, sweetness, we'll check on Annabelle for you. I'll let you know as soon as we hear back from her," he assured me.

I sent my thanks zinging back to him, along with my good luck wishes for Hannah. She had her first Council meeting that morning, and I knew she would be nervous.

Irina's attack on Ruslo was the topic of every conversation around the central fire when Finn and I arrived, bleary-eyed and exhausted, to revive ourselves with cauldron coffee, scrambled eggs, and salt-cured bacon. It became clear, after a few minutes of sitting and listening to the buzz of circulating conversation, that not a single detail of the evening had escaped the gossip mill.

"How do they all know? Is there no discretion in these clans?" Finn grumbled into his tin coffee cup.

"Discretion?" I snorted. "Finn, they're completely isolated here. Flavia once told me there is no such thing as a secret in a Traveler camp, and she's obviously right."

I cocked my head over my shoulder. Many of the faces had now turned in our direction and groups of people were openly pointing at us. I suppose we might have still been objects of curiosity even if we hadn't been involved in the previous night's events, but now it was as though we were sitting under a bright spotlight.

On the far side of the clearing, I spotted Flavia sitting in a small knot of young Travelers. They were all eating and laughing together. The sight of them made me oddly nostalgic for normal, youthful shenanigans. I felt a pang of loneliness as I thought of Tia, and how much I missed just goofing around the apartment together. I'd spoken to Tia several times since Christmas, but I still hadn't told her that Hannah and I would be staying in England indefinitely. I just couldn't work up the courage. How do you admit to your best friend that you're abandoning her to move to another country, possibly permanently? The mature thing to do would have been to tell her right away, as soon as it became official, so that we could start making all the necessary arrangements for the apartment. So naturally, being me, I was running from that conversation as fast as my immature little legs would carry me.

You know that magical moment you envision, when you look around you and think, "I have a place of my own, a job, and I look after myself. I now officially feel like an adult."

Yeah, I was starting to think that moment was a myth.

"Jess!"

I looked up to see Flavia beckoning me over to her with both hands. I nodded and picked up my plate.

"I'll be right back," I told Finn, and made my way slowly through the milling crowd around the fire, holding my plate high above my head lest someone reach out and snatch it from me while there was still even a morsel of bacon on it.

"Hey, Flavia," I said as I reached her.

"Please, sit!" Flavia said, scooting over on her rickety wooden bench to make room for me.

I sat, though a quick glance around the group seemed to suggest that the invitation did not extend beyond Flavia herself. The rest of the group was staring at me with a suspicion that bordered on hostility. There were three other girls and two guys, all—if I had to guess—around my own age.

"Jess, I'd like you to meet my friends," Flavia said, and pointed each of them out with her spoon as she said their names. "This is Jeta." The girl sitting closest to Flavia nodded at me. She was buxom and beautiful, with full lips that sported two gold piercings and a thick, dark braid of hair that fell all the way to the small of her back. "This is Mina." Beside Jeta, a slight, mousy girl with a pointed nose and a scar running the length of her cheek narrowed her eyes at me from above the rim of her coffee cup. She sat on the knee of a broad-chested young man with a pock-marked face and a mane of dark hair pulled into a bun, to whom Flavia pointed next and said, "This is Fennix. He's my cousin. And this is Mairik." From the bench opposite, an extremely tall young man sitting with his legs stretched out in front of him smirked at me, picking his straight, white teeth with the blade of a Swiss Army knife. He winked at me, which made Flavia roll her eyes before she finished, "And last but certainly never least, this is Laini." Just behind Mairik, a girl with a spiky, pixie haircut sat cross-legged on a worn, old stump, tuning a fiddle. She was so slim and slight that she could have been a twelve-year-old boy, but her face was far too beautiful to mistake her as such. One of her eyes was so deeply brown that it was almost black, while the other was a vivid, grass green. I could tell that she was silently acknowledging the moment that I noticed her eyes, relishing the mild astonishment on my face, and basking in the stunningness of her own appearance before her expression closed off with the same suspicious detachment with which the others were now regarding me.

"Nice to meet you all," I said awkwardly. No one returned the sentiment.

"As you can see, they're all really friendly and not at all rude," Flavia said with a sardonic smile, which I returned.

"So, Northern Girl," Mairik said without preamble, flicking his toothpick into the leaping flames. "You're here for the Walker's trial, is that right?"

I swallowed back my annoyance at yet another casting off of Irina's name. Didn't anyone, even her own people, recognize her as a person? Well, she may not have been able to stand up for her own name at the moment, but I could certainly stand up for mine. I plastered on a smile. "Yeah, that's right. And you can call me Jess."

"No, I don't think I can," Mairik said, after a moment of mock consideration. "You'll always be Northern Girl to us."

Flavia rolled her eyes. "Stars alive, Mairik, do you have to be such an insufferable jerk all of the time?"

Laini nodded. "He does. It's chronic."

"Incurable," Jeta agreed.

"I'm just being honest with the girl," Mairik insisted, raising his hands as though in surrender.

"You know, what? Don't even worry about it," I said as Flavia made to open her mouth again. "Call me Northern Girl all you want. But you should know that it doesn't even make sense. I'm not from the North. I'd never even visited the North until three years ago. You're more Northern than I am."

Mairik looked like I'd slapped him in the face. "Me? Northern? There is absolutely nothing Northern about me."

I laughed. "That doesn't make sense. You literally live here. Do you need someone to draw you a map? This," I gestured broadly around me, "is about as 'northern' as it gets."

Mairik was too busy sputtering and looking aghast, so it was Fennix who answered. "We are Travelers. We don't define ourselves by locations, the way that Settlers do. We could never be Northern or Southern or whatever. Our identity is in our wandering, and in the tribe with which we wander."

I briefly considered telling him about my nomadic childhood—about the whirlwind of suitcases and dark interstates and strange apartments in which my mother and I never really unpacked our boxes, but kept them half-full, ready to tape up again at a moment's notice. I'd never had roots in my life, nor barely a tribe to cling to. But then I decided that they did not deserve to know those parts of me. Nothing I could tell them would make a difference in how they viewed me, so what was the point? I swallowed it all back down.

"Suit yourself. I'm only here a few days and then I'm off. Call me what you like," I said.

Rather than seeming placated, Mairik looked disappointed that we weren't going to spar any further. He tried a new tack, smiling obnoxiously at me. "So, you planning any more apocalypses while you're here?"

I groaned. "Aw, shit, I *knew* I forgot to pack something. Maybe next time."

Flavia laughed. Fennix snorted into his coffee.

"What are you, jealous, Mairik?" Jeta asked, pouting.

Mairik's smirk turned to a scowl as he turned around. "Jealous? Of what?"

"Northern Girl here rains down fear and destruction wherever she goes, and you can't even pass your first year of Novitiate training," Jeta cooed.

Mairik shrugged nonchalantly. "I can. I just choose not to. There's a difference."

"And you're sure it's not just because you're an incompetent *bou*?" Laini asked seriously. "Because that's the assumption we were all working under."

Mairik cursed at her in rapid Romanian and chucked a tin plate at her head. She deflected it with an almost lazy jerk of her hand, as though plates flying at her head was not only a regular occurrence, but a boring one.

"Mairik has a point, though," Laini said, her eyes back on her fiddle. "The last time you waltzed in here, you brought fear and destruction and violence the likes of which we had never seen in our camp."

"She didn't bring it," Flavia said sharply. "The Necromancers did."

"The Necromancers were following her," Laini said, pointing at me with her bow. Horsehair dangled from it in a bushy skein. "We suffered greatly because we sheltered her here."

"And it was nothing to the suffering the living and spirit worlds would have endured if we had not sheltered her here," Flavia snapped. "Don't blame Jess for your refusal to understand the wider implications of a prophecy beyond all of our control. Our sacrifices were as nothing to the risks she took on our behalf."

"If you say so," Laini murmured, and shrugged off Flavia's argument as though she didn't believe a word of it.

I pulled my hood up around my face and picked up my mug. "Maybe I should just—"

"Are you crazy?" the girl called Mina suddenly blurted out, holding her cup up in front of her face as though she were keen to keep some kind of object between us as a buffer. Her protuberant eyes did not blink as she stared, waiting for my answer.

I stared back at her, pulled up short. "I... what?"

"Irina is crazy. Are you?" Mina repeated.

Before I had recovered myself enough to respond, however, Jeta rounded on Mina. "What the hell kind of a question is that?"

Mina shrugged, looking totally unabashed. "They say Walkers are driven mad when they separate from their bodies. I want to know if it's true."

"Yeah, but who the hell actually just asks it like that?" Jeta said, rolling her eyes.

"Well, how else am I supposed to find out?" Mina countered with a shrug. She sipped her coffee again.

"Do crazy people even know they're crazy?" Fennix asked the

roup at large. "Like, that's the mark of a crazy person, right? That hey don't even realize they're crazy?"

Flavia turned to me, looking apologetic. "I'm sorry, Jess. I can atch up with you later. They told me they'd behave, but they bviously can't control themselves."

"No, it's fine," I said, squeezing her hand. "Being gawked at like sideshow attraction is kind of my thing." I looked around at the thers, their eyes narrowed, their expressions curious and yet wary. Miles away from Fairhaven, and I was still an object of horrified ascination. And, I realized suddenly, I would continue to be one ntil I demystified myself. I wasn't doing myself—or Hannah—any avors by allowing our reputation to spiral into the stuff of legends. f I wanted people to stop staring and start listening, I guess I better tart talking. I sighed.

"Okay, look. I don't really feel like being gawked at and whispered about for the next few days. I get enough of that at 'airhaven. You all obviously have questions about the Prophecy, so et's have them. Step on up. You ask me, I'll answer."

They all looked at each other, as though silently wondering if it vas a trap.

"Seriously?" Mina asked breathlessly after a few moments.

"Seriously."

"You mean we can ask you whatever we want? About the 'rophecy?" Jeta asked.

"Sure. If it doesn't get too personal, I'll answer it."

"How do we know if you're telling the truth?" Laini shot at me.

"You'll just have to take my word for it," I said. "If the word of a Northern Girl carries any weight around here, that is."

Laini narrowed her eyes at me, but on every other face, ncredulity turned to delight, and the floodgates opened.

"Does it hurt to Walk?"

"No. It's disorienting, but not painful."

"Do you Walk, like, all the time? For fun?"

"Nope, not even once. Haven't done it since I went through to the Aether, and I won't ever do it again, if I can help it."

In a matter of seconds, Flavia's friends had transformed from a uspicious pack of interrogators to a cluster of eager kids at story ime. Even Mairik dropped his confrontational air and listened, ascinated, as I explained what it felt like to fly through the Aether, nd the twisted dark Castings the Necromancers had used, and the

217

unprecedented power of Hannah's gift. Their guards dropped one by one as my own walls came down, and what had started as a necessary chore turned out to be surprisingly cathartic. Only Laini remained stony-faced and silent, tinkering with her fiddle, though I could tell she was listening carefully to every word.

The crowd around the fire dwindled away around us. At one point, Jeta poured a steaming mug of coffee and handed it wordlessly to me as I talked. Finally, after nearly an hour, Flavia's friends had exhausted their well of curiosity and lapsed into a relaxed silence.

"Wild," Fennix whispered as I drained the last of my coffee and set the mug down on a stump.

"Wicked," Jeta agreed in a murmur.

"Does that about cover it?" I asked. "If there's going to be a second round, I'm going to need more coffee."

"I think you've told us much more than we deserved, given how rude we were to you when you sat down," Flavia said, looking sternly around at her friends, a few of whom had the good grace to look sheepish.

"We're nosy and suspicious by nature," Fennix said to me. "Don't hold it against us."

Mina nodded seriously. "Like vultures on carrion when it comes to outsiders."

"You're the most interesting thing to walk into this camp since three years ago, when you were the most interesting thing to walk into this camp ever," Jeta added.

"Interesting is certainly one word for it," said Laini, and she played a long tremulous note on her fiddle. It startled us all and echoed like a lamentation around the clearing.

Flavia leaned over to me and whispered, "Ignore her. Her brother was killed in the Necromancer attack on the camp, and she still hasn't accepted it three years later."

I nodded and looked over at Laini, fighting a rising tide of guilt I knew I didn't deserve to drown in.

Fennix pulled a battered old pocket watch out of his back pocket and swore softly.

"Mairik, we gotta go," he said, holding it up to Mairik's face so that he could see the time. "If we're late again, Dragos will scalp us. We're all going to have to pick up Ruslo's slack today, the stupid wanker."

218

Mairik yawned widely, scratching at his stomach. "I ate too much. I need a nap."

Mina grinned. "Just go tell Dragos that. I'm sure he'll understand."

Mairik kicked some dirt over her shoes and stood up with Fennix. "You want to hang out tonight, Northern Girl?" he asked.

"Hang out?" I repeated in surprise.

"Yeah. Music and general shenanigans at the Scribes' wagon around ten. You in?"

I must have looked wary, because Jeta nudged me with her elbow.

"You should come," she said encouragingly. "It will be fun. Well, as much fun as we can scrounge up around here."

I tried to think of a legitimate reason to refuse, but drew a blank. What other plans could I possibly have at ten o'clock at night in the middle of the goddamn woods?

"Okay, sure," I said. "On one condition, though."

Mairik frowned. "What condition?"

"Can we do something other than sit for an hour and interrogate me?"

Several of them laughed.

"Traveler's Honor," Mairik said, raising his hands in some kind of salute.

"That's swearing on nothing, that is," Fennix said, sticking out his tongue impishly.

Mairik punched him repeatedly on the arm and they ran out of the clearing.

"See you tonight, Jess!" he called back over his shoulder.

I smiled to myself. I'd earned my name back, at least.

"Actually Jess, I do have one last question," Jeta said, leaning in conspiratorially.

"Okay," I said, a bit warily.

"Is your Caomhnóir single, and can you introduce me?" she giggled.

I followed her gaze across the fire to Finn, who had finished his breakfast and settled himself against a rock with one of his little black books in his hands. He must have felt my eyes upon him, because he glanced up and gave me just a shadow of a smile before settling back to whatever image he was weaving out of words with his stump of a pencil.

"No on both counts," I told her.

19

RIFTING

T HE DAY DRAGGED BY, with no word from Annabelle, despite my constant harassment of Milo, who promised me that they would keep trying to get her on the phone. I half-wished that Irina's trial had continued that day, just to get my mind off my crippling worry, but Dragos informed us that the Council would not convene to hear my testimony until the following afternoon, once it had dealt with the fallout from Ruslo's attack.

"Is... how is Irina?" I asked him after he relayed us this information outside the wagon.

He frowned at me as though I had asked something offensive. "What does that matter?"

"It matters because she is a human being," I shot back. "Can you answer the question or not?"

Dragos looked as though he'd rather not answer the question, but obliged anyway. "She remains in her wagon. The protective barriers around her have been reinforced. No one is allowed to stand guard alone, and the perimeter has been widened. She should be unable to hurt anyone else for the time being."

He had not really answered my question at all, but I wasn't about to push the matter.

"And Ruslo?" Finn asked.

"Suspended from duty pending a disciplinary hearing," Dragos said through gritted teeth. "His injuries will heal. His reputation may not." He turned to me and added, curtly, "The Council expects you in the High Priestess's tent promptly at noon tomorrow."

"I'll be there," I said to his already retreating back.

As evening faded into night, with still no word from Annabelle, I lost the capacity to sit still. To stop myself from pacing, I pulled my sketchpad out and flipped past the image of Annabelle, trying not to look at it. With a clean page in front of me, I cast my eyes around for something to draw and my gaze fell upon Finn, reclined in his bunk, tapping a pencil against his lips as he pondered a poem in his little black book. He had unbuttoned his shirt in the warmth of the fire. The glow rippled across the muscles of his stomach and chest. Smiling a bit, I picked up my own pencil and started to sketch.

After a few moments, he felt my eyes on him and looked up, frowning.

"Why do you keep looking at me?"

"Because you're just so gosh-darn adorable," I replied.

"Are you... drawing me?" he asked.

"Yeah. Is..." I hesitated. "Is that okay? I probably should have asked you first. Sorry."

"No, don't apologize. It's fine. Do I... do I have to do anything?" he asked.

I laughed. "Nope. In fact, the less you do, the better."

We sat in silence for a few moments as I sketched. He seemed to have taken my suggestion to do as little as possible as a directive to turn himself to stone.

"Has anyone ever told you that you are weirdly good at holding still? It's actually kind of creepy. Is that a Caomhnóir thing?"

"I'm choosing to ignore the 'creepy' bit and take that as a compliment. And yes, it is a 'Caomhnóir thing.' Standing inspection, staying hidden, masking our emotional affect in public—these are all skills that require a similar measure of control."

"I'm sure you never considered it before, but it makes you an excellent subject to draw," I said. "And sorry about the 'creepy' thing."

"Why do you like it?" Finn asked suddenly.

"Why do I like what?" I asked, eyes still on the sketch. The curve of the jawline still wasn't quite right. I turned my head, examining it.

"Drawing? Why are you drawn to it, if you'll pardon the pun?" he asked.

"I will not pardon that pun. Take it back immediately," I snorted.

He smiled but didn't reply, still waiting for my answer.

"I'm not really sure. I started when I was really young, because something to draw with and something to draw on were two of the only things I could count on no matter where my mother and I ended up next."

"How young, do you think?"

"I don't know. Four? Five? Some of my earliest memories are of drawing."

"What did you draw when you were so young?" Finn asked.

"Faces."

He raised his eyebrows. "Just faces?"

"Yup. Sad faces. Happy faces. Angry faces. Laughing faces. Crying faces. Pages and pages of them."

"That's... a bit odd."

I shrugged. "I was a bit odd."

"Was?"

I punched him on the arm.

"Do you ever wonder why you drew faces all the time? I mean, rather than birds or puppies or rainbows?"

"I didn't live in a world of birds or puppies or rainbows. I lived in world of faces," I said. Finn was still looking very confused, so I sighed and gave up on the jawline, setting my pencil down. "When you're a little kid, people don't tell you things. They just placate you. They tell you what you want to hear, or they tell you a lie, or they tell you it's none of your business—but you almost never get the whole truth."

"I don't recall that I ever felt that way as a child," Finn said.

"Really? You must have had more functional adults in your life than I did."

"What number would qualify as more than you?" Finn asked.

"Well... any functional adults, actually," I said.

"Oh, come now, is that fair?" Finn asked.

I just shook my head. "There are some levels of dysfunction that can't be explained unless you've lived them. Just take my word for it."

"All right, I will," Finn said. "Anyway, I do apologize. I interrupted you. You were talking about how children are always being lied to."

"That's right," I said. "And adults probably think that kids don't realize that, but they totally do—or at least, I did. I knew that no one was telling me the whole story, and I resented it. So, I tried to get the whole story from their faces."

"From their faces?" Finn repeated, frowning.

"Yeah. That's where the real information is. I became an interpreter of faces. Instead of listening to grown ups' words, I started noticing things they did with their faces that gave away their feelings—tilting their heads, arching their eyebrows, pursing their lips, that kind of stuff. Then I started drawing them, I guess to see if I could understand them better that way."

"You mean to say that you started drawing because you thought your drawings would provide you with more truth than living people?" Finn asked.

"Ah, yes," I said, pointing to his face. "Your expression, which I am unusually adept at interpreting, reveals that this realization makes you feel terribly sorry for me."

"Of course it does. Forgive me, but it sounds like a rather cheerless way in which to grow up."

I laughed, trying unsuccessfully to keep the bitterness out of my tone. "Yes, well, I've got the Durupinen and their Prophecy-driven witch hunt to thank for that. Still, in a way, I suppose I owe them a bit of gratitude; if it weren't for them, I might never have discovered this talent of mine."

"Of course, you would have," Finn said. "You are much too full of natural talent for this to have escaped your notice. It would have bubbled its way to the surface regardless."

I shrugged. "Maybe. It was useful, though. It was an anchor for me, in the mercilessly rough sea that was my life. How's that for a metaphor, Mr. Poet?"

"Very appropriate. I'm impressed," Finn said, smirking. "Now explain what you mean. How was drawing an anchor for you?"

"You're asking an awful lot of questions about this," I pointed out.

He shrugged. "I'm just trying to understand you better. I can stop asking, if you'd prefer."

"No, no, it's fine," I said with a sigh, and paused for a moment, trying to regather all the threads of my thoughts so that I could weave them into something coherent. "I didn't have control over very much. I had no control over where or when we moved, no control over saying goodbye to friends or being forced to start over again at a new school. I was a kid, so I was just along for the ride, and I had to make the best of it. But with drawing, I was always in control. I created everything from nothing. I could start over as many times as I wanted if I made a mistake. And if, in the end, I wasn't happy with something, I could just..." I picked up the sketch, crumpled it into a ball, and chucked it over my shoulder.

Finn nodded thoughtfully. "It empowered you."

"Yes. In an out-of-control world I had complete control right here," I said, tapping the new blank page. "And I could start over any time I wanted to. Does that make sense?"

"Perfect sense. Thank you for sharing that with me."

"You're welcome. I've never shared that with anyone else, mostly because no one ever asked me the question, so I never thought about the answer."

"Well then, I'm glad I asked. I think we both learned something about you."

I laughed. "Yeah, I guess so. Anyway, your jawline was all wrong. I'm starting over."

"It's not your fault. I'm difficult to capture. I'm extremely mysterious," Finn said.

I laughed and looked back down at my sketchbook to see that I had revealed the image of Annabelle again. My blood began to thunder through my veins, my palms to sweat. I leapt to my feet. I instantly regretted this decision, as my head collided painfully with a corner beam of the wagon's roof.

"Are you all right?" Finn cried. He leapt to his feet as well, instinctively assuming a defensive stance.

"Yeah, yeah, I'm fine," I grumbled, rubbing ferociously at the throbbing spot on the top of my head. Then I saw what he was doing and laughed. "What are you going to do? Beat the shit out of this piece of wood for daring to hold the roof up?" I asked, pointing to the offending beam.

"I... well, no," Finn said, dropping his hands and slumping a bit. "I just heard the sound; I didn't know what had happened."

"Right. Well, I'll leave you two to duke it out. I know I said I was going to blow it off, but I think I'm going to go hang out with Flavia and her friends," I said.

"Can I come along?" Finn asked, as I shoved my feet into an extra pair of fuzzy socks and my boots.

"You don't need to," I said, shrugging. "I know Traveler Caomhnóir aren't the most impressive we've ever seen, but there will still be several of them there."

"No, I mean..." Finn looked oddly sheepish. "I mean, I'd like to come. I want to come."

"You do?" I asked in surprise.

Finn chuckled. "Look, if you don't want me to..."

"No! No, it's not that, it's just… I'm just surprised, that's all. You don't really *do* social gatherings," I said.

Finn shrugged. "I've never really had much opportunity."

"That's true. I need to get you out more," I said, smiling. "You poor thing, you've never been socialized properly."

"You make me sound like a curmudgeonly pet," Finn said.

I laughed. "A guard dog, maybe. I'm kidding, I'm kidding!" I said quickly as he drew his eyebrows together. "You started the pet analogy, not me. It's not your fault that your childhood playdates consisted of intense martial arts training instead of going to the park like normal kids. But come on. Let's go see for ourselves what kind of mischief these whippersnappers get up to in their natural habitat."

§

It wouldn't have been difficult to find Flavia and her friends even if we didn't already know the way to the Scribes' wagon; their loud and raucous laughter echoed through the cold night air, mingled with snatches of lively fiddle music and the wafting aroma of roasting meat.

"Hey! She actually came!" Fennix yelled over a volley of shouted greetings.

"And she brought the arm candy," Jeta crowed.

Finn's face slackened and he stared at me. "That's Jeta. She thinks you're cute."

"She thinks I'm…" Finn began, looking mystified.

"Cute," I repeated. "Attractive. Foxy. Just go with it, okay?"

He dragged his feet as I yanked him into the clearing after me. "I had to bring him," I said. "I could hardly count on those two fools to keep us safe, could I?"

They all roared with laughter, reaching out and grabbing us and pulling us over to sit by the fire. Someone was ruffling my hair, and someone else was thrusting a mug of something steaming into my hands. It had a heady aroma. I took a tentative sip.

"Mulled blackberry wine with spices," Flavia told me, sitting down beside me. She smiled warmly. "I'm glad you came."

"Thanks for inviting us," I said.

Flavia handed another cup to Finn, who accepted it, but was pulled out of his seat at once by Fennix, who started introducing him to everyone except Laini, who was sitting on the wagon steps. She acknowledged our arrival with a brief look of disgust and went back to picking out tunes on her fiddle.

"It's not much of a party," Flavia said apologetically.

"No, it's great. It's a nice reprieve from sitting quietly in the middle of the woods staring at trees," I said, and then laughed, shaking my head. "Seriously, I'm not trying to be culturally insensitive, but I don't know how you do it. I've been here for two days and I already want to rip my hair out."

Flavia smiled. "I might have, if it wasn't for my work. But like I told you, I'm planning my exit strategy."

"Well, if you ever need a place to stay when you break out, let me know. It looks like Hannah and I are staying in England for the foreseeable future."

Flavia's eyes widened. "Really? You aren't going back to the States?"

I shook my head grimly. "I guess Fairhaven rumors don't spread as quickly as Traveler rumors. Hannah was elected to a Council seat a couple of days ago."

Flavia gasped. "I... that's... wow."

I chuckled. "I know. That's been pretty much everyone's reaction."

"It's rather astounding that, after everything that happened, that your clans found the courage to overcome what I'm sure was a heavy burden of prejudice. I must say, I'm surprised... but impressed."

"So am I. I just hope Hannah can find some peace now. She carries a lot of guilt about the Prophecy, even though she knows deep down that it wasn't her fault. I know she sees this as a way of moving on and proving herself to the rest of the Northern Clans."

I looked over at Finn, who was now examining a long, curved knife that Mairik was showing him. He looked up, caught my eye, and grinned just as Laini struck up a lively tune on her fiddle. It was a favorite, apparently, because the others cheered and began to clap and cheer along. I had never heard music like it before. It had such a stirring depth to it, as though it were somehow in a minor and a major key at the same time. It was as though the song spoke of pain or suffering, but celebrated the resilience in the face of it at the same time. It made my chest ache for reasons I couldn't verbalize.

Jeta was trying to tug Finn to his feet and join a wild, reeling sort of jig they had all started. I burst out laughing at the unmitigated horror in his face as he pulled his arm away, like she had suggested he fling himself into the fire instead. The wine was making me feel warm and sleepy.

The song came to an end. Fennix scooped a clay jug up off of the ground and splashed its contents into the fire, which caused the flames to leap and roar. Mina let out a scream of delight.

"And now we Rift!" Fennix shouted, and the others hooted and hollered and whooped with excitement.

"And now we what?" I asked Flavia, who was looking wary.

"Aw, Fennix, not tonight," Flavia called over the tumult.

"What do you mean?" Fennix cried. "Tonight is the perfect night! Look at the moon!"

The moon hung, a heavy glowing orb, right over our heads. The light, even for a full moon, was unnaturally bright. My hands, clasped around the warm curve of my mug, looked oddly luminescent, as though the moonlight had seeped beneath my skin and lit them from within.

"They aren't Travelers," Laini said, laying her fiddle down and glaring at Fennix. "They don't possess the Sight. They can't Rift."

"Oh, come on, not only Travelers can Rift. Other clans have done it," Mairik said, his voice overly loud and a bit slurred.

"I bet the Walker can Rift," Mina cried eagerly. "Come on, she's been through the Aether! I bet she'll Rift further than any of us!"

As the others talked over each other, arguing, I turned back to Flavia.

"What is Rifting?" I repeated. "What are they talking about?"

Flavia bit her lip. "It's... well, it's hard to describe, but basically it's using a Casting and some herbs to induce a heightened connection to the spirit world. It's meant to clarify communication and deepen understanding."

"What do you mean, herbs?" I asked.

Flavia shrugged. "It's a mixture of herbs and plants that you burn in a small bowl, and inhale the fumes, and—"

"Wait, wait, wait," I said, and I started to laugh. "You mean you're all just going to get high right now?"

Mairik stared at me, looking confused. "Get what?"

"You're... you're going to do some drugs. Trip," I clarified.

"No, not trip, *Rift*," Mina said, as though I had simply misheard he word. "The herbs help open the inner eyes. Lift the veil, you now?"

I couldn't seem to wipe the smirk off my face. "Yeah, I'm familiar vith the concept." I turned to look at Finn, expecting him to share n my joke, but his face was very serious, even thoughtful.

"Oh, come on, Finn, you don't actually want to get high right low, do you?" I asked incredulously. "Doesn't impairing your ucidity violate every tenet of your Caomhnóir upbringing? I was a ittle surprised you even had any wine, not that I'm judging."

Honestly, I was a little surprised I had any wine. I wasn't usually drinker, but I cut myself some slack and made an exception. The voods were boring as hell and bloody freezing, and the wine was ike drinking a blanket.

"No, I don't want to do it, but perhaps you might. I've heard of lifting," Finn said slowly. "I've never done it, but I've learned about t. Those who have done it swear that their connections to the spirit vorld become clearer. Easier to understand."

Under cover of Flavia further explaining the precise history of lifting, Finn jerked his head toward the bag at my feet. The corner if my sketchbook was poking out of it.

I gasped quietly as I caught on to his meaning. The images I lad been drawing, the visions of Annabelle's death: was there a lossibility that Rifting might help me make sense of them?

While Fennix described a recent Rifting experience, I leaned in lose to Flavia. "Flavia, I'm going to ask you a question, but I want 'ou to promise you won't... read into it, or anything."

Flavia frowned. "All right. I promise."

"Does Rifting... is there any evidence that it might help clarify... lrophetic communications?"

Flavia's eyes widened, and I could see the questions forming in heir warm brown depths. But, true to her word, she did not ask ne anything. "Rifting has been known to clarify all kinds of spirit 'ommunications. It was used many times in attempts to gain more larity on prophecies and other spirit communications that were een as warnings or repeated messages."

Finn, who had been watching me closely, came over to stand leside me. "What do you reckon?" he asked.

"Are there any... side effects?" I asked Flavia.

Flavia shrugged. "A bit of dry throat from the fumes, sometimes. Maybe a headache, if you Rift for too long."

I looked up at Finn. He shook his head slightly. "It's up to you."

"But what do you think?"

"I think it's up to you," he repeated.

Ugh. Why would he choose this moment to stop being overprotective the moment I needed someone to tell me what to do?

"It doesn't matter what you decide, Northern Girl. Only Traveler have the Sight, and without it, Rifting will be nothing more than a bad dream followed by a hangover," Laini said scornfully.

"What's the Sight?" I asked.

Laini scoffed. It was Flavia who answered. "It's the connection to our Spirit Guides."

"What Spirit Guides?" I asked. I looked around the clearing as if expecting a Greek chorus of sassy gay spirits to reveal themselves, criticizing my wardrobe in unison. There were no spirits to be seen, sassy or otherwise.

"The Traveler Durupinen believe that there are certain spirits waiting in the Aether that we are connected to. Usually relatives, but not always. They watch over us, and send us signs to guide us along our path."

"We've all got them," Jeta added. "Don't you want to know what yours are trying to tell you?"

"I don't need to Rift to hear what my Spirit Guide is saying," I told her. "Getting him to shut up is usually the problem."

"Huh?" Jeta asked, frowning.

"She's got a sworn Spirit Guide, a guide in the world of the living," Flavia explained. "He was here with her the last time she was in the camp. Milo, wasn't it?"

"Yeah, that's right," I said, nodding. "And trust me, there's never any problem understanding exactly what he has to say. He makes damn sure of that."

"But there's more to be learned, Northern Girl," Mina chimed in, her eyes wide and eager. "They're singing songs for us on the other side of the Gateway. Come dance to them."

"I'm not really the dancing kind," I said. "I'm more the 'stand awkwardly against the wall and nod your head' kind."

"Maybe she's too scared to dance," Laini suggested from her perch. "Maybe the Northern Girl doesn't have the courage to listen to the calls from the other side. Maybe," and she leaned forward, letting her leg swing down out of the tree like the pendulum arm

230

of a great clock, "she's afraid of what the world of the Aether might whisper to her."

I stared at her, and something in the gleam of her eyes made the decision for me. I was a lot of things, but I was no coward.

"Okay, fine. I'll do it. Let's Rift."

20

BROKEN THINGS

FINN AND I WATCHED the preparations with nervous fascination. Mairik and Fennix worked quietly over the fire, measuring and cutting herbs and grinding them together with a mortar and pestle. Jeta and Mina produced a set of tiny ceramic pots, which they lined up on a large, flat rock. Then they poured a small amount of a floral-smelling oil into each pot and began to stir them. I peered over their shoulders and saw that the inside of each pot was a different vibrant color.

"For the runes," Mina explained, looking up at me and grinning broadly.

Once the paints were mixed, we all sat in a circle around the fire, all except for Laini, who continued to watch the proceedings from her perch in the tree, smiling like the Cheshire Cat at my preparations to fall down the rabbit hole.

"Take your jacket off," Jeta instructed me. "And your gloves."

I did as I was told, folding my coat and gloves into a little pile behind me. The leaping flames licked at my bare skin with ripples of warmth, fending off the wintery chill and sending it retreating into the surrounding woods.

Jeta pushed up the sleeves of my flannel shirt, exposing my forearms. Then she dipped a very fine-tipped paintbrush into the pot of blue paint and began to apply it to my arms.

I watched, fascinated, as a pattern of runes and flowers and vines began to blossom across my skin from the tip of her paintbrush. She worked quickly and silently, with broad, practiced strokes, wiping the brush on a rag she kept draped across her knee each time she needed to use a new color.

"This is beautiful," I murmured, more to myself than to Jeta, but she smiled anyway.

"There's a magic in it," she said.

"But there is skill, too," I said, and my eyes traveled up to her tattoos. "Did you design your tattoos as well?"

Jeta nodded. "I do everyone's tattoos in the camp. It's my gift."

There was a note of pride in her voice, a contentment that I envied. It was as though she knew exactly who she was meant to be, and had never even felt the urge to resist what the universe had laid out for her.

"Maybe you could do a tattoo for me before I leave," I said, my eyes falling from Jeta's face to the designs now swirling from my wrists to my palms.

"Tattoos are stories... our stories," Jeta said quietly, tilting her head to the side to examine her handiwork. "If you truly feel you have another chapter to add to yours before setting out, I will gladly record it for you. There. You're done." She held my arms up in front of my face. "Rift-ready."

"Uh, great. Thank you," I said.

Jeta touched a finger to her head in a kind of salute and then turned to Mina who held her bare arms out in front of her, awaiting her own turn.

Despite the intricacy of the artwork, it took Jeta only a few minutes to complete it on everyone who wanted to Rift, including herself. Finally, Mina, Jeta, Flavia, Fennix, Mairik, and I all sat around the fire, each holding a small bowl of herbs. Finn settled himself against a tree stump a few feet behind me, looking both anxious and expectant.

Flavia sat beside me. Her eyes were aglow with excitement. "Are you ready?"

"I don't know. I've never done this before. You tell me," I said, barely able to keep a hysterical edge out of my voice. I was already doubting my decision, wondering if I was a fool to rise to Laini's obvious baiting, but I wasn't about to back out now. I had way too much stubborn pride for that. And if there was any chance, any chance at all that I might be able to understand that prophetic drawing, to heed its warning before it was too late . . .

Mairik circled the fire, handing each of us an instrument that looked like a long-handled tea strainer, except instead of tea, the little metal basket on the end of the handle contained glowing embers from the fire.

"I'll say the Casting," Mairik instructed us all. "When I've finished, hold the embers under your bowl. When the herbs begin

o smoke, just put your face right over it and breathe it in as deeply
s you can. When you feel the Rifting begin, just put the bowl down
nd lay back."

"How do we know when the Rifting begins?" I asked.

"You'll know," Mairik said confidently. "Now when you're in it,
's a bit like lucid dreaming. You can make choices, decide where
ou are going to go and what you want to do. And remember, you
an't get hurt, so do whatever the fuck you want!"

Fennix let out a whoop of exhilaration, which was met by
aughter from the others.

"And when you want to come out of it, just walk out the door,"
Mairik finished.

"What door?" I asked. I tried to sound nonchalant, but my voice
ame out shrill.

"Wherever you go, whatever you do, there is always a door,"
Mairik said. "It won't always look the same, but if you look around
or it, it will always be there, and it will always be open. Just walk
hrough it, and you'll wake up."

I turned to Flavia. "What if I can't find the door?" I muttered.

She shook her head and smiled at me reassuringly. "That's not
ow it works. There's always a door."

I swallowed back a wave of panic and nodded. *Okay. Find the door.*
ven as I thought it, a memory floated to the surface of my mind, a
nemory I only revisited if I absolutely had to. When I went through
he Aether and closed the Gateway from the other side, I had drifted
hrough a kind of dreamscape, but there had always been a door to
ead me to the next place. And, in the end, it had been my choice
o follow Hannah's Call and walk back through a door that had lead
ne home again. I took a deep, steadying breath. If I could find my
vay back through that door, I could do this.

Mairik's voice pulled me back. "Everyone ready?"

Voices rose all around the fire, a chorus of assent. I added my
wn, weakly and a little late. I threw one last look at Finn where he
at nearby. He nodded solemnly to me and I felt a tiny part of my
nxiety melt away. I might be about to take some kind of journey,
ut he would be right there, watching over me, like always.

Mairik began to chant; even in my mounting panic I noticed
strange mixture of Romany dialect and scattered Gaelic words.
t was a jarring, unmelodious mixture, like the same song being
layed in two different keys at once. As Mairik's voice rose and fell,

a tingling began in my arms, and I looked down at the runes and designs Jeta had painted there.

They were glowing.

I stared in utter fascination as a shimmering golden light snaked its way through the designs, lighting up each rune one by one, until my arms looked like a luminous map of constellations.

"Jess! Light your bowl!" Flavia's voice hissed at me, startling me. I was so fascinated by the runes that I hadn't realized that Mairi had stopped speaking. Hastily, I held the glowing, smoking ember underneath my bowl and watched as a fragrant, purplish smoke began to curl up from the contents. I leaned my head directly over the bowl and inhaled deeply.

The first breath of smoke was hot, sweet, and cloying in my throat. I fought down a cough, trying to relax my body so that the smoke would travel downward unimpeded. The second breath, though I felt it go down into my lungs, seemed to also travel upwards, filling my head with a dizzying sensation, obscuring my nerves and leaving in their place a stealing, creeping feeling of relaxation, like a sedative was now coursing through my veins. lost all sense of the others around me. With the third breath came a lightness, an almost weightless feeling, and it was with only the vaguest awareness of the ground beneath me that I managed to lay my head back upon my jacket.

And then there was no jacket. There was no ground beneath me. I was sinking. Sinking straight downward, floating like a molten feather. I felt no fear that I seemed to be falling through space. The descent, I knew instinctively, would not hurt me. The Rifting had begun.

I landed suddenly, yet gently. I felt grass beneath me, and a warm breeze on my face, I inhaled, and the scent of the herbs was gone, replaced by a rich earthy scent like petrichor. Full of anticipation, opened my eyes.

I blinked. I was sitting in the very same spot where I had laid down. In front of me, the fire crackled and popped. I looked to my right and saw Flavia lying on the ground beside me. Her face was twitching and her eyes were moving rapidly back and forth beneath her eyelids. Her bowl of herbs lay beside her limp hand, its contents scattered like ash. I looked to my left and saw Jeta likewise motionless on the ground.

"Oh, you have got to be kidding me," I muttered to myself. "What am I, immune to Rifting?"

I stood up and walked around the fire. All the rest of the Rifters were deep in their trances, insensible to my presence. I knelt next to Mairik and shook his shoulder gently.

"Uh, Mairik? Mairik, can you hear me? I, uh... I did something wrong. It didn't work."

Mairik didn't respond. The muscles in his face were twitching, reacting to whatever marvelous flights of fancy were happening behind his eyes.

"Damn it," I murmured, and stood up. I looked around to where Finn had been sitting and blinked in surprise. His seat was empty. He was gone.

"Finn?" I called.

No response.

I called again and again, circling the fire and casting my eyes out into the gathered darkness of the woods, but Finn did not reply.

I felt my pulse begin to speed up. This was strange. He'd been sitting there only moments before, and he promised he would stay until the Rifting was over. But... had that only been moments before? How long had that falling sensation lasted? Maybe I'd been falling for hours and just hadn't realized it?

A sudden sharp note sounded from a fiddle. I jumped and yelled in shock, spinning to find the source of the sound. A figure sat in the tree nearby.

"Jesus, Laini, you scared the crap out of me."

The figure in the tree let out a soft chuckle.

"Which was probably your intention, of course," I said dryly. "Well, you can take a moment to gloat if you like. You were right. I obviously don't have the 'Sight' or whatever. I Rifted right back to consciousness and didn't see or hear a single thing. What a waste of drugs."

Laini didn't answer. She just laughed again. The laugh was strange. It felt... wrong.

"Laini?"

"Try again."

"What?"

"I am not Laini. Try again."

The figure laughed again. The laugh and the voice were silvery and high, almost like a child's.

237

"Who is that? Who's there?"

I took a cautious step forward toward the figure, but the light from the fire would not penetrate the branches, would not show me who was sitting there. I took another few steps, hesitantly, but it wasn't until I had left the protective ring of the fire that I saw it.

A door.

It seemed to have been carved right into the living wood of the tree the figure was sitting in. It was covered in vines that nearly obscured the hinges and mossy green handle, but there it was, like something out of a fairytale.

The realization hit me. I hadn't woken up at all. I was Rifting right now. The journey—or whatever it had been—had dropped me right down into an exact replica of the place I'd already been. I looked back at the fire. Flavia, Jeta, and the others had vanished.

I turned back to the figure in the tree. It had picked up the fiddle again and was playing upon it, a slow melancholy tune this time. I approached cautiously now, a mixture of fear and excitement bubbling in the pit of my stomach.

I reached the base of the tree and looked up. The song came to an abrupt, screeching end. I sucked in a startled breath.

"Mary!" I gasped.

The Silent Child stared down at me, her sooty face grinning mischievously. I never saw her smile like that when I knew her, trapped on earth.

"Mary, what are you doing here?"

"Me? I'm always here."

"But... you're not trapped in the Aether, are you?" I cried. "I thought... when I saw you... I thought the spirits trapped in the torch were able to Cross!"

"Do not fret. I am at peace. We remain connected, that is all," she said cryptically.

"But why are you—"

"We remain connected," she repeated.

I stared at her. She stared back, utterly at her ease. That was as close to an answer as I was going to get, I supposed. Still, the sight of her sitting there, her little bare feet swinging playfully, left me feeling unnerved.

"What are you doing here?" she countered.

"I'm looking for something, I guess."

"What are you looking for?"

"I'm... not really sure."

Mary cocked her head to one side, staring at me curiously. "How can you find it if you don't know what it is?"

"Good point," I said. "But Mairik told me that this was like a lucid dream and that I could control things, so I would like you to point me in the direction of some answers, if you wouldn't mind."

"Oh, answers," Mary said with a sigh of relief. "Why didn't you say so to begin with? Answers can be found down those two paths."

I squinted into the trees where she was now pointing a tiny, grubby finger. There were two paths winding off through the trees.

"Which one do I take?" I asked her. "If you say the one less traveled, I will shake you out of that tree."

Rather than answering me straight away, Mary sawed a few more chords on the fiddle. They rose from the strings not just as sounds, but as vibrant, twirling strands of color. As I watched them, the bright smoky tendrils twisted themselves into words:

Why don't you ask the path?

I stared up at them, mouthing them. "What do you mean, 'ask the path'? Paths don't—"

My question died in my throat. Mary was gone. The tree was empty, save for the fiddle, which now seemed to be made of embers that were glowing and curling into powdery ash.

"Okay, then," I murmured to myself. "Thanks for your help."

I turned to the two paths in front of me. Both were overgrown with tangles of low-growing vines and creeping groundcover. I swallowed and stepped forward, so that I stood at the very place they split apart, feeling, as I did so, that I had fallen into a videogame.

"Uh, hi," I called into the stillness. "I want to know why I keep getting the vision of Annabelle. Can you please show me which path will lead me to the answer?"

I wasn't sure what I expected would happen? One of the nearby trees to point a branch like a gnarled finger in the right direction? A little furry woodland creature would hop into sight and beckon me forward with a paw? If one thing was for damn sure, even in a drug-induced vision, I was no freaking Disney princess.

I took a step forward and called my question still louder. No answer. No hint. No clue that I could see.

"Okay. Okay, think, Jess," I said to myself. "You can figure this out." I looked around me for inspiration. Mary's colorful words made of music still hung in the air near the tree where she'd been perched.

"Music. Music doesn't have a color," I muttered. As I looked at the words, thinking, I noticed something glinting in the tree just beyond them. An apple, rosy and red, dangling temptingly from a branch.

With a surety that took me by surprise, I walked over, plucked the apple from the branch and took a bite.

The familiar taste I was anticipating did not come. Instead, my ears were filled with musical sounds that sang of sweetness and juiciness and crunch.

"Okay," I said slowly, thinking it through as I chewed and swallowed the song. "Sounds are color. Taste is music. My senses are out of whack. It's like... like drug-induced synesthesia. I'm expecting to hear an answer, but maybe the answer won't be a sound." I dropped the apple on the ground. It sank through the grass and disappeared. Almost immediately a plant began to grow where it had fallen, a tiny tree sprouting leaves and blossoms before my eyes.

I turned my fascinated eyes from its progress and faced the paths again. I hesitated, wondering what sense I should try. Should I pick a rock up off one of the paths and... lick it? I shuddered. Even though I knew the rocks and twigs weren't real, I hardly wanted to start snacking on them. Then another idea occurred to me.

I knelt down and placed my open palm onto the right path. Instantly the feeling of the dirt beneath my hand filled my nostrils with scents I knew: firewood, mahogany, books, coffee, Hannah's mild, fruity perfume. Our room in Fairhaven lay down that path. I pulled my hand back and the smells vanished.

Next, I placed my foot on the left path. Immediately I was overwhelmed with another profile of familiar scents: candlewax, incense, musty old books, ginger tea, cats, even a faint whiff of formaldehyde. My heart broke into a gallop.

Annabelle's shop lay at the end of this path.

I did not immediately break out into a run. Did the other path have answers for me, too? Answers to other questions I didn't know to ask yet? Was there something I needed to know about Fairhaven? About Hannah? I pushed the thought away. That wasn't why I was here. I was here about Annabelle, and I couldn't let myself be tricked or lulled back to the familiarity of home just because I was

:ared that the truth about Annabelle might be just as terrifying as ιy vision.

I stood up, took a deep breath and set off down the left-hand ath. Though the ground beneath my feet was littered with dead ιaves and twigs, I made no sound as I followed it through the trees nd around a bend. I looked around me in fascination as the trees ecame shelves, and the leaves and branches morphed into a quirky ɔllection of spiritual and paranormal curiosities.

Within a few moments, I was standing in the cramped, offbeat uarters of Madam Rabinski's Mystical Oddities. I'd never seen it ɔ empty. Behind me was the door, propped open. Its tinkling little ell that usually heralded the arrival of customers was silent and :ill.

"Annabelle?" I called tentatively. Given what had happened to ιe so far, I hardly expected an answer, and so I jumped in surprise ′hen Annabelle's voice called back at once. "Hey, Jess! I've got ′hat you're looking for right here! It just came in!"

"What?" I replied.

"I'm in the back room!" she called again. "Come on back!"

Curious, I followed the sound of her voice around some shelves nd to the doorway that led into the back room. I couldn't see eyond it, because it was hung with a vintage beaded curtain. I ırned and stared at the door behind me. Instinct told me that ιat was the door that would lead me out of the vision, and that it ′as safe to pass through the beaded curtain. I swung the tinkling :trands aside and stepped through.

Annabelle had her back to me as she rummaged through a large ardboard box on her desk. At the sound of the beads she turned ɔ look over her shoulder. Her face was smudged with dust, but she miled.

"It's on the table," she said, pointing. Her collection of bracelets ιngled like an out-of-tune piano.

I let the beads swing down behind me, unsure whether I should elieve my eyes. Annabelle looked... fine. I scanned her for signs of ιjury—a smear of blood, anything. "Annabelle, are you okay?"

She pulled a voodoo doll out of the box and examined it critically. Of course, I'm okay. Why wouldn't I be?"

"But... what are you doing here?"

Annabelle took her eyes off the doll for a moment to laugh at me. Is that a trick question? Where else would I be? This is my shop!"

"But," I began, taking another step toward her. "You're... you'r okay, aren't you?"

Annabelle put the doll down now and eyed me beadily. "Jessic Ballard, what in the goddess's name are you talking about? It seem like I should be asking you if you are okay, not the other wa around."

I frowned. She obviously didn't know what I was talking about "Yeah. Yeah, I'm fine. What did you say you had for me?"

"What you asked me for. It's in the box," Annabelle said, turnin back to her work.

"What did I ask you for?" I asked, confused.

Annabelle sighed a long, aggravated sigh. "Jessica, what did yo come all the way here for?"

"I came here for answers. I want to know..." I hesitated, bu decided I could tell her here, in this form. She wasn't real. Sh was a manifestation of my own fears and doubts. I wouldn't b frightening the real Annabelle by telling this dream Annabell about the drawing. "I want to know what the drawing means—th one that I keep drawing while I'm asleep. It's about you, Annabelle I'm really scared that something awful is going to happen to you and I'm Rifting so I can try to prevent it."

Annabelle listened to all of this with a completely impassiv face, nodding along as though I were simply reciting some phon messages or a grocery list. When I had finished, she simply smile again.

"I understand, Jessica. Just look in the box!"

Bewildered, I edged through the boxes and baskets and teeterin; piles of unshelved merchandise until I reached the table unde the window. With slightly trembling fingers, I pulled the cardboar flaps apart and looked inside.

The whole world seemed to lurch, tipping me headfirst righ into the box, which now looked less like a box and more like bottomless pit of doom. I was falling, tumbling into blackness Before I could do more than scream, however, I landed, upright an uninjured, in a chair.

I opened my eyes, sucking a breath into my empty lungs, an looked around me. I was sitting in the middle of the Grand Counci Room at Fairhaven, all set up for the Airechtas with its rows an rows of chairs, and the velvet-draped podium up on the platform. I was utterly silent, and completely empty except for me.

I sat for a few tense moments, waiting for something to happen, but when nothing did, I decided that the room was waiting for me to do something. I cleared my throat, tasting the sweet residue of the Rifting herbs, and called out, "Hello? Is anyone here?"

No one answered. My voice didn't even echo, as it should have done in such a cavernous space. It barely seemed to reach a few inches beyond my face.

"I want to know about Annabelle. I want to know about my drawing of her, and what it means."

Still nothing. What was I doing wrong? Didn't I have any Spirit Guides?

Unbidden, Fiona's voice came into my mind. "Your visions and your understanding of them will never become any clearer if you don't own them. You must take ownership, Jess. You must embrace it."

But could I? Was I too scared, too selfish to do it? I thought I might be. God, why couldn't they have given this gift to someone else? Someone who was worthy of it? Someone who could do great things with it? All I seemed able to do was run from it.

I looked down at my hands and found I was holding a crumpled-up ball of paper. Fingers trembling, I unwrapped it, already knowing what I would see. It was the drawing of Annabelle, looking down at her own body.

And I couldn't just let it happen.

I looked up again and called out, "I'm a Seer. I've made a prophecy. I need to understand what it means. Please help me to understand what it means."

Something had changed. This time my voice reverberated powerfully around the room, breaking off and multiplying, so that there might have been a hundred of me, all shouting over each other. Over and over the words bounced back to me:

I am a Seer.

I am a Seer.

I am a Seer.

I caught a slight movement out of the corner of my eye. I turned to look. Someone was now sitting in one of the chairs in the very front row. I could only see her back, but there was something familiar about her. A long thick braid of flyaway silver hair hung down her back.

"Bernadette. Bernadette Ainsley."

Her name came to my lips before I had consciously recognized her. She did not turn or answer me. She simply nodded her head, sending rippling glimmers of light through her hair as the candlelight wavered across it.

I stood up slowly and edged my way across the row of chairs and up the aisle. I wasn't scared to approach her. I knew that she couldn't hurt me here in this dreamscape, and since I had last seen her, I had learned that she, too, had been a Seer. Another Seer. I had never spoken to one before.

I stepped around the last row of chairs and chose one to sit in, leaving a few chairs between myself and Bernadette, just in case. She was staring up at the Council benches, but didn't really seem to see them. Her eyes had a glazed, far-off look. As I watched her, trying to decide what to say, a tear slipped down her face and clung, glimmering, to her chin.

"Bernadette," I said again, very softly.

"Yes," she said, her voice barely more than a whisper.

"Are you here to help me? Can you help me to understand this prophecy?"

Bernadette laughed a tiny, bitter laugh. "Understand? The understanding of my own prophecy eluded me until it was too late. What makes you think I can understand yours?"

"I asked for help and you appeared," I pointed out.

"I came to warn you, not to help you," Bernadette said.

"To warn me? About what? Is it the drawing? Do you know what it means?" I asked quickly, my words tumbling over each other in my eagerness.

"Not about the drawing. About your gift."

"What about my gift?" I asked.

"If you embrace it, you are a fool. It will destroy you, just as it destroyed me," Bernadette hissed, turning a fierce, burning look on me.

"You don't know that," I said. "Many Seers who have embraced their gifts have gone on to help lots of people. Your daughter Fiona told me that."

Bernadette cackled. "You're going to take the word of my mad artist daughter?"

"Your daughter has been a good mentor to me," I said defensively. "And I'd be more likely to take her word than yours, or did you forget that you once tried to stab me?"

The wild smile that had accompanied Bernadette's laughter faded. "I thought only of protecting my sisterhood."

"And that's all I'm thinking of, too," I said. "I know you think that I'm a danger to you, but I'm not. I'm just trying to find a way to live with this legacy I've been given. So, if you can help me do that, I would really appreciate it."

Bernadette laughed again, but the laugh was half a wild sob. "It will break you, Jessica Ballard. Do you hear me? It will leave you broken."

"Don't you dare tell me about broken," I cried, my voice cracking. "I know all about broken. I've been broken. Hell, I've thrived broken. You aren't going to scare me away from this. Now, tell me what I need to know. Please, Bernadette."

We stared into each other's eyes. I watched a fierce battle rage behind her glaze of tears.

"The drawing. Your prophecy. That is how you will keep your promise."

I frowned. "What? What does that mean? What promise?"

"That is how you will keep your promise to the Walker."

"But—"

Bernadette cut me off with a desperate, feral cry. She leapt out of her seat and drew from beneath the folds of her clan robe a long, curved dagger, the same dagger she had once tried to kill me with. She raised it over her head, all reason and meaning gone from her eyes.

"No, Bernadette, no! Please, don't!" I cried, slipping sideways off of my chair and scrambling back from her, arms raised protectively in front of me.

The dagger flashed down through the air, but no pain came. I opened my eyes to see Bernadette still standing in front of me, the handle of the dagger protruding from her own abdomen. A deep scarlet stain was blossoming across her robes.

"No! Bernadette, no! What have you done?" I cried, leaping to my feet and running to her just in time to wrap my arms around her as she sank to the floor.

"Broken things," Bernadette whispered. "Broken things must be discarded."

"Don't say that!" I cried, my own eyes blurring with tears now. "You aren't broken. No one is broken beyond repair."

"Broken…" Bernadette whispered. "Broken things… set free."

An indefinable something was snuffed out behind her eyes, leaving them as vacant and unseeing as the windows of an abandoned house.

"It's all right, Jessica," a voice said.

I looked up and cried out. Annabelle was standing there, smiling at me. "It's all right. Don't be afraid. This is how you keep your promise."

In horror, I looked back at Bernadette, but she was gone, replaced by Annabelle, motionless upon the ground.

"Oh my God, no! Annabelle, no!"

With a cry, I grasped at the place the knife should have been, determined to pull it from her, to reverse the wound, but it was gone. I looked wildly around and saw it lying instead on the ground beside Annabelle's limp, outstretched hand.

"What the hell is this supposed to mean?" I shouted angrily at the spirit Annabelle, who was smiling so serenely down on me. "I'm supposed to let you kill yourself so that Irina can escape? That's insane. I would never do that!"

"All the answers you need are in front of you, Jessica. You must look. You must see it. This is how you keep your promise, Jessica," she repeated.

"So, I'll break my damn promise!" I yelled. "I won't sacrifice you for her, Annabelle."

"Jessica, you must wake up now."

"I'm telling you, I won't let this... what did you say?"

Annabelle smiled again. "I said you must wake up now. Wake up."

"No, I need to know—"

"Wake up."

And before I could say another word, before I could beg another detail from her, the door behind me flew open and, like a leaf in a windstorm, I was plucked from the ground and tossed into the air, whirling and flailing, back through it to the harsh reality of consciousness.

21

UNWELCOME VISITOR

I WAS FALLING, falling again through a vast and airless darkness. As I fell, voices swelled around me, as though I were following their call to the place where I would land.

"Jess! Jessica!"

"Northern Girl, wake up!"

"Come on, come out of it now!"

A group of frightened voices grew louder and louder around me, ntil they were a ringing chorus of fear pounding my eardrums. At ast, with a thud and a gasp, I arrived back in the clearing. I felt ay body twitch against the cold ground, and I shot bolt upright, ay eyes flying open. I could barely see. My vision was blurred with izziness and a haze reminiscent of having just woken suddenly om a deep sleep.

"You think she's still in it?" Jeta murmured to Mairik, who shook is head.

"Nah, she's back. She wouldn't be able to see us if—"

"Look at her eyes," Mina whispered. "Do our eyes look like that hen we do it?"

"Jess," Flavia said in the overly cautious, gentle tones of someone rying to talk someone off the edge of a cliff. "Jess, you're still eeling the after-effects of the Rifting. Don't say anything else, kay? Just drink this."

She held a pewter mug out to me, which trembled slightly in her ngers. Without arguing, I took it and threw back the contents in ne gulp. I wasn't sure what it was, but it burned on the way down, nd sent sensation buzzing into my numb extremities. I closed my yes and tested my senses. Everything seemed to be wired the right ay again. My fingers felt hard, cold earth, not scents. My ears eard the murmurs of frightened voices, not colors. I opened my eyes again, rubbing them vigorously until the blurriness cleared away.

The first thing that came into focus was my own arm. The artwork that Jeta had painted upon it was completely gone, as though it had never been there. I looked at my other arm and saw, with a start, that a single rune remained in the center of my wrist. I rubbed at it, but it did not fade.

"All of the artwork should be gone," said a voice, and I looked up to see Jeta sitting nearest me, staring down in fascination at the rune still marking my wrist. "It disappears—the magic gets used up along your journey. I've never seen one stay behind before."

"But I didn't choose to go through the door," I said. "Someone was calling me back. Someone woke me up."

"That was me," Flavia said. "We all finished ages ago. But you were still in it, and then suddenly you were shouting and flailing, so..." She shrugged apologetically.

"Even so, this should have faded as soon as you woke up," Jeta said, her voice raw with wonder. "And I can't even wipe it off now." She was rubbing at the mark, but it resisted her attempts to remove it.

"I don't recognize that rune. What does it mean?" I asked her.

She lifted her eyes to mine. "To set free."

Broken things. Broken things set free.

My heart stuttered in my chest. My mouth went dry. I focused on the faces around me, one by one: the Traveler kids, their expressions ashen and confused; Finn, his eyebrows drawn together in a severe line over his narrowed eyes; even Laini, who had deemed the situation interesting enough to descend from her perch in her tree and investigate. And . . .

"Annabelle!"

The name escaped my lips in a cry so shrill that everyone around me fell back in alarm. I was no longer Rifting, but there she was, sitting right in front of me beside Fennix, flickering light and shadow from the dying fire playing across her worried features.

"Yes, Jess. It's me," she said warily.

"Why are you... what are you doing here?" I gasped, backing away from her in a frantic crab crawl, sending my bag and my coat skittering across the dirt, until my back hit a tree trunk and I could go no further.

"I... was invited by the Traveler Council," Annabelle said slowly, her face full of concern at the way I was behaving.

"But why? Why now?" I whispered.

"I've been in touch with them since we were here three years ago. I've been trying to reconnect with my history, and I wanted to... Jess, why are you looking at me like that?" Annabelle asked in exasperation. "What is wrong with you?"

"Me? Don't worry about me!" I cried. "It's you! You! You... you have to get out of here!" I struggled to my feet.

"Jess, calm down—" she began.

"I will not! I will not calm down! You haven't seen what I've..." I scrambled to my feet, but had to lean against the tree because my knees felt like jelly. I turned a desperate gaze on Finn. "Finn, please. Get her out of here. Take her somewhere, anywhere else!"

Finn took a tentative step toward me, reaching out a hand. "Jess, take some deep breaths. You've only just regained consciousness. You need to take a breath so that you can process what you—"

"No, Finn, no! You need to get her out of here! Annabelle, please just get out of here! It's not safe for you here!"

Annabelle didn't move, though her expression shifted from bewilderment to fear. It was Flavia who spoke next, her voice calm and soothing.

"Jess, why don't you come with me," she said gently.

"What?" I snapped.

"Come with me. Come into the Scribes' wagon. Let's get you warmed up, and record your Rifting. You've evidently been on a wild ride, and something you saw frightened you. Let's step back. Let's understand it. You can talk with Annabelle when you're feeling more collected."

"No... but I..." I said weakly. My legs were shaking like mad now, and I fought to stay upright.

"That's an excellent idea," Finn said firmly. "Some warmth, some rest, and some interpretation."

I glared at him, betrayal welling up inside me. "Finn! You know what I'm talking about! You need to get her out of here!"

Annabelle opened her mouth, undoubtedly to ask what the hell we were talking about, but Finn silenced her with a look. He turned back to me. "Jess, do you trust me?"

"What kind of a question is that?"

"Just answer it then. Do you trust me?" Finn asked again.

"Yes, of course I do," I said, and the words seemed to take a little of my immediate panic away. "I trust you."

"Good. Then you can rest assured that I will not let anything happen to Annabelle while you go with Flavia. And Annabelle promises to stay with me and heed my warnings, don't you, Annabelle?"

Annabelle's eyes darted back and forth from me to Finn, and then she answered in the same calm, measured tones that Finn had used. "Yes, of course. I'll stay right here with Finn. We will wait for you."

"Very good, then," said Finn, as casually as if we had just decided where to go get dinner. "Flavia, would you be so kind as to bring Jess into the Scribes' wagon? Jess, I'm sure Flavia has some good insight into Rifting that can help you interpret what you saw."

"I..." I glanced nervously around the group. Every pair of eyes was on me, some of them wary, some of them fascinated, but each and every pair was staring at me as though I were something strange. Something different.

So much for a normal night of teenage shenanigans.

"Okay, fine. Let's go," I said shakily.

Flavia smiled tentatively at me and ushered me toward the Scribes' wagon, which was actually an old converted boxcar. I followed her numbly, my eyes continuing to Annabelle, as though I were afraid she was going to vanish the moment I looked away, or else suddenly appear as I had drawn her. At last Flavia closed the door behind me, hiding her from view.

Flavia didn't ask me anything at first. She sat me down in one of the shabby armchairs by the potbellied stove. Wordlessly, she pulled off my boots and tucked a patchwork quilt around me, like a mother tucking a child into bed. Then she made me a fragrant cup of tea, stirred it with a cinnamon stick, and handed it to me. It tasted like ginger and apples and something flowery. I took several sips and let the warmth sink down into me. Flavia let me sit in silence while I drank, never pushing, no expectation, until I was ready to speak. A strong wave of déjà vu washed over me as I recalled the last time I had been inside this wagon. Her counsel then had been thoughtful, comforting, and much appreciated.

"Thank you," I told her at last. I was relieved to hear my voice was no longer shaking or shrill.

"You're welcome. How can I help?"

I looked into Flavia's face. This girl saved my life once. I trusted her. I could tell her.

"Something happened to me recently," I said. "Have you heard about the Shattering that took place at Fairhaven last month?"

Flavia nodded. "Yes, we all heard about that. I had never before heard about one happening in my lifetime."

"Yeah, well, I tend to attract once-in-a-lifetime events every week or so," I said dryly. "Anyway, just before the Shattering happened, I woke up to a spirit drawing of a young Durupinen woman I didn't recognize. It turned out to be the Shattered spirit herself, which I didn't discover until much later. The drawing helped us to identify her and reverse the Shattering."

Flavia's eyes went wide. "She reached out to you before the Shattering even happened?"

I shook my head. "No. That would have been remarkable in and of itself. But that wasn't what had happened. I was able to speak to her before she Crossed. She had never tried to reach out to anyone. She couldn't. She was trapped inside the *príosún* on the Ilse of Skye, under every restrictive Casting you could possibly think of."

Flavia's eyes went, if possible, still wider. I dropped my own gaze to my cup of tea clasped in my hands.

"Then how did she—"

"She didn't. It wasn't a normal spirit-induced drawing. It was a prophetic one," I told the cup. Silence greeted these words. I couldn't bear to look at Flavia's face. It was really much, much easier to keep looking down into my tea and counting the tiny specks of tea leaves settled in the bottom of the cup. Maybe I could interpret them, like Annabelle, and find the answers I needed. Finally, the silence spiraled on for so long that I couldn't stand it anymore. I looked up and found Flavia's face. She'd had time to settle it into a calmly expectant expression.

"Go on," was all she said.

I took a deep breath. "At first I thought it might have been an isolated incident. I've never had a prophetic experience before. But then I woke up to this."

I picked up my sketchbook, opened it to the most recent drawing I'd done of Annabelle, and handed it to Flavia. She took it from me, looked down at it, and gasped.

"But... is this... she's..." she whispered.

"Dead," I finished for her. "I don't know how else to interpret it."

"Nor do I," Flavia replied. "Is that a knife by her hand?"

"Yes. I've drawn that same image in my sleep twice now," I told her. "The sketches seem to be completely identical."

Flavia's eyes flashed in and out of view as the light from the fire flickered against her glasses, turning the lenses opaque. "No wonder you panicked when you saw Annabelle here. And she doesn't know?"

I shook my head. "I just couldn't bring myself to frighten her with a vision I didn't understand. What would be the point? I couldn't tell what had happened, or how it had happened, or where it had happened! It has no context! What am I supposed to say to her? 'Hey, so I had a vision of you dying but that's all the information I have, have a nice day!' I can't do that to her!"

"No, you can't," Flavia agreed. "Does anyone else know you've had this vision? Besides your Caomhnóir, I mean."

"My sister and Milo know, and my mentor at Fairhaven," I told her.

"So this is why you asked me about Rifting and prophecies," Flavia said quietly. "I thought you were still worrying about the Isherwood Prophecy, that there was something still there to interpret. It didn't even occur to me that you were talking about another prophecy entirely."

"I know, right? One prophecy is already one too many," I muttered.

"What did your mentor have to say?" Flavia asked, her studious gaze still poring over the sketch.

"Well, as luck would have it, Fiona's mother is a Seer," I said. "She only ever had one real prophetic incident, a sculpture of my mother's face. Her obsession with interpreting it eventually drove her mad. Fiona has studied prophetic art intensely ever since, in the hopes of helping her mother. She was the one who explained to me that I was a Seer, and that the drawings I had made were actually prophecies."

"And did she have any interpretation to offer for this image?" Flavia asked.

"No. She only encouraged me to open myself to the gift, so that I could be more receptive to understanding what the visions mean."

"Ah, I see," Flavia said, understanding dawning on her face at last. "That's why you wanted to Rift. You wanted help interpreting this particular image."

"That's right," I said.

"And did you? Did the Rifting increase your understanding?" could tell that Flavia was trying to tame her own intellectual riosity, but it bubbled up in her voice nonetheless. Her hunger for ndiscovered niches of Durupinen knowledge was insatiable.

"Yes," I said. "But this leads me to another... uh... delicate piece f information that only a few people know."

Flavia laughed incredulously. "Of course, it does."

I smiled weakly. "You know me. I like to keep things interesting." hesitated again, but I had already made my decision, already ecided that I could trust her. "When I arrived, you told me that you lt sorry for Irina, and that you hoped that the Council would set er free and let her Cross. Is that true?"

Flavia looked taken aback by the sudden shift in topic, but odded her head solemnly. "Yes, it certainly is. In fact," she stood p abruptly, her quilt crumpling to a heap at her feet. She scurried ver to one of the old boxcar tables that was strewn with open ooks and fraying sheaves of parchment, and extracted a piece of eavy yellow paper. She brought it to her chair and handed it over me as she sat back down. "This is a petition to the Council that group of us have created. It asks for mercy for Irina from the ouncil, and asks for consideration for pardon and an immediate rossing."

I scanned the paper, feeling a lump rise in my throat. "There ren't very many signatures on here."

Flavia shrugged helplessly. "That's because most of the Travelers ant to see Irina punished. The Council Elders are livid about he recent string of attacks Irina has committed, especially Ileana. isloyalty is tantamount to treason amongst the Travelers. But we oped that they might consider Crossing her, if we could frame it as he elimination of a threat, rather than giving in to her demands."

"Do you think it will work?" I asked, without real hope in my oice.

"I felt we needed to try something," Flavia replied.

"So, that's a no," I said with a sad smile.

"It's a long shot," Flavia admitted.

I handed the petition back to her. My heart was pounding very ard, considering all I was doing was sitting curled up in a chair. Well, as you know, I was the one who unmasked Irina at

Whispering Seraph. What you may not know is that I tried to Cross her once I realized who she was."

Flavia covered her mouth with her hands. "You did?"

"Yes. And I would have done it, but I was stopped by one of the other Trackers before I could open the Gateway. I had a chance to help Irina, and I couldn't. But before she was taken away, I made a promise that I would find a way to free her, if I could."

Peeking out from over her hands, Flavia's eyes glazed over with tears. "You promised her?"

"I did. And that's why I'm here. To do whatever I can to ensure that she gets to Cross. Obviously, I hope that the Traveler Council will just decide to do so, but if they don't..."

Flavia dropped her hands. "How will you do it?"

"I have no clue," I said. "Well, that's not true. I have one, vague terrifying clue." And I tapped a finger on the sketch in my lap.

Flavia frowned. "I don't understand."

"Neither do I," I said with a bitter laugh. "But I went Rifting with one question in mind: what does this sketch mean? Well, the Spirit Guides had an answer for me: this is how I keep my promise to Irina."

Flavia looked from my face to the sketch several times. I watched the horror slowly blooming on her face, until I felt quite sure that her expression perfectly captured what I was feeling in my gut at that very moment.

"In order for Irina to be free, Annabelle has to..." Flavia's voice shook and faded. She looked down at her petition as though it had transformed into something ugly and malignant in her lap.

"That's what the Spirit Guides told me. And I'm hoping they're wrong. That's why I was hoping you might help me interpret the vision I had when I was Rifting. Maybe I missed something? Maybe they were trying to give me a hint? Maybe I'm interpreting it all wrong? Please, Flavia. I know nothing about Rifting or Spirit Guides or prophecy interpretation, and you're the most knowledgeable Durupinen I know. There's got to be a way to help Irina without sacrificing Annabelle. Help me. Please."

Flavia reached a hand across the small space between us. She grasped my hand where it lay, right on top of the image of Annabelle, and squeezed it. Then she leapt up, returned to her desk, settled herself in front of a blank page, and picked up a pen.

"Tell me everything about your Rifting vision," she said firmly, pushing her glasses up her nose with a bookish determination.

§

When I exited the Scribes' wagon thirty minutes later, I was confident that I had told Flavia every detail I could possibly recall from the Rifting. Unlike a dream, the Rifting did not fade from the memory upon waking, but implanted itself firmly, Flavia told me, allowing the Rifter to ponder and interpret the experience more fully. I was both grateful and disheartened by this fact. On the one hand, clearly recalling details might help save Annabelle. On the other hand, much of the vision had been so disturbing that I longed to forget it entirely.

I saw Finn leaning against a nearby wagon, waiting for me. He leapt to attention as though I were an approaching commanding officer, and perhaps the expression on my face suggested just that.

"What are you doing? Where is Annabelle? Why aren't you with her?" I cried at once.

"I am with her," he said, much more calmly than I deserved. "She's right inside this wagon, asleep. She was dead on her feet. She's been traveling for more than a day."

A cold, iron fist released its grip on my lungs. "Oh. Right. Thank you for staying with her. I know it wasn't easy for you."

"It was where you needed me to be," Finn said.

"Are you sure she's asleep? I need to tell you what—" I began, but a sharp voice cut me off.

"There you are! Where the hell were you? Jess, she's coming! Annabelle is coming to the Traveler camp!" Milo's flustered voice crackled through the connection with a manic energy that made me wince.

"Yes, thank you, Milo, but you're about an hour too late," I replied. "And this isn't a crappy cell phone connection. I can hear you loud and clear as always, so please take it down a notch before you make my head explode."

"Sorry, sorry," Milo said, his voice settling at once. "What do you mean, I'm an hour too late?"

"She's already here," I told him.

"Oh, shit," Milo said. "Damn, sweetness, I'm sorry. I tried to warn you as soon as I found out, but I couldn't reach you for the longest time! It was like the connection was jammed. That's why I was shouting."

"That would be because of the Rifting," I told him. I rubbed at my forehead. Though he was remembering to keep his voice down, my head was beginning to pound. I suspected this was the onset of that Rifting hangover Flavia had warned me about.

"The what?" Milo asked.

"Never mind, I'll explain it later. Just tell me what you found out. How did you know she was coming?"

"She was traveling, which was why it took her so long to get back in touch with us. She was on planes for twelve hours, and then had to switch over to an international cell phone and all that before she could finally call us back. And of course, she didn't rush, because we were trying to play it cool and pretend it wasn't, like a dire emergency, so we wouldn't scare her or make her suspicious that something was going on."

"Well, that plan's out the window," I said dryly. "I scared the ever-loving shit out of her the second I saw her by screaming that she needed to leave because I was putting her in terrible danger."

Milo was silent for a long moment. "Smooth move, sweetness."

"I know, I know," I said. "But I was half-hysterical after a drug-induced dream-vision thing, and—"

"Wait, what now?!" Milo cried. "You're doing drugs? What is going on over there?"

"It's this thing called Rifting," I said impatiently. "The Travelers use herbs and a Casting to deepen their connection with the spirit world and get clearer messages. I tried to so that I could try to understand my vision of Annabelle better."

"And did it work?" Milo asked eagerly.

"Yes and no," I hedged.

"What the hell does that mean?" Milo asked.

"It means that I have some more shit to figure out. But I'll keep you posted, I promise," I told him.

"And... and what about... your promise? Irina?" Milo asked, lowering his voice even though I was the only one who could possibly hear him.

"I still haven't testified. But I'm... working on that, too," I said vaguely.

"Okay. If you need me..."

"I know. Thanks, Milo. Truly."

"You got it, sweetness." I felt the energy pop that meant he had pulled out of the connection. I sighed and rubbed my head again.

"All okay?" Finn asked.

"Yeah. Yeah, Milo was trying to warn me that Annabelle was coming to the Traveler camp."

"Ah," Finn said with a rueful smile. "Too little, too late, then."

"It wasn't his fault. The Rifting sealed off the connection for a while. Is she asleep?" I pointed to the wagon again.

"Yes. I checked. Sound asleep," Finn said.

"Good. You're going to want to sit down for this."

Finn listened calmly while I explained every detail of my Rifting vision, as well as everything that Flavia and I had discussed in the Scribes' wagon. When I had finished, he sat for a few moments with his hands pressed together, his fingertips against his lips.

"We can't keep this from Annabelle," Finn said. "You've got to tell her."

"I know. I just don't know how."

"Regardless, she must be told. It would be unfair to keep her in the dark," Finn said.

My eyes filled with tears despite my efforts to fight them back. "What am I supposed to say, Finn? This is all my fault."

He frowned at me. "How? How is this your fault?"

"I made that promise to Irina, and I set this whole thing into motion. It was a rash promise to make. I had absolutely no idea how I would keep it—I still don't know how I'm going to keep it, except that I seem to be sacrificing one of my good friends in the process."

"You mustn't talk like that," Finn said sharply. "You are not to blame for anything. Every choice we make, every action we take in this life—has consequences. You carry no more blame than anyone else simply because you've been given a glimpse of what those consequences might be."

"But it was still my decision to promise to help Irina," I said.

"And it was the right decision. You should help her. We should all help her. She has been persecuted and tortured for years. It's unconscionable, what's happened to her," Finn said, reaching out and taking my hand. "But don't forget what you know to be true of prophecies."

"What do I know to be true of prophecies?" I asked.

"They are not set in stone. They are not immune to the actions of those they speak of. It was right there in the words of the Isherwood

257

Prophecy: 'she will have the power.' Your agency mattered. Your decisions mattered. You fought for the only outcome you would accept and in the end, you triumphed."

"But that was different. That was about putting myself in harm's way," I said.

"And for most anyone else, that would have been a hundred times harder than risking another," Finn said. "Annabelle is a strong woman, just as you are. Sit down with her. Tell her what you've seen. Give her every detail. Perhaps she will have the answer."

"And if she doesn't?" I murmured.

"Then you will find the answer together. But you cannot carry this on your shoulders, Jess. The burden is not yours alone."

I sighed. "Let her sleep. When she wakes up, I'll tell her everything."

22

BEFORE THE COUNCIL

T WAS ANOTHER SLEEPLESS NIGHT. At this point I would be lucky to stay conscious during my testimony at Irina's trial, let alone make a compelling case for her release.

Around dawn, Flavia emerged from the Scribes' wagon. She arried two cups of strong black coffee, which Finn and I accepted ratefully.

"Have you told her?" Flavia asked us, nodding up at the wagon in hich Annabelle still slept.

"Not yet. We decided to let her sleep. But I'm going to tell her as oon as she wakes up," I told her. The hot mug sent feeling creeping p into my numb fingers. "Have you found out anything? Anything t all that might help us?"

"I'm reviewing as much information about Rifting and Seers as can find, Jess," Flavia told me. "There's a lot to go through, and uch of it is very old and very obscure. But there must be omething there, there must be." She spoke with the certainly of a ibliophile whose beloved books had never yet let her down.

"I hope you're right," I said.

"Is it safe to come out?" a voice behind me asked.

I whirled around. Annabelle was leaning out of the top of the utch door, her hair tousled and her expression wary.

"We'll come in, if that's okay," I told her.

"Sure," Annabelle said cautiously. "But can you tell me what's oing on this time, instead of just screaming at me to leave?"

"Yes," I said. "I'm sorry about that. I didn't mean to scare you." I rned to Flavia. "Will you join us, too, Flavia?"

"Of course," Flavia said. "I'll fetch the sketch book, shall I? And t me get some more coffee. Annabelle, some for you?"

"Yes, please," Annabelle said gratefully. Then she stepped back

and opened the bottom half of the door. "Come on in. Let's hear th
worst."

§

If there is one thing I will never do again for the rest of my life,
is underestimate Annabelle Rabinski.

As I struggled through one of the most difficult conversations o
my life, she simply listened, looking thoughtful and nodding he
head. When I showed her the sketchbook, she did not flinch or cr
out, but drew her eyebrows together contemplatively, poring ove
the details of her own likeness without fear or revulsion.

When I described the Rifting, and what I had learned there, sh
leaned forward, absolutely riveted. Finally, when I had completel
talked myself out, she sat back, let out a long sigh, and smiled a
me.

"Well. No wonder you've been harassing me night and day for th
last week!"

A short, slightly hysterical laugh escaped me. "Yeah. Sorry abou
the low-key stalking, but, as you can see, I had a good reason."

"Jessica." Annabelle reached forward and took my hand in her
squeezing it. "Despite our mutual animosity when we met, we ar
friends now, aren't we?"

"Of course, we are," I said, my voice breaking. "Do you even hav
to ask me that?"

"Friends need to trust each other. Friends need to tell each othe
the truth, always, even in the face of fear or uncertainty. *Especiall*
then," Annabelle said.

"Don't be angry, please," I choked out. "I was just trying to—"

"Protect me," Annabelle finished the sentence for me. "I know
that, and I love you for it. But I don't need your protection. Thi
world of prophecies and spirits is my world, too, Jess. It's my realit
as much as it's yours. And I can handle it. I promise you, I ca
handle it."

"I know. I know you can," I said. "I'm so sorry."

"Don't apologize," Annabelle said gruffly, letting go of my han
again and resuming her usual unflappable demeanor. "First let m
just say that I was here with you three years ago. I witnessed Irina'
torture. I saw the deplorable state they left that poor woman in, an
I have every intention of helping you secure her release, if I can."

"Annabelle, that's kind of you, but seriously, after what you've just seen, you can't possibly want to get involved with—" I began.

"Jessica Ballard don't you dare presume to tell me what I do and do not want to get involved with! I will get involved with whatever I damn well please!" Annabelle snapped. "Besides, it appears that the spirit world has already decided that I have a role to play here. There is no point in denying that, or running away from it. We just need to understand it better. So. Let's be logical about this."

She stood up so swiftly that Flavia, Finn, and I all jumped.

"There are two options here, as far as I can see. Either the Council will free Irina and allow her to Cross, or they will condemn her, and we will have to find a way to free her ourselves. Flavia, you know the Council best. What do you think the chances are that the Council will be persuaded to let Irina Cross?"

Flavia shook her head sadly. "Her betrayal has run too deep to be forgiven. I do not think they will let her go."

Annabelle nodded. "That is as I expected. Even living away from the clans, those same attitudes ran deep in my family. Woe betide the person foolish enough to betray my grandmother's trust."

Flavia smiled gently. "It's in our blood."

Annabelle nodded, then started to pace. "So, it comes down to interpreting this prophetic sketch of Jessica's, doesn't it? If we can understand it, we can move forward."

"But the image is… clear, isn't it?" I asked.

Annabelle shook her head. "Nothing is clear in these matters, Jessica. Nothing is literal, and nothing is set in stone. A single word, a single step, can change everything. Has it occurred to you that this drawing may not even be literal?"

I frowned. "What do you mean?"

"Perhaps the image is figurative? You're an artist, Jessica. You know that art can be symbolic and open to interpretation."

I couldn't fathom a different interpretation of the image than what it showed, but now didn't seem like the right moment to voice that particular thought.

Annabelle did not seem to require a response from me, but turned instead to Flavia. "Flavia, surely you have documentation of prophetic imagery and its eventual interpretation? The Scribes must have made ample study of that."

Flavia nodded. "Yes, of course. In fact, I've spent the last few hours gathering it to analyze. But it's a daunting task. There is so much material."

"Do you think you could enlist the help of any of the other Scribes without attracting suspicion?" Finn asked.

"If I frame it right, I suppose I could," Flavia said, biting her lip. "Everilda doesn't usually ask many questions."

"Excellent. Do it," Annabelle said. "It's important to understand everything we can about how these images present themselves. In the meantime, though, it sounds like much rests on the trial. What time is your testimony today?" Annabelle asked me.

"Noon," I said.

"Let's see what the outcome there is, before we panic," Annabelle said firmly. "A single vote, one way or another, could completely negate this prophecy, whatever it may mean."

"No pressure," I said under my breath. As if enough weren't already resting on what I had to say in front of the Council.

"We—that is to say, several of the other Travelers and I—have been preparing a petition asking for Irina's release. We intend to present it before the Council at the end of trial, after all of the evidence has been heard," Flavia said. "Jess is the last witness on the schedule at noon today."

"So, Jessica will prepare herself for the Council testimony. I will assist Flavia in any way I can until noon. We will all meet up again at the trial," Annabelle said, in the tone of a sports coach reviewing a game plan with her team. I half-expected her to tell us to put our hands in for some kind of cheer.

"Finn," I said sharply, as we all stood. "I want you to stay with Annabelle. Please."

Annabelle smirked. "Oh, come on, Jess. Don't you trust me not to get myself killed between now and noon?"

"I don't trust anything to do with this prophecy, or any other prophecy for that matter," I said.

"I can't blame you for that," Annabelle said, and gave my hand a reassuring squeeze. "So why don't you go back to those Spirit Guides and give them a message from me. Prophecy or no prophecy, I have no intention of dying."

§

The inside of Ileana's tent was abuzz with anticipation as we ntered it at five minutes to noon. It was stiflingly hot. The usual ire was ablaze, and every single Traveler in the camp had crammed hemselves into every corner and crevice of the tent, perched on enches, chairs, upturned crates, trunks, and even each other's acks. A short bench had been placed on either side of Ileana's arved wooden throne, and three women sat on each one, looking usterely out over the excited crowd. Apparently, the Traveler Council consisted of only six members. Ileana sat in the middle, urveying the crowd with her beady eyes.

Not even Finn's reassuring presence at my side, as I took a seat n the front row of benches, could stop my hands from shaking r my mind from racing. On my other side, Annabelle tried to mile reassuringly, but she only managed a pained sort of grimace. Despite her determinedly brave attitude, her nerves were starting o fray as well. She and Flavia had managed to find several nstances of Seer images that had to be interpreted symbolically, ut nothing that could be applied to my own sketch, which was, in ny opinion, terrifyingly literal.

I looked around for some sign of Irina, but there was none. 'erhaps they would march her in, shackled like the prisoner she vas, when the proceedings started? I leaned across to Flavia and sked her.

"They can't safely bring her here. There's no way to contain ter within the confines of the tent, and she's too violent in close roximity to other people," Flavia replied.

"So, they're holding her trial without her?" I whispered ncredulously. "She doesn't even get to hear what's being said gainst her? Or in her defense?"

Flavia shook her head. "You saw what she was like the other ight. No one can get near her."

Somewhere out in the clearing, a gong sounded twelve times, narking the hour. Ileana raised a gnarled old hand, and the tent mmediately fell silent.

"Our proceedings in the trial of Irina Faa will now resume," leana began, and immediately a translator began echoing her vords in a Romanian dialect for the older members of the clans hat did not use much English. "Today we will hear the testimony f Jessica Ballard, Tracker for the Northern Clans," Ileana went on, eckoning me forward and pointing to a carved wooden stool that tad been placed directly in front of the Council.

I stood up and nodded, trying to look—I don't know—responsible? Professional? I was here in an official capacity, I reminded myself. I was a Tracker, with an important job. I was not under attack here. I was not the one on trial, despite the feeling of dread that settled over me as I sat myself on the edge of the chair. The feeling of dozens of pairs of eyes on my back gave me a creeping sensation up and down my spine.

"Elder Oshina will conduct the questioning," Ileana announced. She relaxed back into her throne and picked up her pipe from the arm of her chair, thrusting it between her teeth. She tucked a leg up under herself and I realized with a start that, even in the midst of an official trial, she was barefoot.

The Council member nearest me stood up and cleared her throat. I tore my eyes from Ileana's knurled old toes and focused on her. "Miss Ballard," she began, in a heavy accent that she compensated for by speaking very slowly and clearly, "Thank you for consenting to testify today. Your presence is appreciated."

I nodded stiffly in reply as a round of muttering went through the crowd behind me, including several distinct hisses. My presence was clearly not appreciated by everyone, particularly those who still blamed me for the violence of the Necromancer attack.

Elder Oshina went on. "I would first like to establish your background connection to Irina. For the official record, when did you first meet her?"

"I first met her a little over three years ago, when I sought refuge here in the Traveler camp. After I was informed by High Priestess Ileana that I was likely a Walker, Irina was enlisted to teach me how to Walk."

"How would you describe your first impressions of her?"

"She was... unstable," I said, trying to choose my words very carefully. "She thought of nothing except Walking and escaping her own body, which she described as a prison."

"And when she was Walking? How was she different?"

"She was... happy. No, that's not even adequate. She was... joyful. Elated. She claimed that once I Walked, I would never want to re-enter my body again," I said.

"And was that true?" Elder Oshina asked.

"No," I said. "I found Walking to be disorienting and frightening, at least at first. Even when I got the hang of it, I still never felt so disconnected from my body that I didn't want to return to it."

"I see. So, do you think that Irina was exaggerating the sensation Walking?" Elder Oshina asked.

"No," I said. "No, it was just different for her because she wasn't true Walker."

Elder Oshina and several other Council members frowned at me, ١d the crowd began to mutter. "What do you mean, she wasn't a ue Walker?"

I hesitated nervously. "Well, that's how it was explained to me. ١st because someone can Walk, doesn't mean that they should. he ability to do it does not guarantee the ability to tolerate its 'fects on the mind and body. I am a true Walker, and so my ١nnection to my body remains undamaged by the act of Walking. ina, though able to Walk, could not withstand prolonged absence ٥m her body. That's why she's... well, you've all seen how she is," finished, looking around the room as I said it.

"So, do you believe that Irina's actions are the result of an altered ١ental state, and not a result of willful disobedience and betrayal?" lder Oshina asked sharply, and I could tell from her tone that it as a dangerous question to answer.

"I am sure that this Council has had much more experience with ina than I have. I'm sure that you have interrogated her as a part f these proceedings. I doubt you need my opinion on this matter," ٦edged.

"But we have asked you for it," Ileana said, pulling her pipe from er mouth and scratching her chin with it as she considered me. ١re you refusing to give it?"

"No," I said quickly. "Sorry, I wasn't trying to... Yes, I believe that ina's mental state has been altered drastically by Walking."

"And your mental state? Has it been affected at all?" Ileana ;ked.

The question felt like a trap. "No, I don't believe so. But I've only ⁄alked briefly and, as I explained before, a true Walker—"

"Thank you, that will do," Elder Oshina said, cutting me off. "Let ; move on to the events of October of last year."

I pressed my lips together and swallowed my angry retort. I ٥uld not do Irina or myself any favors by flying off the handle. I ٥uld almost feel Finn's silent pleas behind me. *Keep your temper,* ·ss. *Keep it together.*

"Please explain, in as much detail as you can, how you came into ١ntact with Irina again in October," Elder Oshina prompted.

"I was working on my first case for the Trackers. They sent m
sister, my Caomhnóir, and me down to New Orleans, Louisian
to investigate a spiritual retreat called Whispering Seraph. Th
owner of the property was a self-proclaimed spiritual guru name
Jeremiah Campbell who claimed that an angel had come dow
to earth and was guiding him to help people connect with thei
deceased loved ones."

Anger rippled through the watching Travelers. It was a relief t
know that they looked upon people like Jeremiah Campbell wit
the same contempt as I did.

"As a result of our investigation, we discovered that the 'ange
was, in fact, Irina, guiding Campbell's actions. She was drawn t
Whispering Seraph because there was an old, dismantle
Geatgrima buried in the basement of the plantation house. Sh
used Campbell, in an unsuccessful attempt, to rebuild and reope
that Geatgrima."

Several gasps caused me to look over my shoulder. Mouths wer
agape all through the crowd. Apparently, all of the details of Irina'
escapades had not reached beyond the Traveler Council.

"Was Irina successful in rebuilding the Geatgrima?" Elder Oshin
asked.

"No. We Unmasked her before she was able to reconstruct it,"
said.

"And what was her endgame? Why did she want to rebuild th
Geatgrima?" Elder Oshina pressed.

"She... well, her goals changed. At first, all she wanted was t
be able to Cross. She no longer trusted any fellow Durupinen t
help her do it. But once she began the process, she decided tha
she could create a point of free passage, where spirits could, i
essence, Cross themselves, without the help or permission of th
Durupinen," I explained.

The reaction was predictable. Irina's plan was blatant blasphem
to anyone who believed in the calling of the Durupinen. One olde
woman toward the back of the tent began spewing a steady strear
of curses, and grew so hysterical that a younger woman took her b
the arm and escorted her out of the tent.

I caught Flavia's eye. Her face was full of despair. It was over. I
was already over.

"It would never have worked," I called over the crowd, and the
fell silent. "I tried to tell her as much. The Geatgrima, even if i

266

had been restored physically, could not have been opened without a Durupinen Gateway."

"But her intentions—" began Elder Oshina.

"Her intentions didn't matter. They were illogical. If she had been of sound mind, thinking clearly and rationally, she should have realized that her plan would never work. I tried to reason with her but she was beyond reason."

"Intentions always matter," Elder Oshina said.

"Was there a question in there I'm supposed to answer, or were you just expressing an opinion?" I asked hotly.

She did not acknowledge my question, but continued on as though I hadn't spoken. "What happened, when she refused to heed your warnings?"

I tried to swallow, but my mouth had gone dry. Catriona had prepared me for these questions, but they still made me nervous. "I... I decided to Cross her myself."

Another shocked murmur. Another volley of whispering. I kept my face calm and impassive.

"You decided to Cross her?" Elder Oshina repeated.

"I did," I said promptly. "I'm sure you all had a chance to read the statement that the Tracker Office sent over. I explained it all in my report."

"Perhaps just one more time, for the record," Elder Oshina said. Her tone was decidedly colder than it had been when she began questioning me.

"I assessed the risk of the situation. I did not know how far the other Trackers were from our location or how long it would take them to reach us. I could not guarantee that our Castings would hold Irina until help arrived. I knew that she was incredibly unstable, irrational, and presented a very clear danger to herself and anyone who came into contact with her. I thought the safest thing to do would be to Cross her."

"Without consulting your superiors?" Oshina pushed.

"I've just told you. I could not contact my superiors. I was in a building full of potential victims of Irina's vendetta. I had to make the call to protect everyone there."

"Without consulting the Travelers, under whose jurisdiction Irina would surely fall?" Oshina asked, a note of incredulity in her voice.

"With all due respect, how would I have been able to do that? Not only was the situation extremely precarious and time sensitive, but I didn't exactly have any of you on speed dial. You are notoriously difficult to contact, which I realize is by design, but it does not lend itself to this particular situation. Irina was dangerous and she was in great distress. I had moments to decide what to do. As a Tracker, I had to listen to my instincts and trust my own judgment."

Ileana made a snorting noise through her nose, as though the idea of anyone trusting my judgment was absurd. I was bursting with so many things I wanted to say. What about her judgment, allowing a woman to be needlessly tortured for so many years? It was her fault that Irina became so desperate and that she had resorted to so many wild and violent measures to free herself. Wasn't Ileana's judgment far more questionable than my own?

Luckily, Elder Oshina went on before I had a chance to completely screw myself over by blurting out these observations.

"But you did not have the opportunity to Cross Irina?" she prompted.

"No," I said. "The senior Trackers were much closer than we had anticipated. Catriona arrived and took charge of the situation before I could follow through on my decision. She oversaw Irina's containment from that moment onward. I didn't see Irina again until I arrived here at the camp to testify."

"And when was it that you saw her?" Elder Oshina asked.

"Two nights ago, my first night here, a voice woke me from my sleep. The voice was singing. Finding myself unable to go back to sleep, I decided to follow it. The sound led me to the edge of Irina's clearing, but the Caomhnóir protections around the perimeter prevented me from approaching her wagon. I witnessed her attack on Ruslo."

"And what was your impression of that attack?" Elder Oshina asked.

"I was... horrified," I said. "Those were the actions of a desperate and tortured woman."

"So, you have now borne witness to two different attacks by Irina Faa; one on Mr. Jeremiah Campbell, and one on Ruslo Boswell," Elder Oshina said slowly.

"Yes, that's correct," I said.

"Would it be fair to say that both of those attacks were calculated?"

"Yes."

"Planned out carefully?"

"Yes."

"The products of a sound mind?"

I shook my head. "No. I wouldn't say that."

"But you've just agreed that they were calculated and planned. How could a mad person think things through so meticulously?" Elder Oshina asked.

"I see what you're trying to do," I said. "I spent a lot of time with Irina when she was teaching me to Walk. She was utterly obsessed with Walking, and with procuring her freedom. It was a singular compulsion. Even as she was showing me how to Walk, she was searching for a way out of her enclosure. She even attempted to hijack my body, once I'd learned how to leave it. And it astonishes me that, even after the pain that you've seen her in, the relentless escape attempts, the wild attacks, that you could ever think she has control over her actions."

Elder Oshina pressed her lips together into a tight line of displeasure. It was clear that I had said more than she had intended to let me say, and that I had crossed some kind of unspoken rule by offering my opinion so forcefully. I concentrated on keeping my face smooth and my expression polite as I waited to see if she had any further questions for me.

"Thank you very much, Durupinen Ballard. I have no further questions for you. High Priestess?" Oshina threw the invitation over her shoulder to Ileana who glared at me for a moment, puffing on her pipe, before waving a hand dismissively in my direction.

"Very well, then," Elder Oshina said. "You are dismissed, Durupinen Ballard. We thank you for your testimony. You may leave the proceedings."

I stood up, taken aback by the abruptness of my dismissal. "Uh, thank you. Is it... would it be okay for me to stay and hear the rest of the witnesses?"

"You are not a Traveler. These are not matters of your concern. You may leave the proceedings," Ileana said, a note of finality in her voice now that the invitation to leave was not so much an invitation as an order.

There was nothing else I could do. I walked up the aisle through a sea of hostile glares, Finn and Annabelle close on my heels.

23

DEVIL IN THE DETAILS

"WELL. That couldn't have gone any worse," I declared.

"That's not true," Finn said. "Things can always go worse."

I stared over at him across the fire. We were sitting outside our wagon, waiting for the trial to end. "What is that supposed to mean? Are you writing fortune cookie fortunes in those books of yours instead of poetry?"

Finn grimaced, looking awkward. "I merely meant that you did your best."

"It's true, Jess," Annabelle said. "In fact, given the attitudes of the Council, I'd say that was rather the best you could have hoped for."

"How?"

"Well, you didn't lose your temper and get yourself thrown out or screaming at the Traveler Council, so already you're ahead of your usual pace for this kind of thing," Finn said.

I glared at him, but didn't contradict him, mostly because he was right.

"You stuck to the facts," Annabelle said. "You gave them all the details, and you did it without feeding into the narrative that the Council was clearly trying to build."

"And what narrative was that?" I asked.

"That Irina is the offender rather than the victim," Annabelle said.

"I don't even know why they're bothering to have a trial," I said bitterly. "It sounds to me as though they've already decided that they can't forgive Irina's actions."

"No, forgiveness isn't really in the Traveler repertoire," Annabelle said, a tiny smile tugging at the corner of her mouth.

271

"Nor is admitting when we're wrong. And it would be no small thing for Ileana to admit she's been wrong in handling Irina's situation.

"How so?" I asked.

"To admit that Irina isn't at fault is to admit that the Council needlessly tortured and imprisoned her for decades. Ileana would have to admit to years' worth of poor judgment, not just a single bad decision. It would throw her entire tenure as High Priestess into doubt," Annabelle said.

"Better to take a hit to your reputation than cause anymore unnecessary suffering," I said, but I knew Annabelle was right. Ileana was far too proud to take the fall for Irina; after all, who had farther to fall than the High Priestess?

We stewed in tense silence for nearly an hour before Flavia came walking up the path. Her expression made my heart leap into a panicked gallop.

"They haven't convicted her already?" I asked, jumping to my feet.

But Flavia shook her head. "Ruslo and Andrei testified about their attacks, and I presented the petition. It... wasn't very enthusiastically received," she said delicately.

"Meaning what?" Annabelle asked.

"Meaning I'll be surprised if they even look at it, except to make note of the people who signed it," Flavia said with a defeated sigh. "I've thought before that our court is more about pageantry and public shaming than it is about justice, and today they've proved me right."

"So, now what do we do?" Finn asked. He stood as well, bouncing on the balls of his feet like he was hoping the answer would be to run laps around the encampment.

"The Council is in deliberation now. When they've rendered their verdict, they will send colored smoke up into the air from Ileana's wagon. White smoke if she has been found innocent of treason. Red smoke if she has been found guilty."

"How long will they deliberate for?" Finn asked.

"I'm surprised they need to deliberate at all," I growled. "It couldn't have been clearer to me that they'd already decided."

"Don't forget what I said about the pageantry," Flavia said with a rueful smile. "They will want to make a show of it. Don't expect any smoke for a few hours at least."

272

I groaned, running my fingers through my hair in frustration. All of this waiting was going to drive me mad.

"Let's not waste this time, then," Annabelle said briskly. "We still have a prophecy to figure out."

"Absolutely," Flavia said. "Let's head back to the Scribes' wagon. We can watch for the smoke as easily there as anywhere."

§

If I learned anything about myself in the three hours that followed, it was that I am utterly, irredeemably useless in that kind of a crisis.

Seriously, call someone else. I am not your girl. I am dead weight.

Not that I wasn't trying. I did my best to help Annabelle and Flavia sift through the documents and books about prophecy and Rifting. I sat determinedly down at one of the boxcar tables and set to work at once, but it was as though my brain had temporarily lost the ability to absorb information. I looked down at sentences that danced in front of my eyes, the combinations of letters blurring into meaningless jumbles. Every few minutes, I had to jump to my feet and peer through the little red velvet curtains on the nearest window, so that I could scan the sky for a sign of red or white smoke from Ileana's tent. This was a completely redundant exercise, of course, since Finn was standing right outside the wagon on high alert for the very same thing.

After the tenth time I did this, Annabelle slammed a book shut in frustration and glared at me.

"Do you need to go for a walk, Jess?" she asked me pointedly.

"I... no. Sorry. I'm just..."

"I know," Annabelle said. She did not require the completion of the sentence to understand exactly what I meant. "I am, too. We all are. But couldn't you just... stay still?"

"I make no promises," I said, sinking back into my seat and staring helplessly again at the mountain of papers.

"I thought prophecies were relatively rare," I said to Flavia, gesturing weakly to her own massive pile of scrolls. "Fiona told me they are fairly rare. How is there so much stuff to dig through?"

"But it's precisely because true prophecies are rare that there has been so much documentation about them," Flavia said, and even through the nerves I could hear an edge of nerdy excitement in her voice. "Any time a suspected prophecy is made, scholars jump on the opportunity for interpretation and application, even if the prophecy seems relatively unimportant."

"That must be exhausting for the Seers who make them," Annabelle pointed out.

"Yes, I imagine it must be," Flavia said, frowning as though she had never considered that angle before.

"Fiona's mother drove herself to the point of mental breakdown trying to wring meaning from her only piece of prophetic art," I said quietly.

"Well, you still look impressively sane to me, but I'll let you know if I see you slipping," Annabelle said. Her tone was curt, but when I looked up, she was smirking down at her papers. The smirk faded as she lifted the topmost one, revealing my sketch of her underneath.

"I've got to hand it to you, Jess, your attention to detail is impressive," Annabelle said with a suddenly shaking voice.

"What do you mean?" I asked.

"Well... these clothes you've drawn me in... I've just realized. I'm wearing them right now," Annabelle said.

I jumped out of my seat and stood behind her chair. She pointed down at the picture, her massive collection of bracelets jangling. There was no mistaking it. I'd drawn her entire outfit in exact detail, from the stripes in her shirt to the hole in the elbow of her long wool cardigan.

All at once the walls of the wagon seemed to be closing in, forcing the breathable air from the room and from my lungs.

"Maybe we've been going about this wrong," Flavia said. "Maybe it's not about symbolism and interpretation. Maybe the devil is in the details, so to speak."

I couldn't answer her. I was trying not to pass out. I backed away from Annabelle as though my proximity to her would tear the image right from the page and bring it to life right there in the wagon.

Flavia hadn't noticed my panic attack, though. She was digging furiously through a wooden box that she had pulled down from a nearby book shelf. After a few moments she found what she was looking for: a gold-handled magnifying glass.

Annabelle slid over at once to make room for her on the narrow bench, and the two of them bent low over the image, examining every inch of it for... what?

"What are you looking for?" I asked, a bit hysterically.

"Any other small clues that might help us," Flavia said quietly, as though she might distract herself with the volume of her own voice.

"Why is it going to help to just... just further confirm the inevitability of this?" I cried, choking back tears. "I don't want to know how it happens, I want to know how to stop it!"

Flavia looked up at me, and though her eyes were kind, her expression was rather stern. "Jess, those are not mutually exclusive things. To reveal one is to reveal the other."

I stopped pacing, feeling, for a moment, like a child who had just been reprimanded by a school teacher. She was right, of course. My freak-out was helping no one, least of all Annabelle. I walked over behind them and looked down through the magnifying glass.

Flavia brought it to rest over the image of the dagger. "Jessica, is this the dagger you saw in your Rifting vision?" she asked slowly.

I peered down at it. "Yes. Well, it was the second one I saw. Bernadette had one that she stabbed herself with—it was the same one that she used to attack Hannah and me during the Airechtas. Then, when Bernadette transformed into Annabelle, the dagger transformed, too. That's what the dagger turned into," I said, pointing at the drawing. "Just like that."

"You're absolutely sure?" Flavia asked.

"Yes," I said.

"Why, Flavia?" Annabelle asked. "Do you recognize it?"

"Yes," Flavia said. "Everyone in this Traveler camp would recognize it. Each Caomhnóir is given one upon entering his training. They are identical. You cannot see it at this angle here, but each one is marked with the rune for guardianship on the bottom of the handle."

I gasped. "And you're sure..."

"Oh, yes," Flavia said. "I'm quite sure. There are at least fifty of those daggers right here in this camp."

Annabelle, Flavia, and I looked at each other, then back down at the drawing.

"Its... kind of odd, isn't it?" Annabelle said softly.

"What's odd?" I asked.

"Well, I seem to be dead, and I seem to have been holding that knife, but... where's the blood?"

I looked down at the sketch again. She was right. There was no blood. No visible wound.

"You would think," Annabelle said, "given your incredible attention to detail, that there would be some sign of injury, wouldn't you?"

"I..."

"Jess! Jess, come out!"

Finn's voice rang out sharply from outside. Flavia dropped the magnifying glass with a clatter and we all ran for the door.

Finn said nothing as I came to a stop beside him on the grass. He simply pointed to the sky above the trees, his expression stony.

A plume of red smoke billowed into the air, carrying our last hope for Irina into the night sky and scattering it carelessly up amongst the stars. We all stood silently for a few moments, knowing that Irina, alone in her clearing, would be able to see it, too, and to know what it meant.

"Well," Annabelle said quietly. "That's that."

"Yes, it is," I said. I turned to Finn. "I need to go see Irina."

He stared at me. "Why?"

"I have to go apologize to her," I said. "And I have to break my promise."

Flavia, Annabelle, and Finn all stared at me like I'd just announced I was going to fly to the moon.

"Jess... are you sure?" Finn asked after a moment.

"Am I sure? Am I sure I don't want to sacrifice one of my friends to keep a promise I have almost no chance of keeping? Yes," I said in a vehement hiss. "It was rash and stupid of me to make that promise, which isn't surprising because I'm a rash and stupid person, but I won't let Annabelle pay the price for that. I wish I could have saved Irina. I do. I wish I could have found a way to rescue her from this. But I can't. The prophecy showed me what would happen if I kept the promise. Well, I'm not keeping it. I'm breaking it. That sketch no longer means anything because I won't let it."

"But Jess..." Annabelle began.

"But, what? Show me how to keep this promise and keep you alive at the same time. Show me how to do it, and I'll do it. Please."

She didn't speak. No one spoke.

"Take me to the clearing," I told Finn.

"Wait," Flavia said.

I turned on her impatiently. "Flavia, I know you want to free Irina, too, but—"

"No, it's not that," Flavia said. "It's just... you can't get into the
earing unless you have the right Casting on you, remember? Hang
1."

She ran into the wagon and emerged again a few seconds later
ith a small leather Casting bag. A few muttered phrases and a
1ick rune later, she had finished.

"There. It's the same one that Dragos gave to Finn," Flavia said.
t will get you into the clearing to talk to her, but it won't protect
ɔu from her if she attacks, so keep your distance and be quick. Now
1at her sentence has been passed, they will likely send someone
om the Council to inform Irina of what's happened. You don't
ant to be caught there."

"Thank you, Flavia," I said, "for everything."

She smiled. "You're welcome. I wish we could have solved this
1e."

"Me, too." I turned to Annabelle. "Will you wait with Flavia until
ʒet back?"

Annabelle nodded. "Of course. Jess, I know this isn't easy for you.
·eaking this promise. And I know you're doing it for me. Thank
ɔu."

I didn't answer. Knowing what I was about to do to Irina, that
1ank you felt like a slap in the face—a slap that I absolutely
:served.

§

The clearing was silent. The barrier yielded to my tentative
·uch; I felt my fingers glide through it like a draft of cool air. The
osty grass beneath my feet made a soft crunching noise, but it did
ɔt matter. She was already waiting for me.

She was sitting in the open doorway of the wagon, her knees
1cked up under her chin, manacles on her wrists and ankles. She
·oked older than the last time I had seen her up close in her
ɔdy. Her hair was threaded through with much more gray, and her
·es seemed sunken in the sockets. All the fight had gone out of
:r. That feral, manic energy was gone, dissipated into the night
ith the smoke that had sealed her fate. There was no surprise in
:r gaze as she watched me approach, no gleam of interest. Only
·signation and, perhaps, a bit of contempt.

"I knew you would come, Northern Girl," she said as I planted my feet, still ten feet away from the door of the wagon. "I recognize your Caomhnóir when he intervened to rescue the boy. And then thought I glimpsed you on the edge of the clearing."

"Yes, that was me," I said.

"You could have helped me," she said quietly. "I wouldn't have killed him. All I wanted was the dagger."

"I know. I would have given it to you," I said. "But I couldn't get through the barrier then."

"But you bring me no weapon now."

I swallowed hard. "No."

She laughed. It was a hard, bitter thing, hardly a laugh at all "I see. I thought, when I saw you... but, no. So, all Durupinen promises are worth the same. Even yours."

I didn't respond. What could I say? She was right. I was betraying her as surely as the Travelers had done. I wasn't about to deny it.

"I came to apologize to you, Irina. I tried. Honestly, I did. testified before the Council. I defended you. But they had condemned you before I'd even begun."

"Foolish child," she hissed at me. "Did you truly believe that they would free me of their own accord? They, who have been the source of my torment for so many years? They, who have heard my plea and turned away?"

"Yes," I said weakly. "I had more faith in them than you did. shouldn't have, but I did."

"Then why, now, do you come to me? Simply to stare? To absolve yourself of responsibility? Be gone from this place, Northern Girl."

"I am not absolving myself of responsibility. I am taking it," said. "I'm apologizing not because I need you to accept it, but because I think you need to hear it. I wanted you to know that didn't forget you. I did come here hoping to help you. I... I tried. but the price... the price was too high."

"And what was the price? What would it have cost you?" she asked.

I didn't answer. I wasn't going to tell her that I chose someone else's life over hers. I could hardly admit it to myself. Annabelle's life didn't matter more than Irina's. It just mattered more to me That was the awful, selfish truth of it.

Irina laughed again, and it rose like a shriek into the night. In nearby tree, several startled ravens took flight, cawing madly. "M life, my suffering, is poor currency in the pockets of the Durupinen. I have known this. You do not tell me anything that surprises me."

"I'm sorry," I said hoarsely. "Truly, I am."

Irina leaned forward. I leaned in, too. "Take your apologies and your empty promises and leave this place," she whispered.

What could I do, refuse the only thing she had left to ask of me? I turned, suppressing the urge to look back, but before I had walked even a few paces, I froze.

Ileana stood beside Finn on the edge of the clearing, her pipe dangling from the corner of her mouth. Behind her, half a dozen Caomhnóir hulked in the shadows, daggers drawn. Finn had his hands raised up by his shoulders, a sign of surrender.

"Come with me, Miss Ballard," Ileana barked, and padded off into the woods.

24

THE DORMANT

"So."

The trappings of the courtroom had not yet been cleared from Ileana's tent. Half-eaten food, scraps of paper, and a number of forgotten personal items lay strewn about the place. Several chairs were overturned. A strange scent perfumed the air, emanating from the fire, and a pinkish haze hung in the torchlit gloom—the remains of the red smoke. As I stood amidst the mess, I felt like a teenager, about to be told off by a parent for throwing a raging party in her absence. Of course, I had never done anything of the sort when my mother was alive. In fact, I was generally the one yelling at her for wrecking the place after a binge. All of these thoughts flew through my head in the matter of about three seconds, leaving me with a mad desire to laugh out loud.

"Yes, High Priestess," I said, conquering the laughter and bowing my head respectfully instead.

"Why are you here, Jessica Ballard?" she asked.

The question pulled me up short. It was not the one I had anticipated answering. "What do you mean?"

"I mean what I say. Why are you here, in our camp?"

"I... I was invited here to testify. You invited me," I said slowly.

"That may be true but it does not answer the question. I know why you were invited. I want to know why you accepted the invitation," Ileana said.

"I wasn't aware that I was allowed to refuse it," I hedged.

"Do you refuse to answer the question?" Ileana snapped.

I sighed. I knew what she meant, and she knew that I did. "I came because of Irina. I wanted to help her."

"Help her how?"

"I hoped that my testimony would help to free her."

"You hoped to influence our system of justice," Ileana said.

"I hoped that, when you heard my version of what had happened, it might convince you that this prolonged torture should stop!" cried.

"You think us the monsters and Irina the innocent victim?" Ileana laughed. "What a naïve creature you are, for one that has seen so much of the world."

"I'm not naïve. I know that Irina is dangerous. I know she's done terrible things to free herself. But can't you understand why she's done them? You've driven her to it! Why can't you just find it in your heart to let her go?"

"There are some betrayals that cannot be forgiven," Ileana said sharply. "She would peddle our secrets out in the world. She very nearly breached the Gateway system."

"And she wouldn't have done any of those things if you'd just let her Cross!" I cried. "How can you look at what she's done and not understand that you are partly to blame for it?"

Finn shifted uncomfortably beside me, and I knew from the subtle change in his posture that I had crossed a line. But I didn't care.

"All of your talk about bonds of blood and sacredness of Traveler culture, what does any of it matter if you don't apply it to the most vulnerable amongst you?" I went on. "Irina is only in this state because your Council used her as a guinea pig to test the limits of Walking. Her condition is a result of their decisions, not hers, but now she's being punished for it!"

"You think we should ignore her heinous crimes?" Ileana asked almost amusedly.

"I think you should admit that her crimes could have been prevented by a little mercy on your part. Why couldn't you just have let her die three years ago?"

"We are not in the habit of leaving our own to die. Our code does not allow for suicide or murder. We are here to shepherd spirits, not to play God."

"Oh, so murder and suicide are out, but decades of prolonged torture are just fine?" I asked. I dropped my face into my hands and rubbed at my temples. "Look, I already know I've lost, okay? I understand that you aren't going to change your mind. I'm not going to wipe out centuries of Traveler culture with a single stump speech. I get it. Can I go?"

"I want to know what you said to Irina in the clearing," Ileana manded, her nostrils flaring.

"Why? What are you so afraid of?"

"I am the High Priestess of these clans, and it is my business to ow when someone interacts with one of my prisoners," Ileana ied. Her hands were gripping the arms of her throne like claws. ou have just told me you wished her free. You were just found out bounds speaking privately to her. Now what did you say to her?"

"I apologized to her," I said.

Ileana couldn't have looked more surprised. "You..."

"Yes. I told her that I was sorry. Sorry that my words were not ough to convince you to let her be free at last."

"And that is all?" Ileana pressed. She squinted at me with those arp, cold eyes.

"Yes. That is all," I said, relieved that I could tell her the truth.

"You broke through barriers and risked being caught just to tell r you were sorry?" she demanded again, clearly incredulous.

"Yes. That's part of *my* code," I said coolly.

Ileana glared at me. I glared right back.

"Like so many members of the Ensconced Clans, you do not spect our ways or our laws," Ileana hissed through gritted teeth.)n both occasions that you have set foot in our encampment, you ıve caused undue trouble. I want you to leave these woods and ver return. You will not be welcomed back amongst us, Jessica ıllard. Consider yourself warned."

"Warning duly noted," I replied with a sarcastic inclining of my ad. "Don't lose any sleep over me, though. I have no intention of tting foot here again."

§

Finn and I walked quickly away from Ileana's tent. Dragos llowed closely behind us, Ileana having insisted that he see us rsonally to the border.

"That was foolish," Finn said quietly. "Losing your temper with r like that."

"I know," I muttered. "I couldn't help it."

"The Travelers are not enemies you want to have, Jess," Finn ent on.

"I know that!" I hissed. "*Nobody* is an enemy I want to have. But now that I've been banned from ever seeing them again, I'm no going to worry too much about it."

Finn grabbed my arm and pulled me to a stop.

"Damnit, Finn, what do you want me to do? I can't take it back I've already agreed it was stupid, what else do you want me to—"

"Something's going on. Something's happened," Finn sai tensely.

I looked around. He was right. Caomhnóir were running throug the encampment, telling people to get into their wagons and tent One of them spotted Dragos and sprinted right toward him.

"Dragos, she's gone! The Walker is gone! Escaped!"

"What?" Dragos gasped. "But... how?"

"I was walking the perimeter, like you told me to," th Caomhnóir panted. "And then there were shouts of fire from the fa end of the encampment. I ran to help, and when I came back—I wa only gone a few minutes—she was gone!"

"But she can't have! The Castings!" Dragos cried.

"All broken," the Caomhnóir replied. "Someone has helped her t escape."

"What is the commotion out here?" Ileana had appeared in th entrance to the tent, hands upon her bony hips. "Explai yourselves at once," she barked at the Caomhnóir.

"The Walker is gone, High Priestess. Escaped," Dragos sai leaping to attention.

Ileana's face went white. "That's impossible!"

"It is true, High Priestess," the other Caomhnóir replied. "W responded to a fire in a wagon, and when we returned, she wa gone. The Castings were broken. We cannot find her."

Ileana turned a furious glare on me. "What have you done?" sh hissed.

"Nothing!" I cried. "I've been inside that tent with you!"

Ileana spat on the ground. "Do not lie to me! When you were i that clearing, we found you—"

Dragos stepped up beside Ileana. "High Priestess, we checked a of the Castings when we found the Northerner in the clearing. A of them were intact."

"But she entered the clearing, so she must have broken—"

"I just inked on one of these," I said, holding up my wrist an showing her the rune, and thankful that it was on the other wri, than the one Jeta had drawn on me, so that I did not have to reve

284

hat I'd been Rifting. "It's the same one all the Caomhnóir have to enter the clearing." There was no way that I was going to drag Flavia into this, not after all the help she had given me.

"And how did you know how to—"

"Because I have one, too," Finn said, stepping forward and showing his own wrist. "Dragos himself gave it to me, so that I would have full ability to do my duty in all areas of the encampment."

Ileana stared back and forth between the two of us as though trying to catch one of us in a lie. We both stared stonily back at her. Undaunted, Ileana turned her glare on Dragos instead. "We've only been gone from that clearing thirty minutes at most. She cannot have gotten far. What have you done to secure the borders of the encampment?

"The Castings will alert us if she crosses over the border in human form. And she cannot Walk. The Castings upon her are too numerous and too powerful. She lacks both the knowledge and the materials to undo them," Dragos said.

Ileana let out a defiant cackle. "Then she is as good as caught. But we must find her before she has the chance to damage her body beyond repair. Split up the Caomhnóir. Use half to patrol around the borders, and the other half to search the wagons. But once you have given the orders, I want you to personally escort these two from the camp. I will not allow them to further interfere with our handling of the Walker."

"As you wish it, High Priestess," Dragos said, bowing. He turned to the other Caomhnóir and quietly relayed the orders, then snapped at us: "Come with me. Quickly."

"What about our things?" I asked.

"They will find their way to you," Dragos said, shrugging unconcernedly.

"Meaning someone will send them?" I asked.

"Eventually," he said, not bothering to look at me.

"Great, thanks," I muttered, wondering if I even really needed anything I'd brought. Luckily, my cell phone was tucked in my back pocket out of habit, although I had no service to speak of. I looked over at Finn, but he answered my question before I could ask it by patting his vest pocket. I heard a muffled sound of jingling keys.

We arrived at the central fire, but no one was milling around it.

Instead, faces peeked out from the surrounding tents and wagons, staring at us as we passed.

"I don't see any damage from a fire," I said as we walked. "I wonder where..."

"My Caomhnóir tells me it was the Scribes' wagon that was damaged," Dragos said.

I stopped dead in my tracks. "What?!"

Dragos looked over his shoulder at me, eyebrows raised. "I said the fire was in the Scribes' wagon."

"But... I... was anyone hurt? Is everyone okay?" I gasped.

Dragos shrugged. "It was a very small fire, easily contained."

"You didn't answer my question. My friend who's staying here, the Dormant—"

"Jess! Over here!"

I spun around and cried out in relief. Flavia and Annabelle were coming toward us. Annabelle had her knapsack slung over her shoulder. Both looked sweaty and anxious. Flavia was holding on to Annabelle's elbow as she walked.

"Oh, thank God!" I cried, running over to them. "I heard there was a fire in the Scribes' wagon, and I thought—"

"No, no, it's okay, we weren't in it at the time," Flavia said breathlessly. "I still haven't ascertained how much damage was done, but there will be time for that." She looked at us, and at Dragos. "What's going on?"

"We're being escorted from the camp," I said. "We've been banned."

"Banned? Permanently?" Flavia asked, gaping.

"Yes," I said.

"But why—"

"You two should take shelter in one of the other wagons," Dragos said impatiently. "Haven't you heard? The Walker escaped, and she's a danger to anyone she encounters."

Both Flavia and Annabelle's eyes widened in alarm. Annabelle actually swayed a bit on her feet. Flavia grasped her arm tighter.

Dragos seemed not to notice. "Lock yourself in and do not open the door to anyone until the Caomhnóir instruct you it is safe," he told them.

"No," Annabelle said. Her voice sounded strange, like she was having a hard time forming her words. "If Jess is leaving, then I'm leaving, too. I don't want to stay without her."

286

Dragos snorted. "Suit yourself, Dormant. But you'd do better to be more careful of the company you keep if you hope to reestablish our connections here."

Annabelle didn't reply. She clutched the knapsack more tightly to her back. Her knuckles were white.

"Let us go, then," Dragos said, and continued his march toward the encampment border.

Flavia walked with us, still holding on to Annabelle. I caught her eye and mouthed to her silently, "What is going on?"

She did not answer, merely shaking her head and continuing to walk. Her hand, on Annabelle's arm, was trembling. Annabelle stumbled several times as she trudged forward, but ignored every attempt I made to get her attention.

At last, we reached the edge of the encampment. Dragos waved a hand toward the edge of the trees. "The High Priestess has spoken. Do not return here."

Flavia reached out and pulled me into a tight fierce embrace. As she hugged me, she put her lips to my ear and murmured. "Help her walk. She's going to need your help. Get her out of sight of the woods."

I pulled away, my face full of confusion, but Flavia didn't explain. She planted a tiny kiss on Annabelle's cheek, waved to Finn, and scurried back into the trees and out of sight. I linked my arm through Annabelle's and felt her lean against me. What the hell was wrong with her? She still wasn't looking at me. She seemed to be concentrating with all her might on simply staying upright.

Finn seemed to notice Annabelle's state for the first time, and took her other arm. Together, the three of us shuffled in silence away from the woods and back toward the road. It was nearly a quarter of a mile back to the car.

"Annabelle, what in the world—"

"No," she said, slurring her speech again. "Still too close. Keep walking. We must be completely out of sight."

"But are you hurt?"

"Keep walking!"

Slowly, painfully, we made our way back to the car, Annabelle panting and staggering with the effort. At last the car came into view. Finn pulled his keys from his pocket and clicked the remote starter. The car roared to life, and the headlights cut wide swaths of golden light across the road.

Under cover of the sound of the engine, I turned Annabelle to face me. "Annabelle what in the world is happening? Why are you...?"

But Annabelle, who had collapsed against the side of the car, had begun to laugh.

"Annabelle, please! Tell me what's wrong with you?"

Annabelle looked me fully in the eye for the first time. "Nothing at all, Northern Girl. Except perhaps for the fact that I'm not Annabelle."

I reeled back from her, gasping in horror. I knew the wild look staring out at me from those eyes.

"Irina!" I cried.

"What?!" Finn shouted in alarm.

"These prisons are terribly difficult to work when they don't belong to you, aren't they?" Irina told me through Annabelle's lips. "You'll remember your Spirit Guide had a devil of a time controlling yours when he tried it."

"But... I don't understand. Where is Annabelle? What happened to her? What have you done to her?" I hissed, fighting a wave of terror that threatened to overwhelm me.

"I haven't done anything to her," Irina said. "She did it to herself."

"I... she's not... she would never..." I mumbled.

"Irina, no more games!" Finn snarled. "What happened to Annabelle?"

"Ask her yourself," Irina said, pointing one of Annabelle's violently shaking fingers at something over Finn's shoulder. Both of us turned to see a translucent figure gliding toward us, from a nearby copse of trees. Her familiar face was split into a wide, resplendent smile.

"Annabelle!" I shouted, and the shout was half a sob. "Oh, my God, no! NO!"

Annabelle's smile did not falter. She put up a hand to silence me. "Jessica, don't. It's okay. Let me explain."

"Nothing is okay! This wasn't supposed to happen!" I cried, sinking to my knees. "I broke my promise! I broke my promise to Irina so that this wouldn't happen!"

"Jess, stop." It was Finn who spoke now. His expression was filled with wonder as he stared at Annabelle, and even as I watched him, let out a peal of incredulous laughter. "I can't believe it!" he whispered.

"You can't believe what?" I shouted at him. "And why the hell are you laughing?"

He looked at me, still smiling. "Jess, look at her. She's not dead. *Look at her!*"

Bewildered I looked back at Annabelle. She was in spirit form. Her body was beside me, still shaking with laughter, inhabited by another spirit. There was no way that could be true unless she was dead or . . .

And the truth washed over me. I scrambled to my feet and took a few tentative steps forward, until Annabelle's spirit form stood just in front of me, so close that I could have reached right out and touched her.

"You're Walking," I whispered.

Her smile widened into a sheepish grin. "Not bad for a Dormant, huh?"

"But... I don't understand," I croaked, choking on a sound that was half-sob and half-laugh. "This isn't possible! How... ?" I didn't even know which of a thousand questions to ask.

"It was Flavia who figured it out," Annabelle said. "I wasn't going to bother looking at any more research, but you know her. We went back to the Scribes' wagon right after you left, and she just picked right back up with the magnifying glass. Then suddenly, not a minute later, she shouted, 'Annabelle! Let me look at your bracelets!' Before I could ask her what was going on, she had grabbed my wrist and was going through my bracelets, one by one, comparing them to the ones in the sketch. It was then that she realized you had drawn one that I wasn't wearing."

"Huh?" I asked, perplexed.

"A Soul Catcher. One that had been sliced through," Annabelle said.

A jingling sound behind me made me turn. Irina had lifted Annabelle's wrist and shook back the many bangles to reveal the jingling ends of a knotted hemp bracelet buried amongst the metal ones.

"But... you aren't a Durupinen. You shouldn't have been able to..." I said weakly.

"I know," Annabelle said. "But I didn't stop to question it. The sketch was clear. It didn't show me dead. It showed me Walking. So,

289

we didn't even pause to wonder whether I could do it. You'd alread shown me I could."

"I can't believe this," I said, laughing again.

"Neither can I," Annabelle admitted. "I guess the Durupine should spend a little more time learning to appreciate the possibl latent talents of their Dormants rather than trying to sweep u under the rug."

"But I still don't understand how you managed to..." I jus gestured incredulously at her Walker form.

"Flavia had Soul Catchers right in a drawer in the wagon, le over from when she made them for you three years ago. All w needed was a distraction, a way to get into Irina's clearing withou the Caomhnóir seeing us. So, Flavia lit the fire and we waite for Irina's guard to run toward the commotion. Flavia knew ever single Casting set upon the clearing, because she'd had to researc them all when she helped to build the enclosure that you learned t Walk in. So, she knew exactly how to undo them."

"This is bloody brilliant!" Finn said softly. "Absolutely blooc brilliant."

"And wouldn't you know it, that Caomhnóir was in such a rush t help put out that fire, that he didn't even realize he'd dropped h dagger," Annabelle said, smiling again. "And so, we had everythin we needed, just as your sketch had instructed us."

"But where's Irina's body?" I asked.

Annabelle's smile faltered for the first time. "She... well, as soo as she was out of the confines of the clearing she..." Annabell gestured wordlessly, but I didn't need or want the details. understood. Irina ended her life. Her body was dead now, and sh could not return to it. "The Travelers will surely find it soon, if the haven't already."

"They freed me," Irina cried rapturously, and as she said it, sh rose like a soaring bird out of Annabelle's body, which slumpe unceremoniously to the ground.

"Hey, be careful with that!" Annabelle said. "I'm the one who got to use it!"

But Irina wasn't listening. She was coasting like a leaf on wayward breeze, laughing like a small child.

"But how in the world did you think of putting Irina inside you body?" Finn asked, in awe.

"That stroke of genius was Irina's idea. Flavia and I were tryin o decide how to hide Irina, or else how to get her over the border without the Caomhnóir tracking her down. We knew that Walking was the key, but we couldn't figure out why. Then Irina just... came up with it. She looked over at me and said, 'If I steer that shell out of here, no one will know that I'm inside it.' It was obvious she wasn't keen on the idea, but as soon as she said it, Flavia and I looked at each other and we knew she was right. I wasn't just the Walker. I was the getaway car."

I laughed, but Finn's expression turned suddenly serious. "Speaking of cars, we should really put as much distance between us and the Traveler camp as we can," he said, frowning.

"You're right," Annabelle said. With an almost reluctant sigh she trained her gaze upon her empty body and then flew at it, disappearing into it and then animating it once more.

I ran over and knelt beside her. "Are you all right? How do you feel?"

Annabelle was looking down at her own hands as though she'd never really seen them before. "Wow," she whispered, then looked up at me. "I feel... okay, I think. Weird. A little dizzy, but otherwise... fine!"

I pulled her to her feet and into a fierce hug. "Easy, easy, I'm not quite... adjusted," she gasped.

"Oops, sorry!" I said sheepishly, letting her go, but keeping a hand on her to keep her steady. "I forgot. Let's get you in the car and you can get your bearings back."

Finn stepped forward and offered an arm to Annabelle to help her into the car. I turned to Irina. "Well," I said to her, and smiled. "You're free."

Irina smiled. "So it would seem. And I must take back my words."

"What words?"

"Your promises, Northern Girl," she said coming so close to me that I could see every sparkling facet of the glimmers in her tear-filled eyes. "Your promises are worth their weight in gold."

As the car wound away up the dirt road, Irina soaring along beside it like a canary free at last from the depths of the mineshaft, I reached out into my connection to find Hannah and Milo waiting for me, dependable as always.

"Jess! What's going on? We've been so worried! What's happened?" they cried over each other at once as my energy filtered through to them.

"Can you find Savvy and get a hold of a car?" I asked.

"Of course! But what happened to the Caomhnóir car? Where's Finn?" Hannah asked anxiously, the words tumbling through the connection like a rushing creek over stones. "What about Annabelle? Jess, we've been so worried!"

"Annabelle's fine. Finn is here. We're all okay. But I need you to get in the car and start driving. We've got a very special Crossing to perform, and it's best if we do it away from Fairhaven."

I heard Milo gasp as he understood.

"I don't understand," Hannah said.

I looked out the window at Irina. She was joy personified, coasting on the wind. "A promise is a promise."

EPILOGUE

I STARED DOWN AT MY PHONE and sighed for at least the dozenth time.

"Jess, if I hear you do that one more time, I'm going to pry that phone out of your hand and make the call myself," Hannah said, looking up from her work in exasperation.

"I know, I know," I said, rolling over and burying my face in my pillow. "I'm sorry. I just... I hate doing this to her. She just moved in with us. She was just getting settled. And now I'm abandoning her!"

"Tia will understand," Hannah insisted. "You know that she will."

"I know. But that doesn't make me feel any less shitty about doing it," I said. "I'm not worried about Tia. I know she'll have a new apartment lined up before I've even hung up the phone. I just hope she doesn't have a new best friend lined up, too."

"Jess, don't be ridiculous," Hannah sighed, in a tone that reminded me so much of my mother that I stared over at her with a catch in my throat. I loved when she sounded like our mother, though I would never tell her that. Well, maybe one day, when enough of the wounds had faded to scars.

It had been a week since my return from the Traveler camp, and still couldn't quite believe we had pulled it off. Flavia had sent me a letter letting me know that Irina's body had been found, and that the Traveler Council had, after an exhaustive investigation, at last called off the search for Irina's spirit. They were still trying to piece together how she had escaped, but Flavia assured me that they were no closer to figuring it out than they had been on the day we left. Annabelle had returned to the States and was attempting to resume normal life after discovering her extraordinary talent. She had abandoned her attempts to reconnect with her Traveler relations, and was choosing instead to sever her ties with the camp, lest they somehow discover her abilities and, by extension, her role in Irina's escape. And best of all, Irina was at peace at long last, and the long arm of Traveler law could never reach her again.

Of course, I was still a Seer, and I would have to find a way to deal with that. But I had come to an important realization in the aftermath of Irina's escape; my gift, as frightening as it was, had tried to help me. First it had warned me about Hannah and the Prophecy. Then, it had given me the answer to the Shattering before it even happened. And now, it had showed me the only way to keep my promise to Irina. Perhaps, if I worked with my gift instead of against it, it might just turn out to be a blessing instead of a curse.

Hannah had thrown herself so heartily into her work on the Council that she was quickly earning the respect of her fellows, including many of those who had been so skeptical of her to begin with. She now spent most of her time on the phone and in front of the computer, completing the paperwork needed to transfer to a program in London so that she could finish her degree. In this regard, at least, being a Durupinen was incredibly helpful. Our elaborate network of connections was allowing her to bypass all kinds of bureaucratic red tape in order to make a smooth transition. Our dubiously legal dual citizenship papers had arrived at our door only the day before. I had quit both of my jobs, and had begun sifting through a number of listings for flats that we could move into, though no one seemed to be bothered that we were still squatting in the castle. I was eager to start establishing a life outside of its walls, though; classes were back in session for the newest crop of Apprentices, and I was starting to feel like the creepy alumna who perpetually pretended to still be one of the college kids. The only thing left to do was talk to Tia and tell her we weren't coming home.

My phone suddenly buzzed. I jumped and dropped it, then scooped it back up and looked at the incoming call.

"It's Tia!" I cried.

"Perfect!" Hannah said, smirking. "So, answer it and tell her Jess. The longer you wait, the worse it will be."

I cursed rapidly under my breath for several moments, then answered the call.

"Hey, Ti! Look, I'm so sorry I haven't called you back. I wasn't ignoring you, I promise. I had to—" But I broke off as a volley of sniffs and sobs met my ears. "Tia? Oh my God, are you crying? What's wrong?"

"Jess, he broke up with me! Sam broke up with me!" she managed to stammer, then broke into a veritable storm of crying.

"Oh, no! Oh, Tia, I... I don't even know what to say! I'm so
rry! What... do you want to tell me what happened?" I asked,
ntomiming her news across to Hannah, who gasped and covered
r mouth as she caught on.

"I don't know. He kept wanting me to move in, and I just wasn't
ıdy, and we kept fighting about it," Tia explained between fresh
ıves of tears. "And I just kept telling him that I loved him, but that
.eeded to prioritize school. I mean, I've been working toward this
ıce I was old enough to know what a doctor was, but he wouldn't
derstand."

"How could he not understand that about you by now?" I asked
:redulously. "You've always been goal-driven."

"I know! He used to say it was one of the things he loved about
ə. And so, he just stopped calling me. I was always the one who
d to call him. And he just claimed he was giving me the space I
eded to work, but he felt more distant every time I talked to him.
ıd then this morning he called me to say that he met someone
ɛe and that he wanted to break up."

I think she said something else after that, but I couldn't tell what
was because at that point she dissolved into a blubbering mess. I
. her sob for a minute or so, interjecting soothing words here and
ere, but feeling absolutely helpless in the face of her devastation.

". . . and I feel like I had everything all figured out, and suddenly
ıave nothing figured out at all..."

"Oh, I'm so sorry," I said again.

"And I'm just alone in this apartment, and I'm going crazy," she
iffed. "And I can't stand it. I need to get out of here, but I just
ı't go home to my parents. I can't deal with my mother hovering
my father interrogating me, or—"

"Come here!" I blurted out. Hannah's eyes went wide and she
ırted shaking her head furiously. I turned my back on her.

"What? What do you mean, come there? Aren't you coming
ɔme?" Tia asked.

"Well actually, no," I said. "It's a long story, but the fact is that
ɛ're going to be here for a while. I was working up the courage to
ll you when you called. But that doesn't matter now. You need to
t away. I need to see my best friend. Dig out your passport. Get
ı a plane."

Tia sounded horrified. "I... I couldn't just... I have to plan..."

"What is there to plan?" I asked. "Tia, you just said you have to get out of there. Do it. Get out. Come here. Just be spontaneous an do something crazy."

Tia gave a terrified squeak. "Just... just buy a ticket to England?

"It's England, not the moon! Throw some shit in a bag and get o a plane. You can figure out the rest when you get here. I'm seriou Tia. For once in your life, do what you want to do and not what yo think you're supposed to do!"

Tia was silent. I thought for a minute that the shock considering a spur-of-the-moment decision might have made he head explode, but then I heard her trembling voice reply. "Oka Okay, I'm doing it. I'm buying a ticket right now. Well, I have to tal an exam tomorrow and hand in a paper, but then—"

"Good. Text me your flight details when you have them. We work through this together, Ti. It's going to be okay."

Tia laughed through her tears. "Yeah, the dizzying lack of contr is already dulling my heartbreak."

"Good. I'm here. Call me whenever you need to. Seriously. Lo you, Ti."

"Love you, too, Jess."

I put down the phone. Hannah was looking anxiously at me.

"Is she okay?" she asked.

"Nope," I said. "But she will be."

"I can't believe she agreed to do it," Hannah said, biting her li "That's so... not Tia."

"I know. I wasn't expecting her to actually go through with it I admitted. "There's at least a fifty percent chance that she'll ta herself out of it before she can book a flight. But hopefully tl recklessness that comes with heartbreak will help her see through."

"Look, Jess, I think it's great that you invited her, and I'll be real glad to see her, but..." Hannah gestured around us. "There's no wa she's going to be allowed to come here. The Council made son exceptions about what you could tell her, yes, but to actually let he on the grounds here?"

"I know, I know," I said. "Sorry, I wasn't really thinking tha part through. But, hey, we're Trackers now. I'm sure we can pu some strings for a flat or a hotel room until we get our own livir arrangement sorted out."

"That's true," Hannah said, and finally let her face relax into smile. "I'm glad she's coming, Jess. It will be good for you to have your best friend here."

"Is someone summoning best friends?" Milo asked, floating through the wall and coming to rest on Hannah's bed.

I laughed. "Impeccable timing as usual, Milo, but we weren't talking about you. Tia's coming to visit."

"Fabulous!" Milo squealed, clapping his hands with glee. "But where is she going to—"

"I'm working on that part," I said. "But we're going to need all hands on deck when she gets here, especially you. It's going to be operation cheer up Tia, and we need your expertise."

"Why?" Milo asked, looking puzzled.

"Sam just broke up with her," Hannah said.

Milo's face turned from sunshine to storm clouds in half a second. "Give me one good reason why I shouldn't float right back across the ocean and haunt the ever-loving shit out of that boy," he growled.

"I'll give you two," Hannah said quickly. "You can't possibly materialize that far away on your own, and Sam won't even be able to see you."

"That doesn't mean I couldn't still wreak some havoc," Milo whined.

"But all the nuance of your sass would be lost. Hardly worth it," I said. "Besides, he's going to get an earful from me as soon as I can get him on the phone."

Milo sighed dramatically. "Whatever. But I'm asking Tia for permission when she gets here. That boy clearly needs a dose of afterlife vengeance, courtesy of *moi* and I am only too happy to deliver it. Gift-wrapped."

"Fine. We'll leave it up to Tia," I said, knowing full well that Tia would never let Milo do anything of the sort. "How long do we have until the coronation?"

"About half an hour," Hannah said, checking her watch and then closing her notebook. "We should probably start getting ready."

Though Celeste had been acting High Priestess for several weeks now, her formal ceremony had not yet been held, due to a number of arcane ceremonies and moon-cycle-related conditions that had to be met before she could officially take her position as head of the Northern Clans. But tonight was the new moon, and so with it, we would crown our new High Priestess. And as much as I was not looking forward to the over-the-top displays of pomp and circumstance, I was glad that I would have the chance to watch Celeste ascend the throne. She seemed by far the best choice for the job.

Ten minutes later, decked out in our clan garb, Hannah and I descended the stairs for the entrance hall, where we would line up with the other clans. Each of us had a white candle in a brass holder clutched in our hands, and a triskele pendant bouncing against our throats. The hall was already filled with milling Durupinen, all murmuring excitedly about the ceremony.

"I can't believe you didn't change out of the jeans," Hannah hissed at me.

"I can't believe you thought I would consider changing out of the jeans," I said with a smirk.

"Seriously, Jess. Everyone else is dressed up. There's a banquet afterward," Hannah said, pointing around at the other women. Most of them were wearing dresses and skirts under their clan sashes.

"And I'm really good at eating food in jeans," I replied. "Give it a rest, Hannah. No one cares what I'm wearing."

We arrived at our designated spot and slid into line. I scanned the line of waiting Caomhnóir by the doors, hoping to catch Finn's eye, but I couldn't find him.

"Hannah, do you see Finn?" I asked, scanning the line again.

Hannah craned her neck and stared for a few moments before frowning. "No."

I started to search the rest of the hall, but Hannah tapped my shoulder and pointed back to the line of Caomhnóir. "Who is that, holding our clan colors?"

I followed her finger and saw a tall, hulking, unfamiliar man standing with our clan banner on a pole. Mystified, I counted the number of Caomhnóir and the number of Durupinen clans. They matched.

"What the hell?" I muttered. I thrust my candle at Hannah. "Here, hold this. I'll be right back."

I shunted my way through the crowd, my mind running in a hundred different directions. Was he sick? Had Seamus put him on some other kind of security duty? It seemed strange, given that all the Durupinen were meeting together in the Grand Council Room, that there would be a need for security anywhere else, unless

298

eleste needed some sort of special guard? Maybe that was it.

walked along the line of Caomhnóir, all of whom completely gnored me, until I was standing right beside the one whose banner natched the sash I currently had flung over my shoulder.

"Excuse me?"

He didn't look at me, merely grunted to acknowledge he had eard me.

"Where is Finn Carey?" I asked him.

He shot a quick look at me from the corner of his eye, and then hrugged. "Dunno," he said.

"Well, you're currently doing the job that's supposed to be his," I aid, stepping around so that he was forced to look at me. "He's our aomhnóir, not you. He is sworn to our clan, you're not. Why isn't e here, holding this banner?"

Again, the Caomhnóir just sort of grunted and shrugged.

I felt my anger rising in me, an anger tinged around the edges rith just a hint of panic. "Are you seriously incapable of answering simple question, or do you need me to—"

"Jessica."

I turned to see Fiona standing at the bottom of the stairs, her face xpressionless.

I threw the Caomhnóir one last dirty look and stalked over to neet Fiona.

"Fiona, do you know—"

"Celeste asked me to fetch you. She's waiting for you in here," iona said, her face and voice still oddly blank. She pointed to a arrow door set into the same wall as the Grand Council Room ntrance. "She needs to see you immediately, before the ceremony egins."

"Why? What's going on?" I asked, the panic spreading now, uickening my pulse.

"It will only take a moment," Fiona said, her voice still nconcerned. It occurred to me, as I looked at her, that she was eeping our interaction intentionally boring, trying to not draw ttention from the surrounding crowd. I thought I saw a flash of omething in her eyes, too, a plea not to make a scene.

"Okay," I said, as calmly as I could. "Should I get Hannah, or..."

"No, that won't be necessary. She only asked for you," Fiona said, esturing to the door again.

Swallowing hard, I followed her to the door and walked through it.

Celeste stood in the center of the room, looking like the fairy queen at the heart of a high fantasy novel. Her long dark hair spilled down her back, and her slender form was clad in a long, silvery white gown that spilled out behind her like enchanted water. Delicate gold jewelry adorned her wrists and neck, and a circlet of intricate gold vines and leaves clung to her hair. She quite literally took my breath away. Which meant I had no air left in my lungs to gasp when I saw who was standing beside her.

Ileana, High Priestess of the Traveler Clans had come to Fairhaven.

My mind was spinning as I stared at the two of them together. Ileana knew. She had to know. Why else could she possibly be here? Had they forced the truth out of Flavia, or tracked down Annabelle, or else found some other evidence that tied us to Irina's escape? My palms began to sweat.

"Jess. Thank you for coming," Celeste said. Her expression was very serious.

"Of course," I said, inclining my head. I was relieved to hear that my voice sounded calm even as my insides writhed with fear. "And High Priestess Ileana. To what do I owe the pleasure?"

Ileana did not answer my question, but gave an ironic little bow as she smirked at me, her pipe clutched between her teeth.

"Jess, as you can see, Ileana has come to see me with concerns about your recent visit to her camp," Celeste said. "I have just been discussing her concerns, which I agree are valid and need to be addressed at once."

My mouth was horribly dry. I tried to swallow before I spoke, but my voice still sounded cracked when I spoke. "And what concerns are those? If she has any issues with how I handled myself in regard to my role as a Tracker, I have already given a full report to my superiors."

"This," said Celeste, "has nothing to do with your role as a Tracker. This is about your Caomhnóir, Finn Carey."

I frowned, looking back and forth from one to the other. "What about Finn? He didn't do anything wrong. Look, if it's about the rune I used to get into Irina's clearing, I put that on myself."

"Jessica," Celeste said, holding up a hand to cut me off. "Are you or are you not engaged in a romantic relationship with Mr. Carey?"

"I... what?" I whispered.

"Are you and Mr. Carey involved with each other romantically?" leste asked again sternly.

"I... no, of course not," I replied, trying to think through the nic now coursing through my veins. "Those relationships are rbidden."

"I am well aware of that, which is why I have brought you here," leste said. "We have reason to believe that you have indeed gaged in such a relationship."

"What are you talking about?" I asked.

"When you were escorted from the Traveler camp, you and Mr. rey left many of your belongings behind. When the Traveler iomhnóir went to collect them, so that they could be returned to u, they found these."

She extended both of her hands. In the left one was the umpled-up sketch I had done of Finn, his chest bare. In the other, nn's black book of poetry.

"I'd like to give you the opportunity to explain this," Celeste said lemnly.

"I... it's just a sketch," I said. "I draw people constantly. I have etches of nearly everyone I interact with, spirits included. In :t, I've drawn sketches of both of you," I added, gesturing to ch of them in turn. "And you'll notice that I'm not in a romantic lationship with either of you."

"You surely can agree, though, can't you, that this sketch appears be... intimate," Celeste said delicately.

I shrugged as off-handedly as I could. "Not really, no. I was bored. lrew him because he happened to be there. He's always there. iat's kind of his job. In fact, he's supposed to be here now, but I uldn't find him in the entrance hall. Do you know where he is?"

"Never mind that now," Celeste said. "Very well, then. What out this?" She held out the book.

I shrugged again. "It's a blank book. Finn writes in them all the ne. He has a whole bunch of them."

"And do you know what he writes?" Celeste asked.

"No," I lied.

"You've never once asked him what he writes in these books?" leste pressed.

"Finn is a private guy. Even if I had asked him, I doubt he would ive told me," I said. "He likes to write, I guess, just as I like to

301

sketch. That doesn't mean I'm going to share my work with him or anybody for that matter." My pulse was pounding with the li Was Finn somewhere in another room, being asked these sam questions right now? What if our answers didn't match up? Wh would happen then?

"I find it rather hard to believe that you would not know th contents of Mr. Carey's notebooks, when this one seems to be collaboration," Celeste said coolly. She opened up the cover of th book, and I realized, with a jolt, that it was the one I had illustrate for him for Christmas. Every page was branded with my own wor an undeniable fingerprint of my presence.

I did not say anything. I just stood there, staring down at th book.

"Many of these poems," Celeste went on quietly, "are titled wit your name. Just your name."

"Are they?" I whispered.

"Yes."

I could feel the walls closing in around me, the avenues of escap sealing themselves up. I looked up at Ileana, and she was actual grinning, as though she could hear every desperate thought th was pounding through my brain.

Celeste sighed and closed the book. She set it down on a nearb table, along with the sketch. "While there is no definitive proof th you and Mr. Carey have truly embarked on a relationship that woul be forbidden by our laws, I must say that the evidence that Ilean has provided is compelling. It shows me that your profession relationship with Mr. Carey is likely to be crossing a dangerous lin and that to allow him to continue to act as your guardian would b irresponsible."

"What do you mean?" I asked, the words hardly more than breath. "Where is Finn?"

"I spoke with him last night, when Ileana first arrived," Celest said. "He denied any impropriety on your part, though he admitte that the book was his, and that he had written the poems inside it

"But where is he?" I asked again.

"He is gone," Celeste said. "Seamus has reassigned him, at m request."

"Re—reassigned him?" I stammered. What did that word eve mean? Words had no meaning. They were just sounds that mean nothing.

"Yes," Celeste said, and though her tone was brisk and commanding, her eyes were sad. "I deemed it prudent. Even if, as you both say, there has been no impropriety, it is clear that you have become closer than Caomhnóir and Durupinen ought to be. For the sake of both of our reputations, and to avoid any... issues... down the road, I have ordered him reassigned. A new Caomhnóir has already been assigned to your clan. He will introduce himself when the coronation ceremony is over."

"You... you can't do this..." I whispered.

"It is already done," Celeste said. "And anyway, if things are as you say, what does it matter? One guardian will do as well as another."

I couldn't speak. This was what it felt like to drown.

"Well, High Priestess, I should be letting you get on with your coronation," Ileana said, clapping her hands together and rubbing them. "I apologize for having to inconvenience you on such an important day, but I know how tough your job can be, and I didn't want this situation to complicate things for you in your first days."

Celeste turned to her. "Thank you, Ileana. Safe travels, then."

Ileana gave Celeste a bow, and then turned to swagger out. "Northern Girl," she said, with an ironic salute, and swept through the door. I watched her go, the room spinning around me, unable to catch my breath, a hollow vacuum where my heart had, until just moments ago, been hammering madly.

"Jess," Celeste's voice came from behind me. It was soft, sad. I turned to look at her. It might just have been the reflected gleam of her dazzling ensemble, but her eyes shone as she looked at me. "I'm sorry," she said. "But it is clan law. I'm trying to protect you before it's too late."

I had no words for her. Anger was beginning to stir, rising up through the numbness, forcing it aside. I turned my back on her without replying and ran for the door.

I shoved my way through the entrance hall, knocking people aside, ignoring their cries, blinded by tears. Somewhere behind me, Hannah and Milo's voices called out, but I ignored them. My only focus was on reaching Ileana who had just slipped through the massive front doors.

I stumbled out into the night behind her, panting.

"Ileana."

She turned, her expression triumphant. The smoke from her pipe wreathed her head like a laurel wreath of victory in the battle she had just waged against me.

"Why?" I choked.

"Oh, I would have thought the answer to that would have been obvious, Northern Girl," Ileana said, raising her scraggly eyebrows in surprised amusement. "I cannot prove that you freed the Walker, but I know that you did it just the same. Action had to be taken."

"I see. No mercy for Irina, no mercy for me. Everyone who defies you gets destroyed, is that it?"

She took several steps toward me, leering maliciously.

"We are the Travelers. We are a proud people and we do not brook interference from anyone. I handed down my judgment on Irina. You did not heed it."

"It was wrong," I said through gritted teeth. "*You* were wrong."

"That was not for you to decide," Ileana said. "And so, we have exacted our vengeance. Now we are square, Northern Girl."

She raised her face to the sky and let loose a wild, cawing noise. I leapt back in alarm as a great swooping black something detached itself from a nearby tree and landed lightly on her shoulder. It was a raven, all shining ebony feathers and fierce snapping beak. It turned a single beady eye on me before turning to peck at the hair of its mistress, revealing an empty socket where its other eye had once been.

"A betrayal for a betrayal, Northern Girl," she said softly, stroking the raven's breast. Then she turned and walked away. I stood and watched long after the night had swallowed her, leaving me alone with nothing but the cold, distant stars above my head, and an aching hollowness in my chest.

.E. Holmes is a writer, teacher, and actor living in central Massachusetts with her husband, two children, and a small, but surprisingly loud dog. When not writing, she enjoys performing, watching unhealthy amounts of British television, and reading with her children. Please visit www.eeholmes.com to learn more about .E. Holmes and *The World of The Gateway*.

Made in the USA
Monee, IL
28 February 2021